科技英文
閱讀&練習

English for Specialized
SCIENCE and
TECHNOLOGY

二版

作者 ● JoAnne Juett Ph.D.
譯者 ● 羅竹君／丁宥榆

如何聆聽 MP3 音檔

❶ 寂天雲 APP 聆聽
① 先掃描書上 QR Code 下載 寂天雲 APP。
② 加入會員，進入 MP3 書櫃首頁，點下方內建掃描器
③ 再次掃描 QR Code 下載音檔，即可使用 APP 聆聽。

❷ 在電腦或其他播放器聆聽
① 請上「寂天閱讀網」(www.icosmos.com.tw)，註冊會員並登入。
② 搜尋本書，進入本書頁面， 點選 ◀MP3 下載 下載音檔，
   存於電腦等其他播放器聆聽。

Preface

This is a textbook designed for students studying in science and technology related fields, as well as for general readers interested in scientific and technical subjects. Contained in this book are 46 chapters in 16 units of information about some of the most recent and exciting topics in the scientific and technical area. The chapters in each unit relate to its general topic; for instance, the unit on Nanotechnology contains three chapters addressing the most recent nanotechnology information, including trends such as disruptive nanotechnologies and nanomanufacturing. Additionally, current global concerns, such as climate change and emerging technologies, are explored in different ways among various units in the book, including subjects such as semiconductor environmental safety issues and conservation farming.

The aim of this book is to help students develop basic skills in reading science and technology related publications, including essays, magazines, reports, etc. Each article models a scientific or technical essay and is followed by several sets of exercises designed to help the reader identify vocabulary specific to scientific and technology writing. Using context clues and word analysis, the reader will engage in discovering meaning and use of 17-30 **subject-related words** in each article. By working through each chapter of this book, the student will enhance his or her vocabulary skills and analytical reading skills.

Besides vocabulary and reading skill development, this textbook also provides excellent resources for research on current scientific and technical topics. I would like to recommend some general sources of information that will inform the research process of science and technology students. Sources such as Wikipedia and Webopedia contain vast amounts of resources to begin research from. These are not secondary resources whose credibility lends itself to inclusion in a Works Cited, but they contain excellent bibliographies of information more expert in nature. Additionally, students have available to them sources such as HowStuff Works and About.com, each of which offers in-depth and up-to-date explanations and illustrations on myriad scientific and technical subjects. Again, these resources will help the student begin serious research into a chosen topic.

Finally, I would like to acknowledge my debt to the people and institutions that have helped me complete this book. I wish to thank the University of Wisconsin-Eau Claire Office of Research and Sponsored Programs, who provided a generous grant that afforded me course release time to finish this book. I would also like to thank my English department for their support of my project. I especially appreciate the patient efforts of my editor, Jenny Hung, and all of her hours shaping the text of this book. Perhaps the most patient of all have been my family, Jacqueline, Jarred, and Sam, who have shared in my efforts toward and enthusiasm for this project—thank you.

Contents

Preface 前言 —— 2　　**Introduction** 導讀 —— 6

Unit 1
- Chapter 1　TAIPEI 101 台北101大樓 —— 14
- Chapter 2　Anti-Terrorism in Structural Design 反恐的建築設計 —— 20
- Chapter 3　Green Building 環保建築 —— 26

Unit 2
- Chapter 4　Scooter Engine 機車引擎 —— 32
- Chapter 5　Biomedical Engineering (Mechanical Engineering) 生物醫學工程 —— 38
- Chapter 6　Hybrid Cars 油電混合動力車 —— 44

Unit 3
- Chapter 7　Deadly Infectious Diseases 致命的傳染病 —— 50
- Chapter 8　Obesity Crisis 肥胖危機 —— 56
- Chapter 9　Secrets to a Healthy Life 健康生活的秘訣 —— 62

Unit 4
- Chapter 10　Stem Cells 幹細胞 —— 68
- Chapter 11　Gene Therapy 基因療法 —— 76
- Chapter 12　Orphan Drugs 罕見疾病藥物 —— 82

Unit 5
- Chapter 13　Light-Emitting Semiconductors 發光半導體 —— 88
- Chapter 14　Semiconductors and Environmental Safety Issues 半導體與環境安全 —— 94
- Chapter 15　Semiconductors and Energy Efficiency 半導體與能源效率 —— 100

Unit 6
- Chapter 16　Introduction to Nanotechnology 奈米科技簡介 —— 106
- Chapter 17　Disruptive Technologies 破壞性科技 —— 112
- Chapter 18　Nanomanufacturing 奈米製造技術 —— 118

Unit 7
- Chapter 19　Wireless Network 無線網路 —— 124
- Chapter 20　USB Technology USB技術 —— 130

Unit 8
- Chapter 21　Mobile Computing 行動計算技術 —— 136
- Chapter 22　The Internet 網際網路 —— 142
- Chapter 23　Artificial Intelligence 人工智慧 —— 148

Unit 9
- Chapter 24　Conservation Farming 保育農業 ── 154
- Chapter 25　Food Biotechnology 食品生物技術 ── 160
- Chapter 26　Agrifood Nanotechnology 農業食品奈米科技 ── 166

Unit 10
- Chapter 27　Energy Recovery Systems 能源回收系統 ── 172
- Chapter 28　Nuclear Energy 核子能源 ── 178
- Chapter 29　Renewable Energy 可再生能源 ── 184

Unit 11
- Chapter 30　Earthquakes and Tsunamis 地震與海嘯 ── 190
- Chapter 31　Satellite Oceanography 衛星海洋學 ── 196
- Chapter 32　Volcanoes 火山 ── 202

Unit 12
- Chapter 33　Tropical Weather Disturbances 熱帶天氣擾動 ── 208
- Chapter 34　Water Management 水管理 ── 214
- Chapter 35　Climate Change 氣候變遷 ── 220

Unit 13
- Chapter 36　Forest and Their Threats 森林與森林危機 ── 226
- Chapter 37　Waste Reduction and Management 廢棄物減量與管理 ── 232
- Chapter 38　Human Stress on the Environment 人為的環境壓迫 ── 238

Unit 14
- Chapter 39　Telescopes 望遠鏡 ── 246
- Chapter 40　Spacecraft Systems 太空船系統 ── 252
- Chapter 41　Emerging Space Technologies 新興太空技術 ── 258

Unit 15
- Chapter 42　Light Pollution 光害 ── 264
- Chapter 43　Mars 火星 ── 270
- Chapter 44　High Speed Penetrators 高速穿透鏡 ── 276

Unit 16
- Chapter 45　Types Of U.S. Patents 美國專利類型 ── 282
- Chapter 46　Global Intellectual Property Rights 全球智慧財產權 ── 288

中譯 ── 294
主題單字 ── 344
解答 ── 360

INTRODUCTION

Strategies for Better Reading Comprehension of English in Science and Technology Fields

All readers encounter words they don't know while reading. The first response of the reader may be to look up the word in a dictionary. However, it is not always possible or the best strategy to look up new words in the dictionary when you read. Many sentences and paragraphs include enough information for a reader to use **context clues** and **word analysis** to figure out the meaning of new words.

Strategy 1
CONTEXT CLUES

Readers use the words surrounding the unknown word to help determine the unknown word's meaning. There are many different types of context clues; the clues may appear within the same sentence as the word, or they may be in a preceding or subsequent sentence.

1. Definition

Sometimes a word is clearly defined in a sentence or paragraph.

1. The unknown word can be defined immediately following its use by using a brief definition, separated from the unknown word by punctuation—commas, parentheses or dashes.
2. The use of a "to be" verb indicates that the two ideas are the same.

> **Archaeologists**, anthropologists who study prehistoric people and their culture, search ancient sites for artifacts.

➤ A **chemical bond** is a strong force that holds two or more atoms together.

2. Example or summary

Writers may include examples familiar to the reader to help explain a new and unfamiliar concept or term. A major section or the entire passage may be used. Clue words for examples include

- *such as, for example, for instance*
- *to illustrate*
- *specifically*

➤ Hurricane **hazards**, such as strong winds and high water levels, can cause extensive damage to people and property along coastlines.

3. Description

Sometimes several phrases or sentences help draw a mental picture about a word.

➤ Lula was at her grandmother's farm when a yellow fever **epidemic** broke out in West Tennessee and Mississippi, only a few miles from the farm. An infectious disease of warm regions, yellow fever is carried by mosquitoes. The humid summer air provided the perfect climate for breeding the many mosquitoes that quickly spread the infection to thousands of residents.

→ *The above paragraph demonstrates the meaning of epidemic by chronicling its spread, from its inception to its rapid rate of infection among the residents.*

4. Explanation

An explanation is close to a definition. In the same paragraph, the difficult word is explained, usually in simpler words, to make the meaning clearer. The explanation is generally longer than a definition.

➤ People with macular degeneration may soon be able to be fitted with a **bionic** eye. This artificial eye will contain a battery-powered video processing unit that sends signals to an electronic unit behind the eye. The unit then sends signals to the brain, and the brain will interpret the signals as images.

5. Synonym

Sometimes a difficult word is used with another word or phrase with the same or a similar meaning. Synonym clue words include—

- *in other words*
- *also known as*
- *that is*
- *sometimes called*
- *or*

▶ Patients with fibromyalgia sometimes suffer a sudden onset of **acute pain**, that is, severe pain that lasts a short time.

6. Restatement

Close to a synonym, a restatement differs in that a difficult word is usually restated in a simpler form—usually set of by commas.

▶ After the long drought, the village was **depopulated**, most of the residents dead or moved, but the livestock remained untouched.

7. Contrast

Sometimes phrases or words in the sentence indicate the opposite of the target word. Contrast clue words are—

- *but*
- *in contrast*
- *however*
- *instead of*
- *unlike*
- *yet*

▶ **Cultivated** plants are purposefully grown for their products, unlike uncultivated plants that thrive in the wild without standard agricultural methods.

8. Cause and effect

The cause of an action may be stated using an unfamiliar word. The effect, though, is usually stated in familiar words so that the reader can infer its meaning. Cause and effect context clues include—

- *as a result of*
- *accordingly*
- *because*
- *consequently*
- *for this reason*
- *hence*
- *if . . . then*

▸ The weeds in the garden are so **profuse**, that the neighbors can no longer see the flowers.

9. Inference from general context

Some writers help you figure out unfamiliar words by having you use reasoning and prior knowledge. This context clue is often a little harder to spot.

▸ Sonny refused to accept that his wife's **dementia**, until she didn't recognize the grandchildren when they came to visit.

→ *The second clause of this sentence describes the effects of dementia in order to illuminate the meaning of the word.*

10. Experience or general knowledge

The meaning is derived from the experience and background knowledge of the reader—"common sense" and logic. The context contains information familiar to the reader.

▸ You can usually **cure** a cold by drinking lots of orange juice and getting lots of sleep. If you do that, you should feel better.

Strategy 2
WORD ANALYSIS

Readers analyze elements of written patterns of speech to figure out unfamiliar words.

Words are composed of elements—affixes, which are prefixes, suffixes, combining forms; and root words. The very words *prefix* and *suffix* are examples of word elements. *Pre* means *before* and *fix* means *to fasten or attach*, so a prefix is something attached to something else. *Suf* is a variant of *sub*, *below or under*, so a suffix is something fastened underneath, or in the case of words, behind something else.

prefix	A prefix is a letter or group of letters placed at the beginning of a word to alter the original word in some way, thus creating a word of opposite meaning.	• *un (not)* + *science* → *unscientific*
suffix	A suffix is a letter or letters added to the end of a word to create another form of a word, thus creating a verb from a noun.	• *-ion (result of)* + *infect* → *infection*
combining form	A combining form is part of a word that occurs only as part of a compound word.	• *electro (from electric)* + *magnetic* → *electromagnetic*
root word	A root word is the form of a word after all affixes are removed.	• *act* • *complete*

a group of words	Many root words have a word family, that is, a group of words that share the same root. Each word when combined with affixes becomes a related but different word.	• *action, acting, acted, react, inaction* • *completion, completing, completely, incomplete*

Developing vocabulary, especially for comprehension of difficult scientific and technical texts, is a simple process of memorization. Furthermore, meaningful understanding of vocabulary words involves more than looking up words in the dictionary. In order to fully understand the subject matter, readers must understand the vocabulary words that represent the concepts they are learning.

Engaging multiple vocabulary strategies will help readers to connect unknown words to familiar words and concepts, to understand and apply examples for the meaning of difficult words, and to differentiate between similar words and concepts. Vocabulary strategies enable readers to think about words and ideas in multiple and different ways, and to engage the full range of their cognitive and imaginative skills in the process of reading comprehension.

EXERCISES

A   CONTEXT CLUES

Circle the correct meaning of the bold word based on the surrounding clues.

(____) 1 The nurse enjoyed working in **pediatrics**. The children often responded more quickly to treatments than older patients, and they always seemed to have such positive attitudes.
   a. branch of medicine that deals with women
   b. branch of medicine that deals with children and adolescents
   c. branch of medicine that deals with elderly patients

(____) 2 A cancerous growth may be diagnosed as a **malignant** tumor.
   a. relating to cancer cells that are invasive and tend to metastasize
   b. relating to cuts and abrasions of the skin
   c. relating to broken bones

(____) 3 Inhaling bleach can scar the lungs and inhibit the **respiratory** system.
   a. pertaining to the process of blood circulation
   b. pertaining to the process of digestion
   c. pertaining to the process of breathing

(____) 4 Obesity contributes to heart disease and other physical problems that can shorten one's lifespan, or increase the chances of **premature** death.
   a. happening or done before the normal or expected time
   b. happening according to a normal cycle
   c. happening later than expected

(____) 5 Perimenopausal women should take calcium to prevent the onset of **osteoporosis**. Otherwise, as they age, women may experience thin and frail bones and be prone to bone fractures.
   a. a form of dementia
   b. brittleness of the bones
   c. iron deficiency

B WORD ANALYSIS

Write the prefixes, suffixes, and root words in the blanks. Finally, match each word to its correct definition.

		Prefix or suffix	Root word
a	biochemistry		
b	aquatic		
c	malnutrition		
d	dehydration		
e	inflammation		
f	malpractice		
g	photosynthesis		
h	hemisphere		
i	discharge		
j	imbalance		

(____) 1 combining of compounds with the aid of radiant energy (especially in plants)
(____) 2 a state of disequilibrium or instability
(____) 3 physical weakness resulting from insufficient food or an unbalanced diet
(____) 4 consisting of, relating to, or being in water
(____) 5 pain, swelling, and redness of body tissues in response to illness or injury
(____) 6 the study of the chemical substances and vital processes occurring in living organisms
(____) 7 to release, as from confinement, care, or duty
(____) 8 dryness resulting from the removal of water
(____) 9 half of the terrestrial globe
(____) 10 professional wrongdoing that results in injury or damage

Unit 1

Chapter 1

Taipei 101

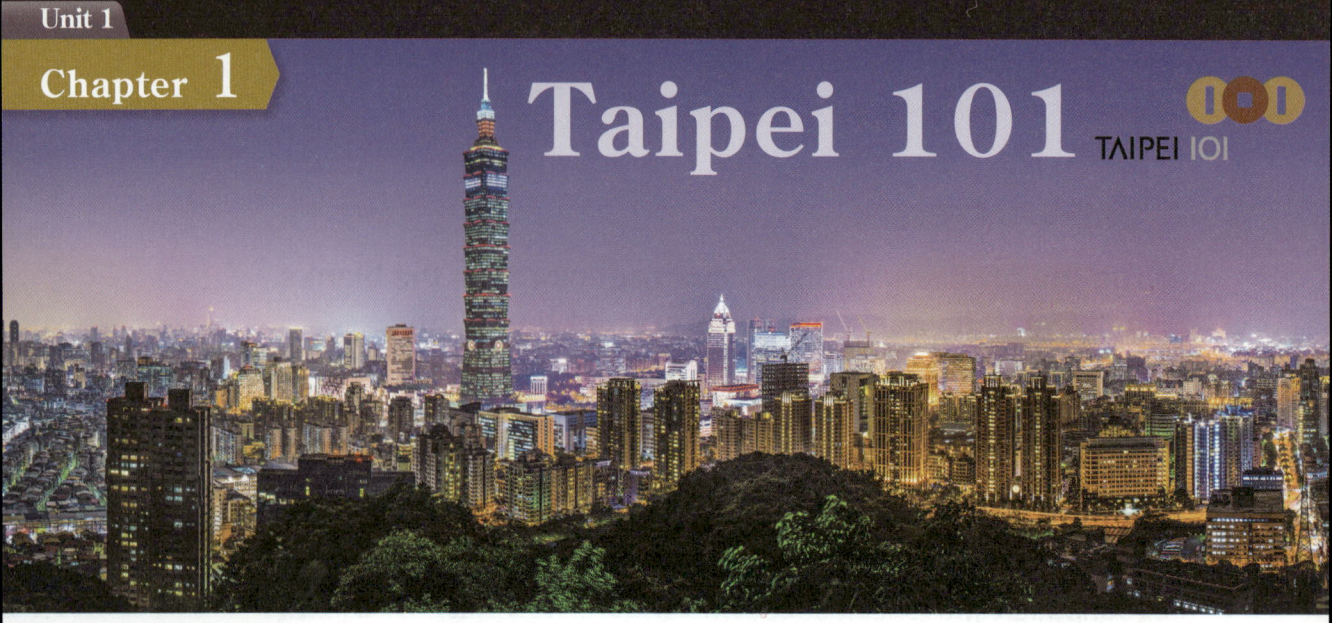

1 From the ancient pyramids of Egypt to the most recent Burj Khalifa, dominating structures have captured the attention and impelled competition among **structural*** engineers. Various categories define the tallest structures, ranging from observations decks (CN Tower of Canada) to glass panels (Burj Khalifa) to towering spires (Taipei 101). On its completion in 2004, Taipei 101 (the skyscraper is so named for its 101 floors) took the title of the tallest building in the world to be fully occupied. However, in 2009, the newly constructed Burj Khalifa took the title with 169 floors occupied, well surpassing Taipei 101.

▲ The 828m tall Burj Khalifa in Dubai has been the tallest building in the world since 2009. (cc by King of Hearts)

▲ the CN Tower in Canada

▲ Taipei 101, rising above the skyline (cc by peellden)

2 The structural achievement of Taipei 101 (formally Taipei Financial Center) was a **collaborative** effort between architects and engineers. Their joint project resulted in a steel and concrete-**reinforced** tower innovatively designed to resist high **seismic** and typhoon stresses. Taipei 101 stands just 508m from a major fault line, and has to potentially

*The blue target words are collected and listed in the Word Book.

counter winds of 100 mph. The architect, C.Y. Lee and Partners, utilized state of the art structural design to defy these extreme forces of nature, while at the same time incorporating traditional Chinese symbols and culture.

3 The architectural innovations of Taipei 101 begin 30m below ground with 380 1.5m diameter concrete piles embedded into the bedrock. The tower superstructure is secured to the foundation with shear studs and supported by eight super-**columns**, primary vertical members of the structural system, two supporting each of the four **perimeter** faces. To the 26th floor, the super-columns share the gravity load with sub-super columns and corner columns to form box sections. All columns are **composites** of steel plates and 10,000 psi reinforced concrete, so that they resist the structural challenge of metal **fatigue**. Four lines of bracing in each direction complete the building's core structure.

1 Taipei 101 during a typhoon (cc by Alton.arts)
2 ruyi symbol as an architectural motif on Taipei 101 (cc by Alton Thompson)
3 feng shui fountain outside Taipei 101 (cc by Alton Thompson)

▲ the base of Taipei 101 Tower (cc by Fkehar)
▼ view from the base of Taipei 101 Tower, looking up (cc by Alton Thompson)

4 Within the **core**, diagonal braces add to core **stiffness**. Inverted V or chevron braces provide passage for elevators as well as allowing elevator lobbies to be more spacious. 4 x 4 concrete shear walls are cast between the core columns, which further provide core stiffness up to the 8th floor. Above the 8th floor, steel **trusses** and inclined moment-resisting **lattices** holding a wall system of glass panels all tie back into the super-columns in order to counter both wind and seismic activity without being damaged. The entire structure is comprised of 8-story **modules**; every 8th story consists of a story-high truss designed to transfer gravity to the super-columns.

▲ Taipei 101 nearing the end of construction, 2003 (cc by Wdshu)

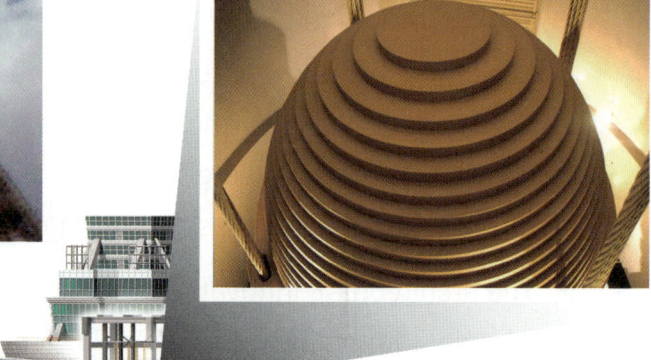

◀ model of the tuned mass damper that hangs between the 88th and 92nd floors of Taipei 101

▶ The world's largest tuned mass damper is used to reduce unwanted vibration from wind and earthquakes.

🎧 02 **5** One of the most unique design aspects of Taipei 101 is the installation of three tuned-mass **dampers**. The primary 730-ton spherical damper, installed between the 92nd and the 88th floors, consists of 41 layered steel plates and is suspended by a **sling** of 8 steel cables. Eight surrounding **viscous** damper devices (VDD) act to **dissipate** the energy (heat) generated when the tuned-mass damper shifts, and an outer bumper ring prevents the ball from ever swaying too far. Because of its weight, the primary damper could not be lifted by crane and had to be constructed on site. Two smaller 7-ton dampers are installed at the tip of the spire to reduce structural response to Vortex Induced Oscillation (VIO), common winds that cause bending moments in the spires.

6 Another unique feature of Taipei 101 is its world's fastest, double-decked, **pressurized** elevators. Traveling between the lobby and the 89th floor observation deck, these elevators rise at 60km per hour and descend at 36.6 km/hour, which means that visitors can travel to the observation deck in less than 40 seconds. Another **observatory** is located on the 91st floor, and the top floor houses a private club, Summit 101. As a multi-use facility, Taipei 101 also houses retail facilities, restaurants, offices, and communication facilities. In addition, beneath the skyscraper you'll find a subway station, which opened in 2013 upon the completion of the Xinyi line of Taipei's Mass Rapid Transit system.

▲ The Outdoor Observatory deck (91st floor, 391.8m) (cc by Michael Apel)

▲ Taipei 101 Mall

◀ MRT Taipei 101/World Trade Center Station

7 Taipei 101 embodies state of the art technology, but its design also incorporates traditional Chinese symbolism. Taipei is **mnemonic** for technology, art, innovation, people, environment, and identity, and 101 connotes the new century in which it arose: 101 is **pluperfect**, one higher than 100, the traditional symbol of perfection. Various uses of eight in the design of Taipei 101 are based on the Chinese interpretation of the lucky number—abundance, prosperity and good fortune. These repeated 8-story segments recall the traditional Chinese pagoda and the bamboo plant, which is a model of strength, **resilience**, and elegance.

8 Taipei 101 stands at the center of the Xinyi Planning District, the only master-planned community in Taipei. The community has become the city center, and even though Taipei 101 has been eclipsed in height by Burj Khalifa, it continues to anchor a thriving business district for Taipei.

▼ Taipei 101 stands at the center of the Xinyi Planning District.

TARGET WORD EXERCISES

A
Match the words with their definitions. The words are in bold in the article—find the definition from the context.

a structural	c composite	e truss	g collaborative	i resilience
b perimeter	d core	f lattice	h pluperfect	j viscous

(____) 1 working together, cooperative
(____) 2 outer limits or boundary of a specific area
(____) 3 more than perfect
(____) 4 sticky, thick, adhesive
(____) 5 used in or necessary to building
(____) 6 a rigid framework designed to support a structure
(____) 7 made up of disparate or separate parts
(____) 8 a central and foundational vertical space, such as in a multistory building
(____) 9 the power or ability to return to the original form
(____) 10 a structure of crossed strips arranged to form a diagonal pattern of open spaces between the strips

B
Fill in the blanks with the correct target words.

pressurized
slings
seismic
composite
dampers
fatigue
trusses

1 Repeated hurricanes were a suspected cause of _____ in the levees.
2 Volcanic eruptions can often cause _____ activities in surrounding areas.
3 The Colosseum in Rome is supported by Corinthian, Doric, and Ionic _____.
4 _____ concrete contains bars or fibers to add strength.
5 Jet airplane cabins are _____ while the plane is in flight to maintain sea level conditions.
6 Pianos contain _____ to stop vibrations of the piano strings.
7 Synthetic fibers are often used to make _____ for lifting and moving heavy equipment.

C
Replace the bold synonyms with the correct target word.

dampers	reinforced	columns	trusses	sling	perimeter
core	composite	structural	resilience	seismic	lattice

1 **Supporting pillars** are the most identifying features of Greek and Roman architecture. → ☐

2 Some engineers specifically study **building design** failure. → ☐

3 A ⁽¹⁾**cross design** of ⁽²⁾**strong concrete and steel members** supports many bridges throughout the world. → ⁽¹⁾☐ → ⁽²⁾☐

4 Fiber-⁽¹⁾**strengthened** plastic is actually a ⁽²⁾**collection of disparate elements** of plastic and glass fibers. → ⁽¹⁾☐ → ⁽²⁾☐

5 **The ability to return to original form** engineering is a new approach to risk management considering adaptation to current conditions. → ☐

6 Landscape architecture contributes aesthetic beauty to the **outer boundary** of many buildings. → ☐

7 The **center of the structure** was aesthetically designed to provide spacious elevators and open lobbies. → ☐

8 In the 1980s, a Major League Baseball World Series game was halted due to **earth vibrations** activity. → ☐

9 **Shock absorbers** dissipate energy or heat in a variety of automotive and industrial machines. → ☐

10 **A suspension strap** enabled the piano movers to lift the piano to the fifth floor apartment. → ☐

D The following words are antonyms to some of the target words. Fill in the correct target words beside their antonyms.

| fatigue |
| collaborative |
| resilience |
| composite |
| viscous |
| core |

1 uncooperative ↔ _____
2 runny ↔ _____
3 inflexibility ↔ _____
4 strong ↔ _____
5 perimeter ↔ _____
6 separate ↔ _____

E True or False. Decide if the target words in the following sentences have been used properly, and place a T or F in the blank.

(___) 1 After the accident, the crooked pole demonstrated its lack of **resilience**.
(___) 2 The **viscous** water poured freely over the levee.
(___) 3 **Dampers** are often used in air ducts to regulate the flow of air.
(___) 4 Some scientists prefer to work independently, **collaborative** from others in their labs.
(___) 5 **Reinforced** glass is designed to be very fragile and shatter immediately upon impact.
(___) 6 A lifting **sling** is essential for moving heavy loads during building construction.

Unit 1
Chapter 2

Anti-Terrorism in Structural Design

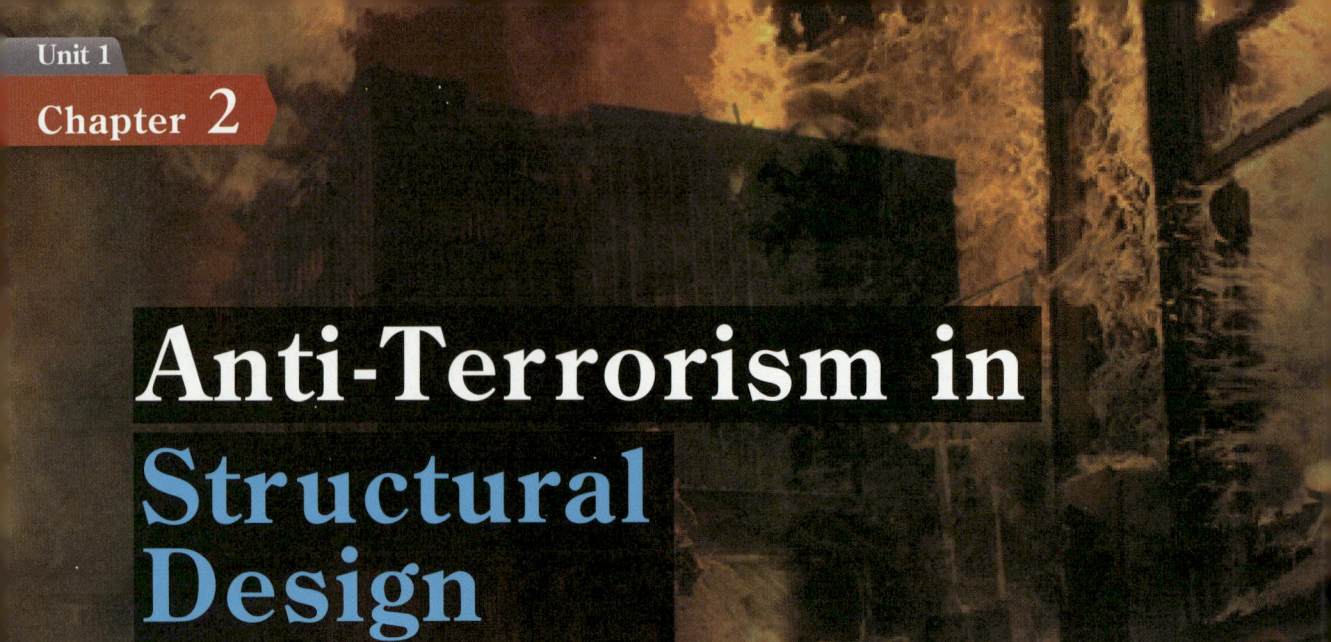

1. In the post 9/11 world, when many countries have become victims of terrorist aggression, enhancing security in the built environment has become a primary public concern. Secure and well-designed environments serve to protect people and structures from many types of dangerous threats and help to maintain high productivity. Throughout the world, councils and agencies examine current building structures to determine if they can withstand a **terrorist** attack, and some countries have already developed codes, design methods, and construction **techniques** to protect both older structures and newly designed buildings.

▲ the 9/11 attacks on the Twin Towers

2. **Blast-protected** or **explosive-resistant** buildings are a first line of defense against terrorist attacks. Although the method and material of any explosion cannot be known in advance, buildings can be designed to withstand both internal and external damage from the effect of a blast. Structural materials need

▲ terrorists

Varied English Spellings

American	British
↓	↓
defen**se**	defen**ce**
cent**er**	cent**re**

20

to be able to withstand both the heat generated from explosive materials, which causes air to blast through walls and windows, and the shock waves created by the actual explosion. The rapid conversion of explosive substances into hot gases places extreme pressure on all parts of a building, compromising its **restraining** capability, thus causing structural collapse. Although some blasts could be caused by gas or nuclear elements, it is more likely that terrorist bombs will be made of some form of TNT (trinitrotoluene), sometimes mixed with other explosive material such as RDX (cyclonite). These bombs are most often delivered in vehicles, but could arrive on foot or through package delivery.

◀ solid trinitrotoluene (TNT), a useful explosive material

3. The initial defense for any building is the use of **deterrence** methods, such as concrete **barricades** and landscaping features that might include permanent planters against the building, statues or concrete seating to prevent vehicular **intrusion**. Structural engineers cannot simply rely on these deterrents, however, and they must plan for resisting damaging explosions in their buildings. The primary goals are to minimize building damage and to prevent collapse of the building, at least until **evacuation** is complete. Another goal is to maintain emergency functions throughout the evacuation process.

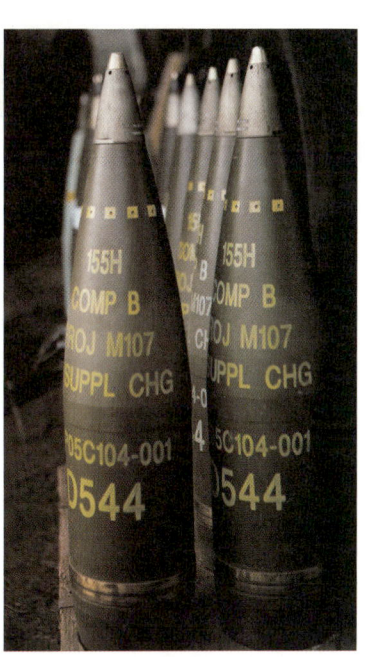

▲ M107 artillery shells. All are labelled to indicate a filling of "Comp B" (a mixture of TNT and RDX).

4. Anti-terrorism designs must exceed specifications for conventional building stress. External components, such as walls and columns, are most vulnerable to air blasts. **Ductile** reinforced concrete walls ensure **flexure** upon sudden blast rather than **fracture**. Load-bearing walls in particular resist blast pressure through mass; large mass will respond after the blast pressure and also wave

▲ Concrete barricades and landscaping features are often used as the initial defense for buildings.

pressure, thus minimizing fracture and wall **deformation**. Ductile reinforced concrete wall construction without columns is most blast resistant, but columns can be used effectively if they are, for instance, concrete encased and not accessible from the building exterior.

5 Air blasts cause the most damage to windows; therefore, windows must be designed to resist explosion and minimize the dangers of **hazardous** breakage. **Glazing** or window design and placement can resist shattering by limiting the number or size of windows, using secondary windows, or using **lamination** to prevent or limit breakage. The use of laminated, **annealed** glass is preferable; the annealed glass should be thinner, allowing for the lamination to hold the shards of glass together or minimize their dispersal. Structural **sealant** should be used around the windows to

◄ Windows are designed to resist explosions and minimize the dangers of hazardous breakage.

22

help hold the window or glass shards in the frame. Window resistance is always weaker than wall resistance; windows should be damaged first, or otherwise the force of the blast will go into the supporting walls, fracturing the building structure instead.

6 Doors are less of a structural concern because of their **transitory** use. However, consideration should be given to use of steel doors and reinforced concrete around the jambs. Ductile reinforced concrete beams are also preferable for roof support. Below-ground portions of a building can be protected by **perimeter** barriers with deep foundations; soil provides a protective barrier for foundation walls.

▲ Steel doors are preferable for anti-terrorist designs.

7 A variety of tools and standards are available to provide structural technology information and codified methods for anti-terrorist building design. The U.S. Department of Defense has developed Unified Facilities Criteria (UFC), which provide minimum anti-terrorism building standards. The Whole Building Design Guide (WBDG) is a non-profit, joint U.S. government and private sector effort which offers a holistic approach to protective building design with an online component. Internationally, ASIS International provides security management information to numerous countries; currently they provide members with a Protection of Assets (POA) manual. The Centre for International Cooperation and Security (CICS) has also begun an international research initiative into security building, especially as it affects poorer nations.

TARGET WORD EXERCISES

A
A successful terrorist attack can cause significant damage. Some of the target words are related to such damage; match them to their definitions.

- a. blast
- b. explosive
- c. fracture
- d. ductile
- e. flexure
- f. terrorist

(____) 1 capable of changing form without breaking
(____) 2 one who frightens or coerces by intimidation
(____) 3 a substance which produces extreme noise, heat, and violent expansion of gases upon a rapid chemical or nuclear reaction
(____) 4 a break or crack
(____) 5 the act of bending or folding
(____) 6 the act of exploding

B
Fill in the following sentences with words from the list on the left.

- fracture
- blast
- explosive
- ductile
- terrorist
- flexure

1. The perimeter statues were badly damaged by the _____ planted in the bed of the truck by an alleged _____.
2. A small _____ was found in an upper window after the seismic activity occurred.
3. Timber does not exhibit much _____ when exposed to extreme stress.
4. Several workers suffered severe burns in a chemical plant _____ in Hebei.
5. In general, two types of engineering materials exist, _____ and brittle.

C
There are many ways that structural design can help prevent the damaging results of a successful terrorist attack; many words from the above text relate to these design processes. Match these target words with their meanings.

- a. techniques
- b. protect
- c. resistant
- d. restrain
- e. deterrent
- f. evacuation
- g. laminate
- h. glaze
- i. anneal
- j. transitory

(____) 1 to keep safe or defend from danger
(____) 2 to furnish or fill with glass
(____) 3 removal of persons or things from an endangered area
(____) 4 methods of accomplishing a task or goal
(____) 5 lasting only a short time
(____) 6 to subject glass or metal to a process of heating and slow cooling in order to strengthen or harden

(____) 7 to hold back, limit or restrict
(____) 8 to cover with layers of material bonded together
(____) 9 able to withstand the action or effect of
(____) 10 something that prevents, checks, or arrests

D Replace the bolded antonyms with the correct form of a target word.

| protect | flexure | deterrents | transitory |
| restrain | evacuate | ductile | resist |

1 The door provided a **permanent** location for the office workers.
   → _____

2 After the typhoon, many villagers were forced to **stay in** their homes.
   → _____

3 Concrete perimeter barriers serve as **encouragement** for vehicular bombings.
   → _____

4 Concrete reinforced window frames are designed to provide **rigidity** when subjected to air blasts or seismic activity. → _____

5 Most steel and concrete columns will **succumb to** the force of an explosion.
   → _____

6 Many governments have designed councils to develop codified building methods to help **harm** their citizens. → _____

7 Floor to ceiling concrete walls help to **release** potential fires in the case of a blast.
   → _____

8 **Brittle** materials are designed to deform rather than rapidly crack and break.
   → _____

E Prefixes: Fill in the blanks with the correct prefixes to create the correct word in each sentence.

| trans |
| ex |
| re |

1 Cross beams helped to make the roof more bomb-_____sistant.
2 Terrorists sometimes carry _____plosives in backpacks.
3 The heat from a blast is _____itory compared to the lasting damage to a building or its occupants.
4 A possible deterrent to terrorists is security personnel designated to _____strain unidentified personnel who seek to enter government buildings.

Unit 1
Chapter 3

Green Building

1 Natural building, or making the most efficient use of natural and local products, is a conscious building process as old as the built **environment** itself. Mud and earth building may date back as long as 10,000 years, and other natural materials, such as straw and wood, were used efficiently hundreds of years ago. In the 21st century, with the additional aid of technology, humanity is now moving toward conscious **sustainable** building or **green** building, which would provide benefits for human health, natural environment, economic and community, as well as limiting or even preventing the waste of natural resources.

2 Worldwide, housing has an enormous **impact** on the environment. According to the US Green Building Council (www.usgbc.org), housing accounts for 17% of fresh water **withdrawals**, 25% wood harvests, 33% CO_2 **emissions**, and 40% material and energy use (45% in China). To help reduce natural resource waste,

▼ natural buildings

the ICC (International Code Council) has produced such building standards as the International Energy Conservation Code, the most commonly adopted energy efficiency code worldwide, and the International Plumbing Code to ensure efficient use of water. Both the USGB and the ICC (International Code Council) provide standards and guidelines for both improved **occupant** health and **productivity** in both living and working environments.

3 Efficient material management, or efficient processing of material left at the end of construction or **renovation** (commonly referred to as **construction** and **demolition** (C&D) materials), is a priority for green building. In the past, the leftover materials have been considered waste, and their **disposal** has been typical for the building process. However, up to 95 percent of the **discarded** materials can be **recycled** into new products or used in new ways to benefit both the construction business and the environment.

▲ ENERGY STAR building label

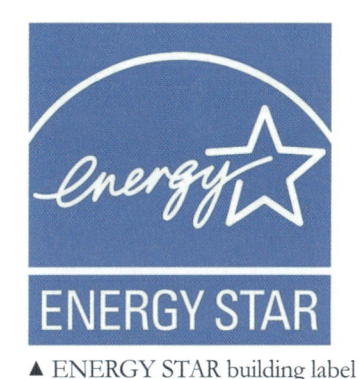

Table 1: Products developed from discarded construction materials

C&D	Recycled Products
Clean, untreated wood	lumber, pressboard or even fuel
Concrete	building projects ranging from homes to nuclear plants
Asphalt pavement and shingles	recycled pavement; in the U.S. there are currently programs called "recycling roofs into roads"
Metals	same metal products; these metals can be recycled indefinitely without losing any of their properties using only 5 percent of the energy used in the initial production
Corrugated cardboard	paper for chipboard, paperboard (i.e., cereal boxes), paper towels, tissues, and printing and writing paper
Drywall	gypsum, which makes up 90% of drywall, recycled into new drywall, cement or fertilizer

27

[06] Green buildings are also designed to meet aggressive energy use targets suggested by the EPA and the ICC. These targets ensure that levels of greenhouse gas emissions are strictly **minimized** or **eliminated**. In the U.S., when structural designs meet or exceed EPA standards designated in their energy performance rating system, they receive an ENERGY STAR building label. In Canada, green buildings are recognized by a BUILDSMART label. In Australia, the Green Building Council (GBC) offers a voluntary rating system called the Green Stars program.

[4] Building green requires effective attention given to **embodied** energy, or the entire amount of energy used in the building process. Embodied energy includes the energy required for the production and transportation of building materials, the construction process, and, if necessary, the demolition of the building. Embodied energy planning includes:
- Measuring the embodied energy
- Considering how the building material is transported
- Reducing and recycling materials
- Considering possible reuse and re**furbish**ing of existing buildings

[5] Australia's GBC has begun the initiative of carbon neutral building or zero net operating emissions, which includes:
- Passive design: **ventilation** and temperature control without mechanical systems
- On-site generation of energy from renewable sources: utilization of solar panels, hot water collectors or wind and water turbines
- Efficient appliances and light fittings: installation of LED

▲ ENERGY STAR appliances

lights, intelligent control systems, and ENERGY STAR appliances
- **Purchasing green power:** purchasing energy from suppliers utilizing renewable energy sources
- **Optimizing or removing HVAC systems:** to include efficient recycling of metals, plastics, or other materials removed or replaced

6 Today, worldwide efforts are being made to create green building standards. In 2008 the ICC created a Sustainable Building Technology Committee (SBTC) to provide oversight and direction for many ongoing efforts in green, sustainable and safe construction. The U.S. LEED (Leadership in Energy and Environmental Design) standards have paved the way for governments' communities from Hong Kong to India to Sweden to develop their own green building guidelines. Building green will ultimately mean more than **negating** environmental impact; built environment can serve as a **restorative** to human health and the natural environment.

▲ Berlin Central Station was constructed with a large glass roof and facade to allow natural lighting.

▲ utilization of solar panels

Varied English Spellings

The U.S. Green Building Council provides much of the information for developing international green building policies, so many green building terms will appear in American English. Two words in the article above have varied spellings:

American	British
↓	↓
optimi**ze**	optimi**se**
alumin**um**	alumin**ium**

TARGET WORD EXERCISES

A The following target words are all basic to the concepts of "green building." Match the words with their meanings based on the reading.

a. sustainable
b. green
c. occupant
d. environment

(___) 1 tenant of an office or house
(___) 2 the air, water, minerals, organisms, and all other external factors surrounding and affecting a given organism at any time
(___) 3 environmentally beneficial
(___) 4 capable of being continued with minimal long-term effect on the environment

B The following target words can all refer to "ways to positively influence something in the environment." Place the correct words in the sentences below.

renovation | restorative | productivity | embodied
impact | recycle | construction

1. Sustainable tourism has had a strong _____ on many national parks.
2. Utilizing natural sources is one way of creating a _____ environment.
3. High efficiency and sensitivity to the environment help define green _____.
4. _____ of older buildings can be more efficient than building new ones.
5. Long-term planning for commercial green construction involves consideration of _____ energy.
6. Environmentally sensitive building contractors recognize that they can _____ over 90 percent of their construction and demolition materials.
7. Worker _____ increases when environmental pollution is reduced.

C The following target words all refer to removing or having an effect of lessening something in the environment. Match these words with their meanings.

a. demolition   e. minimize
b. discard   f. eliminate
c. disposal   g. negating
d. pollution

(___) 1 to put an end to, eradicate
(___) 2 to get rid of as useless
(___) 3 harmful substances or products in the environment
(___) 4 act of tearing down or destroying
(___) 5 to nullify or cause to be ineffective
(___) 6 act of disposing, systematic destruction
(___) 7 to reduce to lowest degree or amount

D Use the correct form of the words from Exercise C to complete the following sentences.

1. The contractors bundled the corrugated cardboard for recycling, because they did not want to _____ it.
2. Asphalt shingles were collected after the _____ of the roof.
3. Outdoor work spaces are one of many ways _____ waste for lighting and cooling.
4. The use of solar energy will significantly increase the chance to completely _____ the need for fossil fuels to generate electricity.
5. The installation of LED lights helped _____ the use of electricity in the new office building.
6. The building contractor was responsible for the proper _____ of hazardous waste.

E In the article, there are many words about green building that contain the prefix "re-." Combine "re" with the following root words in the left column, and match them with their definitions:

a. new
b. sale
c. furbish
d. design
e. cycle
f. store

(____) 1 renovate, brighten
(____) 2 make new again
(____) 3 process for use again
(____) 4 act of selling again
(____) 5 change the appearance of or plans for
(____) 6 bring back to a former condition

F Match the prefixes/suffixes/combining words (some are used more than once) with the target words you've learned in this chapter:

em-
im-
re-
-ive
dis-
-ing
-able

1. _____bodied
2. _____pact
3. negat_____
4. _____cycle
5. _____carded
6. _____posal
7. _____storat_____
8. sustain_____

Unit 2
Chapter 4
Scooter Engine

① In the 1860s serious attempts began to motorize bicycles through the use of fuel engines. More attempts continued through the 19th century:

② **1867:** Sylvester Howard Roper from Roxbury, Massachusetts began demonstrating his steam velocipede at fairs in 1867. His design utilized a charcoal-fired boiler with **alternating cylinders** which operated a crank on the rear wheel.

▲ Roper and his steam carriage

③ **1892:** Felix Millet of France designed what he called a "motocyclette" in 1892. He equipped his bicycle with

▶ The Millet motorcycle (cc by Gérard Delafond)

32

pneumatic tires and a five-cylinder rotary engine built into the rear wheel.

④ **1894:** The first mass produced (actually only about 200 were manufactured) motorcycle was a design by Hildebrand & Wolfmueller of Munich in 1894. They equipped this cycle with a 2.5-horsepower, two-cylinder, four-stroke engine.

▲ 1894 Hildebrand & Wolfmueller model

⑤ **1895:** Then, a French company, DeDion-Buton, produced a three-wheeled motorized cycle equipped with a four-cycle engine that was lighter and more powerful than its predecessors.

⑥ Throughout the 20th century, fuel-driven motor scooters were commonly **powered** by a two-stroke cycle engine, or movements of the **piston** in the cylinder.

▲ De Dion-Bouton tricycle towing a passenger in a carriage

⑦ First stroke: Power/**exhaust** stroke that occurs immediately after the **ignition** of the charge

→ forces the piston down
→ when the top of the piston passes the top of the exhaust port, most of the pressurized exhaust gases escape
→ as the piston continues downward, it compresses the mixture of air, fuel, and oil in the crankcase
→ the mixture rushes into the cylinder
→ the mixture displaces the remaining exhaust gases and thus fills the cylinder with a fresh charge of fuel.

TARGET WORD EXERCISES

A Match the target words with their definitions. The words are in bold in the article—find the definition from the context.

a facilitate	e pivot	i combustion	m alternating
b piston	f compression	j constituent	n durability
c adiabatic	g power	k vacuum	o interference
d intake	h ignition	l alleviate	p exhaust

(____) 1 to make something easy or easier to do
(____) 2 point on which something (e.g., shaft) turns
(____) 3 partly or completely exhausted of gas or air
(____) 4 to perform by turns or in succession
(____) 5 the process of burning; a chemical change, especially oxidation, accompanied by the production of heat and light
(____) 6 to supply with mechanical or electrical energy
(____) 7 to press or squeeze together
(____) 8 steam or gases ejected from the cylinder of an engine
(____) 9 to make (as suffering) more bearable; to partially remove or correct
(____) 10 the act of causing something (e.g., fuel) to burn
(____) 11 the act of obstructing or blocking
(____) 12 able to resist wear
(____) 13 a thermodynamic process that happens without loss or gain of heat
(____) 14 one of the individual parts of which a composite entity is made up; especially a part that can be separated from or attached to a system
(____) 15 the act of taking in
(____) 16 mechanical device inside a cylinder that has a plunging or thrusting motion

B Fill in the blanks with the correct target words.

| interference | adiabatic | ignition | alleviated | pivot |
| combustion | facilitate | constituent | alternating | compression |

1 Gears turn any assembly by _____ their movement.
2 The power unit helps shortening the motor wiring to _____ cost reduction.
3 Gears placed too close together will cause _____ with each other and possibly stop the movement of an assembly completely.
4 Some fossils are the result of extreme _____ in the earth, leaving traces or remains of the original specimen.

5 _____ process is necessary in engines to prevent them from overheating.
6 The fire started with the _____ of combustible materials.
7 An internal _____ engine depends on burning fuel to produce power.
8 Wearing a back brace _____ most of the furniture mover's pain.
9 The shaft was designed to _____ in order to allow maximum flexibility of the bevel arm.
10 The rear wheel is a _____ part of the scooter.

C Write the correct target word beside each prefix, suffix, or combing word.

take	durabil
levi	ternat
stitu	iabat
bustion	haust
terfer	pression

1 ex_____
2 com_____
3 com_____
4 in_____
5 in_____ence
6 al_____ate
7 con_____ent
8 al_____ing
9 ad_____ic
10 _____ity

D Prefixes or combining forms can also create antonyms. Add one of the following prefixes to the following root words and then match with the target antonym.

| un | de | non | ex | out |

a ____interference
b ____take
c ____tinguish
d ____compression
e ____powered

(____) 1 ignite
(____) 2 powered
(____) 3 intake
(____) 4 compression
(____) 5 interference

E Correctly place words a-e from Exercise D above in the following sentences.

1 Patients need to be sure of _____ between multiple drugs that might be prescribed.
2 Lack of air will _____ a fire.
3 Sometimes airplanes take on a sudden burst of outside air, and this causes _____ in the cabin.
4 Air flow control devices assist the flow of outward air with _____ vents.
5 Hang gliders sail through the air with _____ wings.

Unit 2
Chapter 5

Biomedical Engineering
(Mechanical Engineering)

1 Although with vast historical precedent, the increasing **interdisciplinary** relationship between biology and engineering has not gained much momentum until the last decade. Aristotle wrote of mimesis, Leonardo da Vinci mimicked nature in his innovations, and Galileo led the way in exploring relations between mechanics and biology. Not until the 20th century, though, did collaborations between engineers and scientists begin to result in rapid advances in biomedical research and applications.

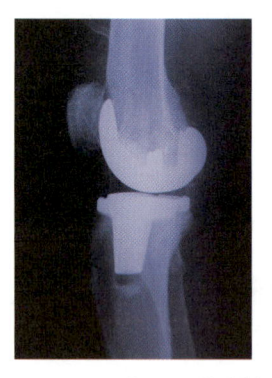

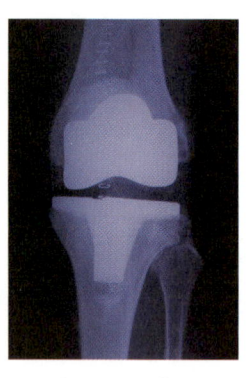

▲ X-rays of an artificial knee replacement from the side (left image) and front (right image)

2 Many new materials have been developed and utilized through **bionic** research, ranging from bone plates to nanotechnology. In the early 1900s, bone plates were **implanted** to assist the stabilization and healing of bone fractures. Implants were usually removed once the fracture healed and the bones could bear stress once again. By the 1950s, blood **vessel** replacement was possible, and by the 1960s many organs and other body parts could be replaced as well.

3 One interdisciplinary example is the application of both fluid mechanics and solid mechanics to resolving biomedical issues. Currently researchers are working on **computational** models designed to better calculate and correct the engineering concerns of **hemodynamics** (physical factors that determine blood flow), durability of the materials, and the biological response of heart valve implant. Collaborations between biologists and physicists have resulted in improved designs for **incontinence** pads, as together the scientists study how urine spreads through fibrous sheets.

4 Integrating solid mechanics with life sciences also contributes to biomedical **innovation**. For instance, in the area of optics, researchers have constructed mechanical devices to study various components and **deform**ities of lenses. Through models of **viscoelasticity** and theoretical modeling of lens structures, researchers are developing new techniques for lens accommodation in human vision.

5 The study of solid mechanics is also essential to determining and preventing stress and wear on artificial joints. In joint replacement, the diseased **articular** surface is replaced by a joint made of **synthetic** material, which could be a metal (such as titanium or cobalt-chromium alloy), ceramic (such as aluminum oxide or zirconium oxide), plastic (such as ultrahigh molecular weight polyethylene), or a combination of these materials. Artificial joints are implanted to restore **impaired** function; however, interface stress cannot be avoided between the bone and the implant. The contribution of solid mechanics research to tribology (the study of wear, friction, and lubrication), is critical, then, for the development of prosthetic materials that are more stress-resistant and biocompatible. With improvements in prosthetic materials and **fixation**, implants have nearly doubled their service longevity.

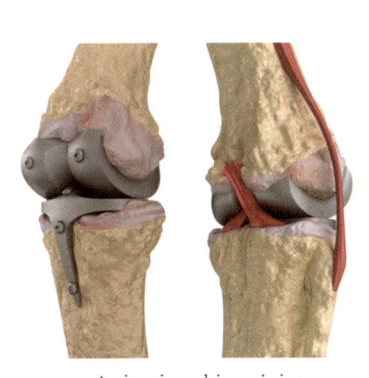

▲ titanium hinge joint

6 There are three main types of biomaterials that elicit tissue responses upon insertion into the human body: **inert**, bio**resorb**able, and bioactive.

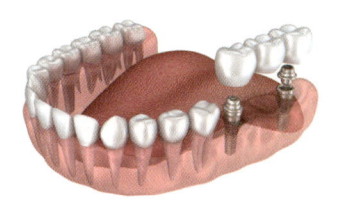

▲ titanium dental implant

- Inert materials exhibit limited chemical interaction with surrounding tissues; titanium and alumina are two such materials used for orthopedic and dental implants. Although inert materials encourage biocompatibility, recent research has shown that some cellular response may be necessary to encourage **adhesion** and healing.
- Bioresorbable materials, such as tricalcium phosphate, are slowly resorbed and replaced by tissue. One example of using bioresorbable materials is scaffold-guided tissue regeneration, which has recently emerged as a very promising advanced **therapeutic** option. Bioresorbable scaffolds of donor cells are created to mimic naturally occurring tissue. These scaffolds, once implanted into a patient, are resorbed and replaced by the patient's own tissue. The entire process may eventually require only minimally-invasive surgery, and can be used for not only artificial implants, but to treat other degenerative, inflammatory, or infectious diseases.
- Some materials, such as bioactive glass and **ceramics**, are capable of forming a chemical **bond** with the surrounding bone or soft tissue. Bonded bone lessens the likelihood of debonding, mechanical loosening and wear due to the reduction of interface motion and resulting friction. Applied principles of interface mechanics continue to improve research into the use of bioactive materials.

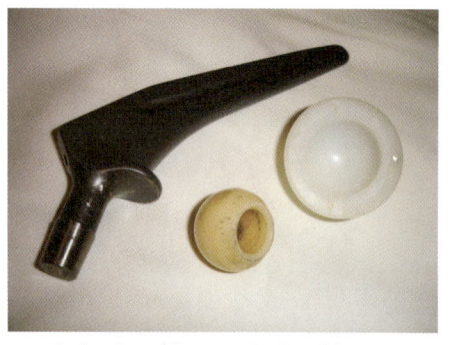

▲ titanium hip prosthesis, with a ceramic head and polyethylene acetabular cup

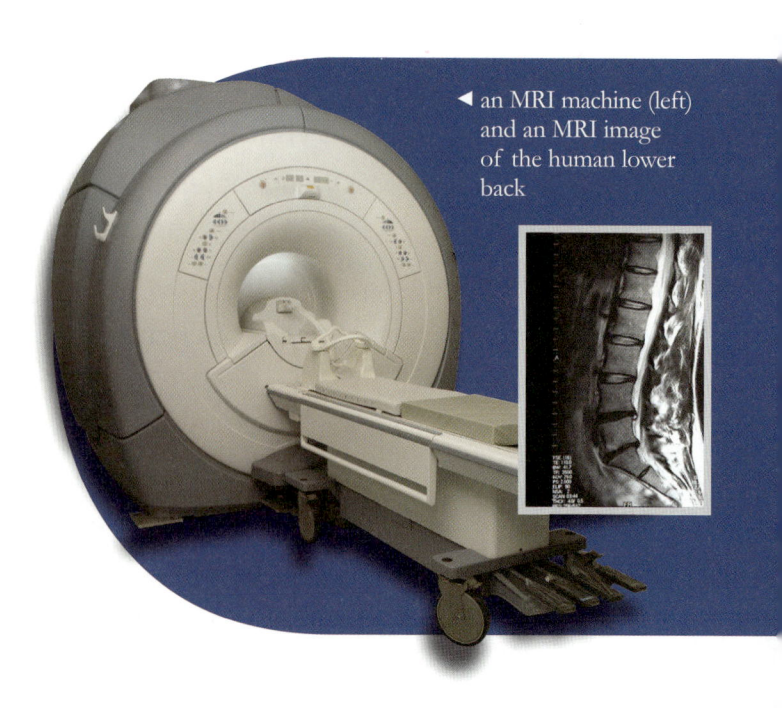

◀ an MRI machine (left) and an MRI image of the human lower back

7 Engineering expertise combined with biological research has also resulted in the development of improved diagnostic devices and procedures to obtain detailed information about internal anatomy:

- **Medical Resonance Imaging:** uses a powerful magnetic field and radio waves
- **Radiography:** uses X-rays to produce photographic images
- **Tomography:** computed tomography (CT) scans body sections, sometimes using dye
- **Ultrasonography:** uses high frequency sound waves

8 Engineers and scientists continue to expand their interdisciplinary work for advancements in areas such as medical imaging and equipment, artificial implants, biomimetics, health care technology, and molecular bioengineering. International and many national conferences annually provide forums for scientists and engineers to share their research and to collaborate in advancing biomedical engineering technology and applications.

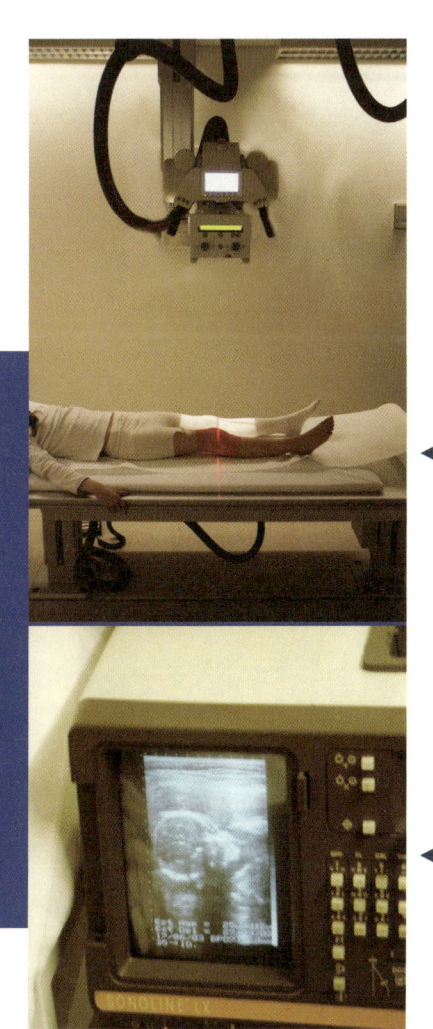

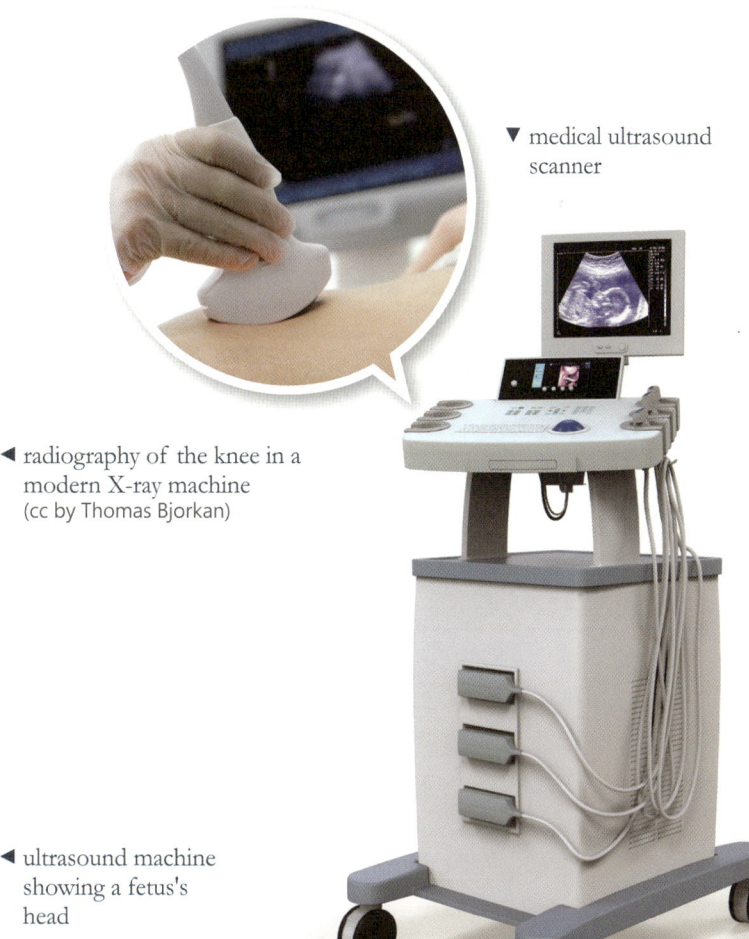

◀ medical ultrasound scanner

◀ radiography of the knee in a modern X-ray machine (cc by Thomas Bjorkan)

◀ ultrasound machine showing a fetus's head

TARGET WORD EXERCISES

A Many words associated with the interdisciplinary work of engineering and biology begin with the combining form "**bio-**" (**life**). Place the correct root words with "bio-" in each of the following definitions.

compatible	logy	medical	active
engineering	resorbable	mimetics	nics

1. Bio_minetics_ is the study and design of synthetic systems that mimic biological systems.
2. Bio_____ is the science of life.
3. Bio_____ science is the application of the principles of the natural sciences to clinical medicine.
4. Bio_____ is the application of engineering principles and techniques to problems in medicine and biology.
5. Bio_____ is the study of biological functions to solve certain types of problems involving use of the body by artificial means.
6. Bio_____ is when something exhibits properties that do not produce a toxic, injurious, or immunological response in living tissue.
7. Bio_____ is any effect on or response from living tissue.
8. Bio_____ is when materials can be broken down by the body and do not require mechanical removal.

B Match the following root words with their proper **prefix** or **suffix** to form the words used in this chapter (the prefixes can be used more than once):

de-	-al	im-	inter-	-ar
ad-	in-	-ion	syn-	

1. articul _ar_
2. _____pair
3. _____hesion
4. fixat_____
5. _____disciplinary
6. _____thetic
7. _____plant
8. _____bond
9. computation _____
10. _____novation
11. _____ert

C Correctly place in the following sentences words you have created in Exercise B.

1. Attending loud rock concerts can _____ one's hearing.
2. The use of nasal drops is a recent _____ for flu vaccine delivery.
3. Natural biomaterials can be _____ in a damaged joint to avoid joint replacement.
4. _____ models are used by researchers to develop virtual designs for new types of joint replacements.
5. The _____ work of researchers across many sciences can have a decisive impact on culture and public policy.
6. Biomimetics is a relatively new field of science devoted to _____ designs based on natural systems.
7. Artificial joints usually replace diseased or damaged _____ cartilage or living tissue.
8. After his hip replacement, the patient had to remain _____ so that the healing process could begin successfully.

D Many names of innovations produced by the collaboration of engineering and biology are known by their initials or acronyms. Match the following acronyms with their proper names (note: some are in the article, and some are related to innovations named above).

a. EROS
b. CAT scan
c. PET scan
d. MRI
e. MRA
f. BME

(a) 1 event related optical signal: a brain-scanning technique which uses infrared light to study changes in neuronal optical properties of active areas of the cerebral cortex

(___) 2 magnetic resonance angiogram: uses a magnetic field and pulses of radio wave energy to provide pictures of blood vessels inside the body

(___) 3 biomedical engineering: the application of engineering principles and techniques to the medical field

(___) 4 computerized axial tomography: an x-ray procedure which combines many x-ray images with the aid of a computer to generate cross-sectional views of the body

(___) 5 magnetic resonance imaging: a radiology technique that uses magnetism, radio waves, and a computer to produce images of body structures

(___) 6 positron emission tomography: an imaging technique that uses short-lived radioactive substances to produce three-dimensional colored images of those substances functioning within the body

Unit 2
Chapter 6

Hybrid Cars

▲ bus fueled by biodiesel

◀ The Bus Rapid Transit of Metz, a diesel-electric hybrid driving system by Van Hoo (cc by Bava Alcide57)

▲ The Saab 9-3 SportCombi BioPower—the second E85 flexifuel model introduced by Saab in the Swedish market (cc by Luftfahrrad)

▲ The 2011 Nissan Leaf was the first plug-in electric car equipped with Nissan's Vehicle Sound for Pedestrians. (cc by IFCAR)

Although **hybrid** cars have just moved into the automotive spotlight over the past decades or so, they actually debuted over 100 years ago. Dr. Ferdinand Porsche developed the first hybrid car, a **gasoline** electric vehicle, at the turn of the 20th century. This vehicle used an internal combustion engine that rotated to charge a generator, which then powered electric motors located in the **hubs** of the front wheels. Unfortunately, the hybrid vehicle was more expensive to produce than a gasoline powered vehicle, so with the development of quieter and smoother running gasoline engines and the self-starter, hybrid cars were for the most part forced out of production.

▲ German automotive engineer Ferdinand Porsche (1875-1951)

② Interest in hybrid cars emerged again in the U.S. in the 1960s, as concerns about pollution began to arise. Soon thereafter, hybrid cars were produced again, but not until the 1990s were hybrids volume produced. The Toyota Prius was introduced into the Japanese market in the late 1990s, followed shortly by Audi in Europe. By 1999, the U.S. had joined the hybrid market with a release of the Honda Insight.

▲ Honda Insight, 1999

▲ Toyota Prius, 1997

③ The hybrid car is a vehicle powered by two or more sources of energy, most commonly gasoline and electricity. Not all gasoline-electric cars contain the same parts or are powered in the same way:

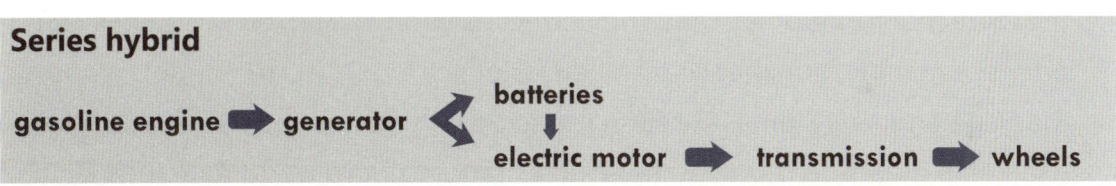

Parallel hybrid

fuel tank ➡ batteries / electric motor ➡ transmission ➡ wheels

Series hybrid

gasoline engine ➡ generator ⬅ batteries ↓ electric motor ➡ transmission ➡ wheels

④ In either system, the gasoline engine ultimately provides power to the wheels for normal driving; the electric motor provides power under increased loads sustained when passing, climbing hills, or **accelerating**. Also, the electric motor provides energy when the car is **idling**, and the gasoline engine restarts when re**engage**d. Combined, the two energy systems significantly reduce **emissions** and increase gas mileage, all without the driver noticing the power **transition**s.

⑤ Another energy efficient feature of hybrids is **regenerative** braking. Conventional braking systems reverse the car's **momentum** through **friction**, a process that creates excess heat energy. The heat energy, which accounts for nearly 30% of the car's generated power, simply **dissipates**. Regenerative braking works to **reverse** the electric motor when decelerating or braking, so that the motor becomes a generator feeding **kinetic** energy back into the batteries for later use.

45

6 Overall, efficiency of hybrid cars can be attributed to the use of smaller, lighter parts. Smaller fuel engines produce fewer emissions, but they also produce less power. Hybrid cars overcome this loss of power through efficient external design, which incorporates lightweight materials, such as aluminum and carbon fiber. Such materials, coupled with low rolling-resistance tires, wheel bearings and brakes, reduce **aerodynamic drag**. Other design elements that contribute to drag reduction are **flush** windows and **recessed** windshield wiper systems, **streamlined** front end and **tapered** rear end, recessed door handles, partially covered rear wheels, and minimized body seams. Proposed future designs include replacing side mirrors with video monitors.

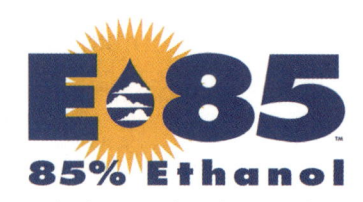

7 Not all hybrid cars are gasoline/electric combination. Other types of engine technology can be utilized to produce hybrid vehicles:

- Natural gas engines: Gasoline engines can be converted to burn compressed natural gas (CNG), liquefied petroleum gas (LPG), or hydrogen. An electronic control unit (ECU) translates information from numerous sensors, and adjusts the correct amount of fuel and the correct ignition timing. Such engines can offer optimal performance and low emissions.
- Methane engines: Biomass used in methane engines can be derived through anaerobic digestion from natural sources ranging from wood to animal manure. The process is similar to that used by waste treatment plants for many decades. The biomass undergoes gasification by subjecting organic materials to low oxygen supply and high temperatures. Biomethane engines are combined with an electric starter to further reduce emissions.
- Biofuel engines: Biological materials can be refined to produce engine fuels. **Ethanol** fuel is derived from corn products and can be combined with small amounts of **petroleum** to run E85 engines, or engines modified to run on 85% ethanol and 15% regular fuel. Research is currently underway to derive ethanol from other sources, including grass and ordinary household waste. Biofuel engines can power electric motors rather than directly powering transmissions, thus further reducing emissions.

▲ the logo used in the United States for E85 fuel

1. biogas
2. The Ford Escape Plug-in Hybrid, with a flexible fuel capability to run on E85 (ethanol) (cc by Mariordo)
3. ethanol plant in West Burlington, Iowa
4. Switchgrass is one of the most promising energy crops in the southern United States.

8 Hybrid cars today provide an efficient and affordable alternative to conventional cars. Some hybrid cars produce up to 90% fewer pollutants than non-hybrid cars, and they are much more economical because they improve mileage, and they continue to show lower depreciation rates than conventional cars. Many governments offer or are considering tax **incentives** for consumers who purchase hybrid vehicles, so the investment in a hybrid vehicle appears to be economically sound as well. Hybrid vehicles have already had a measurable impact economically and environmentally worldwide; as the public increasingly demands fuel efficient vehicles, more hybrids fueled by alternative sources will reach the market.

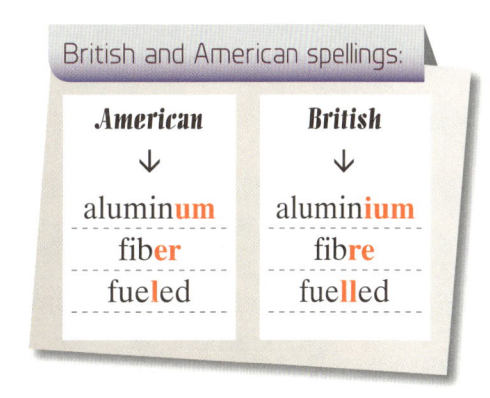

British and American spellings:

American	British
aluminum	aluminium
fiber	fibre
fueled	fuelled

TARGET WORD EXERCISES

A Word puzzle exercise: Fill in the blanks with the correct letters to form a target word from its root word.

1. to increase the speed of: __ac__celer__ate__ *(root: swift)*
2. to interlock or cause to interlock: _____gage *(root: pledge)*
3. energy or a substance given out by something: (emit)emis_____ *(root: to send out)*
4. a change from one state to another: transit_____ *(root: to cross)*
5. relating to or marked by recreating or reconstituting: _____generat_____ *(root: to bring forth again)*
6. force or speed of movement: moment_____ *(root: motion, movement)*
7. the rubbing of the surface of one body against that of another: frict_____ *(root: a rubbing)*
8. pertaining to motion: kine_____ *(root: to move)*
9. to turn or move in the opposite direction: _____verse *(root: to move)*
10. designed with round edges to reduce or minimize the drag caused by air: _____dynamic *(root: force, power)*
11. to place or set in a receding place: reces_____ *(root: a withdrawal)*
12. to construct or design in a form that offers the least resistance: stream_____ *(root: to flow)*

B Several words exist to describe the **petroleum-derived chemical mixture** that powers an internal combustion engine. Fill in the blanks with the correct word choice:

| petroleum | fuel | petroleum spirit | gas | mogas | gasoline | petrol |

1. _____ is a term used to differentiate automotive gasoline from aviation fuel, or avgas.
2. One of the earliest terms for fuel was gasolene, which was later shortened in American English to _____ in 1905.
3. The basic material for fuel is _____, which means "rock oil" or oil from the earth.
4. _____ is a combustible substance that can be consumed to produce energy.
5. When crude petroleum is distilled, it produces a volatile liquid called _____.
6. The fuel for internal combustion engines is a volatile flammable mixture of hydrocarbons, or _____, derived from petroleum.
7. The commonly used British term for gasoline is _____.

48

C **Homographs** are words that share the same spelling, but they have different meanings. The following words are homographs. Using the context of the article, choose the meaning of each target word below that matches its use above.

(____) 1 **Hybrid**
   a. bred from two distinct races
   b. offspring of two different plants
   c. a vehicle having two kinds of components that produce the same results
   d. a word composed of elements from different languages

(____) 2 **Hub**
   a. center of activity, commerce, or interest
   b. the center part of a wheel
   c. computer networking device
   d. center of a city

(____) 3 **Idle**
   a. to run at a slow speed or out of gear
   b. not employed
   c. having no real worth or value
   d. frivolous or vain

(____) 4 **Drag**
   a. to trail on the ground
   b. the scent or trail of an animal
   c. a heavy sledge or cart for pulling loads
   d. the aerodynamic force exerted on an object that tends to reduce its forward motion

(____) 5 **Flush**
   a. to cause to redden or glow
   b. having surfaces in the same plane
   c. having an abundant supply of money
   d. to clean, rinse, or empty with a rapid flow of a liquid, especially water

49

Unit 3
Chapter 7
DEADLY Infectious Diseases

1 Despite the rapid advances of medical research, diagnostics, and treatment through the 20th century, **infectious** diseases remain a deadly global threat. In 2007 alone, infectious diseases were responsible for 26% of global **mortality**. Researchers attribute a variety of factors or causes to the emergence and **transmission** of deadly infectious diseases:

- newly present disease agents, such as bacteria, virus, or fungus
- disease agents recently recognized by improved diagnostic tools and procedures
- increased rates of current deadly infectious diseases
- changes in human behavior, such as shifts in population centers, travel habits, and technology and industry
- increased use of antibiotics
- decreased **compliance** with mandated or available vaccines.

2 One of the most significant disease emergences in the late 20th century was HIV/AIDS, which continues to be a leading factor in worldwide **morbidity**, and the

▲ Nearly 500 million people suffer from malaria each year, most of them are children in sub-Saharan Africa.

most **catastrophic pandemic** historically, alongside bubonic plague and the influenza **outbreak** of 1918. HIV is the acronym for human **immunodeficiency** virus, which in its final stage of infection becomes AIDS, or acquired immunodeficiency syndrome. The HIV virus is unique in that it directly attacks the white blood cells identified as T cells or CD4 cells, which the human immune system needs to fight disease with. HIV cannot be transmitted through casual contact; it can only be transmitted through direct contact with infected bodily fluids, usually through sexual contact or shared needles. There are several antiretroviral (HIV is a **retrovirus**) treatments that can be started immediately upon HIV diagnosis to impede the development of the virus. Even without treatment, it may take years for HIV to develop into AIDS. AIDS carries a high mortality rate, not directly caused by AIDS itself, but as a result of a number of AIDS-related diseases, most notably pneumonia, influenza, and **tuberculosis**. Although initial studies in the 21st century showed declines in HIV, AIDS and AIDS-related deaths in the United States, new diagnostic technologies have noted a U.S. upswing in all three since 2006. HIV and AIDS also continue to

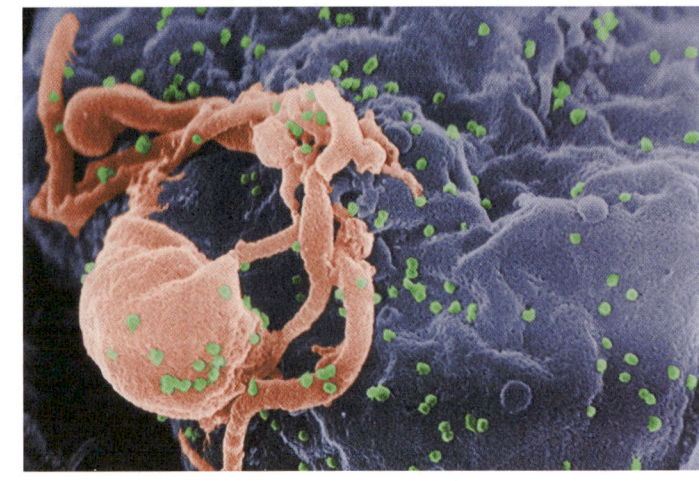

▲ HIV budding on a cell

◄ The HIV virus

Unit 3 Chapter 7 Deadly Infectious Diseases

be diagnosed at an alarming rate internationally, particularly in Africa, where extensive education, treatment and prevention efforts are currently underway.

③ One of the most potentially devastating emerging diseases of the 21st century is SARS, or severe **acute** respiratory syndrome, a viral respiratory illness caused by a **coronavirus** (an enveloped or crowned single-strand RNA genome). SARS emerged in the Guangdong Province of China in 2002, but it was not recognized by researchers until 2003, when nearly 8,000 cases of SARS were identified across 29 countries, out of which 774 deaths resulted. However, the SARS coronavirus was quickly sequenced and public health measures were immediately enacted, such as patient isolation, so that the outbreak was **contained** within months.

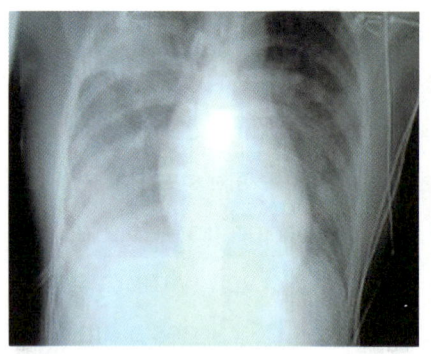

▲ chest X-ray showing increased opacity in both lungs (indicative of pneumonia) in a patient with SARS

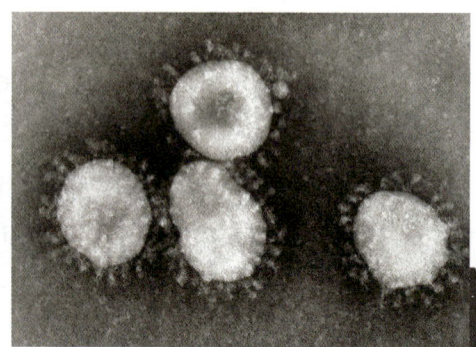

▲ The SARS coronavirus

▼ mycobacterium tuberculosis

④ Some reemerging diseases, such as tuberculosis and malaria, continue at world pandemic infection rates. Cases of tuberculosis (TB), caused by bacteria called *mycobacterium tuberculosis*, have increased 20% in the U.S. since 1980, and continue at roughly 9 million new cases annually worldwide, with nearly 2 million deaths per year. Much of TB's **resurgence** is due to increased antibiotic resistance, but it is also attributable to poverty; most TB-related deaths occur among the poorest and most malnourished in Africa and Asia. Nearly 500 million cases of malaria occur each year, out of which over 1 million people die, mostly young children in sub-Saharan Africa. Malaria, usually caused by an *Anopheles* mosquito bite, progresses rapidly as the **parasites deposited** by the host mosquito first infect liver cells then red blood cells. If not treated right away, the disease can be fatal. Both TB and malaria can be treated and prevented, and global initiatives have been enacted through the U.S. Center for Disease Control and the World Health Organization.

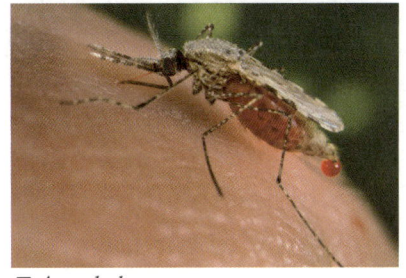

▼ *Anopheles*

5 Beyond natural evolutionary processes, deadly infectious diseases can be transmitted through deliberate acts of bioterrorism. Biological terrorism is the use of dangerous and toxic biological agents as threatening weapons against humans, animals or plants. The Global Preparedness and Response Network is one of many intentional international collaborations working to **mitigate** bioterrorist attacks.

6 Detection, treatment, and preventive measures continue to globally improve, but they are far from **eradicating** many of the deadly infectious diseases that still threaten much of the world, especially children. Recent research improvements include 3-D imaging of viral and bacterial proteins, and new globally-available databases of infectious disease information. Biotechnology offers new approaches to diagnosis, drug developments, and drug delivery.

Although totally eliminating deadly diseases may not be possible, many researchers believe that viral and bacterial threats can be treated and contained through sustained global funding, research, and communication efforts.

▶ M-17 nuclear, biological and chemical warfare mask and hood for a bioterrorist attack

TARGET WORD EXERCISES

A

The prefix "anti-" commonly creates an antonym of the root word with which it is combined. Add "anti-" to the following root words to form words related to infectious disease. Using your knowledge about each root word, match the new antonym to its correct meaning.

a. _____biotic
b. _____viral
c. _____fungal
d. _____parasitic
e. _____histamine
f. _____depressant
g. _____bacterial
h. _____body
i. _____gen (or _____body generating)
j. _____toxin

(____) 1 a substance derived from one biological organism that can destroy or inhibit the growth of other microorganisms
(____) 2 a drug used to prevent or treat mental depression
(____) 3 any protein normally present in the body or produced in response to an antigen which it neutralizes, thus producing an immune response
(____) 4 any agent that destroys or prevents the growth of fungi
(____) 5 an antibody that can neutralize a specific toxin
(____) 6 a drug used to counteract the physiological effects of histamine production in allergic reactions and colds
(____) 7 a substance that, when introduced into the body, stimulates the production of an antibody
(____) 8 destructive to or inhibiting the growth of bacteria
(____) 9 destroying or inhibiting the growth and reproduction of parasites
(____) 10 inhibiting or stopping the growth and reproduction of viruses

B

Place the correct **prefix** or combining form with the following **root words** to form the words you've learned in this chapter, and then place the words in the following sentences.

Prefixes ······▶ out-   a-   com-   re-   retro-
Combining forms ·····▶ in-   immuno-   con-   pan-

a. _____break
b. _____deficiency
c. _____cute
d. _____tained
e. _____fectious
f. _____pliance
g. _____demic
h. _____surgence
i. _____virus

1. After chemotherapy, the cancer was _____ only to the thyroid.
2. Fewer polio vaccinations could lead to a _____ of the disease.
3. Using the internet to provide health messages might lead to greater _____ with vaccine policies, which could lessen the presence of many diseases worldwide.
4. Unlike the emergence of chronic diseases, the onset of _____ diseases are quite sudden, and they require swift action.
5. The 1918 influenza outbreak and HIV are examples of infections that occur in _____ proportions.
6. A _____ is a virus that transcribes its RNA into cDNA and then replicates into the host cell DNA.
7. The _____ of the avian flu has not yet reached pandemic levels.
8. Vaccinations are just one way to prevent humans from _____ disease.
9. An immunocompromised person has an _____, or the inability or absence of the ability to fight infectious disease.

C Choose the correct target word to complete each sentence.

(____) 1 The initial doses of antibiotics helped to _____ the severe symptoms of malaria.
   a. emerge   b. mitigate   c. vulnerable

(____) 2 Because the first cases weren't reported, the _____ rate of SARS was not recognized for nearly a year.
   a. immunodeficiency   b. retrovirus   c. morbidity

(____) 3 Those who live in the direst poverty and most rural areas are the most _____ to infectious diseases.
   a. catastrophic   b. vulnerable   c. contained

(____) 4 An uncontained outbreak of SARS could be devastating and _____ in any country.
   a. morbidity   b. vulnerable   c. catastrophic

(____) 5 New infectious diseases can _____ due to natural microbial mutation.
   a. emerge   b. mitigate   c. retrovirus

(____) 6 The _____ rate among HIV patients steadily declined through the 1990s due to better education, earlier detection, and more effective treatments.
   a. contained   b. catastrophic   c. mortality

55

Unit 3
Chapter 8

Obesity Crisis

1. In the mid-20th century, **obesity** was first introduced into the international classification of diseases. Over 50 years later, obesity may be the most severe global health crisis, earning it the name, "**millennium disease**," from the International Obesity Taskforce. Although some medical professionals continue to dismiss obesity's classification, organizations across the globe, ranging from the U.N. to the World Health Organization to the American Journal of Public Health, all warn that obesity may be the next global pandemic.

- The U.N. reports that in the new millennium, there are more overweight people than starving people in the world.
- The WHO finds that as of 2005, there were 1.6 billion adults overweight; in 2014, more than 1.9 billion adults were overweight. WHO researchers predict that by 2030 obesity may be the number one killer of poor people in the world.
- The American Public Health Association reports that the number of obese children in America has more than doubled over the past twenty years; one in five children in the U.S. are overweight.

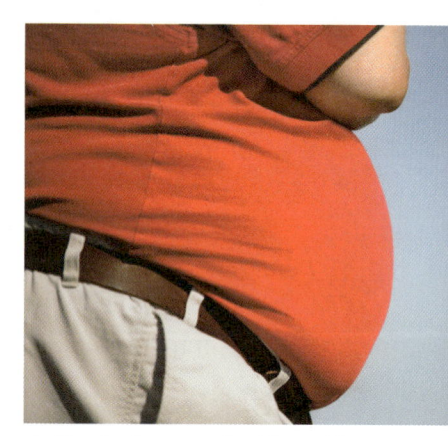

▲ Obesity increases health problems.

▲ One in five children in the U.S. are overweight.

2 More people than ever before appear to be at **risk** for numerous health problems, including **cardiovascular** disease, **diabetes**, and even some cancers. Yet, obesity is preventable through education, food industry, marketing **reforms**, and government support.

3 Obesity is defined as an abnormal and unhealthy **accumulation** of fat resulting in **excessive** weight in relation to height. Obesity, as well as overweight, is measured by body mass index (BMI), an **indirect calculation** of body fat by dividing weight by height squared used for both sexes and for all ages. Health organizations worldwide agree on the **assessment** that a BMI equal to or greater than 25 defines overweight, and a BMI equal to or greater than 30 defines obese. These levels are general **benchmarks** that do not always account for individual differences, and some studies have shown that **chronic** disease **prevalence** increases with a BMI above 21.

4 Obesity emerges from multiple causes, although all ultimately result in an **imbalance** of energy intake and output. Most commonly, obesity results from eating a diet high in fat and calories; the increase of availability of processed foods worldwide has a direct correlation to the global rise in obesity. Global modernization, including upsurge in car ownership, modern appliance availability, and **accessible** technology such as television and computers, contributes to a growing number of **sedentary** lifestyles,

▲ Processed foods have a direct link to obesity.

Unit 3　Chapter 8　Obesity Crisis

57

another factor in rising obesity rates. Other factors for obesity are hormonal, environmental, cultural, and genetic.

🎧 16 ⑤ Carrying extra fat can lead to numerous health problems. Cardiovascular disease is already the world's number one killer, claiming the lives of nearly 17 million people annually through heart attacks and strokes. Obesity has been shown to raise blood **cholesterol** and **triglyceride** levels, to lower HDL "good" cholesterol, and to raise blood pressure levels—all leading factors in heart attacks and strokes. Obesity can also **induce** diabetes, although the link has not yet been clearly defined. It does appear that excess fat increases insulin resistance, which raises blood glucose levels. Diabetes intensifies these cardiovascular risk factors and further increases the danger of heart attacks. Alterations in insulin in obese people may also factor into increases for certain cancers, such as breast and colon. Research continues to also explore a link between sex hormone alteration due to obesity and cancer.

⑥ Worldwide, many organizations are adopting strategies to help mitigate and prevent obesity.

- Healthy People 2010 was launched in January, 2000 by the U.S. Department of Health and Human Services. The project combines health promotion and disease prevention through 28 focus areas, one of which is nutrition and overweight.
- The HOPE (Health Promotion Through Obesity Prevention Across Europe) project is

▲ Foods with a high fat content contribute to obesity the most.

a multidisciplinary network of the European Union. HOPE oversees knowledge integration and policy development in regard to causes, interventions, and prevention of obesity.

- In 2004, the WHO adopted a strategy to promote healthy diets and physical activity. The WHO is engaging public and private international partners in an international effort to:
  - reduce risk of chronic diseases due to obesity factors
  - increase education about healthy diet and physical activity
  - develop sustainable global policies to improve diet and physical activity
  - **monitor** and promote research on healthy diet and physical activity.

▲ A healthy diet and regular physical activity can prevent obesity.

7 Using the recommendations and guidelines from these and other global organizations will be vital to stemming the obesity crisis. Whether it be private food industries developing healthier food choices, or public agencies promoting healthier diets and physical activity, integrated worldwide efforts are needed to reverse the trend and consequences of obesity.

TARGET WORD EXERCISES

A Choose the correct target word for each sentence.

(____) 1 Diabetes patients must _____ their glucose levels several times each day.
   a. adopt   b. monitor   c. accumulate   d. develop

(____) 2 The increased availability of televisions and video games has greatly contributed to the _____ lifestyle of many young people around the world.
   a. busy   b. integrated   c. monitored   d. sedentary

(____) 3 One of the significant contributing factors to Type II diabetes is _____ fat around the abdomen.
   a. excessive   b. indirect   c. imbalanced   d. global

(____) 4 Diets high in fat content put one at a higher _____ for cardiovascular disease.
   a. imbalance   b. risk   c. prevalence   d. accumulation

(____) 5 Obesity can lead to high blood pressure that, when not treated properly, can _____ strokes or heart attacks.
   a. monitor   b. integrate   c. induce   d. calculate

(____) 6 Although technology offered many breakthroughs in disease diagnosis in the 20th century, it also may be a factor in an unhealthy decrease in physical activity in the new _____.
   a. global   b. calculation   c. sedentary   d. millennium

(____) 7 Lack of exercise and obesity has been strongly linked with the development of _____, or insulin resistance, in adults.
   a. influenza   b. malnutrition   c. diabetes   d. laziness

(____) 8 In obese women, the fat tends to _____ around the thighs and buttocks.
   a. accumulate   b. integrate   c. trend   d. promote

(____) 9 Weight gain can be attributed to an _____ between caloric intake and energy expenditure.
   a. accumulation   b. emergence   c. integration   d. imbalance

(____) 10 Many global health organizations are working to make nutritious foods more _____ to people living in rural areas.
   a. excessive   b. accessible   c. indirect   d. reformed

(____) 11 The body mass index is not an exact measurement of body fat, but even as an _____ calculation, it provides a reliable indication of percent body fat.
   a. indirect   b. integrated   c. excessive   d. accumulated

(____) 12 A decrease in child obesity by 2010 is one of the _____ by which the success of the Healthy People 2010 strategy will be measured.
   a. imbalances   b. benchmarks   c. reforms   d. risks

(_____) 13 The _____ of processed foods can contribute to both obesity and malnutrition.
 a. calculation b. assessment c. risk d. prevalence

(_____) 14 Global health organizations have demonstrated a need for the food industry to _____ its marketing strategy to highlight more nutritious food choices.
 a. imbalance b. reform c. prevent d. induce

(_____) 15 A person's BMI can be used to _____ his or her risk of developing a chronic disease.
 a. induce b. indirect c. calculate d. integrate

(_____) 16 Lifestyle factors can be _____ to determine possible links between obesity and depression.
 a. assessed b. excessive c. prevalent d. reformed

B

Add the correct prefix to each word below to create one of the target words, and then match the word with its definition. The definition for the root word is given in parenthesis. Use it as a clue to determine the target word's definition.

a. _____balance (steadiness or stability)
b. _____form (to form again)
c. _____direct (straightforward, in a direct manner)
d. _____valence (having a specified value, widespread)
e. _____duce (to lead, to bring into)
f. _____vent (to come)

(_____) 1 to keep from occurring
(_____) 2 to bring about or cause
(_____) 3 of wide extent or occurrence
(_____) 4 lacking balance, as in proportion or distribution
(_____) 5 to change to a better state or form; improve
(_____) 6 not direct in action or procedure

C

Choose the correct suffix for each root word to create a target word.

Root Word		Suffix		Target Word
1 access	+	tion | ly | ble	=	_____
2 calculate	+	ive | ion | ence	=	_____
3 assess	+	ment | ly | ion	=	_____
4 accumulate	+	ive | ble | ion	=	_____
5 excess	+	ence | ly | ive	=	_____
6 prevail	+	ive | ion | ence	=	_____

61

Unit 3
Chapter 9

Secrets to a Healthy Life

▲ quitting smoking

1 Modern science and medicine have sharply increased life **expectancy** in the 20th century and eliminated the deadly threat of many **infectious** diseases. At the same time, however, an increasingly industrialized world has experienced a rapid and widespread onset of lifestyle diseases. These chronic diseases—primarily cardiovascular diseases, cancer, diabetes, Alzheimer's, and depression—differ from other types of diseases because they are often brought on by one's lifestyle, but they can also be prevented through changes in one's lifestyle.

2 First of all, one can change habits and engage in healthy activities.
- Smoking **cessation**
- Maintenance of a healthy weight
- **Moderate** or no alcohol consumption
- Active lifestyle, such as daily walking and strength exercises
- Healthy **coping** strategies for stress, such as yoga or keeping a journal
- Eight hours of restful sleep each night

▲ moderate alcohol consumption

③ Secondly, one can make wise choices about food, drink, physical activity, and healthcare that help increase **holistic wellness** and **longevity**.

- **Food**
  - Fruits and vegetables, which are low in calories, high in fiber, and high in vitamins and minerals, reduce the risk of chronic diseases and preserve cognitive function.
  - Lean proteins **stimulate** muscle protein synthesis and promote muscle growth.
  - Daily intake of 20-25% of healthy fats, or **polyunsaturated** and **monounsaturated** fatty acids, promotes **absorption** of fat-**soluble** vitamins, such as A, D, and E. Healthy fats, such as omega-3 polyunsaturated fatty acids found in certain fish, have also been shown to reduce mortality linked to cardiovascular disease.

▲ daily walking

▲ Yoga is a healthy coping strategy for stress.

- **Drink**
  - Alcohol in moderation (one to two drinks daily) may provide the benefit of reducing the risk of heart disease, diabetes, and stroke.
  - Drinks high in sugar content should be avoided because of risk of tooth decay and obesity.
  - Drinking 2 liters of water daily helps replenish body fluids and prevent **dehydration**.
  - Moderate intake of caffeine (two to three cups daily) may protect against type-2 diabetes and colon cancer.

▲ eight hours of restful sleep

- **Regular physical activity**
  - Regular aerobic exercise, about 30 minutes daily, strengthens the cardiovascular system and helps maintain healthy weight. Exercise also improves sleep patterns and mental acuity, and boosts sexual desire and performance.

TARGET WORD EXERCISES

A The words in the box all are used to describe discoveries that claim to cure many ills or even prolong life indefinitely. Use these words to fill in the blanks and complete the sentences below. (Hint: the number of spaces corresponds to the number of letters in the correct word.)

| restorative | antitoxin | curative | remedy | balm | serum |

1. A natural herb _____ can be found in health food stores.
2. A soothing _____ can provide relief for almost any wound.
3. Medieval cultures believed that poultices applied with a warm cloth were _____ for most aches and pains.
4. Cosmetic or implant surgery is considered by some to be a _____ of youth.
5. A snake's own venom is a powerful _____ to help fight the effects of a poisonous snake bite. The blood of some animals can be used as _____ to produce antibodies in humans.

B Match the target words with their definitions.

a. prolong
b. cessation
c. moderate
d. cope
e. holistic
f. wellness
g. longevity
h. stimulate
i. polyunsaturated
j. absorption
k. soluble
l. mobility
m. preponderance

(____) 1 long life
(____) 2 a superiority in numbers or amount
(____) 3 to extend in duration; protract
(____) 4 not excessive or extreme
(____) 5 capable of being dissolved
(____) 6 to deal with successfully
(____) 7 concerned with the whole; dealing with integrated systems
(____) 8 to heighten action or increase activity
(____) 9 the ability to move or be moved
(____) 10 of or relating to carbon compounds, especially fatty acids, having two or more double bonds between the carbon atoms
(____) 11 the process by which nutrients enter the tissues of an animal or a plant
(____) 12 to bring to an end
(____) 13 the condition of good physical and mental health

C. Replace the antonyms (in bold) in the following sentences with the correct target word.

1. Proper diet, regular exercise, and other healthy habits help to maintain physical and mental **illness**. → _____
2. Time management is one possible way to **be overcome** with stress. → _____
3. Caffeine ingested just prior to exercise has been proven to **stifle** energy expenditure up to 10%. → _____
4. Sunscreen provides healthy protection from ultraviolet rays from the sun, but at the same time it blocks the body's **emission** of vitamin D. → _____
5. Some studies show that **excessive** daily consumption of red wine may lower the risk of heart disease. → _____
6. Sudden **continuance** of regular exercise can result in adverse psychological effects as well as detrimental physical effects. → _____
7. Recent interest in integrating mind, body and spirit as a **atomistic** approach to health issues is actually a return to practices by many ancient cultures. → _____
8. Due in large part to its vast numbers of fast food restaurants, the United States has the **least amount** of obese children in the world. → _____

D. Identity lifestyle diseases. Place the letter of the correct description beside each lifestyle disease.

a. high blood pressure
b. any malignant growth or tumor caused by abnormal and uncontrolled cell division
c. the sudden death of brain cells in a localized area due to inadequate blood flow
d. abnormalities in the body's ability to use sugar
e. a mental state characterized by a pessimistic sense of inadequacy and a despondent lack of activity
f. a progressive, degenerative disease of the brain that leads to dementia
g. a condition of decreased bone mass
h. a group of chronic diseases in which thickening, hardening, and loss of elasticity of the arterial walls result in impaired blood circulation

(____) 1 Cancer
(____) 2 Hypertension
(____) 3 Diabetes
(____) 4 Depression
(____) 5 Alzheimer's
(____) 6 Stroke
(____) 7 Arteriosclerosis
(____) 8 Osteoporosis

Unit 4

Chapter 10

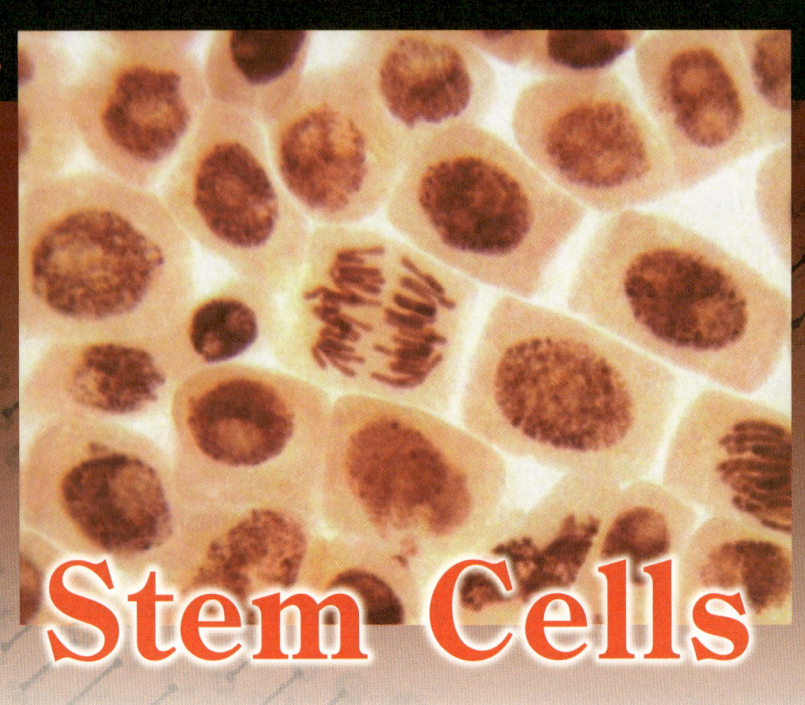

Stem Cells

▲ mesenchymal stem cells

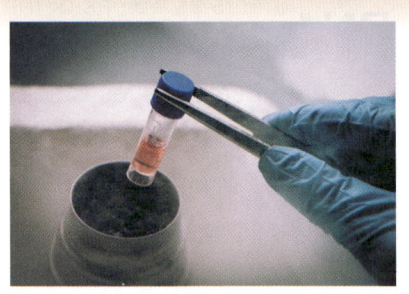

▲ liquid nitrogen bank containing suspension of stem cells

[1] Researchers, led by Dr. James A. Thomson, a biologist at the University of Wisconsin, Madison, first isolated human **embryonic** stem cells (hESCs) in 1998. As both the origin and the framework of the human body, stem cells are prime candidates for research about how the body grows, maintains itself, and in some cases, repairs itself. Understanding how stem cells work and harnessing their power can lead to new and more effective treatment therapies for injuries, diseases and disorders.

[2] Stem cells are **undifferentiated** or unspecialized cells with the **potential** to develop into over 200 different types of cells that make up the human body. **Unspecialized** cells do not have tissue-specific abilities to carry out specific functions throughout the body; however, these cells are **pluripotent**, or carry the potential for **differentiation**. Unlike most cells, such as those in the muscles or blood, that do not **replicate** themselves, stem cells may renew themselves many times over, sometimes ultimately numbering in the millions. Understanding stem cell **proliferation** would help researchers identify and treat abnormal cell division, and enable them to grow stem cells efficiently in the laboratory.

3 Two main types of stem cells exist, embryonic and **adult**, although there are variations of both.
- Embryonic stem cells derive from embryos fertilized **in vitro**.
  ‣ When the embryos are several days old, they contain pluripotent cells that form a hollow ball of cells called a **blastocyst**. The ball is a **tripartite** structure of cells:
    (1) trophoblast cells make up an outer layer
    (2) the blastocoel, or the hollow **cavity** is inside the blastocyst
    (3) the inner cell mass is a collection of cells at one end of the blastocoel that will eventually develop into a **fetus** 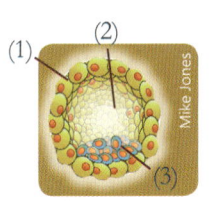
  ‣ Embryonic stem cells can be grown effectively in a lab. The inner cell mass of the blastocyst is harvested and placed into a culture dish where the cells, when provided the proper nutrients, divide and create an embryonic stem cell line. To date, most embryonic cells come from mouse embryos, but human in vitro embryo cells and embryonic stem cells from therapeutic **cloning** are potential resources for stem cell research.
- Adult stem cells, a misleading term since they are present in infants and children as well, are undifferentiated cells that reside among differentiated cells in already-

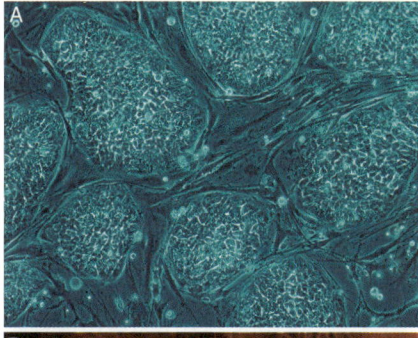

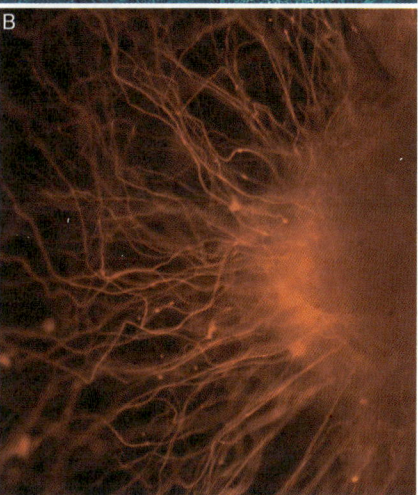

▲ human embryonic stem cells
A: stem cell colonies that are not yet differentiated
B: nerve cells, an example of a cell type after differentiation
(cc by Nissim Benvenisty)

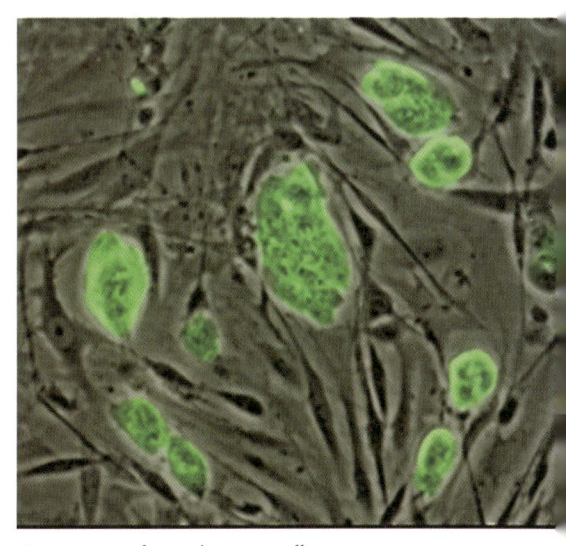

▲ mouse embryonic stem cells

Unit 4 Chapter 10 Stem Cells

69

developed tissues. Scientists understand that the primary function of adult stem cells is to grow or repair tissues throughout life, but they have not yet identified their origin.

- Adult stem cells can differentiate into the **specialized** cells of the tissue in which they reside, but they sometimes have the ability to differentiate into cell types of other tissues, a process called **transdifferentiation** or **plasticity**. If scientists can identify and control the mechanisms of transdifferentiation, they may be able to use the new cells either to test their responses to new medications or to inject them into abnormal tissue for repair and replacement, a process called cell-based therapy.

4 Stem cells hold much promise in helping researchers identify and prevent underlying causes of serious medical conditions. In the future, stem cell therapies may provide renewable cells and tissues to repair and treat **spinal** cord injuries, burns, diabetes, and arthritis. Therapies using pluripotent cells have the potential to repair and replace damaged organs such as the heart or brain cells damaged by Parkinson's or Alzheimer's disease or by stroke. Stem cell therapies to date have had limited success in treating blood diseases such as leukemia, but they hold potential to treat other blood-related diseases such as sickle cell disease.

Human Stem Cell Applications

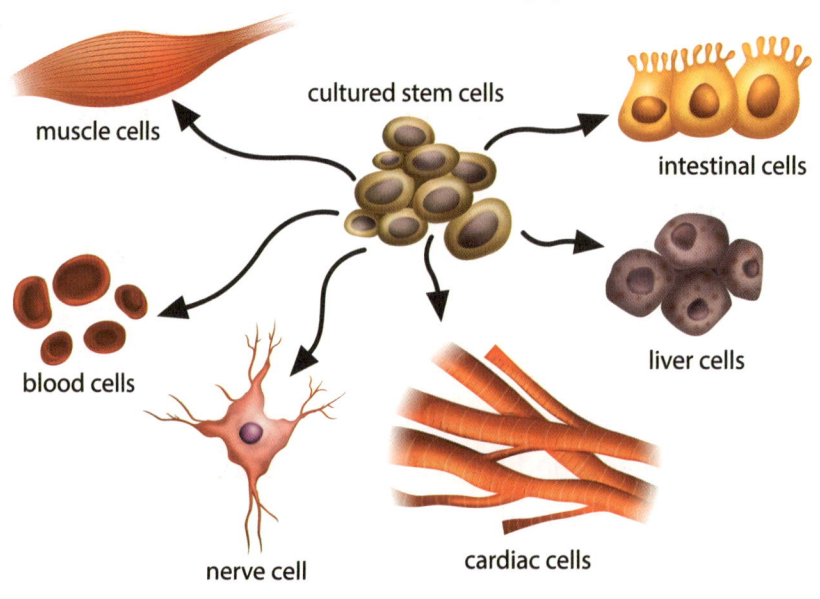

5 One of the most **inhibitive** problems about stem cell research is the ethical controversy that surrounds it.

6 *Opponents:* human life begins at the moment an egg is **fertilized**; therefore, to manipulate or destroy a human embryo is morally indefensible.

7 *Proponents:* many eggs are routinely fertilized that never implant in the uterus for development, and excess fertilized in vitro eggs that would be **discarded** could be used in life-saving research.

8 *Opponents:* adult stem cells can serve the same research and treatment purposes.

9 *Proponents:* the multipotency of adult stem cells is much more limited than the pluripotency of embryonic stem cells, although researchers continue to discover more **flexibility** in adult stem cells than originally thought.

10 Although many governments tightly restrict stem cell research and its funding, scientists continue to advance their knowledge of stem cell functions and potential. Even if many governmental and financial restrictions are lifted, it will be many years before the full potential of stem cell research will be realized.

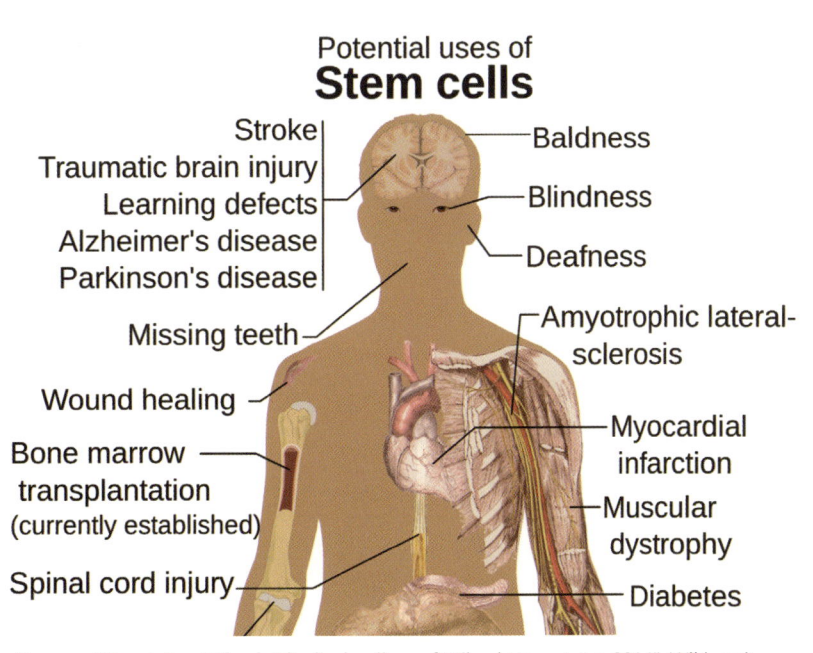

▶ Diseases and conditions for which stem cell treatment is being investigated.

Potential uses of **Stem cells**

- Stroke
- Traumatic brain injury
- Learning defects
- Alzheimer's disease
- Parkinson's disease
- Missing teeth
- Wound healing
- Bone marrow transplantation (currently established)
- Spinal cord injury
- Baldness
- Blindness
- Deafness
- Amyotrophic lateral sclerosis
- Myocardial infarction
- Muscular dystrophy
- Diabetes

(Source: Häggström, Mikael. "Medical gallery of Mikael Häggström 2014". Wikiversity Journal of Medicine 1 (2). DOI:10.15347/wjm/2014.008. ISSN 20018762.)

TARGET WORD EXERCISES

A Fill in the blanks beside each definition with the correct target word.

potential	pluripotent	in vitro	tripartite
plasticity	inhibitive	replicate	cavity
cloning	differentiation	adult	proliferate

(_____) 1 in three parts
(_____) 2 develop from generalized to specialized kinds
(_____) 3 capable of being or becoming
(_____) 4 restrained, suppressed, or prohibited
(_____) 5 made to occur in a controlled environment, rather than a living or natural
(_____) 6 to grow by rapid multiplication of parts
(_____) 7 to repeat or reproduce
(_____) 8 capable having more than one potential outcome
(_____) 9 mature or fully developed
(_____) 10 capable of being molded or made to assume a desired form
(_____) 11 a hollow space
(_____) 12 producing a genetically identical unit

B Replace each of the following phrases with the corresponding target word (or an appropriate form of the target word).

1. Many eggs that never implant in the uterus are routinely **made productive** for development. → _____
2. A blastocyst is a **three-part** structure consisting of trophoblast cells, the blastocoel, and the inner cell mass. → _____
3. Researchers continues to discover more **adaptive capability** in adult stem cells than originally thought. → _____
4. Embryonic stem cells derive from embryos fertilized **in a controlled environment**. → _____
5. Stem cells carry the **capability** for **becoming a specialized kind**.
   ↳ _____   ↳ _____
6. **Mature** stems cells are capable of **assuming a desired form**.
   ↳ _____   ↳ _____
7. Some adult stems cells can become **adapted to specific function** cells.
   → _____
8. One of the most **restrained** problems about stem cell research is the ethical controversy that surrounds it. → _____
9. Most of the cells in the human body do not **reproduce** themselves.
   → _____
10. The blastocoel is a **hollow space** inside the blastocyst. → _____
11. Stems cells have the **potential for more than one outcome**.
    → _____
12. Stem cells are **not changed** or unspecialized cells. → _____
13. Understanding stem cell **rapid multiplication** would help researchers identify and treat abnormal cell division. → _____
14. **Undeveloped** stem cells from therapeutic **identical genetic units** may be resources for stem cell research. → _____
    → _____

TARGET WORD EXERCISES

C **Prefixes and Combining Forms:**
Add the correct **prefix** or combing form to the following words, and then use the words above in the following sentences (a sentence may have more than one correct answer).

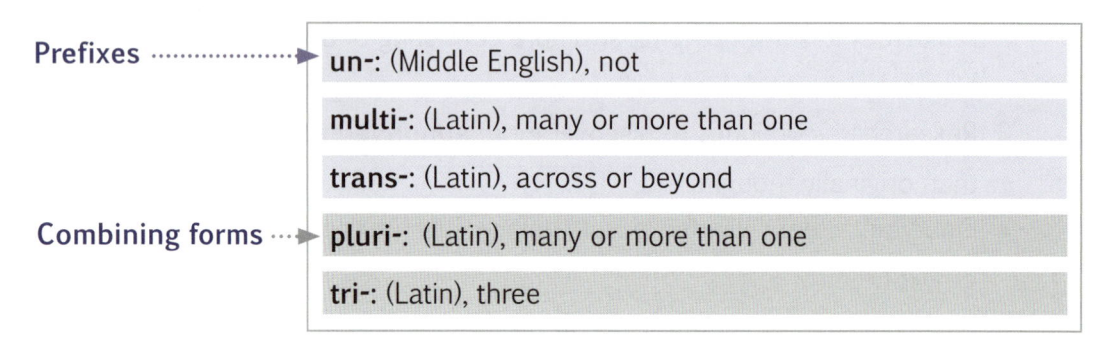

Prefixes:
- **un-**: (Middle English), not
- **multi-**: (Latin), many or more than one
- **trans-**: (Latin), across or beyond

Combining forms:
- **pluri-**: (Latin), many or more than one
- **tri-**: (Latin), three

a. _____differentiated

b. _____genetic

c. _____specialized

d. _____partite

e. _____potent/_____potent

1. A knee joint can have several variations, including a three-part variation called a _____ patella.

2. The cancer cells are a type of _____ cells.

3. Adult stem cells have the capability for limited change, so they are _____.

4. The commercialization of _____ crops is growing worldwide.

Antonyms EXERCISES

D **Antonyms** are words opposite in meaning to another. Some antonyms are created by the addition of **prefixes**. Match the following words with their opposites.

a. embryonic
b. undifferentiated
c. opponent
d. inhibitive
e. unspecialized

(____) 1 differentiated
(____) 2 specialized
(____) 3 proponent
(____) 4 adult
(____) 5 proliferate

Synonyms EXERCISES

E **Synonyms** are words or phrases similar in meaning to one another. Match the following words with their synonyms.

a. fertilized
b. mature
c. differentiate
d. replicate
e. plasticity
f. proliferate

(____) 1 adult
(____) 2 multiply
(____) 3 repeat
(____) 4 elasticity
(____) 5 productive
(____) 6 specialize

Unit 4
Chapter 11

Gene Therapy

1. Through advances in genetic **modification**, scientists have developed techniques to **alter** a person's genetic material to fight or prevent disease. Gene therapy is an experimental process through which manipulated genes are inserted into targeted faulty cells in order to restore or prevent defective genes responsible for disease. Doctors can use gene therapy to forego the use of drugs or surgery.

2. In most gene therapy research, a normal gene is inserted into the faulty cells to replace an abnormal or disease-causing gene. The most common technique is to genetically engineer a **therapeutic** gene, called a carrier **molecule** or **vector**, which then is delivered into the patient's target cells. The most common vector is a genetically altered virus. A genetically altered virus has powerful potential in the body, because it invades cells and forces them to replicate the virus, which is how it spreads. Researchers are able to use this destructive power to alter or destroy abnormal cells, but only if the virus is modified to target solely the abnormal cells. Nonviral vectors have also been developed, but only recently has some success been found for gene repair.

3. Vectors have to be engineered for two specific functions:
- **Gene delivery**: the introduction of viral or non-viral DNA into targeted faulty cells to treat disease or abnormalities

Unit 4 Chapter 11 Gene Therapy

- **Gene expression**: the delivery of DNA instructions into targeted cells to create proteins which can alter the genetic makeup of the targeted cell

- An example of this process is:

  A patient's lung cells are injected with the viral vector

  ⬇

  the vector deposits its genetic material containing the therapeutic human gene into the target cell

  ⬇

  the therapeutic gene generates a **functional** protein product that restores the target cell to a normal state

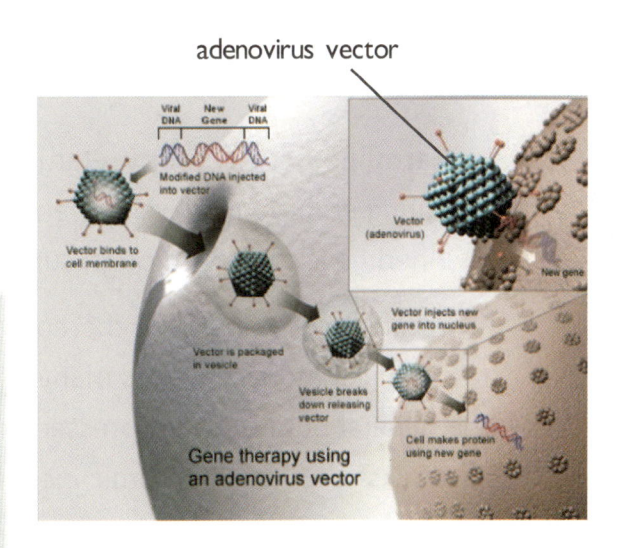

adenovirus vector

Gene therapy using an adenovirus vector

77

5. There are two main types of gene therapy:
   - **Somatic gene therapy**—gene therapy introduced into the human body, specifically the body tissues. Techniques include:
     - **Gene inhibition therapy**: suppresses or interferes with malfunctioning gene activity. This technique introduces a vector to inhibit the expression or activity of **pathogenic** or abnormal genes responsible for infectious diseases, cancer and inherited disorders.
     - **Gene elimination**: the process specifically targets genes in order to force them to express a **toxic** product known as suicide genes. Suicide genes must be uniquely targeted; otherwise, the therapy would result in widespread cell death.
     - Gene **augmentation** is a technique used to treat nonfunctional genes responsible for **inherited** disorders. A functional copy of the missing gene is inserted back into the gene to replicate the production of the missing protein.
   - **Germline gene therapy**—targets eggs or **sperm** for gene modification during embryonic development. This technique has the potential to correct inherited disorders through subsequent generations.

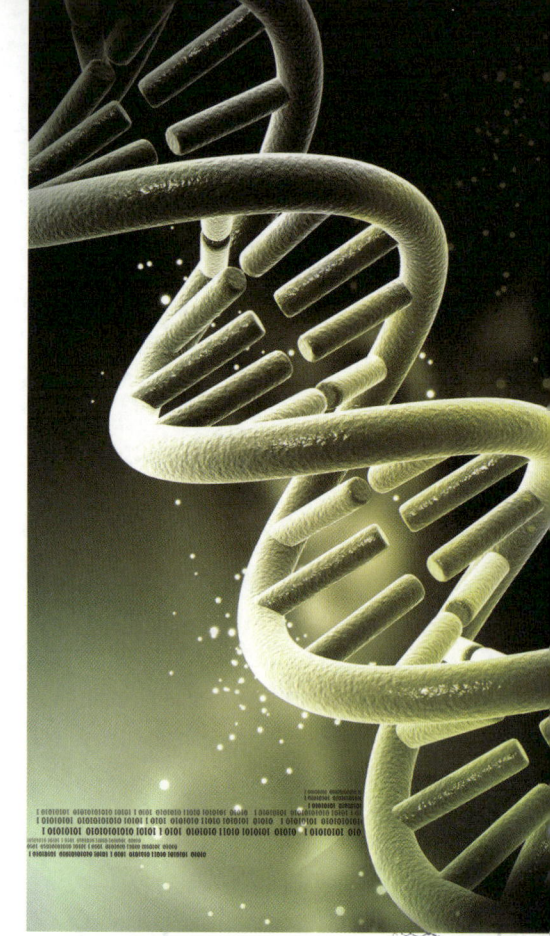

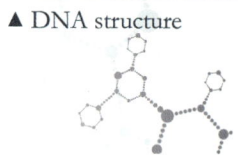

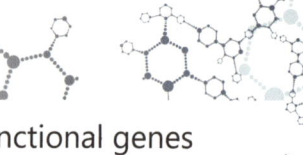

▲ DNA structure

6. Because **germline** gene therapy involves human decisions about changes to genetic material, it raises many unique ethical concerns. Both scientists and the general public have expressed concerns about long-term effects, social **repercussions**, and economic inequities that could inhibit access to germline gene therapy. The main concerns revolve around the use of germline gene therapy:

- **Unpredictability**: in germline gene therapy, the effects of gene modification are unpredictable and, even if the target disease was cured, further defects or **mutations** could be introduced into the embryo.
- **Control**: individuals resulting from germline gene therapy would have no say in whether their genetic material should have been modified.
- **Abuse**: germline gene therapy has the potential to increase desirable traits and **suppress** unfavorable ones. Such use could result in future generations of so-called designer children, with traits chosen by their parents or even result in **eugenics**, which is the manipulation of the genetic properties of an entire population.

7 Researchers must also overcome many technical challenges before gene therapy can become a practical approach to treating disease. Problems with **integrating** therapeutic genes into cells and with the rapidly dividing nature of many cells prevent gene therapy from achieving any long-term benefits. Viruses present multiple potential problems to patients, including **inflammatory** responses, toxicity, gene control, and even the risk that the virus might mutate in a way to cause yet another disease. Also, disorders of multiple genetic defects would be especially difficult to treat effectively using gene therapy.

8 There have been, however, several promising results of experimental gene therapy. Sickle cell disease has been successfully treated in mice, paving the way toward human application. Gene therapy techniques have shown potential to treat the blood disorder **thalassaemia**, cystic fibrosis, Parkinson's disease and some cancers, including **melanoma** and lung cancer. Researchers have also found that gene therapy has the potential to reverse deafness and blindness in humans. Such successes are continuing slowly and methodically, but gene therapy holds promise either as an exclusive treatment or combined with drug therapy to provide a curative or at least long-term therapy for many diseases.

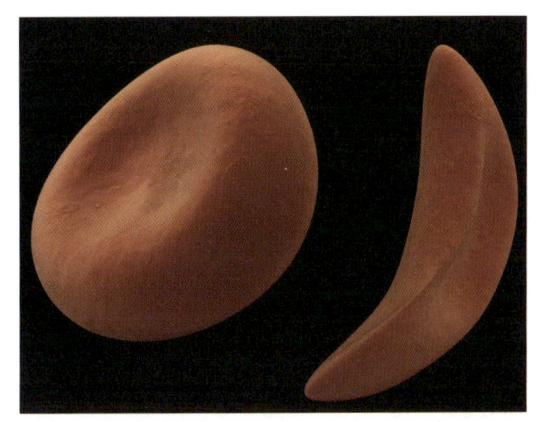

▲ a normal blood cell and an abnormal sickle-cell

TARGET WORD EXERCISES

A Match the words with their definitions. The words are in bold in the article—find the definition from the context.

a therapeutic (adj)	e functional (adj)	i suppress (v)	m eugenics (n)
b augmentation (n)	f inhibition (n)	j integrating (v)	n modification (n)
c pathogenic (adj)	g somatic (adj)	k molecule (n)	o inflammatory (adj)
d toxic (adj)	h alter (v)	l vector (n)	p inherited (adj)

(____) 1 capable of performing; operative
(____) 2 of, relating to, or affecting the body
(____) 3 a restraining of the function of a bodily organ or an agent
(____) 4 to make different without changing into something else
(____) 5 relating to production of good offspring
(____) 6 received characteristic by genetic transmission
(____) 7 an impediment to growth or development
(____) 8 containing or being poisonous material, especially when capable of causing death or serious debilitation
(____) 9 the process of making something greater, more numerous, larger, or more intense
(____) 10 a carrier agent
(____) 11 providing or assisting in a cure
(____) 12 causing or capable of causing disease
(____) 13 incorporating into a larger unit
(____) 14 smallest physical unit of an element or compound
(____) 15 change in an organism due to its environment
(____) 16 causing pain or swelling of an area of the body

B Fill in the blank with the correct unit target word.

| inhibition | molecules | somatic | pathogenic | suppress |
| inflammatory | toxic | functional | integrating | therapeutic |

1 Chemotherapy is _____ for many forms of cancer.
2 Some factories routinely dump _____ waste into nearby rivers and streams, which results in the death of fish and plant life.

3 Most researchers agree that with regard to heart disease, nicotine is _____.
4 A protein extracted from a copperhead snake, contortrostatin (CN), can be used as a form of _____ therapy to prohibit the cancer cell attachment, movement, and migration in the body.
5 _____ new therapeutic approaches with current ones will help expand the possibilities of gene therapy.
6 Replacing the motor made the scooter _____ again.
7 In order to perform well on her test, the student needed to _____ her anxiety.
8 He knew that the pain in his legs was _____ and not purely psychological.
9 _____ bowel disease is a common intestinal problem, especially among women.
10 Biochemistry includes the study of how _____ are made, changed, and function.

C Find a word from the target words with a similar meaning to the word(s) in italics, and replace the word(s).

inflammatory	toxic	modification	augmentation	vector
functional	inherited	molecules	alter	eugenics

1 Plastic surgery can significantly *change* someone's face. → _____
2 Ridge *enlargement* is a process to restore the gums and jawbone placement after tooth loss. → _____
3 Rheumatoid arthritis is a leading *cause of swelling* in the joints.
→ _____
4 *Small particles* are the building blocks of life, consisting of atoms such as oxygen and hydrogen. → _____
5 The color of a person's eyes is *received* from his or her parents.
→ _____
6 A *molecular agent* transported a disabled virus into the liver to help produce normal tissue. → _____
7 Genetic engineering is a type of *environmental manipulation* of genomes.
→ _____
8 One goal of *producing a good gene pool* is to increase human intelligence.
→ _____
9 A knee replacement helps the knee joint become *operative* again.
→ _____
10 Indoor mold can have a *poisonous* effect on the human lungs.
→ _____

Unit 4
Chapter 12
Orphan Drugs

Rare diseases have historically garnered less research attention than more prevalent diseases. These **orphan** diseases, defined as those occurring in less than 200,000 people in the U.S. and less than 5 in 10,000 people in the EU, mean a smaller potential market for new drugs, designated as orphan drugs, to treat them.

To date, over 250 orphan drugs have been developed and made available. However, over 5,000 rare diseases exist in the world. Difficulties exist in the production and availability of orphan drugs because of the uncertainty in production (few of the **molecule**s tested demonstrate **therapeutic** effects), length of time between the discovery of a new molecule and its approval for marketing (an average of 10 years), and expense (orphans drugs are several times more expensive to produce than drugs for more common diseases).

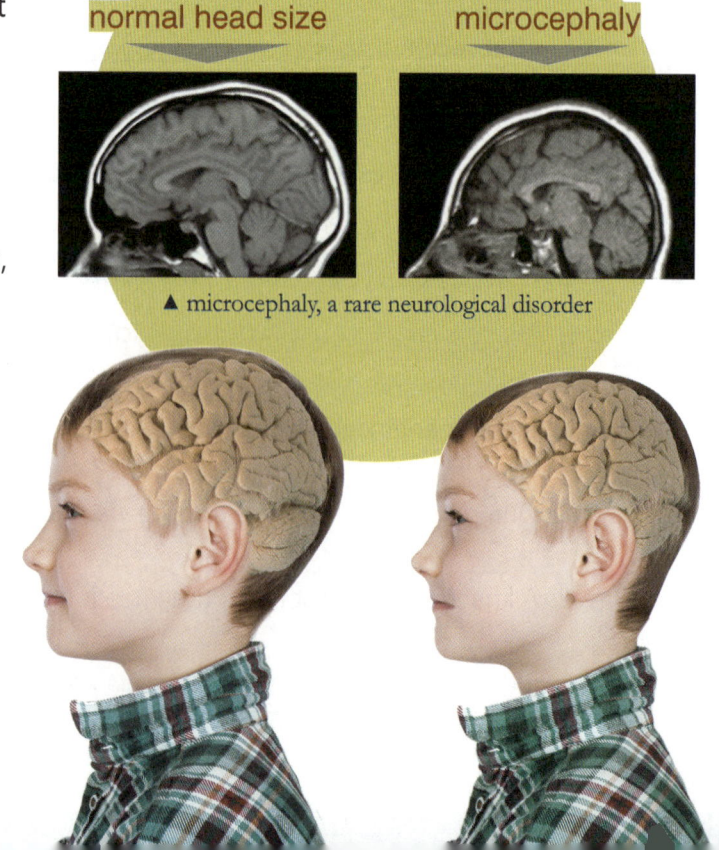

▲ microcephaly, a rare neurological disorder

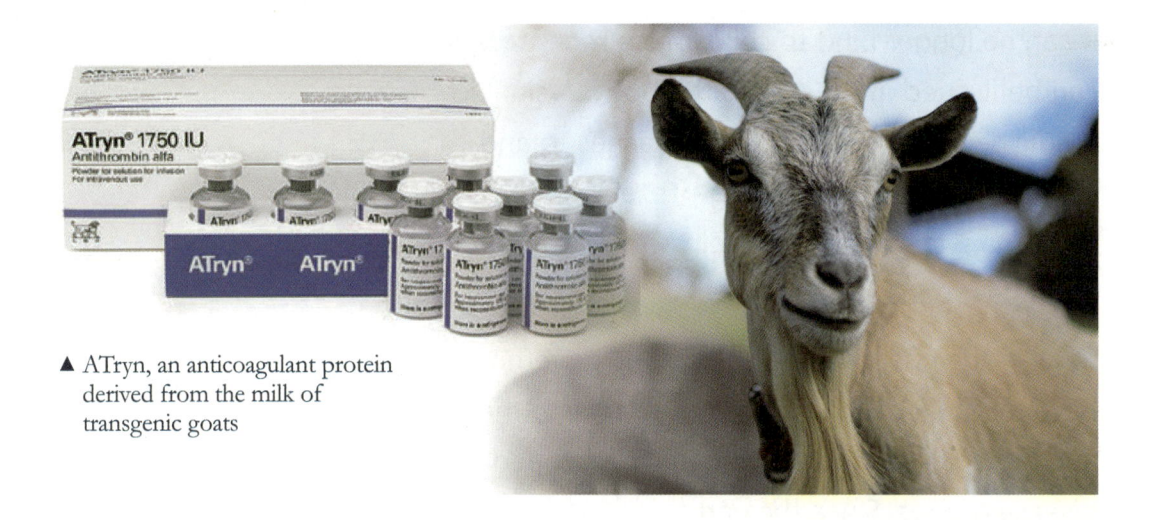

▲ ATryn, an anticoagulant protein derived from the milk of transgenic goats

2 Drugs are often designated as orphan drugs when they are developed in response to public needs rather than for economic incentives. Some drugs are redesignated as orphan drugs when, even though they may be used to treat a more common disease, they are also found effective in treating rare **indications**. Finally, orphan drugs may also be products that have not been marketed, either because the research process for their **development** could not be patented, or because they are targeted for uncreditworthy markets (a particular issue in the development of orphan drugs for third world markets).

3 The vast majority, nearly 80%, of orphan drugs are biologics — drugs that are produced by means of biotechnology. One example is the development of ATryn®, a **recombinant** human **antithrombin** product extracted from the milk of **transgenic** goats. ATryn® functions to moderate **clotting** in the absence of the antithrombin normally found in human **plasma**, and it is often used during high-risk surgical procedures. Another medicine in development attaches to interleukin, a protein overproduced due to mutations in the gene cryopyrin (CIAS1); in excess, interleukin stimulates the **inflammatory** process, often resulting in several rare diseases referred to as cryopyrin-associated periodic syndromes (CAPS). When interleukin attaches to the medicine, though,

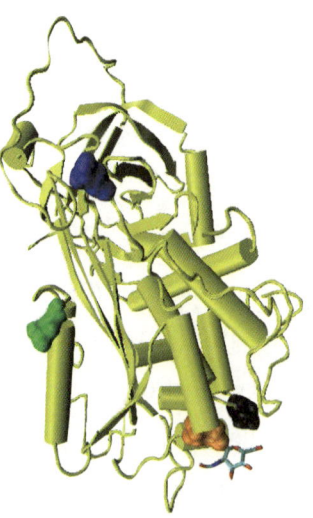

▲ antithrombin monomer

it can no longer bind to cell surface **receptors** and can be flushed instead from the body. A similar medicine under development attaches to and blocks inflammation-causing **proteins** in the body's **immune** system; these proteins can inflame and scar multiple organs in the body.

4 Over the past twenty years, many governments have taken steps to ensure that **adequate** medical and biological products are being developed for rare disease groups. Since the early 1980's, worldwide regulatory incentives to encourage the development of orphan drugs have been initiated. To counter lack of research and **scant** economic incentives, the U.S. passed the Orphan Drug Act in 1983, which offers economic assistance and incentives for clinical research, orphan product **grants**, tax credits, and seven-year exclusive marketing rights on FDA-approved orphan drugs. In the decade prior to 1983, only 10 orphan drugs were produced and marketed; since 1983, over 230 such drugs have been made available in the U.S. A similar initiative was approved by the European Parliament in 1999, and it offers financial incentives and a ten-year market exclusivity for EMEA (European Medicines Evaluation Agency) approved drugs. Japan adopted its Orphan Drug Regulation in 1993, providing marketing incentives and a five-year marketing exclusion for the

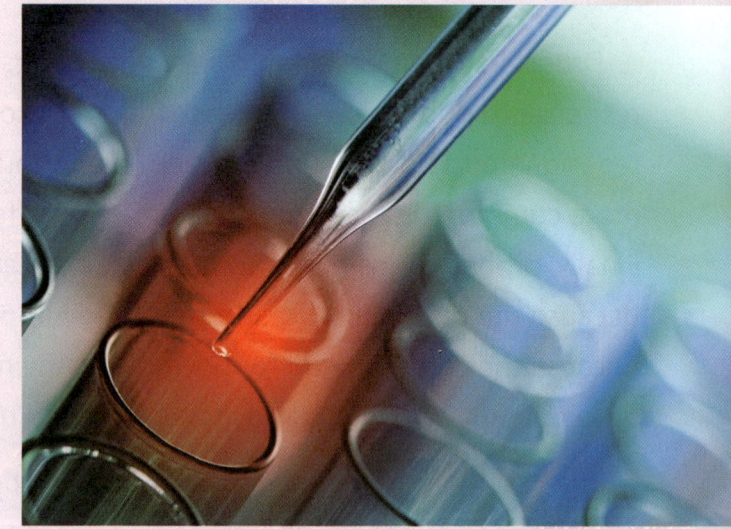

▲ Many governments have taken steps to encourage the development of orphan drugs.

development of MHLW (Ministry of Health, Labor and Welfare) approved orphan drugs.

5 A particular challenge in the **post-genomic** era will be the redefining of orphan diseases. Continuous improvements in **diagnostics** and research will lead to the definition of subgroups of common diseases, thus giving rise to identification of very rare diseases and treatments described as ultra-orphan. The **proliferation** of orphan **designation**s will certainly help to highlight and increase the ethical debates about orphan diseases and products. For instance, the scientific community remains divided on whether or not funding should be provided for special status diseases and treatments. Cost effectiveness continues to be a critical question in orphan drug development. And the issue of **equity**—balancing health benefits with resource use—looms large as research and development allows for increasing orphan identifications. Advances in molecular medicine lead most interested parties to believe that orphan drug research and production will continue to rise through the 21st century. Aside from the ethical issues and possible safety issues, many also find that orphan drugs offer a positive opportunity for global **cooperation**.

TARGET WORD EXERCISES

A Match the following target words with their meaning (use their context from the article).

a. orphan
b. designation
c. adequate
d. indications
e. recombinant
f. clotting
g. immune
h. antithrombin
i. diagnostics
j. development
k. equity
l. post-genomic
m. cooperation
n. transgenic
o. plasma

(____) 1 isolated; not part of a system
(____) 2 substances in blood that inhibit blood clotting by inactivating thrombin
(____) 3 symptom or circumstance that warrants medical treatment
(____) 4 the state of being just or balanced
(____) 5 process of growth and differentiation
(____) 6 act of naming or identifying
(____) 7 coagulation; a semisolid mass
(____) 8 practice of identifying a disease from its signs and symptoms
(____) 9 produced by genetic engineering
(____) 10 liquid part of blood or lymph
(____) 11 sufficient
(____) 12 containing genes transferred from another species
(____) 13 protected from or not susceptible to a disease
(____) 14 working together for a common purpose
(____) 15 current era when researchers achieve higher meaning and function out of raw sequences of data

B Prefixes, Suffixes, and Combining Forms: Match the **prefix**, **suffix**, or **combining form** to the common word forms and their definitions below, and then use some of these words to complete the following sentences.

Prefixes →
- **dia-**: (Middle English), made of, consisting of
- **post-**: (Middle English), subsequent to, later than
- **anti-**: (Middle English), against
- **co-**: (Middle English), with or together
- **trans-**: (Latin), across or beyond

Suffixes →
- **-ment**: (Middle English, suffix), concrete result or agent of a specific action
- **-ing**: (Middle English), action or process

Combining forms →
- **auto-**: (Greek), self-caused or self-induced

a ____gram (a chart, plan, or scheme)	e ____biography (a work about one's self)
b ____form (to change or alter)	f redefin(e) ____ (the process of defining again)
c move ____ (motion or activity)	
d ____operative (after an operation)	g ____worker (partner; fellow)

1. Mohandas Ghandi wrote about his early life in his _____, which he called "The Story of My Experiments with Truth."
2. Some forms of bacteria, when inserted into plant cells, can cause them to _____.
3. A schematic is a _____ using pictures to demonstrate how a machine operates.
4. The doctor charted the improved _____ of John's knee during his _____ rehabilitation.
5. Concerns about the environment are _____ fuel consumption.
6. James Watson and his _____, Francis Crick, solved the questions of the structure of DNA.

C Complete the target words from incomplete letters in the following sentences.

1. Anti_____bin normally is a clotting agent found in human p_____a.
2. Stem cell research will help researchers continue to improve their diag_____ for many diseases.
3. Vaccines enable the human body to remain __m__u____ to many diseases.
4. Rare diseases have historically not received a_____te research or funding.
5. Trans_____ic recom_____ant plants can be produced by DNA manipulation.
6. The patient's medical indi_____ suggest the need for additional therapeutic activities.
7. Medical record imaging is of growing interest in the _____t-_____ic era.
8. Some genetic disorders are of such low prevalence that they are considered __r_____n.
9. Increasingly, hospitals and home care providers work in co_____tion to ensure continued therapeutic activities for patients.
10. When a product receives an orphan drug desig_____ the drug company also receives various economic incentives.
11. Social justice advocates desire e_____ty in research and drug development for third world countries.
12. Hemophilia is a bleeding disorder in which there is inadequate clo_____ing of the blood.

Unit 5
Chapter 13

Light-Emitting Semiconductors

Through **innovations** in technology, natural lighting substitutes have rapidly **proliferate**d over the past two centuries. **Incandescent** light experiments began in the early 1800s. Incandescence is produced by light **photons emit**ted from **atoms** heated to a high temperature (about 2200°C) by electrically-generated **electrons** moving along the **filament** in the bulb. Nearly 90 percent of the heat is lost in this process, creating a soft

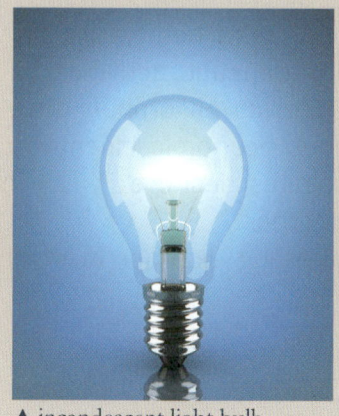

▲ incandescent light bulb   ▲ fluorescent light bulb

light and virtually no energy efficiency. **Fluorescent** lamps soon followed, and they produced a much brighter light by using a coating of **phosphor** powder in the tube. When the heated **mercury** atoms collide with the phosphor, the phosphor atoms heat even hotter, giving off a bright light. Little energy or heat is wasted in a fluorescent lamp, so it is much more energy efficient than incandescent lamps.

2. Far exceeding the energy efficiency of the incandescent and fluorescent light is **solid** state lighting, which utilizes light-emitting diodes (LED) for **illumination**. LED's were first developed in the 1960s, but they did not become widely used until the 1980s. The light of the LED is emitted from a solid semiconductor rather than from a filament or tube. The most common **semiconductor** is **silicon**, although other chemical elements or compounds can be used, and it conducts electricity according to its impurities, either by adding more electrons to create more energy (N-type materials) or by creating holes defined by electron deficiencies (P-type materials). Either **impurity** creates more electron movement, thus generating more energy.

▲ LED lights

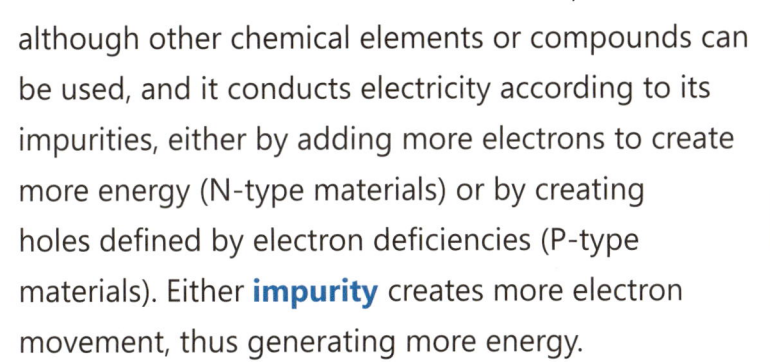

3. The solid semiconductor used to produce light is called a **diode**, which is a combination of n and p materials that conducts electrons from one to the other, but not in **reverse**. When the semiconductor diode is subjected to electrical **current** (it is encased in a housing attached to an electrical current source), it produces visible light. Initially, LEDs emitted only low light and were too expensive for most lighting applications. Early applications, then, were mostly as solid-state indicator lights on devices such as instrument panels, appliances, and dashboards. LED brightness has

▲ light emitting diodes

improved in the 21st century to allow for a wide variety of consumer applications in personal electronics, exterior lighting such as traffic signals and outdoor displays, and even biochemical **detection** processes and in medical devices.

④ The quality of LEDs is not yet **equivalent** to natural sunlight or other lighting sources, based on the color-**render**ing index (CRI) of light sources, which is the ability to reproduce the appearance of an object when illuminated by a true white light. Energy efficiency is measured by the amount of light produced (**lumens**) in relation to the input of electrical power. Future LEDs may be up to 10 times as efficient and long-lasting as incandescent or fluorescent lamps. Greater efficiency and longer lifetimes of LED lighting could potentially reduce lighting costs for consumers by up to 90 percent. LED lighting also holds potential for significant reduction of energy emissions; with LED improvements, global use of electricity for lighting could be cut in half, electricity **generation** savings could be passed on for other uses, and global carbon emissions could be significantly reduced.

Natural sunlight and incandescent lamps	100 CRI
Fluorescent lamps	85 CRI
Future LEDs	80 CRI
Current LEDs	70 CRI

Future LEDs	150-200 lumens	100,000 hours
Fluorescent lamp	85 lumens	10,000 hours
Current LEDs	30 lumens	20,000 hours
Incandescent bulb	16 lumens	1,000 hours

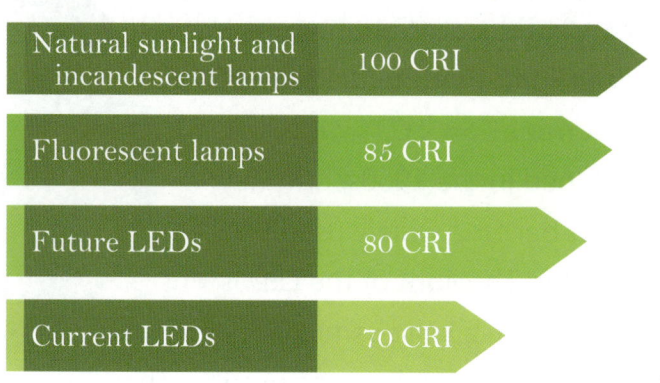

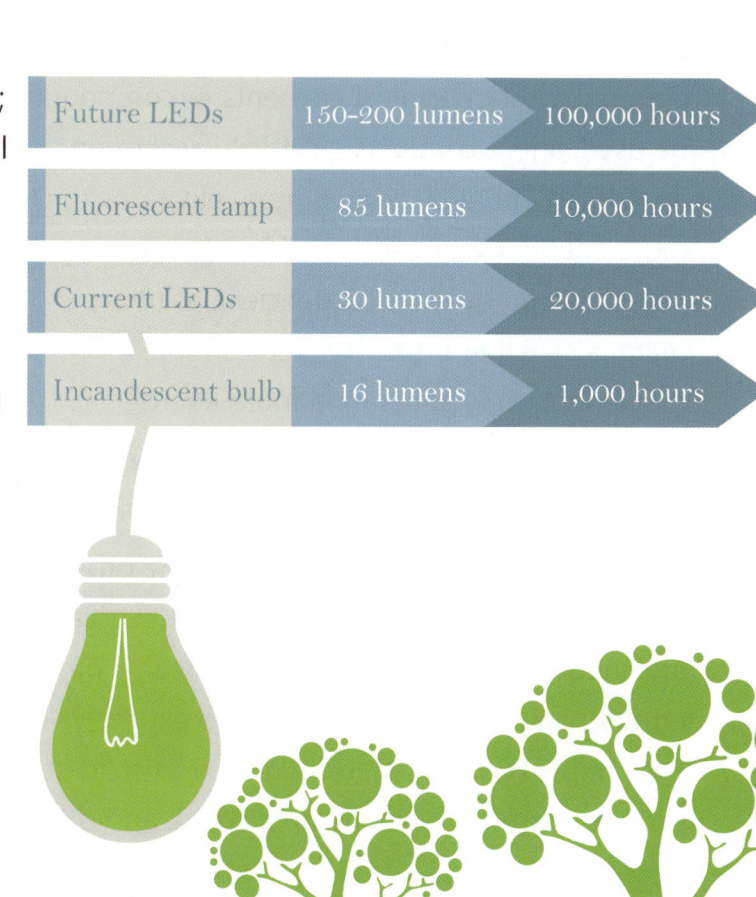

⑤ Most LEDs use inorganic semiconductors, but there is growth in the use of organic LEDs (OLED) as well. OLEDs use organic semiconductor materials—carbon-based small molecules or polymers—which are layered and electrically charged to provide luminescent emissions. OLED materials make semiconductors flexible and thus more **versatile** in application, and OLED lighting is brighter, faster, and more transparent than LED lighting. Already OLEDs are less expensive than LEDs, and when their reliability is improved, they may replace all earlier sources of lighting.

▲ prototype OLED lighting panels (cc by STRONGlk7)

⑥ Future uses of LEDs will cover a broad range of private and public uses. Many researchers predict that soon LEDs will be produced more economically so that they will replace incandescent and fluorescent sources for domestic lighting. The brightness, low maintenance/long lifetime, and energy efficiency of LEDs far surpasses what any other lighting sources will be capable of in the future. Japan has already begun to replace traditional street lamps with LED lighting. Besides energy and cost savings, these lamps produce more uniform light projection and minimal glare. Within the next few years, museums may adopt LED lighting. Besides costs savings, LED lights in museums will help lower temperatures and eliminate **ultraviolet** rays, both of which will improve visitor comfort and artifact preservation. It is possible that within the next few years, traditional lighting will become **obsolete** with the widespread adoption of LED and OLED lighting.

▲ OLED lighting in a shopping mall in Germany (cc by ACBahn)

▲ The Sony XEL-1, the world's first OLED TV (cc by Steve Liao)

▲ OLED TV (cc by LG전자)

Unit 5 Chapter 13 Light-Emitting Semiconductors

91

TARGET WORD EXERCISES

A Each of the words below (not all are found in the information above) describes **an atomic element or particle involved in light production**. Each word derives either from Greek (G) or Latin (L). Match the word and its ancient origin with its current meaning.

- a. proton (G, proton: first)
- b. electron (G, elektron: amber, as by rubbing)
- c. neutron (L, neuter: neither one or the other)
- d. atom (G, atomos: uncut)
- e. photon (G, phos: light)
- f. phosphor (G, Phosphoros: morning star; light bearer)
- g. neon (G, neos: new)
- h. mercury (L, Mecurius: Roman god of tradesmen and thieves)
- i. silicon (L, silex: hard stone, flint)

(____) 1 dark gray solid, non-metallic element used in the manufacture of semiconductors
(____) 2 elementary particle in all atoms that has a negative electrical charge
(____) 3 elementary particle that can appear as a particle of light
(____) 4 positively charged elementary particle, determines the chemical properties of the atom and thus which chemical element is represented
(____) 5 colorless odorless rare gas, used in illuminated signs and lights
(____) 6 neutral subatomic particle
(____) 7 silvery-white, dense, poisonous metallic element used in lamps
(____) 8 smallest unit of matter which can take part in a chemical reaction
(____) 9 chemical element capable of emitting light when irradiated with particles of electromagnetic radiation

B Several of the target words, listed in the box below, directly relate to **a lamp or the process of luminescence**. Fill in the blanks in the sentences with the correct target word.

| incandescent | semiconductor | filament | fluorescent | emit |
| illuminate | solid | current | generate |

1 _____ lamps are cheaper and longer-lasting than filament bulbs.
2 If one is not careful when changing lightbulbs, the electric _____ could pass through the person's body.

3 Tungsten is the typical metal used to make the _____ in an incandescent bulb.
4 Recent improvements in LEDs will _____ less energy waste than ever before.
5 Instead of neon and incandescent lights, LED lights now _____ New York City's Times Square.
6 _____ lights proved to be a significant improvement over kerosene lamps.
7 The availability of new low-cost electronic devices may soon increase due to the use of more organic _____ materials.
8 Metal, which is _____ at room temperature, is an excellent conductor of heat and electricity.
9 Light emitting semiconductors powered by solar power will _____ extremely low levels of energy waste.

C Prefixes, Suffixes, and Combining Forms: Add the correct prefix, suffix, or combining form to their root words to form the target words, and match with the correct meanings.

a _____verse
b _____novation
c _____lifer_____
d _____pur_____
e _____tection
f equival_____
g dur_____

(_____) 1 to increase at a rapid rate
(_____) 2 the process of discovery
(_____) 3 to turn around to the opposite direction
(_____) 4 strong and long-lasting
(_____) 5 something newly introduced
(_____) 6 something that contaminates or dilutes
(_____) 7 equal in value

D Circle the word that is not a synonym of the target word.

1	innovation	novelty	invention	creation	classic
2	reverse	forward	backward	turnabout	change
3	durable	sturdy	resistant	long-lasting	fragile
4	detection	discovery	concealment	find	revelation
5	illuminate	darken	ignite	combust	flare
6	generate	create	induce	prevent	produce
7	solid	hollow	hard	full	opaque
8	emit	absorb	expel	eliminate	release
9	incandescent	luminous	glowing	bright	dark
10	proliferate	multiply	increase	diminish	grow
11	impurity	pollutant	decontaminant	defect	taint

Chapter 14
Semiconductors and Environmental Safety Issues

① Semiconductor **device** manufacturing in the 21st century is a global business. After the first **transistor** was developed in the late 1940s, companies around the world quickly entered the semiconductor industry. By the 1970s, the Semiconductor Industry Association (SIA) was established, and they soon took on the task of developing guidelines for the health and success of a **burgeoning** industry. The semiconductor industry reached global **proportions** as it grew across Europe, and in Japan, Korea, and Taiwan. Together, these countries sponsored the International Technology Roadmap for Semiconductors, a plan to meet new and changing challenges of **quality assurance**, and to assure the economic and environmental health of the industry.

② Although global economic health remains at the heart of various semiconductor industry organizations, environmental health has become a priority as well. Numerous organizations have developed standards and practiced guidelines to improve environment, health and safety throughout the semiconductor industry. Particular issues include environmental management, especially of **hazardous** waste; **occupational** health and safety; and fire and building safety issues.

③ By the early 1980s, the semiconductor industry was globally seeking **alternatives** to hazardous chemicals. The semiconductor **fabrication** process produces significant waste that can be harmful to the overall environment as well as to the workplace environment. A number of **toxic** chemicals are released in the semiconductor fabrication process and **dispersed** in the remaining **wastewater**, including silica, copper, and **fluoride**. The most toxic and dangerous waste product is **arsenic**. An arsenic and gallium alloy (gallium arsenide) has a much faster electron **velocity** and higher electron mobility than silicon, allowing for higher frequencies and higher speeds in electronic products. However, the arsenic, which functions as an **impurity** (**dopant**) for the gallium semiconductor material, is released through the fabrication process as waste.

▲ Arsenic is the most toxic waste product.

◀ gallium arsenide (cc by W. Oelen)

◀ Toxic chemicals released in the semiconductor fabrication process are dispersed in the wastewater.

Unit 5 Chapter 14 Semiconductors and Environmental Safety Issues

95

[28] This waste enters landfills and has the potential to contaminate groundwater. Although many governments regulate arsenic waste, high amounts have been found in the northern U.S., and high levels of arsenic exposure have been noted across Southeast Asia. The U.S. Environmental Protection Agency (EPA) is leading efforts to reduce arsenic waste levels worldwide, and to develop economically **advantageous** and safe ways to recover and reuse gallium, which is a rare and expensive metallic element.

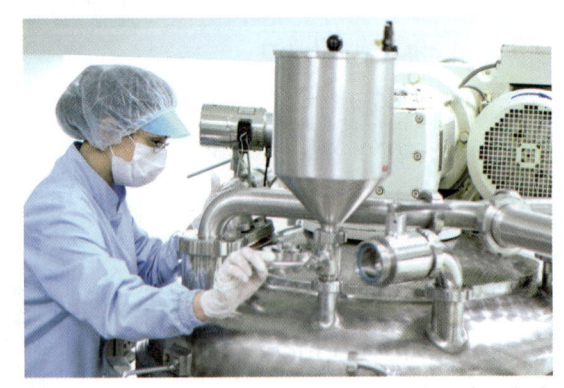

4 In 1995, the U.S. semiconductor industry entered into an agreement with the EPA to significantly reduce high global warming potential gases (GWP), most notably perfluorocarbons (PFCs). PFCs have long atmospheric lifetimes, and have the potential for devastating environmental and climate change, and economic effects. The U.S./EPA agreement has served as a model for similar government and industry agreements worldwide, and in 1999, the World Semiconductor Council adopted a climate protection plan to reduce PFC emissions by at least 10 percent below the industry's 1995 **baseline** level by the end of 2010.

5 Toxic chemicals pose environmental risks to industry employees as well:
- **Acute exposure:** various respiratory, digestive, and skin disorders
- **Long-term exposure: afflictions** ranging from **dermatitis** to several forms of cancer

6 In many countries, government organizations, such as the U.S. National Institute for Occupational Safety and Health, set guidelines for permissible exposure limits (PEL) for hazardous chemicals in the work environment. When administrative and engineering controls are not adequate, workers may be required to wear personal protective equipment. If at any time a worker is exposed to a toxic level of a chemical pollutant, then a **decontamination** process is required for both clothing and personal hygiene.

▲ Industry employees risk being exposed to chemical pollutants.

7 Fire and building safety is also critical to worker health and safety. General building and fire codes do not provide adequate safety for the use of many chemicals in semiconductor fabrication and for the physical requirements of the cleanrooms (a **contaminant**-free room used in the fabrication process). To meet this need, the SIA formed the Fire and Building Safety Committee (FABS) to provide guidelines for the industry and to work with local fire and building codes. The guidelines provide **restrictive** standards for chemical storage, chemical levels at workstations, and for building construction materials. The FABS committee has also had significant impact in all SIA participating countries.

8 In the late 1990s, the World Semiconductor Council created an Environment, Safety and Health (ESH) Task Force to promote global guidelines and performance standards in such areas as:

- Resource conservation
- Pollution prevention
- Decreasing PFC emissions
- Waste management
- ESH conscious design
- Creating safe and healthy work environments
- Establishing global "best practices"

9 **Feasible** targets and performance standards for global ESH issues are evaluated yearly at the annual International Semiconductor Environment, Safety and Health Conference.

◀ Efforts are now being concentrated on creating a safe and healthy work environment.

TARGET WORD EXERCISES

A Circle the correct form of the words at the end of each blank to finish the sentences. Use the article to determine what kind of word is missing (adjective, noun, verb, adverb), and be sure to take into consideration forms using prefixes and suffixes.

(____) 1 In the 21st century, young adults have _____ (burgeon) as a target population for video game manufacturers.
   a. burgeoned   b. burgeoning   c. burgeon

(____) 2 Semiconductor fabrication companies should _____ (assure) their workers that they are protected from toxic chemicals.
   a. assurance   b. assuring   c. assure

(____) 3 The use of organic materials for semiconductor material does not guarantee a reduction in _____ (hazard) waste from the fabrication process.
   a. hazarding   b. hazarded   c. hazardous

(____) 4 An _____ (occupy) in the semiconductor fabrication process can pose potential dangers.
   a. occupation   b. occupational   c. occupied

(____) 5 _____ (Alternate) sources of energy may soon power semiconductors.
   a. Alternative   b. Alternating   c. Alternated

(____) 6 _____ (Dope) some semiconductor materials increases their speed and effectiveness.
   a. Dopant   b. Doping   c. Doped

(____) 7 Creating smaller and less expensive semiconductors has proven very economically _____ (advantage) to the industry.
   a. advantageousness b. advantaging   c. advantageous

(____) 8 Massive sickness and death occurred in Bangladesh when many of its people were _____ (expose) to arsenic poisoning.
   a. exposure   b. exposed   c. exposition

(____) 9 The SIA has developed _____ (restrict) guidelines about the process, location, and time limits of chemical storage.
   a. restricted   b. restrictive   c. restriction

(____) 10 _____ (Feasible) studies of potential technologies, device structures, innovative materials, and unique processing tools help determine how global semiconductor corporations can work together to develop new consumer and industry products.
   a. Feasibly   b. Feasibility   c. Feasibleness

B Place T (True) or F (False) in front of each sentence to indicate whether or not the target word has been used correctly.

(____) 1 Copper used in semiconductor manufacture can be a **velocity** waste at higher levels.
(____) 2 Greenhouse gases that **disperse** into the atmosphere may contribute to global warming and climate change.
(____) 3 Stricter guidelines and standards in the semiconductor industry will decrease the number of workers who develop work-related **proportions**.
(____) 4 Organic LEDs may soon be the standard lighting diodes for mobile and portable electronic **devices**.
(____) 5 Personal protective equipment are standard **wastewater** for employees who may be exposed to poisonous chemicals.
(____) 6 Global semiconductor industry organizations help to **baseline** economic progress and enhance worker health and safety.
(____) 7 Minimizing chemical use in semiconductor fabrication reduces waste disposal costs and worker exposure to hazardous and **toxic** materials.
(____) 8 The correct amount of dopant ensures the highest **quality of** semiconductor material.
(____) 9 Pollutant restrictions need to be financially **feasible** for any company.

C Match the target word with the correct antonym.

a toxic
b disperse
c burgeoning
d advantageous
e exposure
f hazardous
g restrictive

(____) 1 detrimental (causing damage or harm; injurious)
(____) 2 safe (free from danger or risk)
(____) 3 expansive (broad in size or extent; comprehensive)
(____) 4 shrinking (the act of becoming less; restricted)
(____) 5 gather (to assemble; to collect in one place)
(____) 6 nonpoisonous (not producing harmful substances; safe to ingest)
(____) 7 protection (the act of defending from trouble, harm, or loss)

Unit 5
Chapter 15

Semiconductors and Energy Efficiency

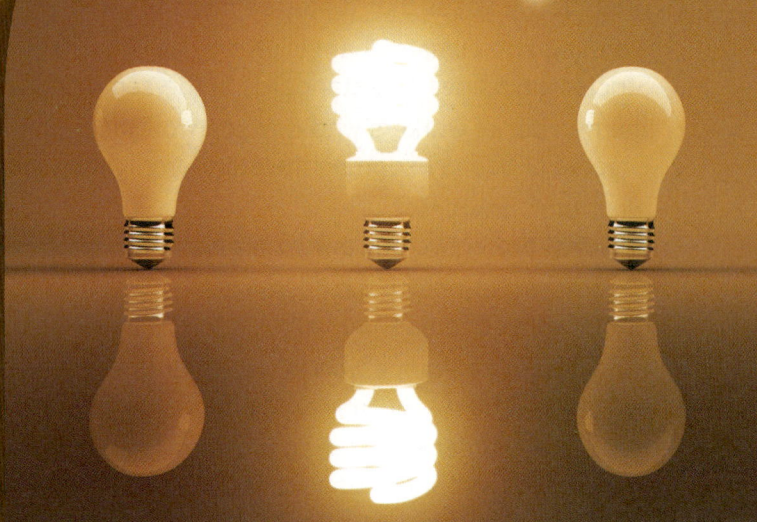

Over 500 billion semi**conductor** devices are sold annually. They range in use from hand-held electronic devices to satellites, and they contribute to the overall efficiency and **convenience** of society. Semiconductor devices have also led the way in clean energy, replacing polluting energy sources, reducing the use of natural resources, and diminishing harmful emissions and waste.

Semiconductors are the basic material for **integrated circuits** (IC), which today drive most of electronic devices. ICs, or what are commonly referred to as chips, are a single **crystal** of semiconductor material, such as silicon, integrated with electronic circuits and **component**s made from the same crystal. ICs can consist of millions of elements, across which short **traces**, or signals, can travel quickly and at low power levels. These **miniature** circuits are relatively

▲ integrated circuits

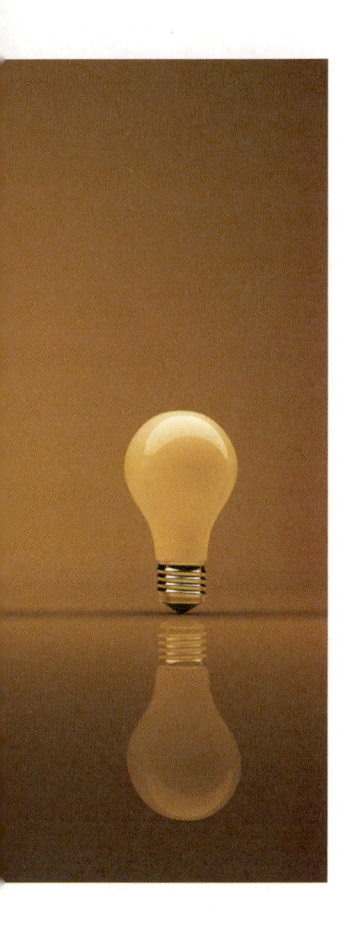

inexpensive to produce in high volume, highly reliable, energy efficient, and capable of very high processing speeds.

3 Integrated circuit advances include high efficiency compressors and **defrost** mechanisms that improve the energy performance of refrigerators and freezers up to 20%. Dishwashers with energy efficient motors consume nearly 40% less energy than conventional models, and they use much less water. Similar savings are possible with clothes washers, in which advanced circuitry can reduce energy consumption and save thousands of gallons of water every year. Digital signal processors allow high levels of energy conversion efficiencies (low energy waste in the process of converting energy input into useful energy output) with HDTVs and other digital electronics.

4 Digital electronics are also equipped with semiconductor-based lighting, or solid-state lighting (SSL), which has **eclipsed** energy savings and emission reduction performance of all previous sources of lighting. Across **consumer** and corporate uses of SSL, a reduction of over 50% energy

▲ More advanced integrated circuits can improve the energy performance of refrigerators and washing machines.

used to power SSL is possible. Additionally, SSL has the potential to reduce total energy consumption upwards of 30% globally, and perhaps even more with its added capability of direct compatibility with battery and solar technology.

5 Solar technology relies on photovoltaic (PV) cells, and although those in solar panels provide another option for renewable energy sources, currently they function only at about 15% energy **conversion** efficiency. PVs made of semiconductor materials absorb sunlight; then, the heat from the solar energy

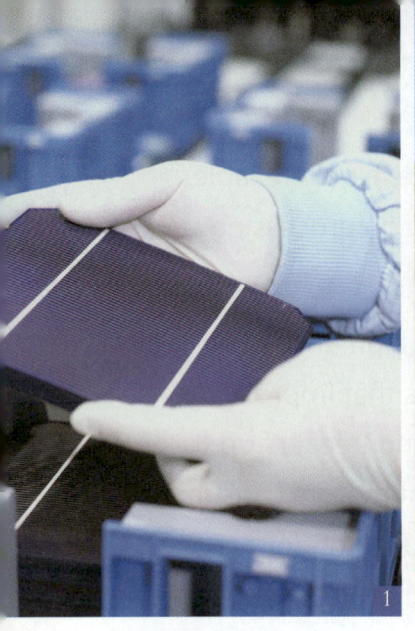

1 Photovoltaics (PV) cells generate electricity directly from sunlight.
(cc by Ersol)
2 solar tree in Austria
(cc by Anna Regelsberger)

◀ solar panels

allows the electrons to flow through the material to produce electricity. Because only certain sunlight energies can motivate the electrons, and because the semiconductor materials also reflect the sunlight, only about 15% of the sunlight actually generates electricity. PV manufactures are currently working to improve solar cell efficiencies.

6 Other advances in chip technology include adaptive **voltage** scaling (AVS), an advanced energy-management process that enables increased voltage for faster performance without boosting energy consumption or limiting component lifespan. In fact, AVS may reduce energy consumption in digital processors by up to 70%. LCD (liquid crystal display) technology creates images on a flat surface by shining light through a combination of liquid crystals and polarized glass, and when applied to portable devices, televisions, and **computers**, provides over a 30% savings in energy consumption. Additional

▲ the LCD display of a digital TV camera

▶ LCD TV

energy savings may soon be realized as many portable devices will be recharged using improved chip technologies that drive solar power systems.

7 Chip-enabled features reduce vehicle energy consumption and improve vehicle performance and reliability. Integrated circuits contribute to fuel savings in numerous ways, including timing and **combustion** controls and gasoline direct injection. Both fuel efficiency and pollution reduction is possible through chip-enabled evaporative emission control systems. Even the need for driving can be reduced through the application of integrated circuits in telecommuting and teleconferencing.

8 Industries can realize energy savings by utilizing **variable** speed drives (VSD) and variable frequency drives (VFD) to adjust the speed of motor-driven systems to match load requirements. Fixed speed drives are often geared to peak loads, which leads to energy inefficiency during times of reduced load or flow. Chip-enabled VSDs match motor speed to load requirements, a process that could realize over 75% energy consumption savings.

9 Numerous organizations across the world are engaged in advancing energy efficiency through advanced semiconductor technology. The **Consortium** for Energy Efficiency (CEE) is a nonprofit North American organization which promotes energy efficient products and encourages structural and behavioral changes in the energy marketplace. The U.S. Department of Energy's Office of Energy Efficiency and Renewable Energy (EERE) is undertaking multinational initiatives to promote renewable energy sources, including those possible through rapidly advancing semiconductor technologies. And the World Semiconductor Council at its 2008 meeting in Taipei produced an international statement stating its commitment to continuing and improving semiconductor contributions to a cleaner environment.

▶ The Solar Settlement, a sustainable housing community project in Germany (cc by Andrewglaser)

TARGET WORD EXERCISES

A The prefixes "**con-**" and "**com-**" derive from the Latin **cum**, or "**with**." Fill in the blanks in the following sentences with the correct "con-" or "com-" target word, based on the article above and the definition given in parentheses.

| consumer | consortium | convenience | computer | contribute | conductor |
| control | conversion | continue | conventional | component | consumption |

1. Energy _____ *(to turn around)* is the transformation of energy from a source such as the sun into electrical energy.
2. Governments will need to _____ *(to give support or money for a common purpose or fund)* economic and personnel resources to industries in order to meet global energy efficiency goals.
3. Alternative energy industries have the potential to soon replace most _____ *(customary; ordinary)* power plants.
4. Semiconductor technologies have significantly improved air pollution _____ *(instruments to regulate a mechanism)* in many industries.
5. Rising fuel costs can create economic hardship for the average _____ *(a person who buys goods or services for personal needs)*.
6. Computers can often be upgraded by replacing some of the hardware _____s *(constituent parts or features of a whole)*.
7. Efforts to reach zero emissions are expected to _____ *(to go on with; persist in)* well beyond the target date of 2010.
8. While metals are very efficient electrical _____ *(substances that allow electricity, heat, sound, etc. pass through them)*, non-metals are efficient insulators.
9. Scientists from around the world have created a global _____ *(a partnership or association)* to rebuild Afghanistan's agriculture.
10. The industry sector of the United States is responsible for over one-third of the nations' energy _____ *(the using up of goods or services)*.
11. Innovations in LCD _____ *(programmable electronic machine that performs high-speed operations or stores information)* screens have made them brighter and easier to read.
12. Cell phones are a modern _____ *(anything that adds to one's comfort or saves work)* upon which many individuals and business rely.

B
Acronyms are abbreviations formed by using the initial letters of words of a phrase or title. The following acronyms are related to semiconductor technology and efficiency. Fill in the blank with the correct target word according to the article and the definitions.

| Variable | Trace | Integrated | Crystal | Circuit | Energy |

1. **IAD**: _____ Access Device (A device installed at the customer premises that enables multiple services to share a single circuit)
2. **PCB**: Printed _____ Board (A flat plastic or fiberglass board on which interconnected components are laminated or etched)
3. **VFO**: _____ Frequency Oscillator (a component in a radio receiver or transmitter that controls and changes the frequency to which the apparatus is tuned)
4. **LCoS**: Liquid _____ on Silicon display (a reflective technology in which liquid crystals are used to control the amount of reflected light)
5. **ETBA**: Energy _____ Barrier Analysis (a procedure intended to detect hazards by focusing in detail on the presence of energy in a system and the barriers for controlling that energy)
6. **WEEA**: World _____ Efficiency Association (an organization of the World Energy Council charged with increasing energy efficiency, especially in developing countries)

C
Use the correct form of the target words used in Exercise B in the following sentences:

(___) 1 Electronic _____ allows electrons to flow through wires generating energy.
　　　　a. circuitry　　　　b. circuitous
(___) 2 Alternative sources may soon be used to _____ LED and LCD screens.
　　　　a. energize　　　　b. energy
(___) 3 A microprocessor is an _____ circuit that processes all information in the computer.
　　　　a. integration　　　b. integrated
(___) 4 A signal _____ is a device used to test for the presence of a signal.
　　　　a. tracing　　　　　b. tracer
(___) 5 The bond formed when silicon _____ can easily be broken by adding impurities.
　　　　a. crystallizes　　　b. crystal
(___) 6 Power _____ can be adjusted by semiconductor devices designed to detect the changes.
　　　　a. variability　　　　b. variable

105

Unit 6
Chapter 16

Introduction to Nanotechnology

1 The most basic definition of nanotechnology is the process of **assembling** and manipulating materials discovered at the nanoscale level. The nanoscale measures materials smaller than **microscopic** objects on a scale ranging approximately from 1-100 nanometers (nm). A nanometer is one millionth of a millimeter; to put this into perspective, one sheet of paper is 100,000 nanometers thick. The atomic scale is actually smaller than the nanoscale (a nanometer is roughly the size of three or four atoms), but the nanoscale is the first point at which any materials can be assembled. Nanoscience is the research to discover the properties and behavior of these nanoscale materials and to develop beneficial ways to use them.

2 Materials at the nanoscale level often **behave** differently than large scale materials. Nanoscale materials have a larger surface to volume ratio, meaning that nanomaterials have more exposed surface area in relation to their volume or size than larger materials. Nanomaterials, then, have more area to **interact** with their environment, thus increasing their capability to **react** in some specific ways, such as conducting heat or reflecting light. Carbon nanostructures, when **incorporated** into such products as bicycles or baseballs, are not only many times stronger than structures from conventional

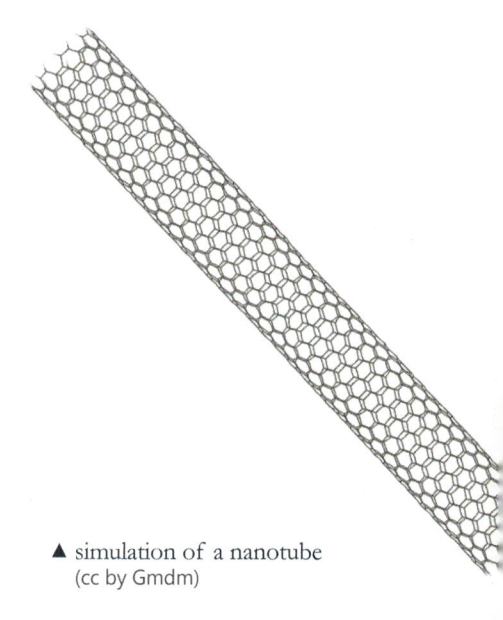

▲ simulation of a nanotube
(cc by Gmdm)

materials such as wood or aluminum but are, in fact, the strongest structures known. Carbon nanotubes also have **novel** superconductivity properties that will most likely in the future **eclipse** the speed and productivity of elements such as silicon and gallium, which are currently utilized in semiconductors.

▲ Nanotechnology can make golf balls fly straighter.

▲ Eric Drexler popularized the potential of molecular nanotechnology. (cc by Eric Drexler)

3) Nanotechnology originally meant building items starting from their atomic properties, or from the bottom up, as **envisioned** by the Noble prize-winning physicist Richard Feynman as early as 1959. In the 1980s, Eric Drexler built upon Feynman's ideas and popularized the term "nanotechnology," but he referred specifically to the possibility of building machines on the molecular scale, or molecular manufacturing. The definition of nanotechnology has since expanded to mean a **multidisciplinary** field engaged in research and development from nanoscience to nanomanufacturing.

4) Nanotechnology derives from what is already successfully taking place in all of nature. One example of natural nanoengineering is the basic process of **photosynthesis**. Scientists are developing artificial photosynthesis to create clean energy. Another example is the nanostructure of the lotus leaf, which creates a waterproof barrier. The lotus leaf structure has been copied to produce various water **repellent** materials. Spider silk is naturally reinforced with nanoscale crystals, which can stretch by 40 percent of its length and absorb a hundred times more energy than steel without breaking. Researchers believe

that they can not only replicate this silk **artificial**ly, but they can also **rearrange** the crystals into even stronger silk fibers; and, because spider silk is spun with only protein and water, this eco-friendly reproduction process could replace the harsh chemicals now used to produce strong artificial fibers such as Kevlar.

▲ Kevlar
(cc by Kevin dicelis)

▲ The nanostructure of the lotus leaf creates a waterproof barrier.

5 The National Nanotechnology Initiative (NNI), created by the U.S. government to oversee a **comprehensive** nanotechnology research and development program, describes at least four generations of nanotechnology, of which only the first two are fully underway.

▲ Spider silk is naturally reinforced with nanoscale crystals.

- **Passive** nanostructures—nanostructures with **steady** structures and functions, used to improve various product components.
  - golf balls that fly straighter
  - battle **fatigues** that are chemical resistant
  - cosmetics with improvements in skin protection from harmful rays
- **Active nanostructures**—nanostructures that **fluctuate** during operation.
  - laser-emitting devices
  - drug delivery particles that change chemical composition upon delivery
- **Systems of nanosystems**—systems created through bioassembly or self-assembly.
  - scaffolding for tissue engineering
- **Molecular nanosystems**—**heterogeneous** molecular systems in which each molecule has a distinct structure and plays a specific role.
  - a molecular assembly with the ability to control interaction between light and matter in order to conserve energy

6 The benefits of commercial nanotechnology applications include global water purification and **filtration**, clean and efficient energy generation and distribution, and a healthier environment through precision farming, reduced fuel consumption, and pollution monitoring. However, with the increase of research and application in nanotechnology also comes increased risk. Nanomaterials also have potential for abuse, such as **intrusive surveillance**, terrorist applications such as weapons of mass destruction, and broad economic disruption from proliferation of low cost nanomaterials. Foresight Nanotech Institute, the Global Issue in Nanotechnology working group, and other worldwide institutions work to ensure beneficial development of nanotechnology, to provide a broad based education about the challenges and risks of nanotechnology, and to help improve global nanotechnology policies.

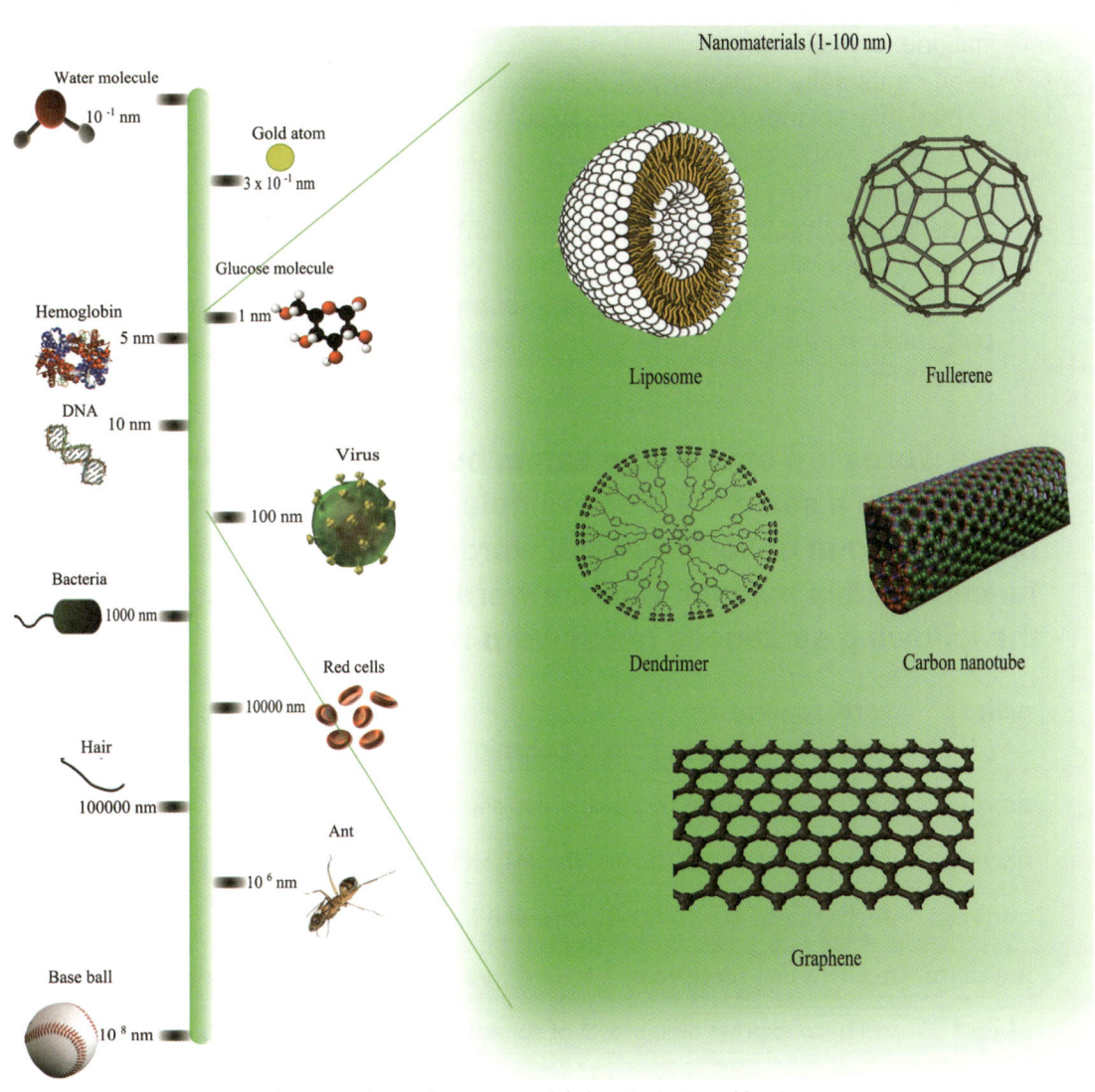

Unit 6 Chapter 16 Introduction to Nanotechnology

Nanomaterials (1-100 nm)

Water molecule 10^{-1} nm
Gold atom 3×10^{-1} nm
Glucose molecule 1 nm
Hemoglobin 5 nm
DNA 10 nm
Virus 100 nm
Bacteria 1000 nm
Red cells 10000 nm
Hair 100000 nm
Ant 10^6 nm
Base ball 10^8 nm

Liposome
Fullerene
Dendrimer
Carbon nanotube
Graphene

▲ comparison of nanomaterial sizes (cc by Sureshbup)

TARGET WORD EXERCISES

A Matching the target words with the correct meanings.

a assemble	e react	i artificial	m fluctuate
b microscopic	f incorporate	j rearrange	n filtration
c behave	g envision	k comprehensive	
d interact	h repellent	l steady	

(____) 1 resistant or impervious to a substance
(____) 2 so small as to be invisible except through a microscope
(____) 3 to act in response to an agent or influence
(____) 4 of broad scope or content
(____) 5 put into a different order
(____) 6 imagine; conceive of
(____) 7 to be continually changing
(____) 8 to take in or include as a part or parts
(____) 9 to act on or with something
(____) 10 to fit together the parts or pieces of
(____) 11 made by humans; produced rather than natural
(____) 12 to act in a specific way
(____) 13 the process of passing liquid or gas through a specific device to remove particulate matter
(____) 14 without much change or variation

B Some words are spelled the same, but can have different functions in a sentence. For example, "compress" can function both as a noun or verb. Several words in the article above function in this manner. Use the words listed below correctly in the following sentences (each word is used twice):

eclipse	verb: to surpass
	noun: the partial or complete obscuring of one celestial body by another
novel	adj: new noun: fictional prose narrative
harvest	verb: to collect noun: the season for gathering crops
convert	verb: to change noun: one who has changed beliefs
measure	noun: a unit specified by a scale verb: to ascertain the dimensions of
object	verb: to express disapproval of something noun: a material thing
conduct	verb: to manage or control noun: behavior

1. Nanofabrication products may one day _____ the use of silicon semiconductors in electronic products.
2. Researchers are studying how to use sound to _____ heat into electricity.
3. One process of nanotechnology is to build up an _____ by combining atomic elements.
4. Carbon nanotubes _____ both heat and electricity better than any metal.
5. One should only photograph a solar _____ with the proper eye protection.
6. Surgeons often _____ veins to replace arteries that are diseased.
7. Richard Smalley strongly disagreed with Eric Drexler, so he never became a _____ to the possibility of molecular nanotechnology.
8. Nanometers are the unit of _____ in nanoscience.
9. For farmers, the _____ marks the end of the growing season.
10. The Euro Nano Trade Alliance helps to monitor proper _____ in nanotechnology research and commercialization.
11. Michael Crichton's *Prey* is a _____ that warns of the dangers of nanotechnology.
12. Some critics _____ to nanotechnology for religious reasons.
13. Newly developed nanotechnology materials may provide a _____ way to clean up oil spills and polluted waterways.
14. Scientists have now developed a molecular ruler to _____ the smallest of life's particles.

C

The words "filtration" and "envision" are nouns formed by the suffix "-ion" (Latin: being, the result of). Correctly form a noun from the root words below and place them in the following sentences.

| interact | react | incorporate | comprehend | fluctuate |

1. Many universities are researching the possible _____ of nanoscience into the K-12 curriculum.
2. One of the challenges of drug delivery through nanotechnology devices is the uncertain _____ of nanostructures within the body.
3. The possible impact of nanotechnology just on curing and preventing chronic and degenerative diseases is at this point beyond human _____.
4. The larger surface area of nanomaterials allows for greater _____ with the environment.
5. Nanotechnology advances provide sensors which can monitor heartbeats, breathing rates, _____ in blood pressure, and other subtle body changes.

Unit 6
Chapter 17
DISRUPTIVE Technologies

The term "**disruptive** technology" was first used by Clayton Christensen, a Harvard Business School professor, in 1997. He used the term to describe technology that **displaces** established technology and ultimately **revolutionizes** consumer use, product value, and economic **competition**. Disruptive technologies change the status quo and the market for particular technologies. In the 21st century, examples of disruptive technologies include flash memory, which replaced other types of personal data storage, and digital photography, which has largely replaced film photography in all but the professional marketplace. Nanotechnology innovations, such as nanotubes, nanospheres, nanowires, are the most recent disruptive technologies under development for commercialization.

▲ The term "disruptive technology" was defined by Clayton Christensen. (cc by World Economic Forum)

disruptive technologies

▲ flash memory

▼ digital photography

▲ nanotechnology (nanowires)

112

② Biomedical technology, energy efficiency, and bioterrorism are three **critical** areas in which nanotechnology is disrupting production and delivery. For biomedical technology, nanotechnology is quickly emerging as a disruptive technology in cancer diagnosis and treatment:

- Quantum dots (nanocrystal semiconductors) hold the potential for optical detection of genes and proteins and for tumor and lymph node **visualization**.
- Nanoshells (silica core and metal shell) may soon be capable of deep tissue tumor cell **thermal ablation** (heat destruction) and tumor-specific imaging.
- Nanowires and carbon nanotubes will be capable of disease protein biomarker detection, DNA mutation detection, and gene expression detection.
- Dendrimers (spherical nanostructures that carry molecules) will diagnosis cancers through **image contrast** agents, and they will assist treatment through controlled release drug delivery.
- Nanocrystals will improve formulation for poorly **soluble** drugs.
- Nanoparticles will be capable of multifunctional therapeutics and targeted drug delivery.

③ These disruptive technologies will radically change the speed and reliability of cancer cell detection through much more **sensitized** and specific processes, including increased localized sensing of cancer cells. Although currently the cost of cancer research, treatment and morbidity continues to **trend** upward, in the future, more economical production of nanodevices will dramatically cut the costs related to cancer through increased prevention and reduced detection and treatment costs.

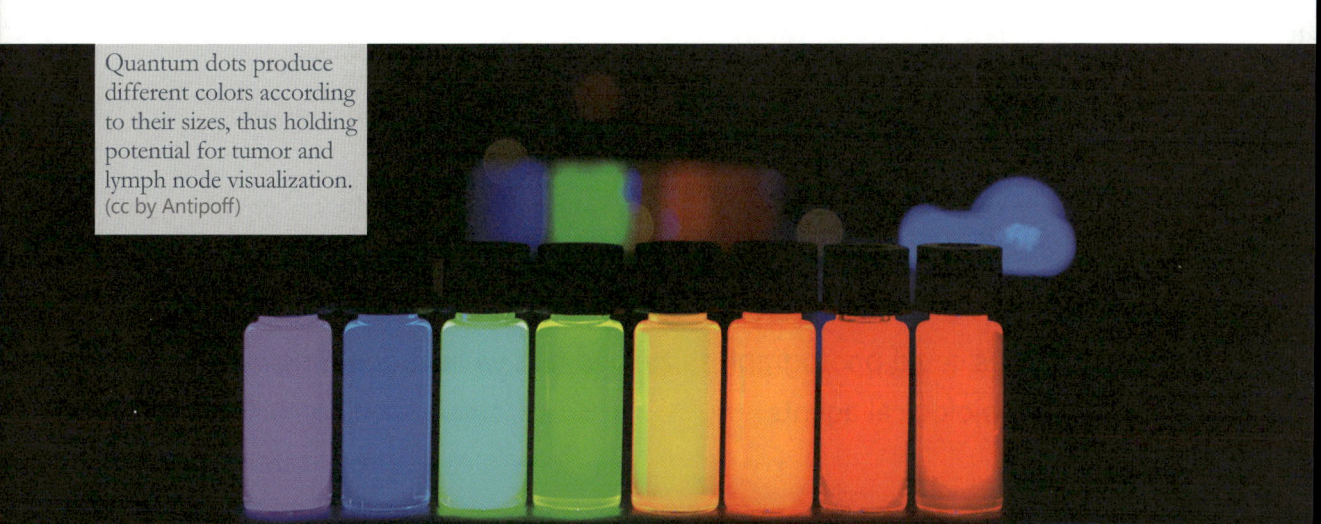

Quantum dots produce different colors according to their sizes, thus holding potential for tumor and lymph node visualization. (cc by Antipoff)

4 Energy efficiency technology and energy storage devices may radically shift energy sources away from fossil fuels in the early 21st century:
- **Nanobatteries**: silicon batteries with the potential for integration of other electronic components into a single device, allowing power generation on the nanoscale and enabling power on demand only. Both of these enhancements dramatically reduce power dissipation, which would significantly improve battery life and reduce energy output.
- **Solar energy**: development of ultra-thin **amorphous** solar cells derived from nanocrystals with the **capacity** for much higher sunlight-to-electricity conversion efficiency. These organic and inorganic cells are stronger, more flexible, and can be produced inexpensively.
- **Wind energy**: nanocoatings, including de-icing and self-cleaning technologies that reduce **impediments** to power generation.

5 Disruptive technologies include products to detect and warn against biological dangers that may be used for bioterrorism purposes.

- Sensing technologies may soon be able to detect trace amounts of chemical and biological elements, providing protection against infectious diseases, such as SARS.
- Detectors may be able to track or locate Alzheimer's patients or workers at risk in dangerous environments.
- Warning systems may soon be available for agricultural threats such as mad cow disease or avian flu.

6 Disruptive technologies may soon have additional impact on global security issues, providing **proactive** rather than reactive technology by allowing security systems to adapt to incoming threats.
- Biometrics offers the possibility of facial recognition and multifactor **authentication** (such as **iris** scans and fingerprint imaging).
- Searchable **surveillance** systems could prevent cyber attacks on government information and infrastructure.
- Nanosatellites will be able to gather terrorist activity intelligence; for instance, such satellites could photograph suspected labs while monitoring traces of chemical or biological agents.

7 However, with the significant benefits of disruptive technologies, potential risks also emerge.

- **Health**: toxic elements and materials, biohazards, ultrafine nanoparticles, unknown safety risk of nanoproduced foods, such as anti-nutrients and allergens. The Environmental Protection Agency has noted that current chemical identification and characterization may be inadequate for nanomaterials.
- **Environment**: unknown behavior of nanomaterials in the atmosphere, in soil, and in water; unknown potential mechanisms of biodegradation
- **Security**: biological attacks, such as widespread pathogen release; bioweapons, such as radiological bombs
- **Economic**: disruption to trade relations; displacement of current commodity markets; disruption from abundance of inexpensive products; inequities in economic and social policies

8 Nanotechnology is a disruptive technology that is widely expected to significantly impact global markets within the next few years. Although nanotechnology will negatively disrupt some established industries, such as biomedical device and automotive equipment production, its long-term impact will bring cost reductions and efficiency improvements in such industries as energy, health, and the environment.

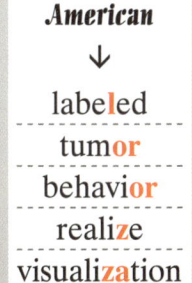

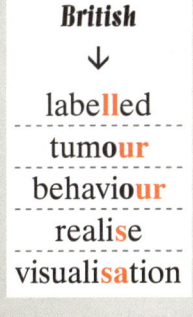

Unit 6 Chapter 17 Disruptive Technologies

American and British Spellings:

American	British
labeled	labelled
tumor	tumour
behavior	behaviour
realize	realise
visualization	visualisation

◀ ▲ biometrics

TARGET WORD EXERCISES

A Choose the word that is **not a synonym** of the target word in each of the following sentences:

(____) 1 Global innovations show a growing **trend** toward shrinking electronic devices.
   a. movement   b. decline   c. incline

(____) 2 Nanotechnology has significantly enhanced visual possibilities through improved **image** manipulation tools.
   a. graphic   b. picture   c. misinterpretation

(____) 3 Digital imagery provides a much higher level of color **contrast** than analog technology.
   a. similarity   b. range   c. differentiation

(____) 4 A web-operable scanning probe microscope enables researchers to engage in nano-**visualization**.
   a. imaging   b. representation   c. blocking

(____) 5 Computers have proven to be **disruptive** technologies for many jobs in banking, from tellers to bookkeepers.
   a. interrupting   b. upsetting   c. continuing

(____) 6 Tiny elevators that could be used as drug delivery systems may be the most **complex** molecular machines yet built.
   a. simple   b. complicated   c. intricate

(____) 7 New nanofabrication technologies could soon **displace** traditional manufacturing methods.
   a. supplant   b. supersede   c. install

(____) 8 **Amorphous** semiconductors lack a definite crystalline structure.
   a. definite   b. shapeless   c. formless

(____) 9 Educating consumers is a **proactive** approach to marketing nanotechnology.
   a. passive   b. intentional   c. calculated

(____) 10 New **thermal** technology has significantly improved heat shielding on space shuttles.
   a. heating   b. cooling   c. warming

(____) 11 Nanoparticles may soon play a **critical** role in cancer detection and treatment.
   a. insignificant   b. important   c. crucial

(____) 12 Therapeutic **ablation** through heat or radiofrequency helps to destroy cancerous tumors.
   a. excision   b. erosion   c. introduction

B Root words stand on their own and have their own meaning. Identify which of the following words are root words below.

1. a. visualize
   b. visual
   c. visualization
2. a. compete
   b. competition
   c. competitive
3. a. critic
   b. critical
   c. criticize
4. a. transition
   b. transit
   c. transitional
5. a. revolution
   b. revolutionary
   c. revolt
6. a. disruptive
   b. disrupt
   c. disruption
7. a. act
   b. proactive
   c. action
8. a. displace
   b. place
   c. replace

C Adding a prefix, suffix or combining form to a root word changes its meaning and sometimes its function. For example, adding "nano-" to technology changes its meaning to "extremely small technology." Add one of the prefixes, suffixes, or combining forms listed below to the root word of a target word to create a new word, and then match the word to its correct meaning.

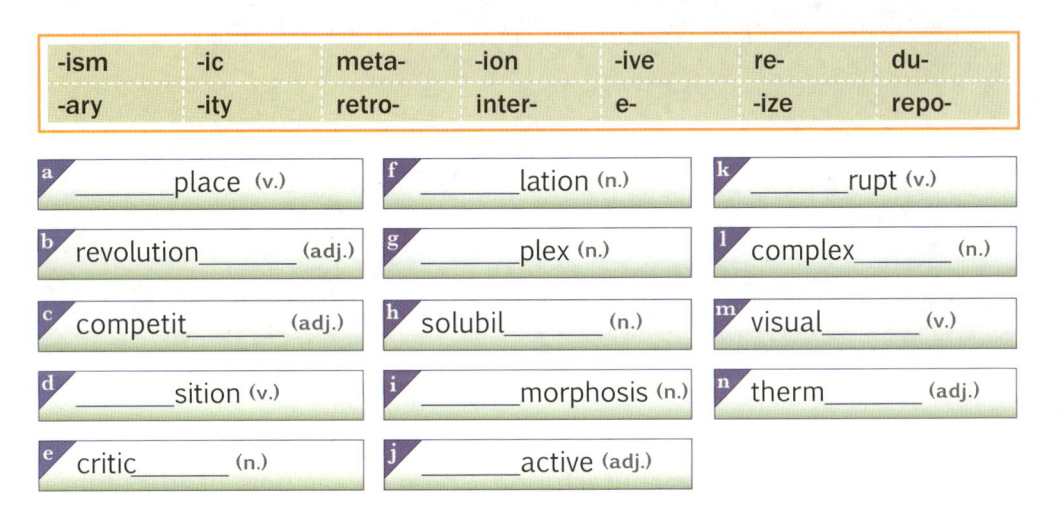

| -ism | -ic | meta- | -ion | -ive | re- | du- |
| -ary | -ity | retro- | inter- | e- | -ize | repo- |

a. _____place (v.)
b. revolution_____ (adj.)
c. competit_____ (adj.)
d. _____sition (v.)
e. critic_____ (n.)
f. _____lation (n.)
g. _____plex (n.)
h. solubil_____ (n.)
i. _____morphosis (n.)
j. _____active (adj.)
k. _____rupt (v.)
l. complex_____ (n.)
m. visual_____ (v.)
n. therm_____ (adj.)

(____) 1 a feeling of great happiness or excitement
(____) 2 to put into another place or location
(____) 3 general character, aspect, or appearance
(____) 4 the act of making a judgment or analysis
(____) 5 to conceive of; to make visible
(____) 6 radically new or different
(____) 7 the quality of being able to be dissolved
(____) 8 relating to or associated with heat
(____) 9 a complete change of physical form or substance
(____) 10 twofold; double
(____) 11 influencing or applying to a period prior to enactment
(____) 12 to break the continuity or uniformity of
(____) 13 involving rivalry
(____) 14 to put back into a former position

Unit 6 Chapter 17 Disruptive Technologies

117

Unit 6

Chapter 18

NANO manufacturing

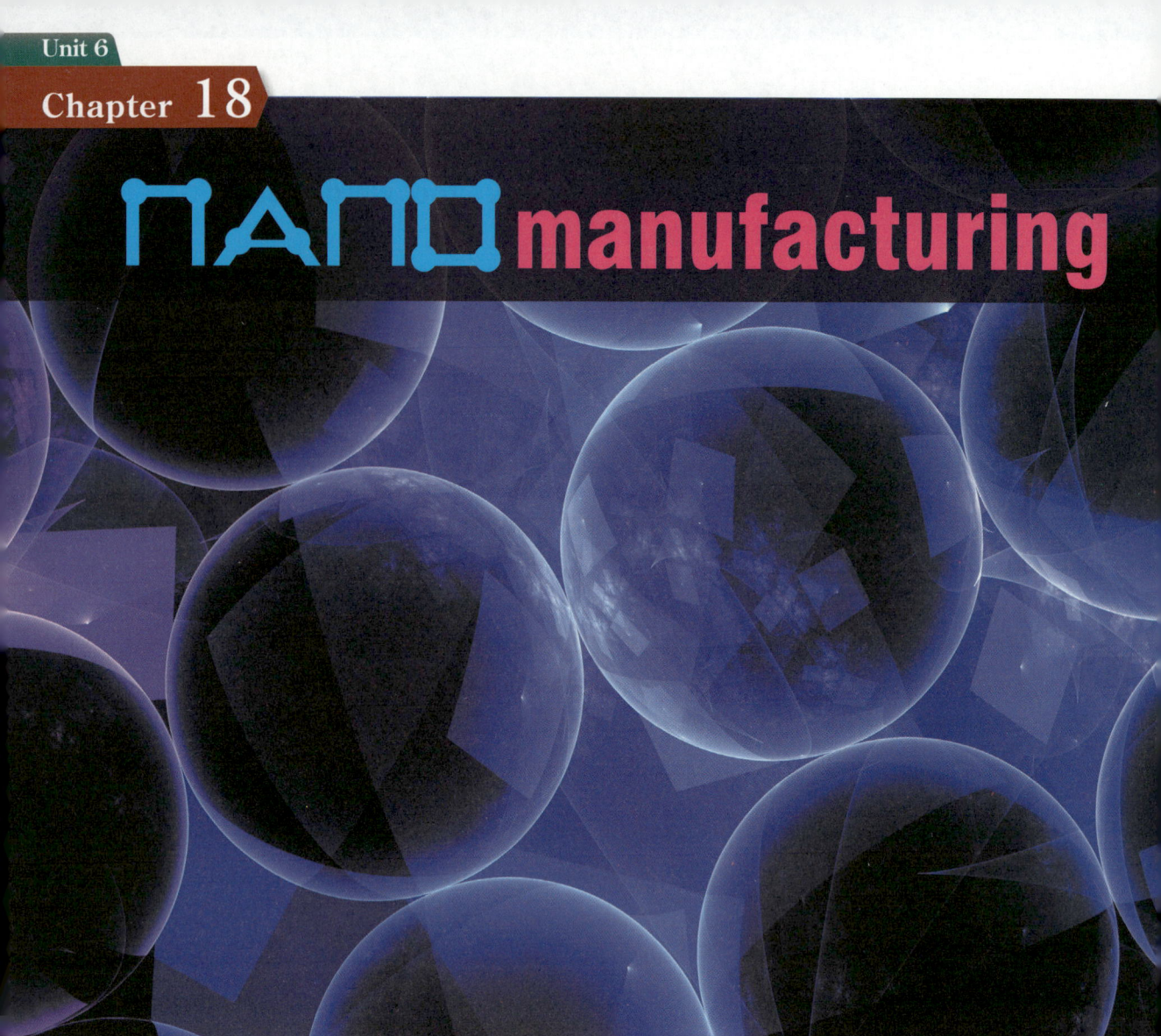

🎧 35 ❶ As nanotechnology evolves, one of the emerging areas of potential applicability is in manufacturing. Some researchers **predict** that within the next decade, up to one half of the **innovations** in manufacturing and materials will be at the nanoscale level. Nanomanufacturing is both the production of nanomaterials and the use of nanotechnology to create larger-**scaled** products. Nanomanufacturing research and development is moving so quickly that many industry leaders believe that it could be the global industrial **revolution** of the 21st century on.

❷ The goal of nanomanufacturing is to effectively translate the discoveries of nanoscience into innovative, applicable and responsible technologies. Nanomanufacturing is **poised** to revolutionize global productivity, energy efficiency, and economics. Various applications for processed nanomaterials currently exist, such as:

- **Nanocoatings, thin-films, and nanocomposites:** nanomaterials, such as nanocrystals, applied to large-scale products for heat, **wear**, **corrosion**, and scratch resistance. The benefits range from strengthening cutting devices to scratch resistant **optical** devices to wear resistance and energy efficiency in various types of vehicles.

- **Nanocatalysts:** nanoparticles or **clusters** of nanomaterials that create chemical reactions for production of larger-scale productions. Nanocatalysts speed up or intensify chemical, petroleum, **pulp** and paper, and energy production. The benefits include reductions in cost and environmental pollutants.

3 The nanomanufacturing process involves five main stages: **synthesis**, separation, **purification**, **stabilization**, and **assembly**. The material properties change in each stage, so they must be checked for quality assurance.

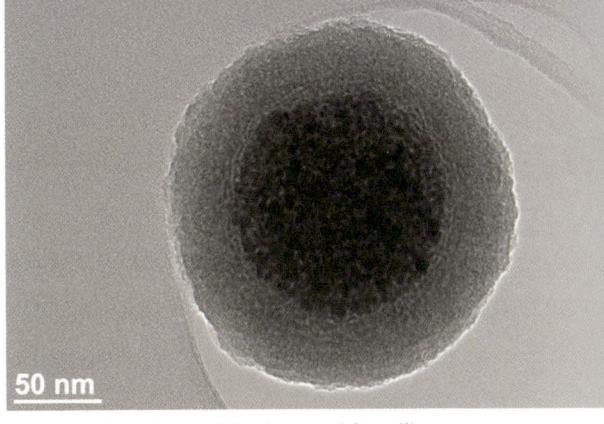

▲ magnetic nanoparticle cluster with a silica shell (cc by Marko Petek)

▲ water droplet resting on a nanocoated material surface (cc by P2i)

▲ Cars made with nanomaterials have better wear resistance and energy efficiency.

- *Synthesis*—creating **specific** property reactions to transform nanomaterials for application.
- *Separation*—removing waste materials without affecting the properties—quality and structure—of the nanoproduct. One of the most common required separations is the de-**aggregation** of the nanomaterial particles.
- *Purification*—Some nanoproducts must be further isolated, depending upon the intended application, such as electrical or optical.
- *Stabilization*—modification may be required for storage and handling or specific applications. One of the challenges of nanomanufacturing is to retain the unique properties of nanomaterials, such as thermal and magnetic, while modifying surface materials.
- *Assembly*—integration directly into products or additional modification before integration into a nanotechnology-enabled product.

4 Nanomanufacturing faces unique challenges. Currently, nanomanufacturing methods only **yield** limited numbers of products without proven increased performance, and the methods are currently inefficient to prevent large amounts of **precursor** waste. Research and development in nanomanufacturing are working to develop processes to mass produce nanoproducts without weakening the unique properties of nanomaterials and with large-scale reductions in hazardous waste. Responsible development is a critical issue in nanomanufacturing; risk assessment research must discover and address the potential effects of both engineered and natural nanomaterials, address potential toxicological issues in the manufacturing process, and address the other societal dimensions of nanomanufacturing, including legal and ethical issues.

5 Nanomanufacturing also requires new techniques in order to assure the highest quality of production. For instance, innovations are needed to control the assembly of nanostructures and nanocomposites. **Accurate** measurement of

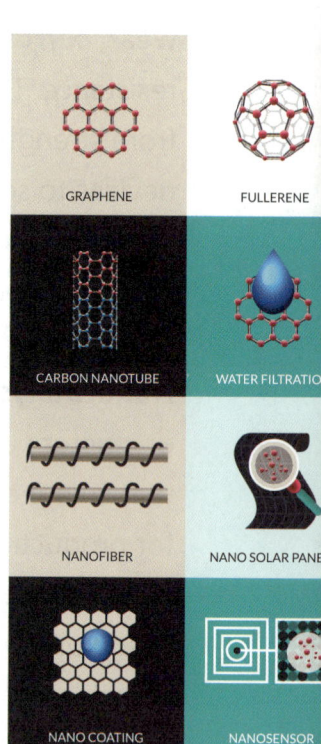

nanomaterials demands new applications from measurement science (metrology) and advances in instrumentation and other computational tools.

6 Nanomanufacturing techniques will eventually be integrated in all types of manufacturing, resulting in developing numerous products for everyday use and enabling innovative products in the future. Ultimately, nanomanufacturing will revolutionize industry in regard to health, safety, and the environment. Nanotechnology will enable low-cost and energy efficient manufacturing processes that will result in a vast **array** of revolutionary products, for example:

- improved energy storage
- affordable solar energy
- light-weight energy efficient vehicles
- clean coal plants
- water purification equipment and processes
- drug delivery devices
- nanoscale biosensors to detect disease

7 Although the economic and environmental savings potential of nanomanufacturing appears significant, currently nanomanufacturing poses substantial cost and investment risks. Strategic global partnerships and incentives are needed to help **mitigate** the risks to both larger industries and start-up companies. Government programs can help by clearly defining and upholding intellectual property rights for nanotechnology development. Both private and civic organizations can also help by producing favorable policies that could range from financial incentives to government-sponsored publication of innovative research. Multidisciplinary and global partnerships can provide tools for sharing information that will help nanomanufacturers to use emerging nanotechnologies to **bridge** the gap from research labs to commercial use.

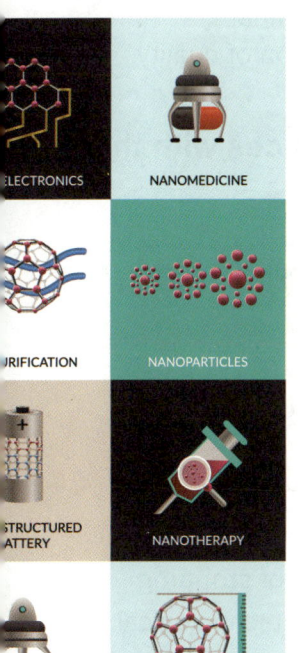

American and British Spellings:

American	British
stabilize	stabilise
oxidize	oxidise
fiber	fibre

TARGET WORD EXERCISES

A Match the correct target word with its definition.

a. predict f. yield
b. poised g. bridge
c. corrosion h. scale
d. pulp i. wear
e. specific j. array

(___) 1 oxidization, rust
(___) 2 to be ready and waiting
(___) 3 product, return
(___) 4 to connect or reduce distance between
(___) 5 an orderly arrangement
(___) 6 particular, distinguishing
(___) 7 a standard of measurement
(___) 8 to foretell
(___) 9 mixture of cellulose material
(___) 10 deterioration or reduction of quality

B Replace the synonym in each of the following sentences with the correct target word.

| aggregate | array | corrosion | specific | predict |
| poised | accurate | wear | stabilization | |

1. Nanotechnology has the potential to provide the most **precise** cancer diagnostics available. → _____
2. Coatings developed through nanotechnology provide **oxidation** protection for stainless steel products. → _____
3. Recent research has shown that gold nanoparticles are capable of **stopping the fluctuation of** enzymes to create biocatalysts for use in biotechnological applications. → _____
4. Many researchers **forecast** that nanotechnology will revolutionize industry in the next generation. → _____
5. Top-down nanomanufacturing uses traditional fabrication methods to **accumulate** materials with external tools. → _____
6. Nanocoatings provide protection from friction and **deterioration** for many metal devices. → _____
7. Pulsed lasers may be able to enable metal nickel to self-assemble into an **arrangement** of nanodots. → _____
8. **Particular** sizes of nanostructures may prove to be more fragile than others. → _____
9. Nanomanufacturing is **in position** to soon dominate global economic markets. → _____

C
Some of the target words can be used as nouns or verbs. Correctly use the target words listed below in the following sentences. Each word is used twice as noun or verb.

predict   poised   corrosion   pulp   stabilization   aggregate

yield   accurate   scale   wear   array   bridge

1. Wood _____ (n.) is utilized to make many different types of paper products.
2. Self-assembly will revolutionize how millions of atoms _____ (v.) to become nanoparticles that can be used in large-scale products.
3. Nanoparticles are an _____ (n.) of millions of atoms.
4. Semiconductors have allowed the electronics industry to exponentially _____ (v.) down the size of its products.
5. Many industries have goals for the application of nanotechnology that include developing high rate, high _____ (n.), and environmentally safe processing technologies.
6. Residents of humid climates may soon be able to _____ (v.) anti-mosquito clothing as the result of nanomanufacturing techniques.
7. Traditional processing technologies will someday be outdated, and they will need to _____ (v.) their superior output to nanomanufacturing techniques.
8. Nanomanufacturing research often must _____ (v.) the gap between science and the economy.
9. Nanotechnology may provide answers to both strength and flexibility in _____ (v.) building across rivers and highways.
10. New research in nanotechnology may result in precision on the atomic _____ (n.).
11. Nanoassembly methods will be able to _____ (v.) wood and fiber using significantly less energy.
12. Many fabrics can now be enhanced by nanotechnology to be breathable and _____ (n.)-resistant.

Wireless Network

Unit 7 — Chapter 19

Although wireless technology seems a very recent emergence in tele**communications**, **wireless** services have actually existed for more than a century. In 1896, after Guglielmo Marconi successfully produced radio waves over extended distances, he established the Wireless Telegraph and Signal Company Limited. In 1901 radio signals carried across the Atlantic, and by the mid-20th century, wireless technology had already become a **dual** purpose technology, proving to be an invaluable military tool. Wireless signals could be **encrypted** to send and receive plans and instructions without risking **unauthorized** access.

▲ Nobel Prize-winning physicist/inventor Guglielmo Marconi developed the first effective system of radio communication.

❷ In the 1970s, wireless began to be adapted by business and institutions. Computers and other electronic devices that until that time had to be connected by wires in order to share information, could be linked through radio **frequency** (RF) technology instead. Alternating electric currents are supplied to an **antenna**, which creates an **electromagnetic** field, sometimes called a **radio wave**, that **broadcasts** through space.

❸ Wireless **networks** can **span** a relatively small area, such as a home or office, or they can be international in scope. Computer networks in one area are called local area networks (LANs). LANs connect individual nodes, or CPUs, giving each unit **access** to devices and data across the system. Two or more LANs can be connected to become wide area networks (WANs); WANs usually span a large geographic area, and their individual nodes often connect through a public network such as a telephone system or satellite. The largest WAN in existence is the Internet.

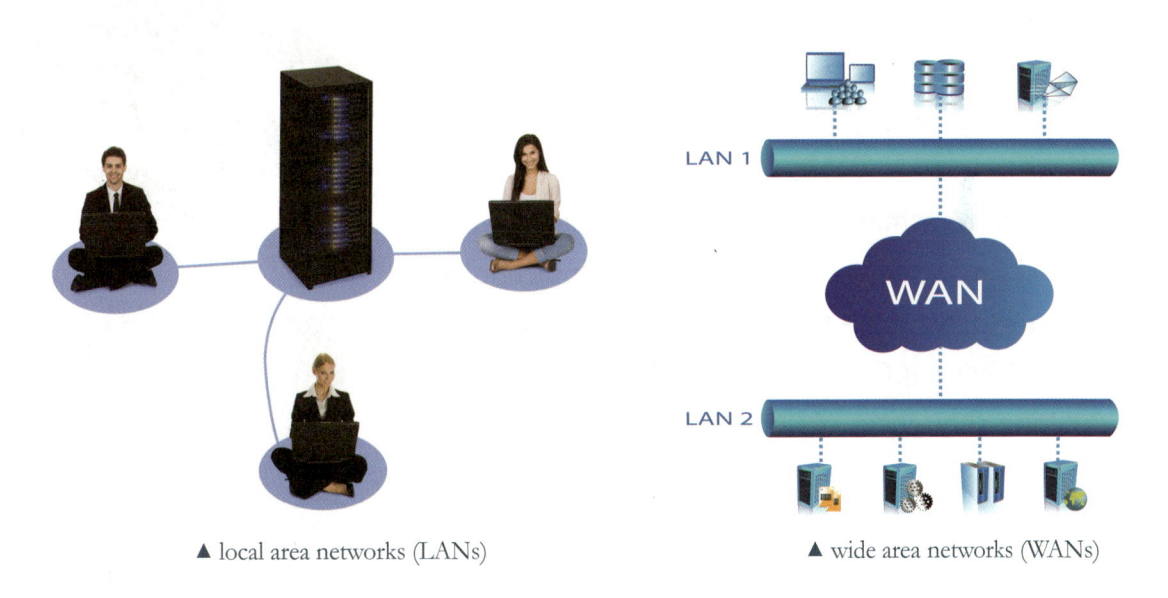

▲ local area networks (LANs)

▲ wide area networks (WANs)

❹ No network is completely wireless; at least one device will be wired. For instance, in a home computer networking system, one computer may be wired to a router. The **router** serves as an access point (AP) to broad**cast** a wireless signal that other computers in the home can detect and tune to its frequency. The router links to resources available on the wired network, in particular an Internet connection. The wireless computers connect to the router or access point using wireless network **adapters**. These are either built into the computer hard**ware** or plugged into an empty **expansion** slot, USB port, or on a notebook computer, a PC Card slot.

5. The Institute of Electrical and Electronics Engineers (IEEE) has developed wireless networking standards to which networking devices must **adhere**. Certification of devices that meet IEEE standards is referred to as Wi-Fi or Wireless Fidelity. Wi-Fi transmission is considerably stronger than that of cell phones and televisions. Wi-Fi devices transmit either in the 2.4 or 5 GHz frequency band of the radio **spectrum**, and they transmit data in a range from 11 to 270 megabits per second (Mbps). There are several Wi-Fi variants:

- 802.11b transmits at the 2.4 GHz frequency. This is the slowest transmission at only 11 Mbps and the least expensive standard. It uses complementary code keying (CCK) **modulation**, a process of pairing sequences of finite data to improve speeds.
- 802.11a transmits at 5 GHz and up to 54 Mbps. It uses a more efficient modulation method called orthogonal frequency-division multiplexing (OFDM), a coding process that splits a radio signal into several sub-signals before they reach a receiver, thus improving speed and reducing **interference**.
- 802.11g transmits at 2.4 GHz, but it can handle up to 54 megabits of data per second, because it uses OFDM.

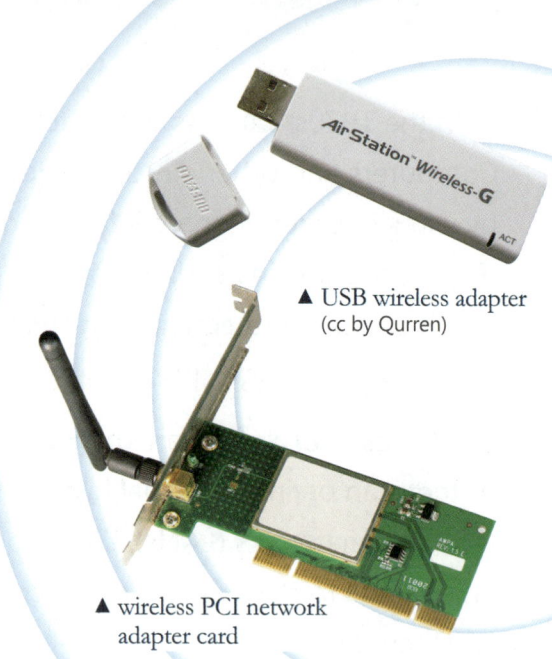

▲ USB wireless adapter
(cc by Qurren)

▲ wireless PCI network adapter card

▲ Wi-Fi logo

▲ outdoor Wi-Fi access point
(cc by Robo56)

- 802.11n is the most recent standard available, reportedly with the capability of achieving 140 Mbps. The IEEE has formally approved this standard sometime in 2009.

6 Wireless networking is subject to interference, often because various building materials, such as concrete or glass, can either **deflect** or absorb radio waves. Sometimes other electronic devices in a building, such as cordless phones or microwaves, can cause interference because they operate on the same frequency bands. Interference can usually be corrected by using special antennas to redirect the radio waves or by relocating the wireless networking hardware.

7 Without an encryption feature, any wireless network is vulnerable to connections by unauthorized users. Wireless network **encryption** scrambles the data so that only the user with the correct key code can access the information. Several standard encryption schemes are:

- **Wired Equivalent Privacy (WEP)**: requires authentication on both ends, but the encryption process has been found inadequate, because the coded data, sent over a limited set of values along the key**stream**, or shared secret key codes, changes infrequently, allowing hackers to **decipher** the code.
- **Wi-Fi Protected Access (WPA)**: requires a pass**phrase** used to generate unique encryption keys for each wireless client, and the encryption keys change frequently, providing additional security.
- **Wi-Fi Protected Access 2 (WPA2)**: requires Advanced Encryption Standard (AES) for encryption of data. AES uses a dedicated chip to handle the encryption and decryption, so upgrades to WPA2 security may require new or additional hardware.

8 Wireless networks continue to evolve rapidly. Currently, research has shifted from coverage to capacity. With the development of faster networks, users are doubling their data transmission almost on an annual basis. To meet this challenge, researchers are now focusing on cross-layer and hybrid network designs that integrate cellular and computing networks.

▲ Various building materials, such as concrete or glass, can either deflect or absorb radio waves.

TARGET WORD EXERCISES

A A **compound word** is a new word that is created by putting together two or more smaller words. Using the words and their definitions in parenthesis, create compound words and correctly place them in the following sentences.

a. **wire** (a slender flexible strand of metal used to carry electric current in a circuit)	**work** (duty, task)
b. **key** (answer, secret)	**phrase** (group of words)
c. **pass** (to gain passage despite obstacles)	**communications** (a system for sending and receiving messages)
d. **tele** (abbreviated form of "telephone", meaning operations performed remotely or by telephone)	**cast** (to throw out, hurl)
	ware (articles of the same kind or material)
e. **broad** (having great breadth or width, of vast extent)	**less** (without, lacking)
f. **net** (web, mesh)	**stream** (a continuous series or succession)
g. **hard** (firm, solid)	

1. The videotaped lecture was _____ on several web sites.
2. In order to upgrade to the 208.11n standard, many companies will have to purchase new _____ for their network systems.
3. Some systems need extreme security, so they employ a _____ for data access, rather than a simple password.
4. All of the computers on the University's _____ had access to online materials from the library.
5. Mobile computing depends on _____ access to remote networks when one is away from the office.
6. With the expansion of wireless _____, including mobile, satellite, and broadband, wired computer and telephone systems are becoming obsolete.
7. A _____ can be a line of bits, numbers, or A-Z characters used to create an encrypted message.

128

B

Fill in the prefixes with the following root words to form the target words in the article, then match the target words with their correct meanings. The meanings of the root words are noted in parentheses.

| ex- | ad- | de- (twice) | inter- | un- | en- | re- |

a. _____flect (to bend)
b. _____authorized (author)
c. _____here (to stick)
d. _____crypted (to hide)
e. _____pansion (to spread)
f. _____cipher (nothing, to be empty)
g. _____ference (to strike)

(_____) 1 be compatible or in accordance with
(_____) 2 decode, translate
(_____) 3 done without official approval
(_____) 4 hindrance, obstruction
(_____) 5 to turn or cause to turn aside from a course
(_____) 6 increase, enlargement
(_____) 7 to encode or encipher

C

Choose the word that is not a synonym for the following target words:

1 **dual**	double	two-fold	singular	binary
2 **frequency**	wires	wavelength	radio wave	oscillation
3 **span**	cross	traverse	cover	limit
4 **access**	obtain	hide	locate	find
5 **antenna**	monitor	receiver	transmitter	aerial
6 **modulation**	variation	transmission	interference	shift

D

Some words can be used as different parts of a sentence and still retain their basic meaning. Identify the part of speech of the target word in each sentence (noun, verb, etc.).

(_____) 1 The history of wireless technology **spans** more than one century.
    a. noun   b. adjective   c. verb

(_____) 2 The administrator's goal was to create a **network** infrastructure across campus.
    a. noun   b. adjective   c. verb

(_____) 3 Over 6 million people have internet **access** in their homes.
    a. noun   b. adjective   c. verb

(_____) 4 Satellite radio has expanded the popularity of radio **broadcasts**.
    a. noun   b. adjective   c. verb

Unit 7
Chapter 20

USB Technology

1 Universal Serial Bus (USB) is a **universal** interface, or interconnection, for computers, designed to eliminate the need for **adapter** cards and **peripheral** interfaces, such as parallel and serial **ports**. USB ports are built into computers (over 90% of all computers produced integrate them) to accommodate USB cables that connect to external devices. USB provides versatility because devices can be added to or removed from the computer, or **host** device, while it operates. A USB controller supports virtually all types of peripheral devices available:

▲ USB ports

- keyboards
- printers
- joysticks
- mice
- game pads
- external hard drives
- external optical drives
- mass storage devices
- cameras
- **cellular** phones
- audio-visual devices
- numerous **gadgets**, such as toasters, **humidifiers**, and alarm clocks

❷ Several companies, including Compaq, IBM, Intel, and Microsoft, joined forces and created the first USB in the early 1990s. These companies developed a nonprofit called the USB **Implement**ers Forum (USB-IF) to oversee marketing, standards, and compliance programs for USB. By 1997, USB was incorporated into many PCs, and soon afterwards Windows 98 became the first operating system equipped with USB. In that same year the iMac became the first Apple computer to incorporate USB.

❸ USB technology allows information to be shared between the computer and peripherals through communication channels called pipes. Usually there are 32 pipes per connection, 16 to the host controller and 16 from the host controller. Each time the host powers up, it **queries** all attached peripherals and assigns them an **address** through a particular **driver** installed by the peripheral device. Then, throughout operations, the pipes will continuously **poll**, or check the status of the host to see if additional or different information needs to be shared.

❹ USB devices can support up to 127 peripheral devices, through a star-**tiered** or star-**topology** structure supported by multi-port USB hubs with USB **sockets**.

❺ *USB hub*: A USB used to increase the number of USB ports. For instance, a three-port hub consists of one hub that plugs into the computer USB and two hubs that can support two external devices.

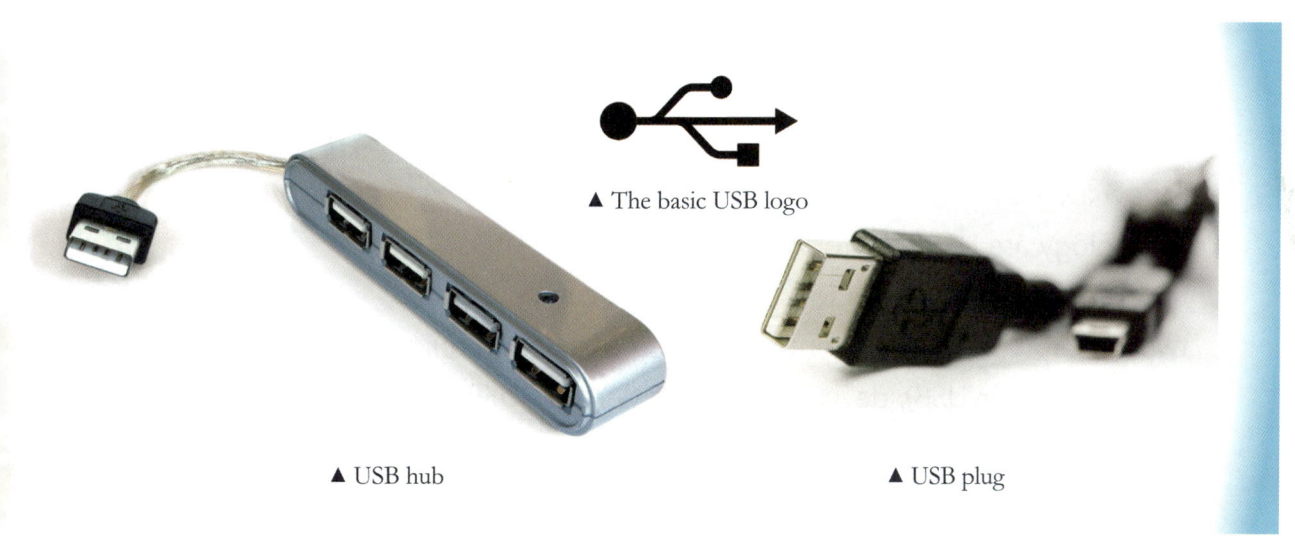

▲ The basic USB logo

▲ USB hub

▲ USB plug

▲ USB socket

6 *USB sockets*: USB plugs are connected through various types of sockets—Type A, Type B, mini-sockets, and micro-sockets.
- Type A: rectangle connections found on the computer or hubs
- Type B: square connections found on the input end of hubs and on peripherals
- Mini-sockets: designed the same as standard A and B sockets; used for smaller devices such as PDAs, cell phones, and cameras
- Micro-sockets: smaller plugs to replace mini-sockets in cell phones and smaller handheld devices

7 USB technology has evolved through several generations. The first generation was USB 1.0 and 1.1, which consisted of data transfers in the range of 1.5 Mbps (megabits per second) to a full speed of 12 Mbps. USB 2.0 improved the speed of data transfer to 480 Mbps and was made standard in 2001 by the USB-IF. Super-speed data transfer of 4.8 Gbps (gigabits per second), which is 10 times faster than USB 2.0, is now available with USB 3.0. Other forms of USB technology are USB OTG (on the go), a dual-role USB that can connect a device to a computer or can connect two **portable** devices without **mediation** of a computer, and USB Wireless (WUSB), developed by the Wireless USB Promoter Group in 2004 to provide the same functionality and structure as USB 2.0, but without wired cabling.

[8] The introduction of USB technology has increased the speed, power and convenience of computers and their peripheral devices.

- USB technology is "hot plugged," meaning the user does not need to shut down the computer or use specific software or drivers.
  - Peripherals are "plug and play," which means that they plug into the USB port and are immediately fully operational.
    - USB cables are limited to 5 meters in length. Cables can be extended by using USB hubs with multiple USB slots, extension cables through which signals are actively passed, or a USB bridge, designed to join two PC computers.

[9] Technology continues to move ahead to accommodate larger amounts of data transfer, such as digital images and music files, and higher speeds of transmission. The shift from wired to wireless USB may soon allow USB to become the standard for data transmission across electronics from PCs to mobile technology.

TARGET WORD EXERCISES

A Match the following target words with its correct meaning.

a tier	e poll	i host	m peripheral
b driver	f topology	j address	
c query	g implement	k mediation	
d universal	h adapter	l port	

(_____) 1 to search for information, to question
(_____) 2 a point of physical access between a host and a device where data can pass in or out
(_____) 3 an auxiliary device that works in conjunction with a computer
(_____) 4 one of a series of rows placed one above another
(_____) 5 the configuration of a communication network
(_____) 6 to carry into effect, fulfill, accomplish
(_____) 7 not restricted in application, can be used for many kinds, forms, sizes
(_____) 8 a piece of software specifically controls peripheral devices
(_____) 9 inquiry
(_____) 10 a computer containing data or programs that another computer can access by means of a network or modem
(_____) 11 a name or number used in information storage or retrieval that is assigned to a specific memory location
(_____) 12 a device that makes different pieces of apparatus compatible
(_____) 13 the initiating communication between entities

B Many words, when adopted for technical applications, take on slightly different meanings. Each of the words below will be used in two of the following sentences; use the context of the sentence to determine the correct technical and non-technical use of the target words.

| driver | topology | address | port | peripheral | host | adapter |

1 The ships docked in the _____ to weather the typhoon.
2 China was a recent _____ for the summer Olympics.

134

3 The police officer gave the _____ of the vehicle a ticket for speeding.
4 A USB, parallel, or serial _____ may be integrated into a notebook computer.
5 Geologists have studied the _____ of the Andes mountains for centuries.
6 The musician made his living working as an _____ of many orchestral scores.
7 In the early days of computer applications, the _____ computer would fill an entire building.
8 The brain tumor took the woman's central vision, leaving her with only _____ sight.
9 Only a specific utility software program contained the _____ for the old printer.
10 The old monitor could only be used with the new computer when it was attached through an _____.
11 Some computer networks are configured in a loop _____, in which the components are serially connected in such a way that the last component is connected to the first component.
12 When I moved, I sent my new _____ out to all of my friends.
13 A _____ device on a computer can be either internal or external, as long as it is not an essential part of the computer.
14 One computer needs to access the _____ of another computer on the network in order to share information.

C Suffixes: Fill in the correct target word from exercise A after its root word, and then choose the correct part of speech for the target word.

Ex.: apply application ✓a. noun   b. adjective   c. adverb

1 universe _____   a. noun   b. adjective   c. adverb
2 drive _____   a. noun   b. adjective   c. adverb
3 mediate _____   a. noun   b. adjective   c. adverb
4 periphery _____   a. noun   b. adjective   c. adverb
5 inquire _____   a. noun   b. adjective   c. adverb
6 adapt _____   a. noun   b. adjective   c. adverb

Unit 8
Chapter 21

Mobile Computing

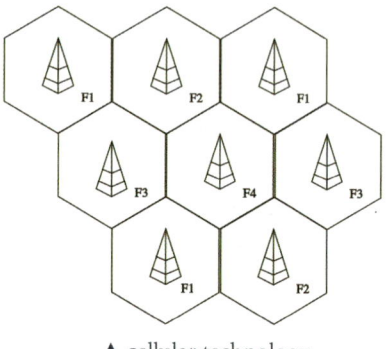

▲ cellular technology

1 Mobile computing means the ability to utilize a computing device while traveling. Mobile computing is much more than portable devices, though. Wireless communications, advanced microprocessor technology, and hardware advances, such as PDAs and wearable computers are all important components of mobile computing as well. The technology of mobile computing is designed to meet myriad human demands ranging from business and government to social contacts. Through advances in wireless technology and in computing device **miniaturization**, mobile computing is rapidly expanding and changing the way people live and interact on a global scale.

2 A global **infrastructure** of wireless networks provide the technology necessary for mobile computing. Some wireless networks operate within a limited range, such as wireless LANs (local area network) and Bluetooth technology; other wireless networks, such as wireless WANs (wide area network), are designed for broad coverage. The most common wide area network is cellular technology, first introduced in the mid-1980s. Some WANs are only designed for very limited and relatively slow speech transmission. The most recent generations of WANs can support complex, **broadband** multimedia applications that operate at exponentially faster speeds.

▶ A smartphone is an example of a mobile computing tool.

3 The architecture or design of a mobile computing environment consists of both the wireless network system and the mobile device. The network system, regardless of its **range**, includes a base station **equipped** with wireless interfaces for transcoding and switching communications with mobile devices, location **registers** to track the location of the mobile device. Examples of mobile devices or equipment are mobile computers or mobile phones. Communication is possible between network systems and mobile devices through mobile computing **platforms**, or operating systems. Platforms support three types of services:

- *Network transport services*: usually provided by Internet services, specifically mobile IP (Internet Protocol) for mobile devices. Mobile IP technology binds or combines a home address and a **temporary** address; the service then forwards the temporary address to the new host, which enables **constant** connectivity.
- *Middleware services*: software designed to allow interaction between wired networks and mobile device applications. Some of the services include data format transformation or compression, detection of device characteristics in order to **optimize** data output, encryption for security purposes, and troubleshooting of devices and networks.
- *Local platform services*: operating systems and other software services designed for mobile devices.

🎧 42 ❹ Security is a significant issue for wireless networks, because they operate from a public-shared infrastructure that can be vulnerable to **interception** or compromise. There are several wireless security principles that directly relate to mobile computing:

▲ Security is a significant issue for wireless networks.

- *Confidentiality*: keeping information secret from unauthorized persons.
- *Integrity*: keeping the information intact.
- *Availability*: maintaining availability only to **legitimate** users.
- *Non-**repudiation***: identifying and verifying sender and receiver.
- *Authorization*: matching user's **properties** to information access.
- *Accounting*: calculating the fee for a service **rendered**.

❺ There are many preventative techniques and measures that can be employed to maintain wireless communication security:

- *Encryption*: **algorithms**, or key codes assigned to a particular user.
  ‣ symmetric key **encryption**: same key for encryption and decryption
  ‣ public key encryption: decryption key is different from encryption key

▲ password protection

- *Password protection*: a string of characters that serve as an **authentication** tool for user or device identification and to verify the user's level of privilege.

▲ digital signature

- *Digital signature*: an electronic signature used to authenticate the sender's identity and to ensure originality of the sent document.
- *Digital **certificate***: an electronic identification card, issued by a certification

authority (CA) that establishes **credentials**, such as:
- name
- device serial number
- **expiration** date
- digital signature

- *Audit trails*: records of computer system access and recent operations.

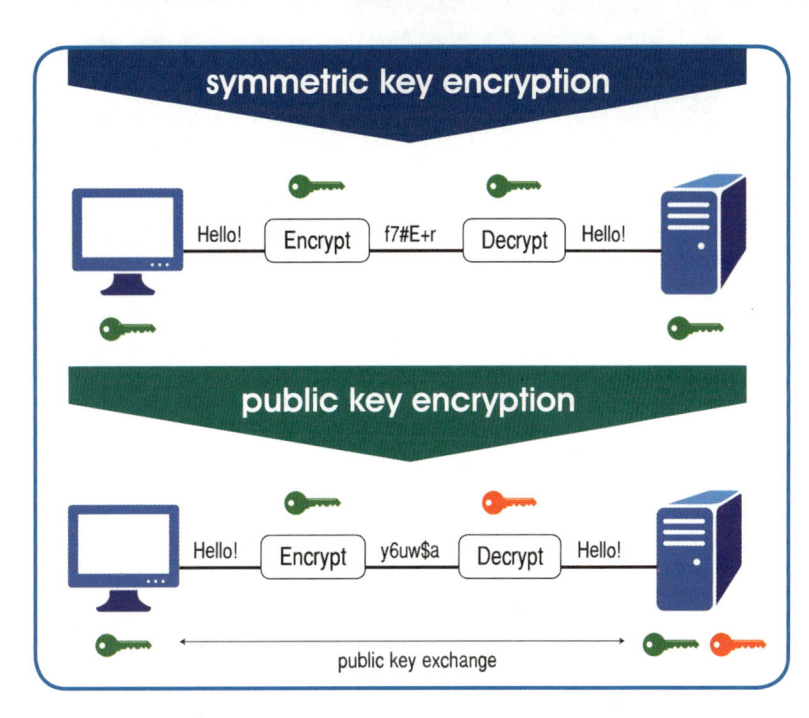

symmetric key encryption

Hello! → Encrypt → f7#E+r → Decrypt → Hello!

public key encryption

Hello! → Encrypt → y6uw$a → Decrypt → Hello!

public key exchange

▲ Battery power conservation remains a limitation for mobile computing.

6 Mobile computing has nearly unlimited future potential. However, as it currently exists, it also has some limitations that will need to be overcome:
- network performance **variations**, including range and **bandwidth** limitations
- lower level of security on wireless networks
- limited memory, power, and processing capability in mobile devices
- small device display
- limited battery power **conservation**

7 Despite its current limitations, many innovations are already on the horizon for mobile computing, such as laser keyboards, advanced **transcriber** technologies, and enhanced display technologies. Soon, 5G wireless networks will increase the speed of mobile computing to 10 Mbps or more. Future mobile computing devises will contain increased storage capacity and faster processors with more features, such as video conferencing and data processing software. Additional improvements will include increased battery capability, increased energy efficiency, and increased mobility, such as wearable mobile devices. The paradigm of computing and communications is quickly shifting to a truly mobile environment with these innovations and many more slated to appear within the next few years.

TARGET WORD EXERCISES

A Match the target words below to their correct meanings.

- a. encryption
- b. range
- c. properties
- d. equip
- e. expiration
- f. transcriber
- g. platform
- h. authentication
- i. render
- j. register
- k. optimize

(____) 1 device or application that transfers information from one system to another

(____) 2 to supply something for a specific purpose

(____) 3 the activity of converting data or information into code

(____) 4 a part of the central processing unit that stores specific information

(____) 5 an operating system, software, etc. having a standard design for use with compatible programs or applications

(____) 6 to get the most of out, to make the best use of

(____) 7 to offer or make services available

(____) 8 the full extent over which something operates or is perceivable

(____) 9 the process of identifying and confirming an individual, message, file, and other data

(____) 10 the point in time at which something ends

(____) 11 characteristic traits or attributes peculiar to a person or thing

B Choose the correct target word to replace its antonym in the following sentences.

(_____) 1 The **enlarging** of handheld devices has demanded the development of micro-USB cables to fit smaller ports.
  a. range　　　　　b. miniaturization　　　c. encryption

(_____) 2 The delay in repairs of the storm damage caused a **permanent** loss of cellular service for many in the community.
  a. temporary　　　b. expiration　　　　　c. constant

(_____) 3 Security issues are a **fluctuating** concern for the mobile computing environment.
  a. temporary　　　b. conservation　　　　c. constant

(_____) 4 When the digital certifications verified the digital signatures, the corporation knew the online participants were **unauthorized**.
  a. legitimate　　　b. equipped　　　　　c. rendered

(_____) 5 Unauthorized people should theoretically not be able to read or access any data that has been converted through the process of **decoding**.
  a. variation　　　　b. encryption　　　　　c. miniaturization

(_____) 6 Recent developments in software applications will allow the software to adapt to the **constant** between the many different mobile computing devices currently available.
  a. register　　　　b. expiration　　　　　c. variation

(_____) 7 Semiconductor technology will help promote battery power **waste** in handheld electronic devices.
  a. conservation　　b. encryption　　　　　c. authentication

Unit 8
Chapter 22

THE INTERNET

[1] The Internet is a global networking infrastructure that connects millions of computers located in over 100 countries. Internet architecture is a **decentralized**, complex combination of hardware and various software applications that can be accessed in a variety of ways through thousands of **available** service providers.

▲ The Internet is a global networking infrastructure.

[2] In 1969, the first network was constructed by the U.S. Department of Defense ARPA (Advanced Research Projects Agency) by connecting four computers, or Interface Message Processors (IMP) to share information. This network, known as ARPANET, was designed to **route** information by sending information in **packets**, or pieces of information that

◄ the first Interface Message Processor (IMP) for the APRANET
(cc by Steve Jurvetson)

142

could flow through the system, to be **reassembled** at their **destination** into a complete message.

3 Initial uses of the Internet involved developing **static** sites and applications. Early web pages contained information that a user might find useful, but the user could not interact with or change the information in any way. Also, early web software could be downloaded by users, but these applications could not be modified. In essence, the Internet was initially developed as an online storage system for information.

4 The financial future of the Internet seemed dismal following the **drastic** drop in stock prices for Internet companies in the early 21st century. However, in 2004 Tim O'Reilly and his company, O'Reilly Media, coined the term Web 2.0 for a new web environment that has been emerging since 2000. Web 2.0 (so named to distinguish it from its **predecessor**, now known as Web 1.0) is actually an evolving set of practices and principles upon which an interactive online environment is built. The most significant characteristic of the Web 2.0 world is that it is a form of **hypermedia**, or a dynamic environment in which users can link to any number of external sources and even **modify** the existing text or objects. Wikipedia is among the most famous of hypermedia sites; it is an online

▲ ARPANET (1988)

▲ DARPA (renamed from ARPA) headquaters in the U.S.

▲ Wikipedia is the most famous hypermedia site.

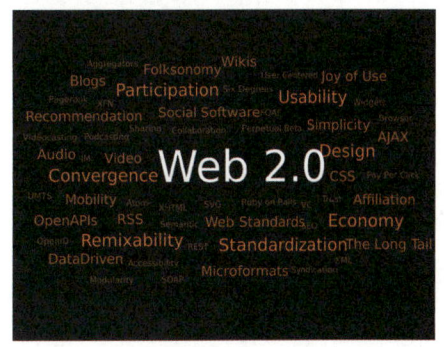

▲ word cloud with terms related to Web 2.0 (cc by AnonMoos)

Unit 8 Chapter 22 The Internet

143

encyclopedia driven by user **content** creation and modification. Although Wikipedia actually has numerous editors who regulate the information, theoretically any user can add or change any entry.

5 One of the most important principles of the Web 2.0 is collaboration. O'Reilly Media identified that users who could participate in content development were most likely to continue to return to certain sites. So, driven by numbers and economics, Internet developers quickly pioneered concepts that would enable user **interactivity** with both the site content and other users. A good example of user **collaboration** is Flickr, an online photo management and sharing application. Flickr is based on a concept sometimes called *folksonomy*, a type of collaborative categorization where multiple users chose their own keywords to identify the photos. These keywords are called **tags**, which allow for multiple associations among users. Also, web applications, in particular open source (or public **domain**) applications, are driven by peer production. Software such as Linux and Python are projects in which any user can download the code, modify it for his or her purposes, and share the modifications to **propagate** an ongoing evolution of open source software.

▲ the edit box interface through which anyone can edit a Wikipedia article

▲ Flickr

144

6 As technology rapidly changes, along with a growing organic shift in software design to increased user-created content, the Web will soon move beyond its current 2.0 environment. Already in use is the **semantic** web, meta-databases that analyze and compare databases to process universal meaning from otherwise **disparate** information. Virtual worlds, already a staple in video gaming, are quickly being adapted for routine purposes such as mapping directions or even identifying items in rows in grocery stores.

7 As companies develop higher quality pictures and sound for television and mobile phones, they will also adopt more online services for their users. Already, television has moved to digital broadcasts, and they may soon revolutionize TV viewing through interactivity that goes far beyond the current ability to purchase programs or shop for advertised items. Mobile phones already utilize tens of thousands of online applications, and usability increases with each generation of mobile web phones.

8 All current web products are available worldwide, but less than 20% of the world has access to and uses the Internet. Challenges to Internet use are generational (the elderly are less likely to use the Internet), self-image (some people feel they aren't "smart" enough to use the Internet), and wealth. Many predict, though, that Internet use could **quadruple** or more over the next 50 years as international communication increases and services such as Google provide Internet use information and language **translation**.

TARGET WORD EXERCISES

A Match each target word below to the correct definition.

a destination	e drastic	i content	m disparate
b translation	f packet	j tags	n route
c decentralized	g modify	k available	o collaboration
d static	h reassemble	l domain	p semantic

(____) 1 to undergo redistribution away from a central location or authority
(____) 2 obtainable or accessible and ready for use or service
(____) 3 send documents or materials to appropriate destinations
(____) 4 a small package or bundle
(____) 5 to gather together again, especially in a different place
(____) 6 the place to which something is going
(____) 7 of or relating to the meanings of words
(____) 8 the state of being rendered in another language
(____) 9 the subject matter of communication
(____) 10 fixed; stationary
(____) 11 fundamentally distinct or different in kind; entirely dissimilar
(____) 12 a label assigned to identify data
(____) 13 severe or radical in nature; extreme
(____) 14 to change or alter slightly
(____) 15 to work together, especially in a joint intellectual effort
(____) 16 field or sphere of activity or influence

B Find the correct pieces and put them together to form the correct target word. You will have to alter the form of some words. Some pieces may be used more than once.

| de- | state | destine | avail | pack | translate | con- |
| -ion | -able | collaborate | -ic | tent | -et | centralize |

1 _____   5 _____
2 _____   6 _____
3 _____   7 _____
4 _____   8 _____

C Some words can be used interchangeably as different parts of speech. Also, when a suffix, such as -ion, is added, the word performs a different function in the sentence. Identify the correct part of speech for each target word or form of a target word used in the sentences below.

(____) 1 Digital technology **route** information in many packets that are reassembled at their destination.
   a. noun   b. verb   c. adjective

(____) 2 Many online photo albums allow the users to **tag** their pictures.
   a. noun   b. verb   c. adjective

(____) 3 The student had to browse many Internet sites to find enough **content** for his report.
   a. noun   b. verb   c. adjective

(____) 4 The company's new Internet use guidelines were published in several **translations**.
   a. noun   b. verb   c. adjective

(____) 5 A young team of computer experts agreed to **collaborate** on the company's latest software development project.
   a. noun   b. verb   c. adjective

(____) 6 When the network failed, the information technology team made **modifications** to the server.
   a. noun   b. verb   c. adjective

(____) 7 My university **decentralized** our network system by employing several servers rather than a main server.
   a. noun   b. verb   c. adjective

(____) 8 The city placed all of their public information on a **static** web site so that important documents could not be altered.
   a. noun   b. verb   c. adjective

(____) 9 She purchased a new computer when she noticed a **drastic** drop in prices.
   a. noun   b. verb   c. adjective

(____) 10 Because of his love of video games, his parents knew he was **destined** to have a career in computer technology.
   a. noun   b. verb   c. adjective

Unit 8
Chapter 23

Artificial Intelligence

1 A copy machine automatically adjusts to maintain copy quality; a computer calculates when to buy and sell stocks according to market fluctuations; robots assemble and paint vehicles on an assembly line; an **automated** system detects credit card fraud; a physician digitally **accesses** a patient's health records to recommend proper treatment. These **tasks** and many others like them are all made possible through **artificial** intelligence (AI). AI is a branch of computer science concerned with the **possess**ion and production of intelligence by machines. Over the past five decades, though, AI has expanded into many other fields and impacted numerous technological **advancements**.

2 AI emerged out of a 20th century **quest** to produce intelligent machines. Such a quest is, in fact, an ancient one, but with the development of the computer in the mid-20th century, the possibility of engineering such a machine became a reality. The term artificial intelligence first appeared in 1956. Early research in the development and application of AI came in the form of replicating human tasks requiring high levels of intelligence. One of the most famous AI **applications**

occurred in the 1960s, when machines were **programmed** to play high quality chess. Current AI research falls into three basic categories:

- **Strong AI:** machines whose intellectual ability matches or surpasses that of a human being.
- **Applied AI:** production of commercially viable intelligent machines for tasks such as **biometrics**, medical diagnosis, and stock trading.
- **Cognitive Simulation (CS):** machines test theories about how the human brain works, such as facial recognition or solving abstract problems.

3 The progress of AI rests on how to define "intelligence." To date, although intelligence is understood and observed in **vary**ing degrees in humans, animals and machines, it is limited in AI to human intelligence, and even this definition is problematic. Human intelligence that can currently be **replicated** by machines includes:

- learning
- reasoning
- problem solving
- **perception**
- language understanding

▲ The humanoid robot AZIMO was equipped with sensors to detect obstacles in its way and to walk up and down stairs. This ability is described as "perception," one aspect of the human intelligence that can be replicated by machines.

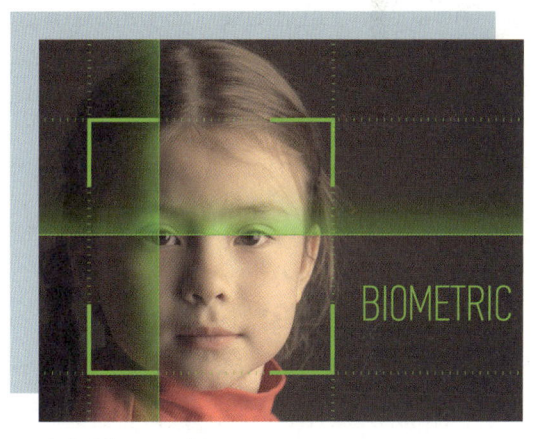

▲ facial recognition

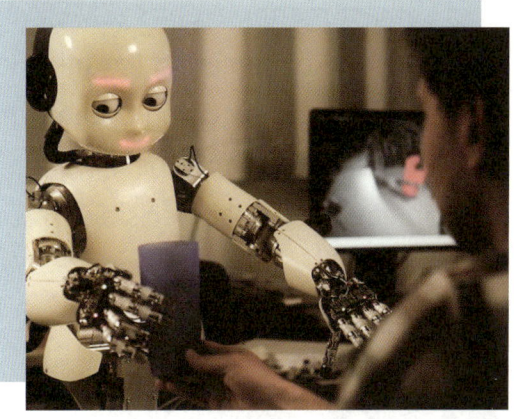

▲ The iCub humanoid robot at IDSIA's robotics lab in Switzerland trying to reach for a blue cup

4 Recreating human intelligence in computers occurs in two basic ways. The first approach is called *bottom-up*, and involves simulating the network of **neurons** that carries information in the brain. Just like the brain, computer neural networks carry and store information via electrical signals. To date, such computer networks have been inhibited by size. Replicating the human brain would demand a computer several thousand times larger than what is now available. Computer neural networks are also cost **prohibitive**. In the 21st century, though, new computer architectures and **parallel** computing (utilizing several computers for the same function) might yield new results in computer neural networking.

5 The second approach to recreating human intelligence in machines is to replicate cognitive functions of the human brain. These *top-down* computers simulate human decision making, often based on accumulating knowledge.

- **Expert systems:** computer architecture that replicates human behavior in two basic ways: knowledge representation (gathering knowledge of subject matter experts (SME)) and knowledge engineering (codification of SME information). Using the information and formulation, an expert system can solve problems and make decisions.

◀ Artificial intelligence makes it possible for computer programs to play highly competitive chess.

- **AI-based game playing programs:** combine intelligence with entertainment. These programs get progressively smarter as they gather past information to synthesize in response to new situations.
- **Frame theory:** packets of information, or frames, are accessed for application to a given situation. The use of frames also allows the computer to add knowledge.

▲ Kismet, a robot with rudimentary social skills (cc by Polimerek)

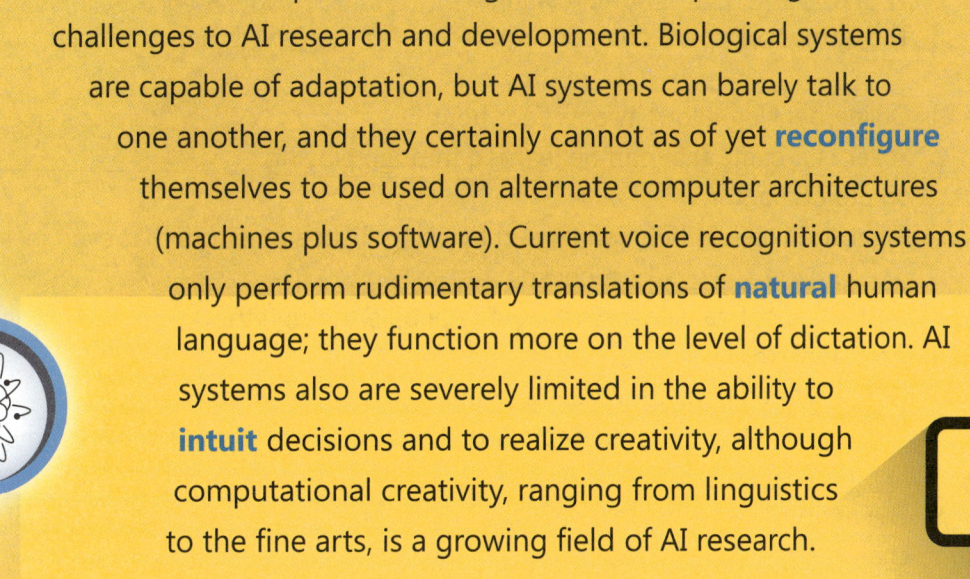

6 There are some aspects of intelligence that still pose significant challenges to AI research and development. Biological systems are capable of adaptation, but AI systems can barely talk to one another, and they certainly cannot as of yet **reconfigure** themselves to be used on alternate computer architectures (machines plus software). Current voice recognition systems only perform rudimentary translations of **natural** human language; they function more on the level of dictation. AI systems also are severely limited in the ability to **intuit** decisions and to realize creativity, although computational creativity, ranging from linguistics to the fine arts, is a growing field of AI research.

7 The practical impact of AI is already wide-reaching; AI systems monitor their surroundings, capture and process **expert** knowledge, and assist humans in a wide array of tasks from planning to tutoring. On the horizon are **expansive** educational systems, complex security systems in homes and vehicles, and information processing systems to inform everything from shopping to artistic creations. The future may be limitless when self-improving AI technology becomes available.

TARGET WORD EXERCISES

A Fill in the blanks using words in the list below.

| expansive | access | artificial | program | simulation | vary |
| perception | reconfigure | natural | neural | replica |

1. AI enables computer systems to understand, analyze and generate _____ human languages.
2. Some people believe that transplants and bionics are creating _____ human beings.
3. The composer could compose and score his music with one computer _____.
4. Online banking allows twenty-four hour _____ to one's account.
5. Poker is a game that can be learned through playing _____ games on the computer.
6. Flight training has been enhanced by using flight simulators that even include the _____ of a cockpit.
7. AI enables optical sensors to identify people through the _____ of facial features.
8. In case of equipment failure, the robot was programmed to quickly _____ the adapters on the control panel to get the assembly line moving again.
9. The multi-player role-playing game had a very _____ list of characters.
10. Artificial _____ networks model biological networks.
11. Computer-operated traffic light systems _____ from city to city.

B In each sentence below, circle the correct target word to replace the antonym.

(____) 1. When the program crashed, the company needed a(n) **novice** to reinstall the software.
   a. simulation   b. expert   c. automated

(____) 2. Many linguists were hired to contribute their expertise to the **limited** list of languages the robot would be able to translate.
   a. expansive   b. replica   c. synapse

(____) 3. The bank laid off nearly half of its tellers because it now used a(n) **manual** teller machine.
   a. expert   b. automated   c. expansive

(____) 4 The robot provided **natural** respiration for the patient during surgery.
   a. artificial   b. access   c. neural

(____) 5 He learned to play chess from the computer by running **natural** techniques for specific situations.
   a. task   b. program   c. simulation

(____) 6 Even with AI applications, a medical diagnosis could **remain constant** between doctors.
   a. access   b. perception   c. vary

(____) 7 Many AI applications are intended to replicate **artificial** human behaviors.
   a. natural   b. automated   c. vary

(____) 8 Some people have ethical questions about scientists' ability to create a(n) **original** of the human body as well as the human brain.
   a. access   b. synapse   c. replica

C Choose the correct form of the target word to complete each sentence.

(____) 1 The program _____ stock information on a daily basis.
   a. access
   b. accessed
   c. accessing

(____) 2 The new robot would _____ more humanlike qualities than the previous model.
   a. possessed
   b. possession
   c. possess

(____) 3 Standards for entering medical histories _____ from hospital to hospital.
   a. vary
   b. varying
   c. varies

(____) 4 The summer intern _____ the computer to sort client files.
   a. programming
   b. program
   c. programmed

(____) 5 A short in the wire led the technician to _____ the switchboard.
   a. reconfigure
   b. reconfigured
   c. reconfiguring

(____) 6 Robots that assist in surgical procedures are examples of the use of _____ systems.
   a. expertness
   b. expertly
   c. expert

(____) 7 Because the computer contained information from thousands of professional chess tournaments, it could perform an _____ search before every move.
   a. expansion
   b. expanse
   c. expansive

(____) 8 Many jobs in the factory were _____ and no longer required human intervention.
   a. automation
   b. automated
   c. automating

Unit 8 Chapter 23 Artificial Intelligence

153

Unit 9

Chapter 24

Conservation Farming

Conservation farming or **husbandry** is a type of farm management that **preserves** natural resources and potentially increases crop production. One of the primary tasks in conservation husbandry is soil management, which includes specific **tilling** practices, or conservation tillage, and appropriate crop **rotation** patterns. Other significant conservation practices are water and pest management.

▲ conservation farming

154

2. Conservation tillage is any planting system in which after planting at least 30% of the soil surface remains covered with residue — the material left after harvest and processing of crops. The residue cover helps to reduce soil erosion, control weeds, and improve **nutrient** levels in the soil. There are several types of conservation tillage available to farmers.

- **No-till:** leaves the soil and crop residue undisturbed except for the crop row where the seed is placed in the ground. Weeds are controlled by small amounts of **herbicides**.
- **Ridge-till:** roughly 10-15 centimeter high ridges are formed and rebuilt during row **cultivation** for weed control. Residue is left on the surface between ridges.
- **Mulch-till:** entire fields are tilled before planting, but at least 30 percent of the soil surface is left covered with residue after planting.
- **Reduced-till:** entire fields are tilled before planting, but 15-30 percent of the soil surface is left covered with residue after planting.

▲ Soil erosion is a serious problem for farmers.

▲ Young soybean plants both thrive in and are protected by the residue of a wheat crop. This form of no-till farming provides good protection for the soil from erosion. (Wikipedia)

▲ corn harvest on a field planted with the ridge-till method in southwestern Minnesota

▲ the mulch-till method used on a sugar beet field, Switzerland (cc by Volker Prasuhn)

③ An additional benefit of conservation tillage may be decreased **seepage** of agricultural chemicals into groundwater, but more research is needed to determine its effectiveness.

④ Soil conservation can also be achieved through crop rotation (**alternating** crops) or crop **sequencing** (alternating crops in an established pattern). Typical patterns involve two or three year sequences:

- **Row crop/small grain rotation:** combination of row crops and small grains are planted over the three-year period.
- **Rotation with meadow crops:** hay, pasture, or other use in 1 or more previous years.
- **Idle or fallow in rotation:** idle, **diverted**, or **fallowed** land in 1 or more of the previous years.

▲ crop rotation (cc by Lesław Zimny)

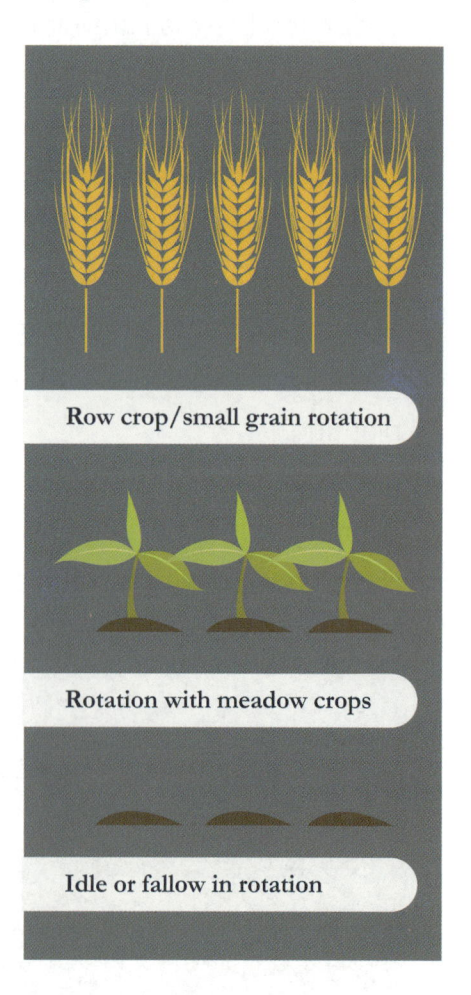

⑤ Crop rotating or sequencing helps maintain or even increase nutrient levels, and increased nutrients can encourage longer plant growth periods. Rotating or sequencing crops is also one way to prevent weed **infestation**, combat plant disease, and manage pests. On an economic level, crop rotation and sequencing can serve as a buffer against fluctuations in the economic market.

⑥ Management practices, such as crop rotation, crop residue management (including cover crops), and conservation tillage practices must be used together with water management practices in order to most effectively control erosion and preserve soil nutrients. Farmers may choose to construct buffer zones or areas of undeveloped land. These areas allow for surface water to be captured onsite or diverted from the field **via** waterways or channels. Agricultural water management also includes planting more water-conserving and drought-resistant crops and using low-volume and water recycling irrigation systems.

7 Land husbandry is also realized through a practice called Integrated Pest Management (IPM). Farmers inspect and monitor crops for damage, use mechanical devices and other insects to control pest damage, use substances to regulate insect growth and disrupt mating behaviors, and, in limited amounts, use pesticides.

▲ IPM uses mechanical devices to control pest damage and regulate pest growth.

8 Conservation farming practices are promoted, researched and developed by organizations around the world, such as the International Institute of Rural Reconstruction, World Agroforestry Center (ICRAF), the International Fund for Agricultural Development, and the UN Food and Agricultural Organization. Through these international organizations, farmers, private sector enterprises, scientists, development organizations, donor organizations and policymakers can meet to develop new practices and policies for conservation agriculture. In the 21st century, the main goal of all of these organizations has been to double agricultural production while substantially reducing the **degradation** of natural resources, in particular biodiversity, soil, and water. Also, through international conferences, **stakeholders** in conservation agricultural practices work with governments around the world to develop universal policies and incentives for farmers to change their production system to conservation farming. Furthermore, global efforts are underway to ensure that around the world agricultural practices are adapted to meet the challenges of climate change.

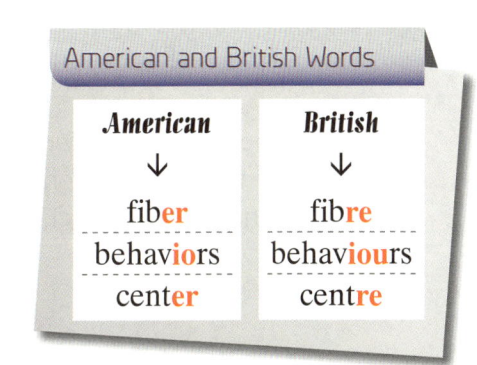

American and British Words

American	British
fib**er**	fib**re**
behav**iors**	behav**iours**
cent**er**	cent**re**

Unit 9 Chapter 24 Conservation Farming

157

TARGET WORD EXERCISES

A
Circle the suffix in each of the target words listed below. Then, match the word with the correct meaning of its root word.

a. husbandry
b. tilling
c. rotation
d. cultivation
e. sequencing
f. fallowed
g. infestation

(____) 1 a following of one thing after another; succession
(____) 2 to inhabit in numbers or quantities large enough to be harmful or threatening
(____) 3 to use sparingly or economically; conserve
(____) 4 the act of tending or tilling
(____) 5 characterized by inactivity
(____) 6 to prepare land for the raising of crops
(____) 7 the process of taking turns or alternating

B
Choose the correct part of speech for the target words used in the sentences below.

(____) 1 Intense **cultivation** of the field over the years depleted many of its essential nutrients.
   a. noun   b. adjective   c. verb   d. adverb   e. preposition

(____) 2 The farmer needed to **routinize** the tilling methods so that the laborers consistently performed their tasks.
   a. noun   b. adjective   c. verb   d. adverb   e. preposition

(____) 3 The state took over the farm so that it could create a nature **preserve** for the wildlife.
   a. noun   b. adjective   c. verb   d. adverb   e. preposition

(____) 4 Planting corn and soybeans in **sequential** order increased the annual crop yield.
   a. noun   b. adjective   c. verb   d. adverb   e. preposition

(____) 5 The danger of many herbicides is that they can remain **residually** active in the soil for years.
   a. noun   b. adjective   c. verb   d. adverb   e. preposition

(____) 6 Without proper buffers, surface water **runoff** after heavy storms can cause extensive soil erosion.
   a. noun   b. adjective   c. verb   d. adverb   e. preposition

(____) 7 New farming methods can more easily be implemented because information is now easily accessible **via** the Internet.
   a. noun   b. adjective   c. verb   d. adverb   e. preposition

(____) 8 The farmer **diverted** water from a local stream for irrigation purposes.
   a. noun   b. adjective   c. verb   d. adverb   e. preposition

(____) 9 Cover crops often host **beneficial** insects.
   a. noun   b. adjective   c. verb   d. adverb   e. preposition

(____) 10 Farming **intensively** may deprive some species of an adequate habitat.
   a. noun   b. adjective   c. verb   d. adverb   e. preposition

C Choose the correct target words to replace the synonyms in italics in the following sentences.

(____) 1 The farmer prepared the land in order to *(grow)* crops.
   a. cultivate   b. till   c. fallow

(____) 2 The farmer *(prepared)* the land, but did not raise crops that year.
   a. sequenced   b. decomposed   c. fallowed

(____) 3 The farmer *(plowed)* the land in order to grow crops.
   a. cultivated   b. tilled   c. fallowed

(____) 4 Crop remains are often left after the harvest for *(decaying)*, a process that allows nutrients to seep back into the soil.
   a. decomposition   b. diversion   c. runoff

(____) 5 Crop remains are often left after the harvest, but in the event of heavy rains, they may be lost as *(agricultural drainage)* if not protected by buffers.
   a. decomposition   b. rotation   c. runoff

(____) 6 Crop *(remainder)* is often left after the harvest in order to allow nutrients to seep back into the soil.
   a. sequencing   b. residue   c. infestation

(____) 7 Crop *(growing dissimilar crops alternatively in a specific order)* can save the soil from nutrient depletion.
   a. sequencing   b. rotation

(____) 8 Biannual crop *(growing dissimilar crops alternatively)* can save the soil from nutrient depletion.
   a. sequencing   b. rotation

Unit 9 Chapter 24 Conservation Farming

159

Unit 9
Chapter 25

Food Biotechnology

For centuries, plant and animal species have been **crossbred** to produce hybrids. The process, however, was **laborious** and took many generations to complete. In the late 20th century, modern biotechnology was introduced into agriculture and food **hybrid** production with exponential savings in time and effort. Currently, food biotechnology includes both traditional cross breeding and modern biotechnology techniques, such as genetic engineering, to breed plants and animals for better taste, stronger disease resistance, and higher **yields**. Agricultural genetic **alteration** goes by many names:

- agricultural biotechnology
- biotech crops
- genetically **modified** (GM) foods
- genetically engineered (GE) foods
- plant biotechnology
- animal **genomics**
- **cloning**
- **novel** foods (typically genetically altered foods that have yet to be proven safe for human or animal consumption)

▲ genetically modified foods

2 Genetic alteration involves two steps: first, the genes are modified; then, the changes are passed on to the descendents of the organism. The alterations are designed to produce specific results or traits, such as increased crop yields or improved taste. Genetically modified crops fall into three basic categories or generations, based on their specific enhanced **traits**.

▲ Transgenic plums contain a gene that makes them highly resistant to plum pox virus.

- **First generation or enhanced input** (designed to **boost** yield) **traits:** **herbicide** tolerance, insect and virus resistance, and tolerance to environmental stressors, such as **drought**.
- **Second generation or added-value output or use traits:** nutrient enhancement, such as increased levels of omega-3 fatty acids or lysine for animal **feed**.
- **Third generation: pharmaceutical** production or contribution to improved processing of bio-based fuels.

▲ GE foods have attracted several criticisms and concerns.

3 Animal biotechnology also has potential environmental and health benefits through various biotechnology techniques.
- **Animal genomics: selective** breeding based on animal genotypes; determining **optimum** nutritional needs for consistent production of high-quality foods.
- **Cloning:** assisted reproduction of an identical twin of the best available animals, which is used to breed future generations.
- **Genetic engineering:** the **deliberate** modification of the animal's genome using techniques of modern biotechnology.

4 Animal biotechnology produces pharmaceuticals, tissues and organs for **transplantation**, materials for surgical **sutures**, antimicrobials to target disease-causing bacteria, and healthier foods. Animals benefit from biotechnology tools that can improve animal health, and cloning can assist in wildlife conservation.

5 Critics of GM foods range from environmental activists to religious organizations. Most social concerns about GM foods fall into three categories: human health risks, environmental issues, and economics. Human health concerns focus mainly on the safety of biotech foods and on allergy issues, which include the dangers of **allergic** reactions to the new foods and the creation of new **allergens**. Environmental hazards may include **toxins** from GM foods, pests that develop resistance to GM crops, transference of **pesticide** resistance to weeds through cross-breeding, and threats to wildlife by cloned animals. Economically, food biotechnology involves long and costly production processes, which can lead to affordability issues for developing countries. Patent **infringement** also poses an economic threat. Additionally, some critics continue to call for tighter regulations on technology evaluation.

6 Genetically modified foods also raise significant ethical questions. Some religious and ethnic groups object to GM foods based on their core belief that humanity should not control life issues. For other groups, genetic engineering poses a threat to the traditionally defined categories of plants and animals. Another ethical

issue is the debate about whether or not society has sufficient knowledge to manage and control a technology that **manipulates** genetic material from two different species. Finally, the question has been raised about the ethics of human behavior. This issue points out the possibility of human selfishness leading to unintended outcomes of genetic modification and to possible misuse of research results.

7 Increasingly, consumers are becoming more favorable toward food biotechnology. In the United States, many consumers are aware of biotech foods available in stores and are likely to purchase them. Most consumers expect benefits from food biotechnology, including quality and safety. Worldwide consumer knowledge of food biotechnology is not as high as in the U.S., so it is imperative that the global community have greater access to the science, the potential benefits, and the risks of food biotechnology. Currently, over 20 countries besides the U.S. are actively engaged in food production through biotechnology techniques. Furthermore, many countries throughout the world now have agencies dedicated to **regulatory** oversight of agricultural biotechnology.

▲ Most consumers expect benefits from food biotechnology and are becoming more favorable toward it.

8 Food biotechnology has the potential to help solve many health and environment issues. Higher and healthier food yields can counter hunger and **malnutrition** issues. Higher levels of resistance can reduce potential pollution issues. Food biotechnology will continue to make a significant impact on the global community, as long as research and development makes every effort to keep the public trust, provide economic fairness, and protect the health of the ecosystem.

American and British Spellings:

American	British
↓	↓
fav**or**able	fav**our**able

TARGET WORD EXERCISES

A Match the target words with their correct meaning.

a laborious	e traits	i selective	m infringement
b modified	f boost	j optimum	n regulatory
c cloning	g drought	k deliberate	o malnutrition
d feed	h pharmaceutical	l sutures	p allergy

(____) 1 an abnormally high sensitivity to certain substances, such as pollens, foods, or microorganisms
(____) 2 to increase; raise
(____) 3 food for animals or birds
(____) 4 involving great exertion or prolonged effort
(____) 5 genetically determined characteristics or conditions
(____) 6 restricting according to rules or principles
(____) 7 physical weakness resulting from insufficient food or an unbalanced diet
(____) 8 a long period of abnormally low rainfall, especially one that adversely affects growing or living conditions
(____) 9 the process of reproducing or propagating asexually
(____) 10 of or relating to drugs used in medical treatment
(____) 11 the most favorable condition for growth and reproduction
(____) 12 changed in form or character
(____) 13 done with or marked by full consciousness of the nature and effects; intentional
(____) 14 tending to choose carefully or characterized by careful choice
(____) 15 fine thread or other material used surgically to close a wound or join tissues
(____) 16 an act that disregards an agreement or a right

B Unscramble the target words in each sentence.

1 Growing plants for medical use is sometimes referred to as **amcperaulahic** farming. → _____
2 Making innovative farming equipment affordable for the small farmer could **osbto** agricultural production in many countries. → _____
3 **Noniglc** chickens has the potential to significantly increase egg production throughout the world. → _____
4 Crop rotation should be a planned, **tblidearee** process to ensure maximum results. → _____

5 Critics of agricultural biotechnology claim that organic farming could **edef** all of the world's citizens. → ☐
6 A recent increase in production of genetically **diefdomi** maize has resulted in a drop in organic maize production. → ☐
7 Tilling soil with a hoe is a very **iourosalb** task. → ☐
8 The USDA is a **rogyeraltu** agency for biotechnology farming practices in the United States. → ☐
9 Often the most immediate effects of a **gohudtr** is a drop in crop production. → ☐
10 Drinking farm milk may help prevent **galelry** in children. → ☐
11 Large, industrial farms are not always the **iompmtu** size for the best agricultural biotechnology practices. → ☐
12 Agricultural biotechnology provides possible solutions for combating poverty and **umatinlonrit** in developing countries. → ☐
13 A new gene introduced into sheep udders may produce silk that could be used for surgical **rsetusu**. → ☐
14 Competition among food biotech companies has lead to cases of patent **nenintmerifg**. → ☐
15 Pesticide use can be reduced by **vsecletie** spraying of weeds. → ☐
16 Biotechnology can be used to change milk **irtast**, such as color and taste. → ☐

C From the choices given, choose the parts of speech for the variations of each target word below.

1 **allergy:** noun adverb adjective
   allergen: noun adjective adverb
   allergic: noun verb adjective

2 **nutrient:** noun adverb adjective
   nutritious: adverb verb adjective
   nutrition: noun verb adverb

3 **laborious:** noun adverb adjective
   laboriously: adverb verb adjective

4 **regulatory:** noun adverb adjective
   regulation: noun verb adjective
   regulate: noun verb adjective

5 **selective:** noun adverb adjective
   select: verb adverb
   selection: noun verb adjective

6 **modified:** noun adverb adjective
   modification: noun verb adjective
   modify: noun verb adverb

7 **clone:** noun adverb adjective
   cloning: noun adverb adjective

8 **optimize:** noun verb adverb
   optimal: noun verb adjective

Unit 9
Chapter 26

Agrifood Nanotechnology

Nearly 10 billion dollars are spent globally each year on nanotechnology research and development, and the global market for nanotechnology produced goods and services could exceed 1 trillion dollars before 2020. One revolutionary area for nanotechnology is agrifood—the production and processing of food and agricultural commodities. Nanotechnology has the potential to replace existing agricultural technologies, from detecting, altering plant and animal health, to ensuring food safety. Agrifood nanotechnology can possibly alter all aspects of the food industry through applications that will change plant and animal growth, food processing, packaging, and delivery systems.

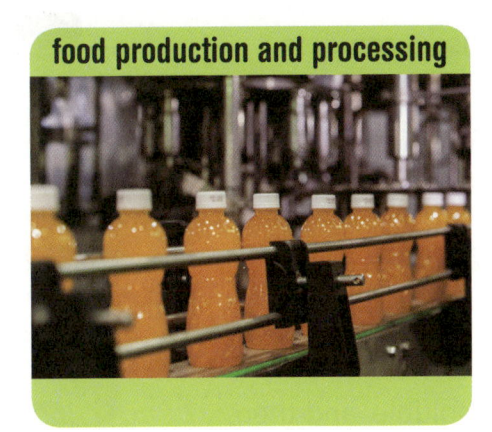

▲ Nanotechnology is set to revolutionize the agrifood industry.

2 Nanotechnology can be applied to agrifood in various ways, such as **smart** packaging systems that **sense** changes in temperature and moisture, are antimicrobic and antifungal, and could even repair tears or holes. Smart food packages could be **embedded** with tiny materials specifically designed to **alert** consumers that a product is no longer safe to eat. Other packing materials used for bottling and packing beverages could be composed of nanocomposite plastics that provide for a longer shelf life.

▲ Packing materials could be composed of nanocomposite plastics.

3 Another major area of growth in agrifood nanotechnology is in the development of food **supplements**. Nanomaterials can be added to solid foods, liquids, or as a **coating** to deliver many different types of **nutrients**. For example:

- nanoparticles of carotenoids (antioxidants) can be added to fruit drinks
- nanoparticles can deliver healthy fatty acids through canola oil
- nanoclusters, tiny particles 100,000th the size of a grain of sand, can be **suffused** with pure cocoa to enhance the taste of a chocolate drink without sugar or other sweeteners.

◀ Nanoparticles of carotenoids (antioxidants) can be added to fruit drinks.

167

- smart foods embedded with nanosensors can detect nutrient **deficiencies**
- nanocapsules that will remain **dormant** until **activated** by the nanosensors

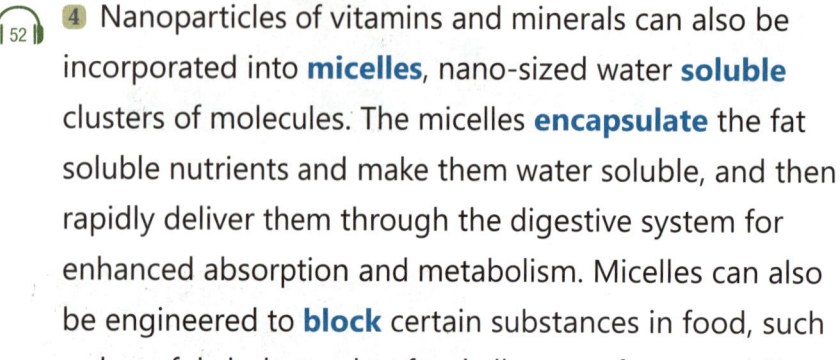

4 Nanoparticles of vitamins and minerals can also be incorporated into **micelles**, nano-sized water **soluble** clusters of molecules. The micelles **encapsulate** the fat soluble nutrients and make them water soluble, and then rapidly deliver them through the digestive system for enhanced absorption and metabolism. Micelles can also be engineered to **block** certain substances in food, such as harmful cholesterol or food allergens, from reaching certain parts of the body. **Conversely**, micelles can be engineered to carry harmful cholesterol to targeted areas, such as the brain, to combat certain cancer cells. In addition, the many potential health benefits of food nanotechnology also include increased energy, improved cognitive and immune functions, and reduced effects of aging.

▲ Nanoparticles can deliver healthy fatty acids through canola oil.

▲ Food nanotechnology can bring benefits such as increased energy, improved cognitive and immune functions, and reduced effects of aging.

5 Nanotechnology can also provide benefits for agricultural systems. For example, nanoscale devices may identify or even prevent plant health issues. Nanotechnologies are also being developed to encapsulate and control nanoparticles that can be used for numerous types of applications:

- targeted pest reduction
- **dosage** regulation of growth hormones in livestock production
- animal **pathogen** detection and neutralization prior to reaching consumer markets
- pollution reduction through efficient use of water, pesticides, and **fertilizers**
- fertilizer and pesticide delivery systems that respond to environmental changes, such as heat and moisture.

6 Agrifood nanotechnology will have numerous economic benefits. The food supply can be monitored and tracked by nanodevices that can also maintain historical environmental records about all phases of production. Sensing devices that restore freshness will reduce food waste. Location identification, reporting, and remote control of the food supply will streamline and secure food delivery. The cost of agrifood nanotechnology still remains high, but with continued innovations and more devices and food available, the costs could drop significantly below that of traditionally grown and processed foods.

7 The next few decades should see a marked rise in the application of nanotechnology to agrifood. Natural agricultural systems will be preserved and enhanced. Transportation of food products will be safer, and retail environments will be more attractive, safer, and more educational. The consumer will be better protected from food-borne illnesses, including benefiting from nanotechnology that can detect illness from food after its consumption.

8 However, because agrifood nanotechnology is still in its nascent stage, many uncertainties exist about its potential effects on human health and the environment, and, to date, few risk assessments have been undertaken. Limited information is available about the human body's ability to absorb, **distribute**, and **excrete** nanoparticles. Procedures to detect and measure nanomaterials in food, feed, or the body are still in the developmental stage. Furthermore, new research has still to adequately address questions of potential side effects and even toxicity of nanomaterials. For agrifood nanotechnology to succeed, global initiatives must work together to facilitate and regulate research and development that will result in sound practices and policies.

American and British Spellings

American ↓	British ↓
agrifood	agri-food
nanotechnology	nano-technology

TARGET WORD EXERCISES

A Choose which definition matches the use of the target word in the article, based on what the part of the speech each word is and its context.

(____) 1 **smart** (paragraph 2)
   a. sharp or stinging, as pain
   b. intelligent, clever

(____) 2 **sense** (paragraph 2)
   a. to detect automatically; perceive
   b. any of the faculties by which stimuli from outside or inside the body are received and felt

(____) 3 **alert** (paragraph 2)
   a. to warn of danger; to make aware of a fact
   b. mentally responsive and perceptive; quick

(____) 4 **supplement** (paragraph 3)
   a. to provide an addition to something
   b. an addition designed to make something more adequate

(____) 5 **coating** (paragraph 3)
   a. a layer of a substance spread over a surface for protection or decoration
   b. cloth for making coats

(____) 6 **block** (paragraph 4)
   a. a solid piece of a hard substance, such as wood, having one or more flat sides
   b. to impede the passage or progress of; obstruct

B Identify the correct target word in each of the sentences below.

(____) 1 Manufacturers can _____ silver nanoparticles into plastic storage bins to kill harmful bacteria.
   a. excrete   b. encapsulate   c. embed

(____) 2 Nanoparticles can _____ an entire shake with chocolate flavor.
   a. suffuse   b. soluble   c. encapsulate

(____) 3 Nanotechnology can make some vitamins, such as A and K, _____ in water.
   a. embedded   b. soluble   c. suffused

(____) 4 Nanoparticles can _____ pesticides and only release them under certain environmental conditions.
   a. soluble   b. distribute   c. encapsulate

170

(____) 5 Organizations that oversee nanotechnology regulations should be sure to
_____ their information to countries around the world.
   a. excrete   b. embed   c. distribute

(____) 6 One of the uncertainties in agrifood nanotechnology is how animals
dosed with nanoparticles will _____ them.
   a. suffuse   b. excrete   c. embed

C Fill in the correct **prefix**, **suffix**, and/or combining form of each root word listed below to form the target words. Then, match the target word with the correct origin and its meaning.

a. nutri_____
b. dorm_____
c. activ_____
d. _____verse_____
e. supplem_____
f. coat_____
g. _____bed
h. solu_____
i. _____capsul_____
j. _____tribute
k. _____crete

(____) 1 *cote*: a coat
(____) 2 *nutriens*: to nourish
(____) 3 *bhedh*: to dig
(____) 4 *solvere*: to loosen, release, free
(____) 5 *supplere*: to fill up
(____) 6 *dormir*: to sleep
(____) 7 *cretus*: to sift out
(____) 8 *actus*: a doing or moving
(____) 9 *capsula*: box
(____) 10 *tribuere*: to allot
(____) 11 *convertere*: to turn

D Using the choices below, add, delete or change the **prefix** or **suffix** on the target word to make the correct word for each sentence.

| -ion |
| -ive |
| con- |
| re- |
| -al |

1 Nanotechnology will help improve the *(nutrient)* _____ of many people in developing countries.
2 Nanomaterials allow better release efficiency of *(activate)* _____ food ingredients.
3 The application of nanotechnology will continue to *(distribute)* _____ to food quality and safety.
4 Agrifood technology provides a possible *(soluble)* _____ to hunger and poverty across the globe.
5 Researchers still do not have any *(excrete)* _____ evidence as to whether or not the absorption of nanoparticles is harmful to the human body.
6 Nanodevices delivering nanomaterials may have the potential to *(conversely)* _____ cancer.
7 *(Supplement)* _____ vitamins will someday be delivered directly to targeted parts of the body for their most efficient absorption.

Unit 10
Chapter 27

Energy Recovery Systems

1 In the 21st century, new energy **recovery** technologies have emerged in a global effort to mitigate the devastating effects of harmful pollutants on the environment. Some of these technologies utilize renewable sources of energy, while some work to recycle energy that is already being produced. Energy consumed by industry, vehicles, or homes normally produces a significant amount of **waste**, but with new technologies, this energy waste can be captured and reused, recycling energy back into these systems. **Recycled** wasted heat from industry, for instance, **generates** over 50% of Denmark's total electricity needs. Recycled energy accounts for nearly 40 percent of electricity in other parts of Northern Europe and about 35% in Germany. In the U.S., however, less than 10% of electrical power is provided by recycled energy.

2 Energy was first recycled over 100 years ago. The first system was a combined heat and power system (CHP) or cogeneration system that simultaneously generates electricity and recovered **thermal** energy. The electricity generation produced heat, and a thermal recovery unit **captured** that heat to be used for heating or cooling space, for operating equipment, or for producing steam or hot water. Thomas Edison built the first CHP plant in the world, and the system is still in use today.

▲ Masnedø CHP power station in Denmark

3 Over the past century, industry has developed other systems for energy recovery. Industrial plants produce waste heat, most of which could still be reused for different purposes. For instance, hot flue gases are generated by ovens and furnaces at high atmospheric pressure. The pressure has to drop in order for the gases to burn; the gases are then usually released, or **flared**, into the atmosphere. Turbines can be installed, though, that react to the pressure drop by spinning and thus driving a generator which produces several megawatts of electrical power. Pollutants from released gases are reduced or even stopped, and plants can be powered fuel-free.

4 In addition, industry may soon use an energy recycling process called gasification. Gasification converts low value carbon-containing materials or **feedstock**, such as coal, into synthesis gas, or syngas. The gasification system **relies** on a gasifier that applies heat and pressure to break apart the chemical bonds of the feedstock

▲ gasification plant in Güssing, Austria

to produce raw syngas. After impurities are **removed**, syngas can then be burned as a fuel to generate electricity or further processed for use in the petrochemical and **refining** industries. Minerals that don't gasify or other impurities stripped from the syngas can be released as harmless, **inert** matter. Occasionally these by-products are converted into solid products that can be marketed as **slag**, or a non-hazardous glass-like product that can be used in roofing or road construction materials.

Syngas

5 Vehicles also have the potential to recover energy and reduce fuel consumption and emissions. Hybrid vehicles already recover energy through regenerative braking: when a hybrid vehicle slows, or in effect the engine reverses, the energy resulting from the **friction** is captured rather than wasted, and stored in a battery for later use. Even lighter and faster is a new **kinetic** energy recovery system that captures kinetic energy during vehicle **deceleration**. The system then transfers the captured energy into a mechanical **flywheel** system that could more quickly **boost** power and reduce emissions.

▲ hybrid car

6 Homes can be equipped for energy recovery systems as well, such as energy and heat recovery ventilation systems. Energy recovery **ventilation** systems capture energy that would normally be exhausted through the ventilation system, and transfers the energy from the exhaust into the **incoming** air stream. Energy recovery ventilation recovers both temperature and humidity, while heat recovery ventilation recovers only thermal energy. Both energy and heat recovery ventilation systems can recover up to 85 percent of the energy in the exhaust air.

7 **Drain**-water (or greywater) heat recovery systems can capture hot water that goes down the drain, carrying with it most of the energy used to heat water in a home. Drain-water heat **exchange**rs can recover heat from the hot water that drains from showers, bathtubs, sinks, dishwashers, and clothes washers. Some heat exchangers have **storage** capacity for recovered heat for later use, and some directly transfer energy from the warm drainwater to the cold supply water, which is either directed to the incoming cold water and/or to the water heater.

8 Energy recovery innovations continue globally at a rapid pace. Energy efficiency may improve nearly 100 percent through energy recovery devices and methods. Future efforts to improve energy recovery will include enhanced hydrogen fuel cell technology, new bioprocessing techniques, and innovative nanotechnology applications.

— Cold Water
— Pre-Heated Water
— Hot Water
— Drain Water

▲ diagram showing how a drain-water heat recovery unit can be installed into a house (cc by Ashp uk)

TARGET WORD EXERCISES

A
Match the correct meaning with each target word.

a. thermal
b. flue
c. incoming
d. turbine
e. capture
f. flywheel

(____) 1 relating to, using, producing, or caused by heat
(____) 2 the act of entering or arriving
(____) 3 a heavy wheel that regulates the speed of a machine
(____) 4 a conduit to carry off smoke
(____) 5 a machine in which power is produced by a stream of water, air, etc., that pushes the blades of a wheel and causes it to rotate
(____) 6 to take, seize, or catch

B
The prefix "re-" means "again" or "to go backward." Using the meaning given below, add the correct root word to make a word from the article above.

1. re_____ (the act of regaining or saving something lost)
2. re_____ (to respond to a stimulus)
3. re_____ (to use again)
4. re_____ (to process or cycle again for further use)
5. re_____ (capable of being restored to a new or fresh condition)
6. re_____ (set free or let go)
7. re_____ (to be dependent for support, help, or supply)
8. re_____ (taken out of or extracted)
9. re_____ (relating to or marked by regeneration)
10. re_____ (turns about or moves in the opposite direction)
11. re_____ (coming about as a consequence)
12. re_____ (to bring down, as in extent, amount, or degree; diminish)

C
Add or change a suffix to create the correct form of the target word in each sentence.

1. Energy _____ (recover) can result in zero emissions.
2. Hybrid vehicles are equipped to store energy produced during _____ (decelerate).
3. Many energy recovery systems use a heat _____ (exchange) to produce electricity.
4. A combined heat and power system uses two power sources for energy _____ (generate).
5. Heat recovery systems can be used to control whole house _____ (ventilate).

D Some words are spelled the same but used as different parts of a sentence. Use each of the target words listed below in the correct form as indicated in each sentence. The words can be used more than once.

| flare | drain | waste | exchange | boost |

1. The _____ (noun) from the smokestack produced visible flames.
2. The racecar driver wanted to _____ (verb) his speed with the new kinetic energy recovery system.
3. Recycled _____ (noun) can come from many forms, such as solid and gas.
4. A copper pipe attached to a shower _____ (noun) can capture and recycle hot water.
5. Some energy recovery systems _____ (verb) both heat and moisture.
6. People living in the United States _____ (verb) many solids instead of recycling them.
7. We saw the flames _____ (verb) from the smokestack.
8. A copper pipe can capture and recycle water that _____ (verb) from the shower.
9. The new kinetic energy recovery system should provide a _____ (noun) to racecar speeds.
10. Some energy recovery systems involve only the _____ (noun) of heat.

E Homophones are words that are pronounced the same but differ in meaning and sometimes spelling. Circle the correct homophone in each sentence.

1. The engineer had a natural (flare/flair) for engine design.
2. The (flare/flair) from the smokestack lit up the sky.
3. The exhaust left the vehicle as (waste/waist).
4. He attached his cell phone pouch to the belt around his (waste/waist).
5. The chimney (flue/flu) had to be cleaned each fall.
6. School was cancelled because so many children had the (flue/flu).

177

Unit 10
Chapter 28

NUCLEAR ENERGY

▲ nuclear power plants

1 Research and application of the power of the atom began in the 20th century. Atom splitting, or nuclear **fission**, as a theory emerged in the 1930s, both in Europe and in the U.S., but the technical reality of the process did not occur until the 1940s. At that time, the power of a nuclear reaction was quickly **harnessed** for military use. Soon after World War II, the U.S. established the Atomic Energy Commission (AEC) to develop nuclear energy for peaceful, civilian purposes. In 1951 the first nuclear reactor generated electricity, and since that time, efforts have grown around the world to utilize nuclear energy as an alternative source of power. Like other sustainable energy sources, nuclear fission is a low-carbon method of producing electricity.

2 The process of nuclear fission originates from the **splitting** of uranium atoms. Fission is induced by bombarding a uranium atom with free neutrons. The uranium nucleus absorbs the neutron, splits, and produces roughly 2.5 more neutrons, plus an

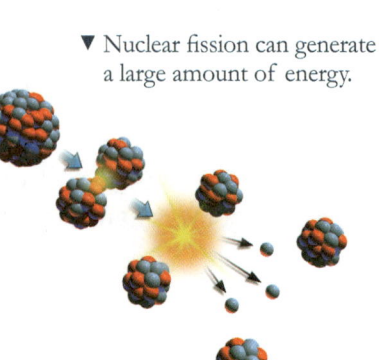

▼ Nuclear fission can generate a large amount of energy.

178

amount of energy. These neutrons can be absorbed by other uranium atoms, and thus the reaction becomes **self-sustaining** or a **chain** reaction.

③ In order to control the reaction conditions, small, hard **pellets** of uranium fuel are arranged in long tubes. Bundles of these tubes are inserted into the reactor and **submerged** in water. Control **rods** inserted among the tubes slow or accelerate the nuclear reaction. The heat produced by the reaction turns the surrounding water into steam; the steam drives a **turbine**, which spins a generator to create electricity.

▲ German stamp honoring Otto Hahn and his discovery of nuclear fission (1979)

Unit 10 Chapter 28 Nuclear Energy

▲ uranium fuel pellets

▲ fuel pellets ready for assembly

▶ magnox fuel rod (cc by Geni)

▲ The Advanced Test Reactor at Idaho National Laboratory (cc by Argonne National Laboratory)

④ All nuclear reactors are designed for one of two purposes, research or power.
- **Research reactors**: operated at universities and research centers, for research, testing, and producing radioactive material for **non-energy** purposes.

179

- **Power reactors**: generally used in nuclear power plants for electricity production, although in a smaller form they can power ships.

▲ small nuclear reactor used for research at the EPFL in Switzerland (cc by Rama)

▲ U.S. nuclear-powered ships

5 Nuclear energy is the most cost efficient of all electricity generating technologies, with a low-cost fuel source and use of a very small amount of land for facilities. In addition, the benefits of nuclear energy cut across broader energy concerns. For instance, nuclear energy may be used to generate hydrogen for hydrogen fuel cells and electricity for electric-powered vehicles. Additionally, nuclear power can generate high heat temperatures that can aid in chemical production and the transformation of seawater and groundwater sources into freshwater.

6 A benefit of the production process of nuclear energy is that the amount of waste generated by nuclear plants is significantly smaller than waste generated in traditional power plants. Currently, waste is processed into a solid form, encased in airtight concrete **canisters** or concrete vaults filled with water, and stored at nuclear facilities. Scientists have considered other storage options, including **disposal** in the sea, in space, or in ice-sheets.

7 An international scientific **consensus** is emerging for deep underground disposal, or what is called a **geologic repository**. Research is also underway to develop recycling technologies to capture the vast amount of energy in the used fuel and to further reduce by-products requiring disposal.

8 By-products of nuclear power production that might be accidently released into the worksite or the community pose the greatest concern among nuclear power critics. Other nuclear power criticisms include the disruption of aquatic and wildlife habitats by the building of nuclear power plants, and the creation of unrecoverable land where contaminated radioactive waste is stored. Land **reuse** after a plant is shut down may in the future pose contamination risks, although after closing, the plant must undergo **decommissioning**, which involves **decontamination** and/or removal of radioactive materials.

9 Despite its potential dangers, nuclear power also provides numerous benefits. The use of nuclear power has the potential to significantly reduce global dependence on fossil fuels, such as coal and oil. Additionally, nuclear power in small amounts of radiation can also provide benefits ranging from medicine to space. Radioisotopes can be used in diagnostic procedures for **mapping** blood flow or the spread of cancer, and they can help treat various cancers. Watches and smoke **detectors** use tiny radioactive materials to produce light or sound, and radiation can **sterilize** medical and cosmetic products. **Irradiation** of food kills **disease-causing** bacteria, insects and parasites without altering the food or making it radioactive. Also, generators driven by radioactive materials provide power for unattended space vehicles.

▲ The use of nuclear power has the potential to reduce global dependence on fossil fuels.

10 Nuclear power is a growing source of energy throughout the world. Around 130 power reactors provide nearly 30% of the European Union's electricity. Nuclear power accounts for almost 20% of the United States' electricity production; there are more than 100 nuclear generating units in the country. Both South Korea and Japan already produce around 30% of their electricity through nuclear power. Fourteen countries in Asia also currently support research reactors.

181

TARGET WORD EXERCISES

A
Hyphens sometimes join two words (including prefixes and suffixes) to create new words. Examples are "anti-inflammatory" or "fuel-efficient." Join the words below to create the correct hyphenated words, and then fill them in each sentence below.

| sheet | non | disease | by | sustaining | use |
| energy | re | ice | product | causing | self |

1. Proper decommissioning procedures allow for land _____ after a nuclear power plant is closed.
2. Nuclear medicine is one example of the _____ use of nuclear power.
3. Antarctica has a ban against placing nuclear waste under its glacial mass or _____.
4. Nuclear fission produces more neutrons than it needs, creating a _____ or chain reaction process.
5. Researchers hope to generate hydrogen as a clean _____ from nuclear power.
6. Irradiation of food products promises to eliminate _____ germs from food.

B
Match the correct target word with the described action.

a. govern
b. split
c. submerge
d. decontamination
e. harness
f. sterilize
g. decommission
h. mapping

(____) 1. what you do when you control something to make use of it
(____) 2. what you do when you place something completely under water
(____) 3. when you are charting or following the flow of something
(____) 4. when you make something free from bacteria or other microorganisms
(____) 5. when you exercise a determining influence over something
(____) 6. when you withdraw something from active service
(____) 7. what you do to make something safe by eliminating poisonous or otherwise harmful substances
(____) 8. what you do when you divide or separate something

C Replace the synonyms in the following sentences with the correct target words.

(____) 1 A concrete cylinder can serve as a **storage container** for nuclear waste.
   a. pellet   b. repository   c. chain   d. ice-sheet

(____) 2 Uranium **densely packed balls** used in fuel tubes are about the size of a fingertip.
   a. mapping   b. irradiation   c. pellets   d. chains

(____) 3 The self-sustaining energy from a **series of closely linked things** reaction can be generated by either nuclear fission or fusion.
   a. chain   b. geologic   c. cargo   d. mapping

(____) 4 Scientists have researched placing nuclear waste in **structure of a specific region of the earth's crust** areas such as glacial ice and sea beds.
   a. sterilized   b. repository   c. geologic   d. govern

(____) 5 Food **exposed to a radioactive substance** serves a similar purpose as heat or freezing to rid the food of harmful bacteria.
   a. irradiation   b. cargo   c. pellets   d. repository

D The root words of target words are listed below. Add a suffix or prefix (or both) from the table below to each root word to form the correct target word. Then, identify its correct part of speech.

| -ion | de- | self- | re- | -ory | by- | -ize | -ic |

1 **geology**: _____
   a. verb   b. noun   c. adjective

2 **reposit**: _____
   a. verb   b. noun   c. adjective

3 **sterile**: _____
   a. verb   b. noun   c. adjective

4 **commission**: _____
   a. verb   b. noun   c. adjective

5 **decontaminate**: _____
   a. verb   b. noun   c. adjective

6 **sustain**: _____
   a. verb   b. noun   c. adjective

7 **produce**: _____
   a. verb   b. noun   c. adjective

8 **use**: _____
   a. verb   b. noun   c. adjective

Unit 10

Chapter 29 Renewable Energy

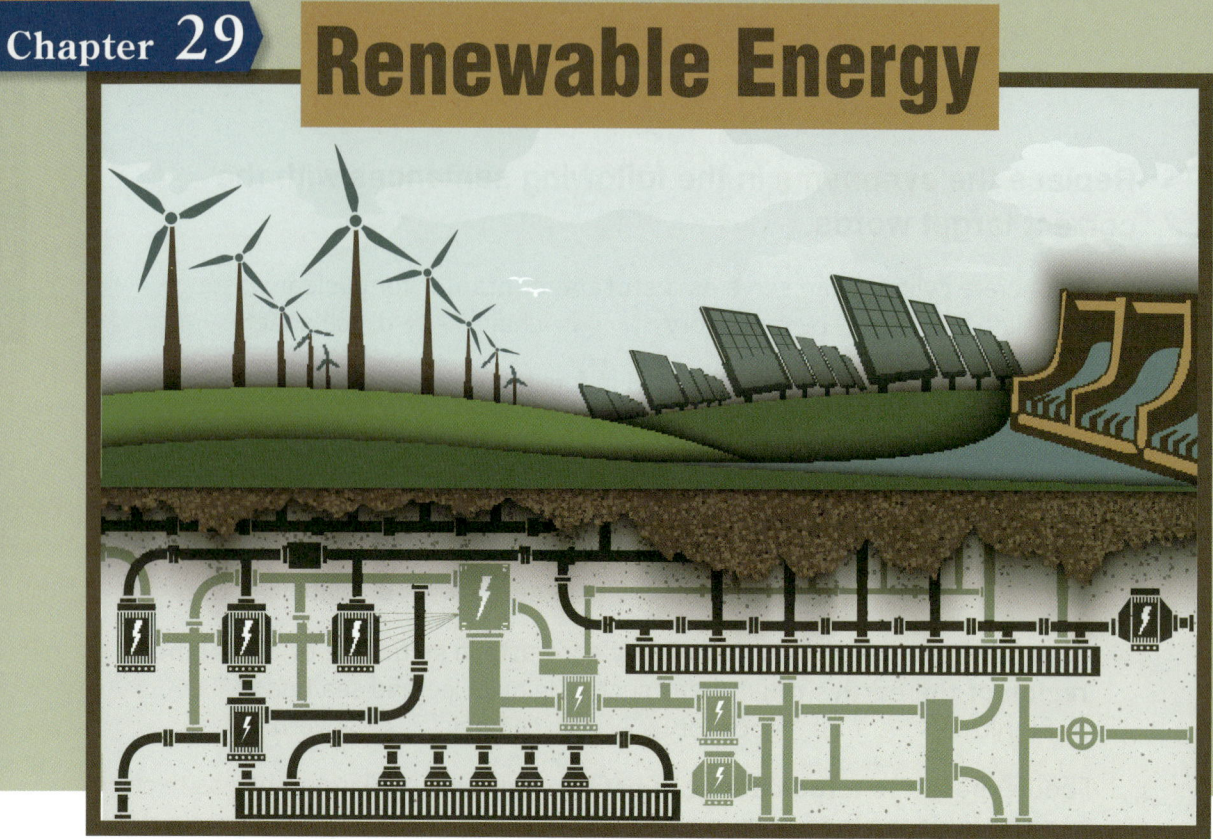

1. **F**ossil fuels (coal, oil, natural gas), formed from plant and animal remains from millions of years ago, provide more than 85 percent of the world's energy. Fossil fuels, however, are not renewable resources. Once the supplies are **depleted**, these resources are gone. Also, the emissions from burning fossil fuels can have **harmful** effects on the environment. Because of expanding global energy needs and growing concerns for the environment, it is becoming increasingly necessary to turn to alternative sources of energy.

2. Renewable, clean energy production is the most **viable** solution to fossil fuel concerns. These resources are naturally regenerated and produce few or no hazardous emissions.

- Solar energy systems use solar **radiation** to produce heat and electricity.
  - Solar thermal systems—solar collectors absorb solar radiation to heat water or air for space and water heating.
  - Solar thermal-electric systems—solar collectors focus the sun's rays to heat

▼ solar thermal plants in Spain (cc by Koza1983)

184

Total World Energy Consumption by Source (2013)
(cc by Delphi234)

Fossil Fuel 78.4%
- Petroleum
- Coal
- Natural Gas

Nuclear 2.6%

Renewable 19%

Renewable
- Traditional biomass — 9%
- Bio-heat — 2.6%
- Ethanol — 0.34%
- Biodiesel — 0.15%
- Biopower generation — 0.25%
- Hydropower — 3.8%
- Wind — 0.39%
- Solar heating/cooling — 0.16%
- Solar PV — 0.077%
- Solar CSP — 0.0039%
- Geothermal heat — 0.061%
- Geothermal electricity — 0.049%
- Ocean power — 0.00078%

Unit 10 Chapter 29 Renewable Energy

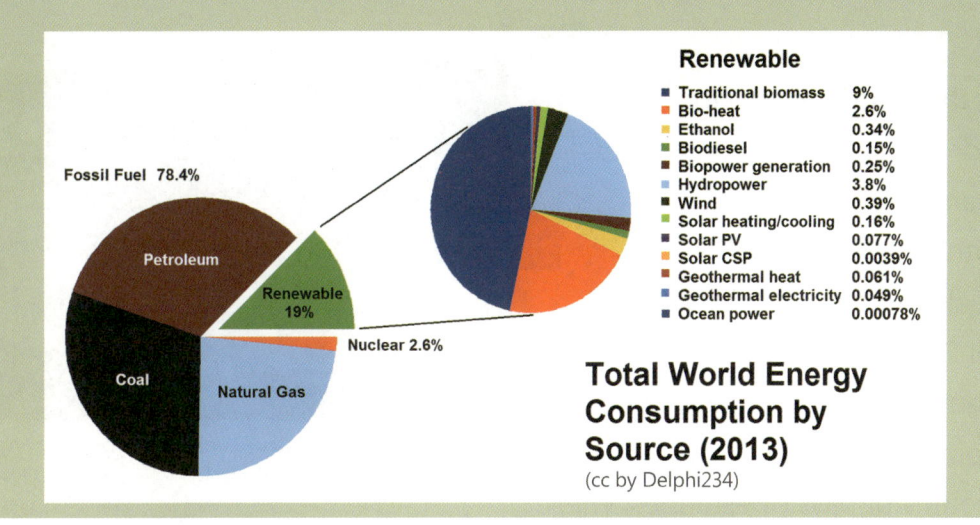

fluid to a high temperature. This working fluid can then generate steam to operate a turbine, which is then used to produce electricity in a generator.
- Photovoltaic systems—solar electric cells convert solar radiation directly into electricity, which can be used to **power** watches or even large **installations** with hundreds of modules for electric power production.

• Wind can be captured by wind turbines. The energy of the wind turns the **blades** on a rotor. This rotational motion spins a **shaft** which is connected to a generator that produces electricity. Over 75% of installed wind capacity is in only five countries, with Europe having over two-thirds of these wind turbines.

• **Flowing** water can also be used to power machinery or produce electricity. Water is diverted or released from a dam or **reservoir** into turbines and generators which convert the energy into electricity. **Hydropower** produces 20%

▲ photovoltaic power plant in Nevada, USA

▲ wind farm near Arlington, Oregon, USA (cc by Steve Wilson)

185

of the world's electricity; Norway produces more than 99% of its electricity with hydropower and New Zealand uses hydropower for 75% of its electricity.
- Another form of water energy comes from **tidal** stations located in the mouths of bays or estuaries. These stations are equipped with turbines that spin as the tide flows through them, generating electricity. Tidal power plants currently operate in France, Russia, Canada, and China.
- Geothermal energy, heated water and steam generated in the **interior** of the earth, can be accessed by drilling through the rock **layers**. Used for heating purposes and for producing electricity, geothermal energy is already an important alternative energy source in the United States, Iceland, and parts of Europe. Concerns about geothermal energy persist, though, because of released chemicals that can pollute air and harm aquatic habitats.
- Non-fossilized plant materials (biomass), such as wood, **municipal** waste and **methane** gas, and biofuels, can all be used to produce heat energy. Pulp production

▲ The Three Gorges Dam on the Yangtze River in China (cc by Le Grand Portage)

▲ Rance Tidal Power Station, France

▲ steam rising from the Nesjavellir Geothermal Power Station in Iceland

▲ geothermal plant at The Geysers, California, USA

residue, burning **rubbish**, and methane gas can be re-used to produce electricity. Biofuels, such as ethanol, and "biodiesel," a fuel made from grain oils and animal fat, are used for fuel enhancers, alternative fuel sources, and for heating.

- Hydrogen gas can be produced by separating water into hydrogen and oxygen in a process called electrolysis. Fuel cells are devices that produce electric power from the interaction of hydrogen and oxygen gases. These are potential sources of fuel for automobiles, heat, and electricity.

▲ CHP power station using wood to supply 30,000 households in France (cc by Bava Alcide57)

▲ sugarcane plantation to produce ethanol in Brazil (cc by José Reynaldo da Fonseca)

3 A range of global incentives are available to help encourage investment in and use of renewable energy. Various national and international agencies are developing energy policies for sustainable economic development. Some countries, such as those in the European Union, are developing plans to increase energy supply security. Other initiatives, such as the Sustainable Energy Finance Initiative of the United Nations, are creating economic incentives for energy investments. Because of the sense of global urgency to develop alternative energy, solutions are quickly moving from research to development. For instance, tests are underway on generators for hand-held electronics that are powered by body movement or blood circulation, and a winged car may be reality by the second decade of the 21st century. Another inventive concept is to repave road and highways with solar **panels** in order to capture solar energy for home and business use, as well as power electric vehicles that would travel on them. These energy alternatives and other new resources will help to lessen the global environmental and economic energy burden.

TARGET WORD EXERCISES

A Match each target word with its correct meaning.

a fossil	e security	i pose	m layer
b harmful	f rubbish	j tidal	n installation
c viable	g residue	k blade	o power
d radiation	h interior	l municipal	p flow

(____) 1 of, relating to, or located on the inside; inner
(____) 2 capable of success or continuing effectiveness
(____) 3 freedom from risk or danger; safety
(____) 4 the act of connecting or setting in position and preparing for use
(____) 5 matter that remains after something has been removed
(____) 6 injurious or damaging
(____) 7 related to the alternate rise and fall of sea level caused by the gravitational pull of the sun and moon
(____) 8 refuse; garbage
(____) 9 to create or to present (as in a problem, threat, etc.)
(____) 10 of or relating to a town or city or its local government
(____) 11 a single thickness of a material covering a surface or forming an overlying part or segment
(____) 12 the emission of energy as particles, electromagnetic waves or sound
(____) 13 an arm of a rotating mechanism
(____) 14 preserved from a past geologic age
(____) 15 a source of physical or mechanical force or energy
(____) 16 to move as a liquid does; move in a stream, like water

B Create a target word by adding to or removing a suffix from the following words. Then, place the correct target word in each sentence.

a install _____	g lay _____
b flowing _____	h radiate _____
c harm _____	i fossilize _____
d municipality _____	j secure _____
e powerful _____	k viability _____
f rub _____	l tide _____

1. Nuclear fusion has not yet been developed as a _____ source of renewable energy.
2. Tons of material from garbage or _____ heaps burned as a source of energy.
3. The recovery and recycling of solid waste from _____ sites can produce significant amounts of electricity for cities and states.
4. New nuclear power plants have not been constructed recently in the U.S. because many citizens consider them a _____ risk.
5. Europe has several successful offshore wind _____ providing power to several countries.
6. If nuclear _____ leaks from a nuclear power plants, it can be very dangerous for people and the environment.
7. Fossil fuel pollutants have contributed to the depletion of the ozone _____.
8. Politics could compromise the security of some sources of energy, especially _____ fuels.
9. The _____ of water in rivers and streams provides a constant source of available kinetic energy.
10. _____ plants must be located near a waterway, because they depend on the rise and fall of the tide.
11. Alternative energy sources cause little or no _____ effects to nature.
12. Geothermal _____ is the use of geothermal heat to generate electricity.

C Replace the antonyms with the correct target word.

1. Greenhouse gases emitted by fossil fuels are **beneficial** to the atmosphere.
   → _____
2. Steam generated from the earth's **exterior** can be used to generate electricity.
   → _____
3. Global initiatives are providing more and more funding for alternative sources of **powerlessness**. → _____
4. International regulations will help guarantee the **insecurity** of energy sources in the coming decades. → _____
5. Someday researchers will be able to harness the power of nuclear fusion for an **unworkable** source of energy. → _____

Unit 10 Chapter 29 Renewable Energy

189

Unit 11
Chapter 30

EARTHQUAKES and Tsunamis

1 Since scientists began to track seismic activity at the beginning of the 20th century, the amount of such activity has fluctuated little. This activity results, though, in such destructive **geophysical phenomena** as earthquakes and **tsunamis**. Their **catastrophic** damage continues to rise due to increased population and environmental damage.

2 An earthquake occurs when masses of rock shift below the earth's crust, sending out waves of energy that can cause trembling or even dramatic shaking of the ground. Earthquakes can occur any place in the world, but most occur along **fault** lines, or places where the **tectonic plates** (the outer layer of the earth's crust) have become **brittle** and begun to shift. Ninety percent of all earthquakes occur along faults, which can rupture when pressure builds between the brittle plates.

3 The following terms describe the location and type of energy waves that result from an earthquake.

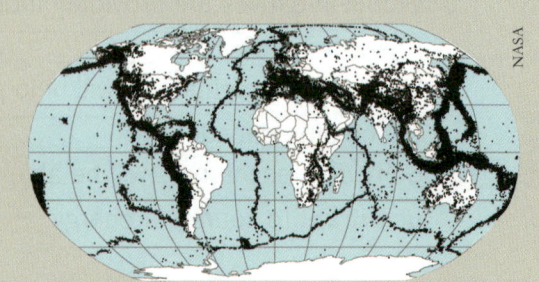

▲ global epicenters from 1963 to 1998

- **hypocenter or focus**: location of the initial **rupture**, where the energy is released.
- **epicenter**: lies directly above the focus; where the effects of the earthquake are usually the most severe.
- **seismic waves**: **vibrations** transmitting the shock of an earthquake.
- **body waves**: earthquake vibrations that travel only through the earth.
  - primary (P) waves stretch and compress the rock in their path through Earth, moving at up to 6.4 km per second.
  - secondary (S) waves move the rock in their path up and down and side to side at about 3.2 km per second.
- **aftershocks**: vibrations, often weaker, that occur after an earthquake due to the readjusting of the earth's surface.

▲ p-waves and s-waves shown on a seismograph

4. Earthquakes are measured by size and effect with the following two methods:
- **Richter scale**: measures the **magnitude** of an earthquake, or how much energy is released, and assigns it a decimal number, such as 6.0. Magnitude is measured by using a seismograph to record the size of seismic waves.
- **Mercalli scale**: measures the **intensity** of an earthquake, or the level of shaking, which varies in location. Intensity measurements are based on human observation and are assigned numeric values from I to XII.

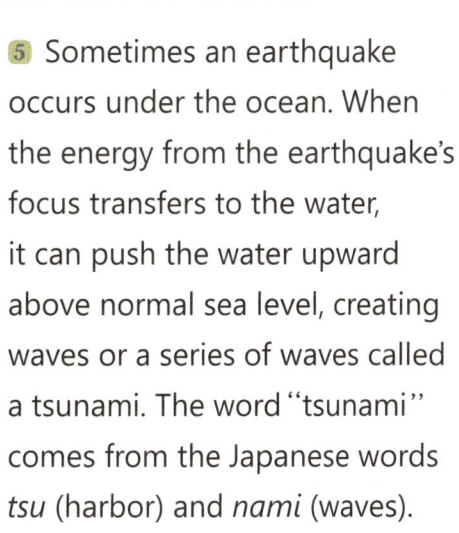

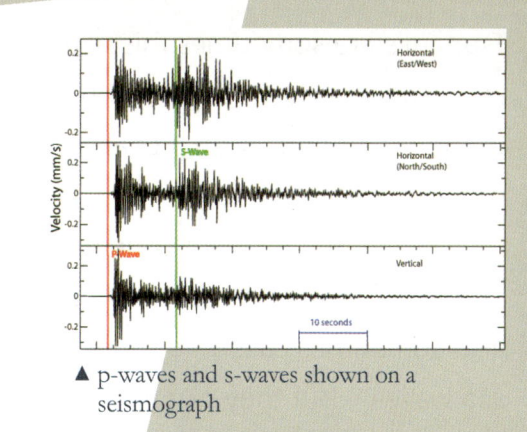

◀ Charles Francis Richter (1900-1985), the creator of the Richter magnitude scale

5. Sometimes an earthquake occurs under the ocean. When the energy from the earthquake's focus transfers to the water, it can push the water upward above normal sea level, creating waves or a series of waves called a tsunami. The word "tsunami" comes from the Japanese words *tsu* (harbor) and *nami* (waves).

🎧60 Tsunamis are sometimes mistakenly referred to as "tidal waves," but even though their impact on a coastline depends upon the tidal level when they **strike**, they are not otherwise affected by the tides. Tsunamis are also sometimes called "seismic sea waves," but they can also be caused by nonseismic activity, such as submarine rockslides or **meteorite** impact.

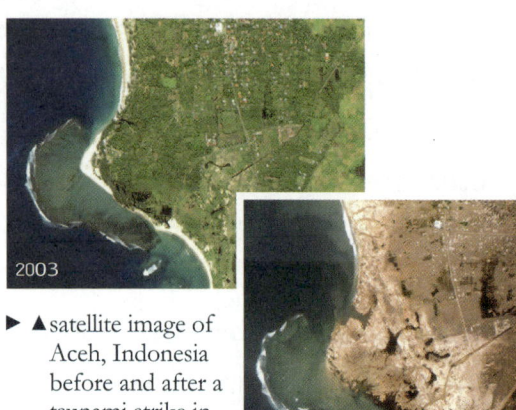

▶ ▲ satellite image of Aceh, Indonesia before and after a tsunami strike in December, 2004

▲ tsunami

▲ the tsunami caused by the 2004 Indian Ocean earthquake

▲ the aftermath of the 2004 tsunami in Aceh, Indonesia

6 A tsunami can be hundreds of miles long, travel as fast as 480 kph, and last up to an hour. Tsunamis differ from wind-generated waves, which generally have a very short length, travel up to 90 kph and last just seconds. Tsunami waves often reach above 100 km. The height of a tsunami wave as it approaches the coastline becomes much greater than the depth

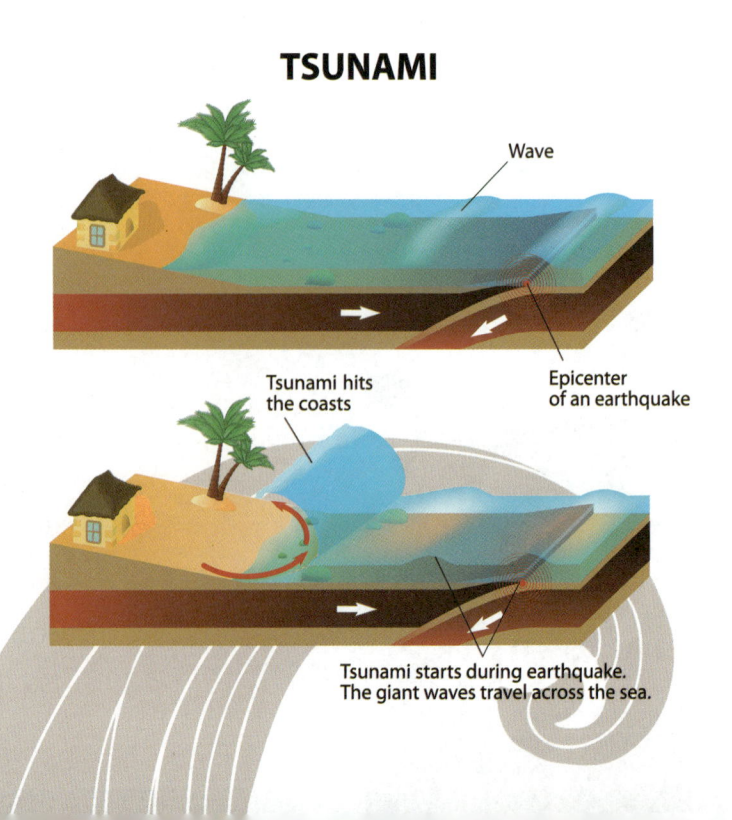

TSUNAMI

Wave

Tsunami hits the coasts

Epicenter of an earthquake

Tsunami starts during earthquake. The giant waves travel across the sea.

of the water, thus tsunami waves are called **shallow**-water waves. Although a tsunami slows as it moves into shallower water, its height allows it to retain much of its energy.

7 The damage from a tsunami can be extensive, eroding an entire coastal region, stripping away sand and vegetation, and causing significant property damage and loss of life. Several types of tsunami detectors are now available to help reduce the impact of tsunamis.

- Tide **gauges** measure sea and tide levels and **warn** when levels rise.
- Satellite altimeters measure the height of the ocean surface directly by radar.
- Short-term **Inundation** Forecasting for Tsunamis (SIFT) combines seismic and sea level data with numerical models to predict time, height and arrival of a tsunami.
- Deep-ocean Assessment and Reporting of Tsunamis (DART) uses **buoys** to detect and transmit sea level measurement information to tsunami warning centers.

▲ tide gauge building in Russia

▲ tidal gauge ready to be installed in a harbor (cc by David Monniaux)

8 The ability to accurately predict earthquakes and tsunamis is limited. Although scientists can accurately diagnose the level of stress of a fault, they cannot predict specific locations, dates or times. The National Earthquake Prediction Evaluation Council reviews predictions, but as of yet has not developed methods for accurate predictions. Communities located near faults are working to minimize damage and injuries through educating the public about safety precautions and by instituting earthquake-resistant structural standards. In high-risk tsunami areas, such as in Japan, communities are engaging in educational programs about warning systems and evacuation plans.

▲ Japanese tsunami warning sign

▲ tsunami evacuation route sign in Thailand

193

TARGET WORD EXERCISES

A Each of the words below is related to the **earth's structure and movement**. Replace the definitions in the following sentences with the matching words.

geophysical	tectonic	plate	brittle	fault
rupture	focus	seismic	magnitude	

1. Researchers gather annual statistics about many *relating to the physics of the earth and its environment* events, including earthquakes and tsunamis. → _____

2. Interactive maps allow geologists to track *subject to or caused by earth vibration* events across the world. → _____

3. The Earth's outer layer contains a mosaic of *one of the sections of the earth's upper mantle that is in constant motion along with other sections* that interact to create mountains, volcanoes, and earthquakes. → _____

4. Most earthquakes occur in the *having a tendency to break when subject to high stress* sections of the earth's crust. → _____

5. San Andreas is a major *a fracture in the continuity of a rock formation caused by a shifting or dislodging of the earth's crust* line that runs nearly 800 miles through California. → _____

6. Researchers have found that the weight of some volcanoes could cause a *the state of being broken open* in the earth's crust. → _____

7. Earthquake waves are shock waves that originate at *the point of origin of an earthquake* of an earthquake and are sent out in various directions through the earth. → _____

8. Until the 20th century, the earth's outer shell was thought to be continuous and unbroken; we now know it is made up of many *pertaining to the structure or movement of the earth's crust* plates. → _____

9. The greater the *a measure of the amount of energy released by an earthquake* of an earthquake, the greater the chance that it will cause extensive damage. → _____

B

From the jumbled words below, create compound words which can be found in the article, and correctly use them in the following sentences.

shallow	quake	coast	earth	after	wind	rock
line	water	risk	shocks	high	slides	generated

1. An _____ is usually caused by the rupture of a fault, but could result from a volcanic explosion or landslide.

2. Tsunamis are _____ waves, which means that their height is much greater than the depth of the water they arise from.

3. _____ waves last only a few seconds because the wind doesn't have enough energy to continuing pushing the water.

4. Melting glaciers could put massive pressure on underlying rocks to produce underwater _____ and tsunamis.

5. Even though a tsunami may lose some energy as it moves from the open ocean toward land, it can still do extensive damage to property and land along a _____.

6. Property owners who live along the San Andreas fault are in a _____ area for earthquakes.

7. _____ usually occur within two days of an earthquake.

C

Place the correct target word with its meaning.

catastrophic	shallow	strike	phenomena
inundation	warn	buoy	gauge

_____ 1 causing or capable of causing extreme harm

_____ 2 a part of a body of water of little depth

_____ 3 to damage or destroy, as by forceful contact

_____ 4 occurrences, circumstances, or facts that are perceptible by the senses

_____ 5 the state of being covered with water, especially floodwaters

_____ 6 to make aware in advance of actual or potential harm or danger

_____ 7 a float moored in water to mark a location or warn of danger

_____ 8 an instrument for measuring or testing

195

Unit 11
Chapter 31

Satellite Oceanography

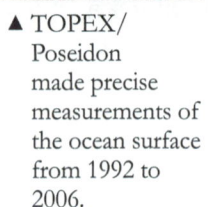

▲ TOPEX/Poseidon made precise measurements of the ocean surface from 1992 to 2006.

▲ The Ariane 4 rocket, with TOPEX/Poseidon on board

1 More than 70 percent of the earth's surface is covered by water. These waters constantly interact with the **atmosphere**, exchanging heat and moisture. The complex currents of the world's oceans **circulate** heat from the tropics to the poles, and release heat back into the atmosphere as they return to the tropics. These waters are **turbulent**, vast, and dense; the constant fluctuations make the waters difficult to study in detail. Until the early 1990s, oceanography (the scientific study of oceans) utilized information gathered by ships and ocean buoys about water temperature, surface heights, **salinity**, and ocean **current** patterns. With the launch of the first satellite to map ocean topography, TOPEX/Poseidon in 1992, ocean dynamics could be observed and measured in a much more accurate and detailed way.

2 Satellite oceanography involves the use of satellite radar altimeters. Altimeters send a microwave **pulse** to the ocean's surface and measure how long it takes to return, providing data about changes in sea surface height. The strength and **shape** of the returning signal also provides information on wind speed and the height of ocean waves. These data allow scientists to identify the speed and direction of ocean currents, to distinguish between warm and cold water current, and to chart wind speed and the size of waves.

TOPEX/POSEIDON MEASUREMENT SYSTEM

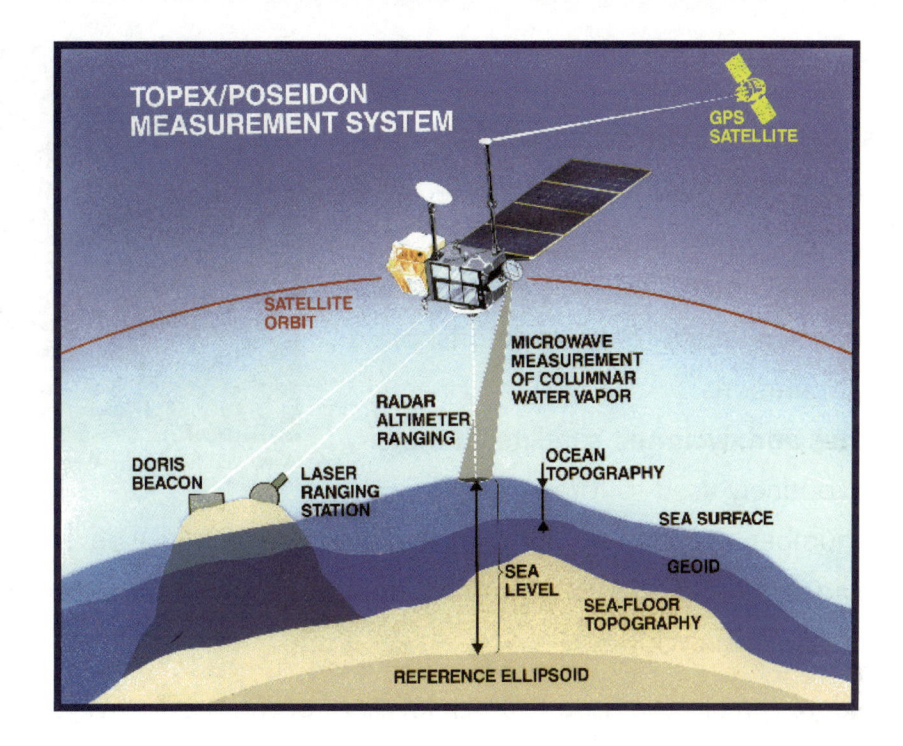

③ Satellites are capable of detecting forceful energy and current patterns in the oceans that significantly affect marine life and weather phenomena. For instance, satellite altimetry provides data about the change in location of cold and warm water masses along a coast, such as the western United States coastline along the Pacific Ocean. These masses affect the path of the jet stream, the line of weather that determines storm locations across land. Satellite oceanography helps predict seasonal weather activity based on these masses, and helps communities prepare for weather phenomena such as eddies and hurricanes.

- **Eddies**: circular currents of water producing turbulence. The force of an eddy, which can span hundreds of miles and last for years, can **displace** marine life and change weather patterns in that area. Satellites provide a range of information about eddies:
  ‣ Researchers can study the dynamics of an eddy to predict weather.
  ‣ Scientists can detect eddies caused by pollution, such as oil spills, that disturb the ecosystem of the area.

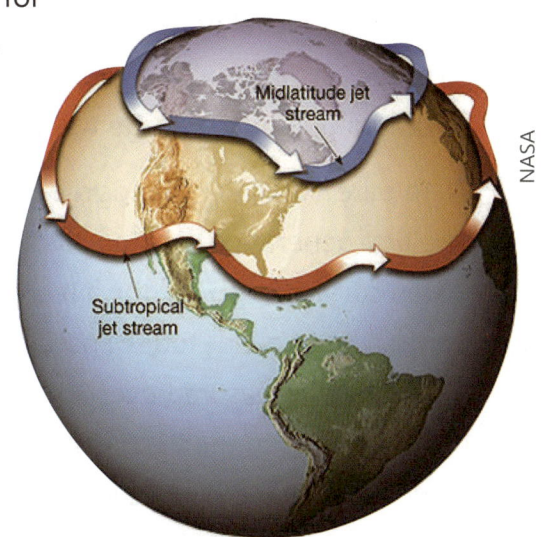

▲ two jet stream systems over the northern hemisphere

- Sailors use information on eddies for **navigation**, ship routing and even for planning **yacht** racing.
- Many offshore industries study eddy currents for worker safety and to schedule offshore drilling operations.
- **Hurricanes and cyclones**: satellite altimeter data are routinely used to forecast the number and strength of hurricanes over an entire season. Data can also provide information about stored heat in oceans with the potential to **cause** and **sustain** cyclones.

▲ two eddies in the Weddell Sea

4 Satellite data can also be used to track levels of ocean productivity.
- Biologists can use measurement of ocean color to track the redistribution of nutrients, such as concentration of phytoplankton, zooplankton, and shrimp.
- Fronts, areas where sea temperatures and colors **abruptly** change, can be clearly distinguished in ocean waters. Such sudden changes commonly indicate areas of high fish concentrations. **Acoustic** properties of water are heightened in front areas. If these areas can be accurately detected by the military, then personnel can be warned of possible listening devices in the area.
- The **migration** patterns of marine life can be detected with satellite technology, providing essential data for fishermen and fishery managers. The water level of rivers and lakes can be monitored by **satellite** altimeters, especially in **remote** regions. The data may be used to forecast floods, draught, and to manage water resources.

5 To date, satellite oceanography has seen several generations of **altimetry**. The first generation was the NASA Seasat satellite, launched in 1978 to measure ocean surface **topography**. Nearly two decades later, in 1992, NASA and the Centre Nationale d'Etudes Spatiales (CNES) joined in the TOPEX/Poseidon mission that measured over 95 percent of the Earth's non-frozen water surface every 10 days. In the 21st century, two ongoing altimetry missions have been launched jointly by NASA and CNES—Jason-1 (2002) provides near real-time and long-range (multiple decade) forecasting, and Jason-2 (2008) continues the data record of Jason-1 with improved accuracy and **precision**. The latest observation satellite, Jason-3, launched on January 17, 2016.

6 More satellites are planned for launch in the near future, each with advanced imagery and remote sensing capabilities for retrieval of information such as sea surface height, salinity, temperature, and vector winds. Future satellites will also provide a **holistic** view of the ocean. As satellite oceanography continues to improve methods of ocean modeling and data **assimilation**, it will provide important information about the Earth's dynamics, especially climate change.

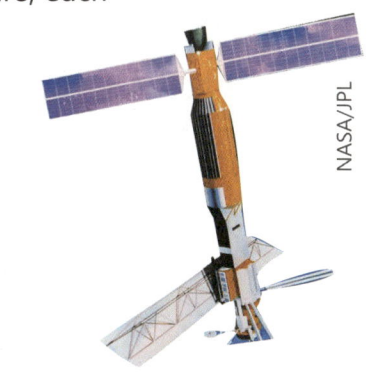

▲ artist's drawing of the Seasat satellite

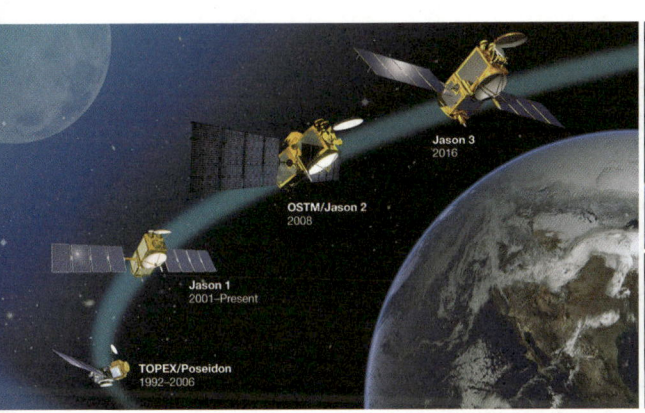

▲ Artist's rendering of the TOPEX/Poseidon satellite and its follow-on Jason series of satellites

▲ Jason-2 just before launch

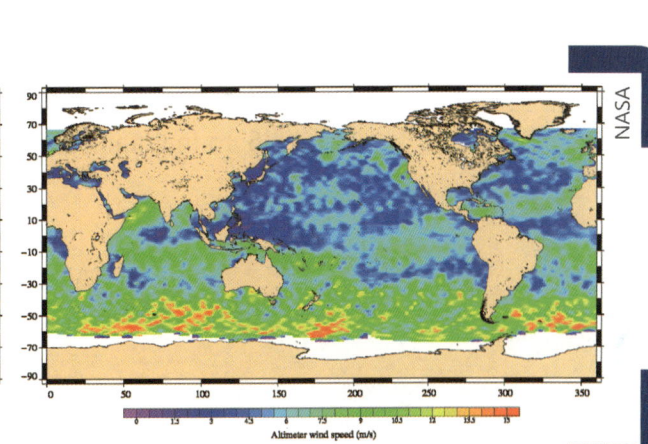

▲ sea wind speeds maped by Jason-1 (right) and Jason-2 (left) on the same 10-day period

199

TARGET WORD EXERCISES

A   Match the target words to the correct definitions.

yacht | current | sustain | precision | turbulent | cause
salinity | acoustic | displace | migration | circulate
pulse | navigation | abruptly | shape | remote

(salinity) 1 the relative proportion of salt in a solution
(precision) 2 the quality of correctness or exact measurement
(shape) 3 the characteristic surface configuration of a thing; an outline or contour
(displace) 4 to move or shift from the usual place or position
(current) 5 a flow of water or air in a particular direction
(remote) 6 inaccessible and sparsely populated
(migration) 7 the movement of a complete population of animals from one area to another
(turbulent) 8 full of violent unpredictable currents
(pulse) 9 a sharp transient wave in the normal electrical state
(yacht) 10 a large boat with sails or an engine, used for racing or pleasure cruising
(abruptly) 11 quickly and without warning
(acoustic) 12 of or relating to sound, the sense of hearing, or the science of sound
(cause) 13 give rise to; make happen
(navigation) 14 the guidance of ships or airplanes from place to place
(circulate) 15 to move in or flow through a circle or circuit
(sustain) 16 to maintain or continue for a period of time

B Determine whether the target word in each sentence is a noun or verb.

noun	verb	1	The waters **pulsed** with energy as the waters pushed the ship toward the shore.
noun	verb	2	The sailors believed that supporting the hurricane survivors was a good **cause**.
noun	verb	3	The changes in water temperature forced a **migration** of many types of fish.
noun	verb	4	Sailors use satellite altimetry to help them **navigate** shorter routes.
noun	verb	5	Technology has helped **shape** the future of oceanography.
noun	verb	6	Ocean currents **circulate** in a clockwise direction in the northern hemisphere.
noun	verb	7	The force of an eddy can **cause** weather patterns to change.
noun	verb	8	Ocean currents are modified by the **shape** of continents.
noun	verb	9	The U.S. Navy uses satellite altimetry for **navigation** and mapping.
noun	verb	10	Satellite oceanography can precisely measure the complex ocean **circulations**.
noun	verb	11	Microwave **pulses** from satellite altimeters can measure the roughness of the ocean's surface.
noun	verb	12	Satellite altimeters provide data to relate when fur seals **migrate** to oceanographic conditions.

C Match root words with suffixes to create the target words. Then, create new words from the root words by adding a different suffix from the list below. You may have to add or remove letters from the root words to create the target or new words (it is possible to create more than one new word for each root word).

Suffixes: -ion   -ity   -ate   -ly   -ent   -ing   -ed   -ence   -ness

Root Words	Target Words	New Words
1 circle	+ _____ = _____	+ _____ = _____
2 turba	+ _____ = _____	+ _____ = _____
3 salt	+ _____ = _____	+ _____ = _____
4 abrupt	+ _____ = _____	+ _____ = _____
5 navigate	+ _____ = _____	+ _____ = _____
6 migrate	+ _____ = _____	+ _____ = _____
7 precise	+ _____ = _____	+ _____ = _____

Unit 11
Chapter 32

Volcanoes

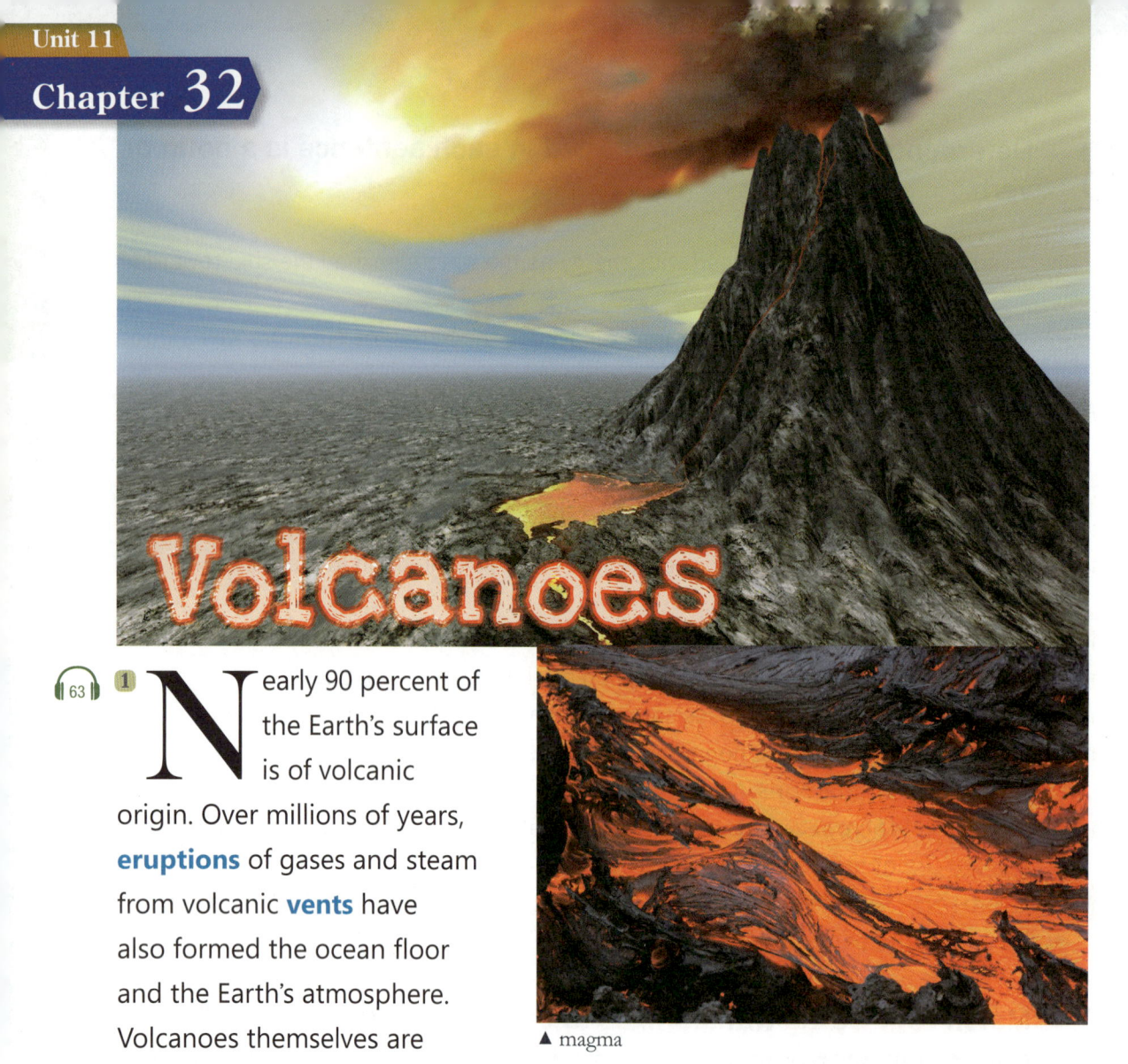

1 Nearly 90 percent of the Earth's surface is of volcanic origin. Over millions of years, **eruptions** of gases and steam from volcanic **vents** have also formed the ocean floor and the Earth's atmosphere. Volcanoes themselves are

▲ magma

produced by the products of their own eruptions. The word volcano can refer either to the vent or opening through which **molten** rock and gases are **ejected**, or to the cone-like mountain formed around the vent from ejected materials.

2 Molten rock, known as magma, usually forms at the boundaries of the loose plates that shape the earth's crust and its underlying mantle layer. Where these plates interact, the **mantle** melts and forms **magma**. As magma is liquid and lighter than its surrounding rock, it rises. Some of the rising magma collects in **reservoirs** or chambers. The pressure in the chambers is lower, allowing the gases in the magma to expand. This expansion forces the magma through openings in the Earths' crust, an event called a volcanic eruption. When the plates **diverge**, the heated magma fills the gap; this process is called spreading center volcanism. The exception to plate interactions is hotspot volcanoes, which occur when hot mantle material wells up to form a **plume**. The plume is activated when a continental plate moves over it.

3 Volcanic eruptions are classified both by **frequency** and behavior. Active volcanoes erupt regularly; **dormant** volcanoes have erupted during recorded history; extinct volcanoes have never erupted in historical times. Volcanic eruptions exhibit several different types of behavior:

- **Phreatic** (steam eruptions): magma encounters groundwater or surface water, resulting in an explosion of steam, water, ash, and rock fragments (called pyroclastic material), which does not reach the surface.
- **Hawaiian**: non-**explosive** eruptions produced by gas **discharges** that shoot eruption columns up to 1 kilometer above the vent, producing lava, but little pyroclastic material.
- **Strombolian**: mildly explosive eruptions producing some **lava** flow and low levels of tephra (ash and dust) and bombs (lava fragments).

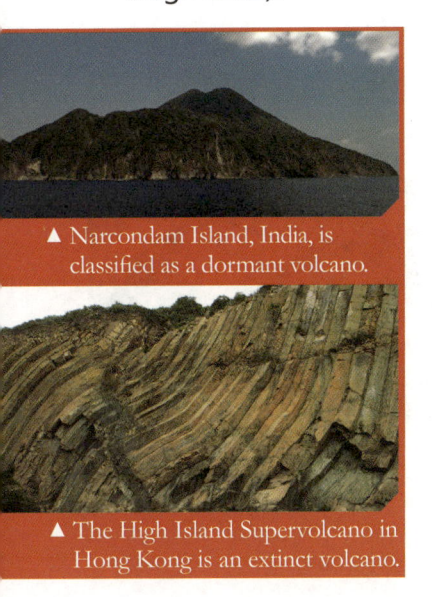

▲ Mount St. Helens is an active volcano.

▲ Narcondam Island, India, is classified as a dormant volcano.

▲ The High Island Supervolcano in Hong Kong is an extinct volcano.

- **Vulcanian**: very explosive eruptions, characterized by eruption columns up to several kilometers above the vent and significant pyroclastic flows.
- **Pelean**: violently explosive eruptions, producing glowing **avalanches** of pyroclastic flow.
- **Plinian**: violent eruptions resulting from sustained eruption columns up to 45 kilometers above the vent. Eruption columns produce widespread pyroclastic flows and ash clouds that can quickly encompass the Earth.

[64] **4** Types of volcanoes range from perfectly-shaped cones to deep depressions filled with water, but are characterized by three main types.

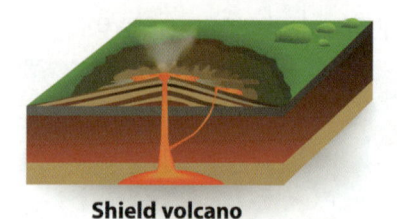

- **Shield**: a broad, flattened **dome**-like shape created by layers of very fluid, slow-moving lava flowing over its vent.
- **Composite** (also called stratovolcanoes): steep-sided cones formed by alternating layers of lava and rock fragments accumulated from their own lava flows, pyroclastic flows, and dangerous mudflows called lahars.
- **Caldera**: **basin**-shaped depression formed when magma so violently erupts as to empty the vent and leaving no structural support. The vent sinks or collapses, and little pyroclastic material falls nearby to build up the ground, leaving depressions of several kilometers in diameter. Calderas are the most dangerous volcanoes, producing significant pyroclastic **surges** and even tsunamis resulting from ground collapse.

▼ Skjaldbreidur Volcano: a shield volcano in Iceland, whose name means "broad shield"

▲ Mount Fuji: a stratovolcano in Japan, also an active volcano

▲ Mount Aniakchak: a 3,400 year old caldera in Alaska

[5] Volcanic eruptions pose major health threats, including death from **suffocation**. Volcanic eruptions can **trigger** other natural hazards, such as mudslides, floods, and wildfires; they can also **contaminate** drinking water and cause power outages. Adverse health effects from a volcanic eruption include burns and other injuries, **respiratory** illness, and the possibility of infectious disease. Pyroclastic materials ejected in volcanic eruptions are also extremely damaging to the environment, particularly due to the presence of toxic gases. Gases such as carbon dioxide, which is a greenhouse gas, **sulphur** dioxide gas, a main cause of acid rain, and sulphate **aerosols**, contribute to the destruction of the ozone layer.

▲ Volcanoes can trigger mudslides.

▲ the official logo of the United States Geological Survey

▲ the logo of the United States National Oceanic and Atmospheric Administration

[6] Agencies throughout the world monitor volcanic activity and provide warnings when possible. The USGS and NOAA use technology such as thermal **infrared** technology and weather satellites to determine when and how violently volcanoes will erupt. Volcanic Ash Advisory Centers around the world also use satellites to track volcanic ash clouds. One of the most recently developed satellite methods of volcanic activity detection is called Robust Satellite Technique. This technique compares past information with present activity in order to more accurately identify and track volcanic ash clouds, as well as to detect and monitor dangerous thermal changes. Improvements in the sensitivity of monitoring techniques are needed to help provide warnings for aircraft and communities, and to mitigate the damage of volcanic activity.

TARGET WORD EXERCISES

A Choose the meaning for each target word that best matches its context in the article.

(____) 1 eruption
a. an appearance of a rash or blemish on the skin.
b. the emergence of a tooth through the gums
c. the sudden occurrence of a violent discharge of steam and volcanic material

(____) 2 vent
a. to release (an emotion) in an outburst
b. the opening of a volcano in the earth's crust
c. a duct that provides ventilation

(____) 3 eject
a. forcefully eliminate a substance
b. to evict
c. leave an aircraft rapidly, using in an ejection seat or capsule

(____) 4 plume
a. a token of honor or achievement
b. a feather, especially a large and showy one
c. an upwelling of molten material from the earth's mantle

(____) 5 dormant
a. temporarily quiet, inactive, or not being used
b. lying with head on paws as if sleeping
c. not active mentally

(____) 6 discharge
a. electrical conduction through a gas in an applied electric field
b. a substance that is emitted or released
c. a formal written statement of relinquishment

(____) 7 explosive
a. a volatile situation with troops and rioters eager for a confrontation
b. sudden and potentially violent
c. a chemical substance that undergoes a rapid chemical change

(____) 8 basin
a. a large, bowl-shaped depression in the surface of the land or ocean floor
b. a washbowl; a sink
c. a round wide container open at the top

(____) 9 trigger
a. to set off; initiate
b. the lever pressed by the finger to discharge a firearm
c. a device that activates, releases or causes something to happen

(____) 10 surge
a. an instability in the power output of an engine
b. to improve one's performance suddenly, especially in bettering one's standing in a competition
c. a sudden onrush

B Choose the correct word for each definition.

(____) 1 melted or liquefied by heat
  a. suffocation   b. molten   c. explosive

(____) 2 to go or move in different directions from a common point or from each other
  a. trigger   b. surge   c. diverge

(____) 3 the number of times any action or occurrence is repeated in a given period
  a. frequency   b. dormant   c. erupt

(____) 4 the sudden fall or slide of a large mass of material down the side of a mountain
  a. explosive   b. dome   c. avalanche

(____) 5 a circular or elliptical area of uplifted rock in which the rock dips gently away
  a. dome   b. discharge   c. trigger

(____) 6 killing by depriving of oxygen
  a. vent   b. suffocation   c. basin

(____) 7 having to do with the act or process of breathing
  a. dormant   b. respiratory   c. diverge

C Add or replace a **prefix** in each of the following target words, and then match the new word to its correct meaning.

Prefixes: dis-, re-, pre-, non-, con-

a. eruption _____
b. eject _____
c. explosive _____
d. surge _____
e. diverge _____
f. vent _____
g. discharge _____

(____) 1 that will not explode
(____) 2 to keep from happening
(____) 3 to load or fill again
(____) 4 a disorderly outburst or tumult
(____) 5 to move towards or meet at the same point
(____) 6 to refuse to accept, submit to, believe, or make use of
(____) 7 rise again; to take on form or shape

Unit 12

Chapter 33

Tropical Weather Disturbances

1 Tropical weather **disturbances** typically begin as areas of rough weather and thunderstorms in the tropics, geographically defined as the area 23.5° north and 23.5° south of the equator. Throughout the year, this area receives high quantities of solar insolation (exposure to sunlight). The heated tropical seas release moist warm air that produces **bands** of rain and low pressure areas around the equator. A **convergence** of moisture, heat, and wind systems in the tropics can lead to thunderstorms—weather disturbances that produce heavy rains and **gusting** winds.

▲ thunderstorm

2 A group of thunderstorms can organize as the winds increase around the moist, low pressure air. When the winds reach a **constant** between 20 and 34 **knots**, the disturbance is classified as a tropical depression. Each year, hundreds of tropical depressions occur worldwide, and each one is numbered.

▲ tropical cyclone

3 As a tropical system strengthens, its winds **spiral inward**, concentrating moisture near the center. When the winds **swirl** counter-clockwise in the northern hemisphere or clockwise in the southern hemisphere around a low pressure system, this is called cyclonic flow. As these winds move away from the equator, they can take advantage of curving winds **deflected** by the Earth's **rotation** (a phenomenon called the Coriolis Effect). The tropical system gains **intensity** from the winds, and it can become a tropical storm, cyclone, typhoon, or **hurricane**. When a tropical storm organizes to the point where its sustained winds are more than 34 knots (39 miles per hour), it is **designated**, by international agreement, a tropical storm. Once the intensity of a tropical weather disturbance exceeds 63 knots, it becomes a tropical **cyclone**. These storms are characterized by a dark spot found in the middle of the storm the eye. Around the eye are intense winds and bands of rainfall that make up the eye wall. Extending hundreds of kilometers outward from the eye are spiral rain bands — long, narrow bands of clouds, heavy rain, and high winds.

4 Tropical cyclone is a **generic** term; it is called a typhoon in the western north Pacific basin and Asia (Japan) and a hurricane in north and central America. These storms are categorized by **maximum** sustained wind speed. Three basic classifications exist for levels of typhoon intensity, separately developed and used by the World Meteorological Organization

▼ the WMO in Geneva (cc by Mark Parsons)

▲ the Japan Meteorological Agency (JMA)

(WMO), the Japan Meteorological Agency (JMA), and the Joint Typhoon Warning Center (JTWC) in the United States.

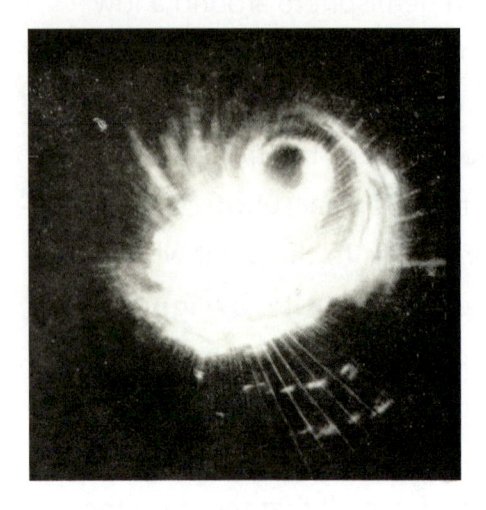

▲ radar image of Typhoon Cobra

Three basic classifications for levels of typhoon intensity	
WMO	
Typhoon	64+ knots
JMA	
Typhoon	34-63 knots
Strong Typhoon	64-84 knots
Intense Typhoon	85-104 knots
Violent Typhoon	105+ knots
JTWC	
Category 1	64-82
Category 2	83-95
Category 3	96-113
Category 4	114-135
Category 5	135+

5 Typhoon names are numbers, assigned upon their birth or when they achieve wind speeds for classification as a typhoon. The **determination** of the birth and death, or the life **span**, of a typhoon is one of its most unique characteristics. Because of differing international standards for determining typhoon life spans, typhoons are often known by different numbers in different locations.

6 Typhoons occur throughout the year, but their **peak** season is between July and November, and they occur least frequently during February and early March. About 80 typhoons are reported annually, with the majority and the strongest arising in the area of the south China Sea. Besides wind damage, other dangers posed by typhoons are landslides and flooding.

▲ typhoon

7 Hurricanes are tropical storms that exceed 64 knots, located in the Atlantic and eastern and central Pacific Oceans. Hurricanes are classified by wind speed as Categories 1-5 on the Saffir-Simpson scale, like JTWC classifications of typhoons. Hurricanes in categories 3, 4, 5 are known as major hurricanes. About eight hurricanes annually occur, nearly triple the annual number 100 years ago.

8 Hurricanes move with the **trade** winds into the Caribbean and can turn north to move over the United States, and at times even affect Canada. Over 97 percent of hurricanes occur between June 1 and November 30 each year, with maximum activity in early September. Hurricanes are capable of extensive damage as a result of high winds, heavy precipitation, and strong storm **surges**.

9 Sophisticated satellites and radar help meteorologists predict and track tropical weather disturbances, and meteorological agencies send regular weather bulletins to local governments and mass media outlets. These forecasts, advisories, and warnings about current weather conditions help ensure that appropriate measures can be taken against possible hazards. Although it is still difficult to know exactly where a tropical cyclone will hit and with what strength, **meteorologists** are able to issue early warnings that help the public to prepare.

◀ damage caused by tropical cyclones

Unit 12 Chapter 33 Tropical Weather Disturbances

211

TARGET WORD EXERCISES

A Unscramble the syllables to create a target word. Then match the word with the correct definition.

a. ig + des + nate = _____
b. bance + tur + dis = _____
c. ral + spi = _____
d. stant + con = _____
e. ta + tion + ro = _____
f. mum + i + max = _____
g. mi + de + tion + na + ter = _____
h. si + in + ty + ten = _____
i. ner + ge + ic = _____
j. ward + in = _____

(____) 1 applicable to an entire class or group
(____) 2 consistent; unchanging
(____) 3 something that follows a winding course or has a twisting form
(____) 4 toward the inside, center, or interior
(____) 5 to give a name to or describe as
(____) 6 the act or process of turning around a center or an axis
(____) 7 exceptionally great concentration, power, or force
(____) 8 a variation in normal wind conditions
(____) 9 the act of making or arriving at a decision
(____) 10 the greatest possible amount or degree

B Below are target words and other one-syllable words that rhyme with them. The words are incorrectly matched with definitions. Place the correct word beside each definition.

1	gust	to push or drive quickly and forcibly	thrust
2	thrust	a hard crisp covering or surface	_____
3	crust	a strong, abrupt rush of wind	_____

212

4	band	small loose grains of worn or disintegrated rock	_____
5	land	the course along which something moves or progresses	_____
6	sand	an agricultural or farming area	_____

7	span	moved on foot at a rapid pace	_____
8	ran	method thought out for doing or achieving something	_____
9	plan	to extend across in space or time	_____

10	trade	to walk slowly and with difficulty through water or mud	_____
11	made	a wind blowing almost constantly in one direction	_____
12	wade	produced or created artificially	_____

13	peak	lacking strength or power	_____
14	weak	to cause chaos or damage	_____
15	wreak	approaching or constituting the maximum	_____

C

Combine the following root words with their scrambled prefixes, suffixes, and/or combining forms to make the correct target words, and correctly place them in the sentences below.

rotate	con-	-ic	dis-	ward	-ence	in-
-mum	verge	turb	-ion	design	-ity	stant
con-	-ance	tense	maxi-	in-	gener	-ate

1. The rough winds indicated the beginning of a tropical weather _____.
2. Wind _____ over a relatively small area causes an upward air current that will form clouds.
3. A hurricane is a tropical storm with winds that have reached a _____ speed of 64 knots or more.
4. The _____ of the earth deflects winds, causing them to curve rather than move straight toward the poles.
5. Tropical weather disturbances are classified by the _____ or increasing strength of their winds.
6. Different meteorological agencies use varying standards to _____ levels of typhoons.
7. Tropical cyclone is a _____ name for intense tropical storms that occur in various regions of the world.
8. When a tropical storm intensifies, the winds spiral _____ toward the center.
9. Tropical cyclones are ranked according to their _____ sustained winds.

213

Unit 12
Chapter 34

Water Management

Approximately 70 percent of the earth and nearly 65 percent of the human body is water. These numbers demonstrate that water is essential for human health and the health of the planet. Globally, water supplies are abundant, because water sources are continually **replenished** by an **evaporation** and precipitation cycle. Yet, nearly 700 million people live in locations that are experiencing water **scarcity**. Water supply can be naturally affected by climate, drought, and floods, but problems with **misallocation** of water resources, pollution of water sources, and difficulty in accessing and developing available water contribute to a growing water crisis in the 21st century. The most effective means for confronting this crisis is better development and management of the world's water resources.

◀ ▼ Water supply can be naturally affected by drought and floods.

▲ flood

▲ drought

2 Increasing **affluence** in the world brings greater water consumption. However, only about 3 percent of the world's water is fresh; the rest is **undrinkable** seawater. Of this 3 percent, 80 percent is frozen and not available. The remaining 0.5 percent provides for agriculture (about 70 percent), industry (about 20 percent), and **domestic** activities, including human **consumption** (about 10 percent). Nearly 40 percent of the world does not have access to clean drinking water or **sanitation** facilities. Each year nearly 1.5 million people die because of unsafe water, **hygiene**, and sanitation (WSH), 90 percent of whom are children. As access to safe WHS improves, though, competition grows among water users for a water supply that remains constant or even declines because of eroding quality or climate change.

▲ Nearly 700 million people in the world experience water scarcity or exposure to unsafe water.

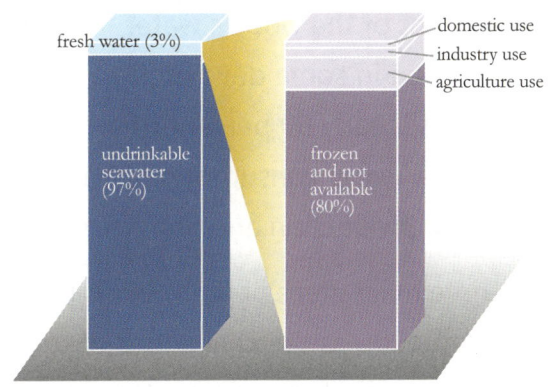

▲ global water distribution

3 Business and industry expansion, along with rapid **urbanization**, also **accelerate** demand for limited water supplies. Business activity needs range from production to consumer.

- Energy production—such as water used for cooling in thermal energy production
- Products—water is necessary for finished products ranging from food to medicine
- **Consumers**—polluted industrial wastewater limits clean water supplies

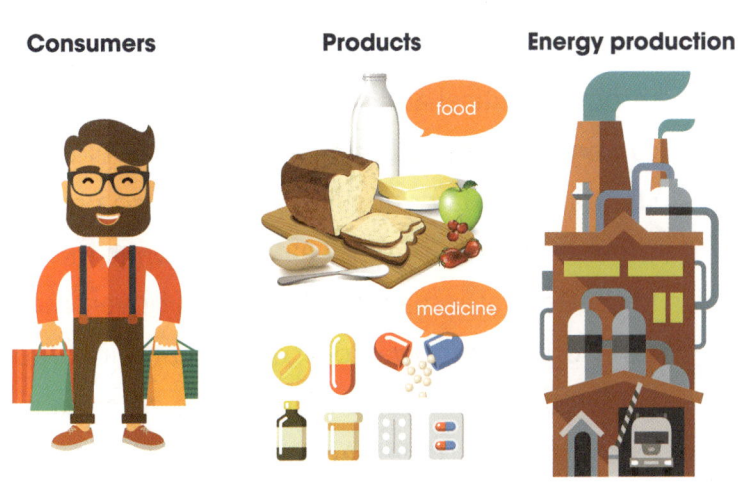

▲ Business and industry expansion accelerate demand for limited water supplies.

215

4 As agricultural demands rise to meet the needs of a growing world population and changing **dietary** habits that require more fresh foods, water efficiency and production must increase. Irrigation claims nearly 70 percent of the world's water supply, and in some developing countries, nearly 90 percent of their total water consumption. Water supplies also provide for livestock production and fish **commodities**.

▲ Irrigation claims nearly 70% of the world's fresh water supply.

5 Three main areas need to be improved globally in order to address the challenges of the current water crisis. First of all, environmental changes need to take place, such as reducing the overall amount of water used, and reusing more untreated water for **irrigation** and industry. Off-peak water use for irrigation will reduce water demands from delivery systems. Also, countries need to develop water shortage contingencies in the event of drought or seasonal shortages.

6 The water crisis can also be addressed through political and social changes. Governments can ensure fair sharing of resources and higher standards of water quality. They can also provide water rights security, as well as economic **incentives** for better water management. Local government agencies can work to empower local citizens and incorporate traditional knowledge for more comprehensive community strategies to combat local water shortages. Additionally, **transboundary** cooperation between communities will enhance regional economic development, advance cultural **preservation**, and avoid conflicts linked to water shortages.

▲ Icebergs may become an efficient water source in the future.

7 Global economic policies are another way that governments may address declining water supplies. Various types of financing could be made available for communities and individual farmers, such as government subsidies (especially with regard to seasonal need), microfinancing (financing for poor and low-income); private investments, and community partnerships. Both governments and private investors need to provide equitable water markets and trading practices that guarantee water availability and delivery. They can also participate in best practice water pricing. Furthermore, global water resource accounting can develop uniform standards for proper measurement, monitoring and reporting systems for water in every community.

8 Various organizations, such as the United Nations, the World Water Council, and the Global Water Partnership, all have and continue to sponsor global forums and **initiatives** to develop and sustain a comprehensive approach to water management. Integrated water resources management implemented through a worldwide network will be able to combine financial, technical, and human resources to address the critical issues of sustainable water management.

◀ Various organizations continue to sustain a comprehensive approach to water management.

Unit 12 Chapter 34 Water Management

TARGET WORD EXERCISES

A The suffixes **-ion**, **-er**, when added to a root word, create a noun; **-able** and **-ary**, when added to a root word, often create an adjective. Combine the following root words with their noun or adjective suffixes to create the target words. Then, use each word correctly in the sentences that follow.

a. consume + ion =

b. evaporate + ion =

c. sanitize + ion =

d. urbanize + ion =

e. preserve + ion =

f. consume + er =

g. sustain + able =

h. diet + ary =

i. *bound + ary =

*You also need to add a prefix to this word to create a target word.

1. Cities are growing rapidly in the 21st century as a result of _____.

2. Water management in developing countries will help to improve hygiene and to produce food for better _____ health.

3. The per capita growth of water _____ includes the increased numbers of people who drink beverages made with water.

4. Individual water management will be possible when the _____ is educated and given helpful resources.

5. The restoration and _____ of wetlands will help communities achieve sustainable water management.

6. Although plants and soil will absorb much of the natural rainfall and irrigated water, some water will be lost into the atmosphere due to _____.

7. Countries who can agree on water rights and sharing resources will have a greater chance for long-term, _____ water management.

8. For some communities, improved _____ means having indoor plumbing and toilets.

9. Agreements between neighboring countries, or _____ agreements, are necessary for water management success on a global level.

B Many of the target words are related to the role of human beings in **water use and management**. Match the words to the human actions or circumstances listed below.

a undrinkable	d misallocation	g hygiene	j dietary
b domestic	e affluence	h urbanization	k incentives
c consumption	f sanitation	i consumer	

(_____) 1 in my home
(_____) 2 my water use
(_____) 3 when I distribute water unequally
(_____) 4 ways I can keep my body and environment clean
(_____) 5 when I practice the principles of personal health and cleanliness
(_____) 6 the state of a liquid that I will not or cannot ingest
(_____) 7 my state of being wealthy
(_____) 8 when my community moves in large numbers to the city
(_____) 9 what I am when I shop and buy things
(_____) 10 my habits of eating and drinking
(_____) 11 these are rewards or motivations for me to take action or work harder

C The combining form "**hydro**" comes from the Greek word for "**water**." Combine "hydro" with the following root words to make new words, and then match the new words to the correct meanings.

a hydro + power =	d hydro + logist =
b hydro + phobic =	e hydro + graphy =
c hydro + electricity =	f hydro + logy =

(_____) 1 electricity generated by the conversion of the energy of running water
(_____) 2 scientific study of water
(_____) 3 abnormally afraid of water
(_____) 4 energy generated with water
(_____) 5 the study, description, and mapping of oceans, lakes, and rivers
(_____) 6 a geologist skilled in the scientific study of water

Unit 12
Chapter 35

Climate Change

[1] Weather, or short-term atmospheric changes, affects life on Earth daily. Average atmospheric conditions over an extended period of time are called climate. The climate is influenced by both **natural factors** and human-related activities. Significant long-term alterations in global weather patterns, such as shifts in temperature, precipitation, or wind, are generally classified as climate change.

▲ Significant long-term alterations in global weather patterns are classified as climate change.

[2] Changes in the Earth's climate occur when the **balance** between electromagnetic radiating energy from the Sun and radiant heat from the Earth

220

is disturbed by varying forces. There are two basic types of climate **forcing** processes.
- External processes occur beyond the Earth, such as **slight** variations in the Earth's orbit around the sun or changes in the sun's intensity.
- Internal processes take place inside the Earth's climate system, including changes in ocean **circulation**, volcanic eruptions, or in the makeup of the Earth's atmosphere. Perhaps the single most critical cause of climate change over the past 50 years has been pollution and alteration of the composition of the Earth's atmosphere.

❸ Human activities appear to be the most **substantial** cause for changes in the composition of the Earth's atmosphere, including burning fossil fuels, deforestation, and urbanization. Such environmental disturbances or abuses produce pollutant gases that **intensify** the natural **warming** cycle of the earth. An overabundance of gases such as carbon dioxide or methane forces the earth to **trap** infrared heat energy that should naturally escape the atmosphere, making the atmosphere behave much like a greenhouse. The trapped heat raises the temperature of the lower atmosphere and the Earth's surface, and produces what is known as global warming.

▲ Urbanization is a significant cause of climate change.

❹ Since 1750, the climate has been on a warming trend, but the most **considerable** changes have occurred within the last fifty years or so. Most of the years since 1995 have ranked among the warmest years recorded since 1850, when global surface temperatures were first measured. The impact of climate change is **extensive**:
- Higher atmosphere and oceanic temperatures adversely **impact** agriculture, forest management, and marine life. In Latin America, for instance, the tropical forest could be replaced by savanna and much tillable land could become desert (desertification) in the future.
- Habitat loss is caused by higher surface and ocean temperatures. As much as

25 percent of mammals and 12 percent of birds currently endangered could become extinct.
- Ice **covers** in both hemispheres have been declining, contributing to the rise of the global sea level. The melting of the Greenland ice sheet could raise sea levels by as much as seven meters.
- Global changes in precipitation amounts could increase flooding, soil erosion, and groundwater pollution.
- **Dilution** of ocean salinity at the poles and increased salinity at low latitudes will directly effect ocean currents and may trigger more climate changes.
- Increased ocean acidity could damage coral reefs and threaten marine life.
- Extreme weather events, such as droughts and tropical cyclones, could reduce crop yields and cause property damage and loss of life in local communities.
- Infectious diseases may spread in the wake of floods or drought; malnutrition will result from food shortages or shifts in food production, and heat or cold-related injuries or even death may occur.
- The economy of many countries may be severely affected with loss of **revenue** from tourism, decreases in crop and fishing harvests, and a shortage of water resources.

5 Initial efforts to effectively address climate change focused on **ambitious**

▲ Climate change may lead to desertification.

▲ Higher ocean temperatures could lead to habitat loss.

▲ Ice covers in both hemispheres have been declining due to climate change.

▲ Increased ocean acidity could damage coral reefs and threaten marine life.

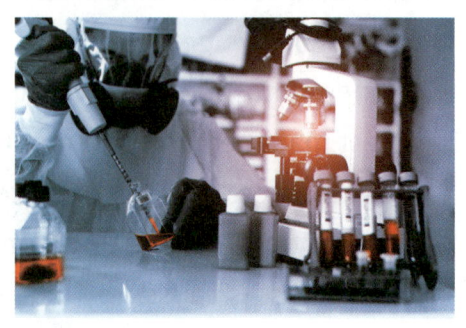

▲ Infectious diseases may spread in the wake of floods or drought.

mitigation strategies. The goals were to decrease or eliminate sources of greenhouse gas emissions and to conserve water and energy resources. A number of successful strategies have been implemented and continued on the local as well as international level. Many individuals are reducing consumption of fossil fuels, and local communities are investing in more efficient infrastructure, such as upgrading buildings and roads. Local and national **legislatures** are also adopting comprehensive energy plans.

6 More recently, efforts have expanded to include adaptation strategies. Societies have traditionally adapted to natural climate changes, but the **rapidity** and intensity of the current climate change demands more innovative strategies. Governments can fund public health resources, ensure water **allocation equity**, and provide water rights security. Various government agencies, along with private organizations, are already working to preserve coastlines and wetlands, as well as to improve agricultural practices and pest control. Local communities can expand early warning systems and emergency response systems. Individuals might adjust their clothing and activity levels. For instance, in increasingly warmer weather, individuals may choose to wear lighter weight clothing that also covers more of the body for protection from the sun's damaging rays. People may also choose to **forego** outdoor activities during the peak hours of intense heat during the day. Ultimately, global efforts toward comprehensive research, adaptation, and mitigation policies will help return the Earth to natural cycles of climate change.

▲ People may choose to wear lighter weight clothing that also covers more of the body for sun protection.

TARGET WORD EXERCISES

A Each definition below contains a form of one of the target words. Identify the related word, and then add one of the following **suffixes** to create the target word.

| -al | -ing | -fy | -able | -ive | -ion | -ous | -ity | -ure |

Example: of, relating to, or concerning nature
 Related word: *nature*
 Target word: *natural*

1. use of force or coercion
 Related word: _____
 Target word: _____

2. of large or relatively large substance
 Related word: _____
 Target word: _____

3. preserving or imparting warmth
 Related word: _____
 Target word: _____

4. to make intense or more intense
 Related word: _____
 Target word: _____

5. worthy of consideration; significant
 Related word: _____
 Target word: _____

6. large in extent, range, or amount
 Related word: _____
 Target word: _____

7. the act of diluting or reducing the concentration of something
 Related word: _____
 Target word: _____

8. marked by ambition; challenging
 Related word: _____
 Target word: _____

9. assembly possessing high legislative powers
 Related word: _____
 Target word: _____

10. a rate that is rapid
 Related word: _____
 Target word: _____

B In each sentence below, the target word may be used as a noun, a verb, or an adjective. Identify the correct use of the target word in each sentence.

(____) 1 Emissions from coal producing industries **factor** heavily into climate change processes. a. noun b. verb c. adjective

(____) 2 Some countries would consider it a **slight** if they were not included by the U.N. in discussions about climate change. a. noun b. verb c. adjective

224

(____) 3 Even the smallest changes in temperature can have a negative **impact** on the Earth over time.   a. noun   b. verb   c. adjective

(____) 4 Certain gases present in the atmosphere **trap** heat that should be allowed to escape to prevent unnatural warming.   a. noun   b. verb   c. adjective

(____) 5 Many countries must carefully **balance** economics and environmental concerns when they work to address climate change.   a. noun   b. verb   c. adjective

(____) 6 Burning coal is an important **factor** in climate changes.
    a. noun   b. verb   c. adjective

(____) 7 **Slight** changes in weather occur everywhere on a daily basis.
    a. noun   b. verb   c. adjective

(____) 8 The atmosphere acts as a protective **cover** over the Earth.
    a. noun   b. verb   c. adjective

(____) 9 Certain gases act like a **trap** in the atmosphere, keeping the Earth's heat from escaping.   a. noun   b. verb   c. adjective

(____) 10 Addressing climate change can call for a delicate **balance** between economics and environment concerns in many countries.
    a. noun   b. verb   c. adjective

(____) 11 Even the smallest changes in temperature can negatively **impact** the Earth over time.   a. noun   b. verb   c. adjective

(____) 12 Although some of the host nation delegates did not show up to climate change talks, they did not mean to **slight** their guests.
    a. noun   b. verb   c. adjective

(____) 13 Warm temperatures may mean that snow will **cover** the ground for shorter periods each winter.   a. noun   b. verb   c. adjective

C Combine the jumbled words below to form compound words found in the article.

short	coal	green	related
lands	up	term	land
ground	cold	long	Green
coast	wet	producing	term
make	house	water	line

1 _____
2 _____
3 _____
4 _____
5 _____
6 _____
7 _____
8 _____
9 _____
10 _____

Unit 12 Chapter 35 Climate Change

Unit 13
Chapter 36

Forests and Their Threats

▲ A forest is land with at least 10% tree cover.

Nearly one third of the world's land is covered by forests. Forests are defined in various ways, but in general, a forest is land with at least 10 percent **canopy**, or tree cover. Over 60 percent of the world's biodiversity is contained in forests, providing essential ecological, cultural, and economic resources. For instance, trees **perpetuate** the water cycle to enhance **rainfall**. They absorb carbon dioxide to help regulate both the natural and the **human-induced greenhouse** effect. Also, forests help prevent flooding and soil erosion, and provide opportunities for recreation and tourism. Many economic resources, including **medicinal** plants, fruits, meat, firewood, and lumber, come from forests. For **indigenous** peoples, forests represent cultural identity and provide a place for special ceremonies or customs.

▶ Over 60% of the world's biodiversity is contained in forests.

226

▲ ▶ Many economic resources come from forests.

▼ Forests represent cultural identity for indigenous people.

2 Forests are **periodically** threatened by natural forces, such as weather disturbances, fire, or volcanic activity. Although these events can cause **widespread** forest damage, the loss is never complete. Forest biodiversity has a remarkable ability to regenerate relatively quickly (usually in less than 150 years) and return to or **exceed** its previous levels.

3 The greatest loss of forests, or deforestation, comes from human activity. Deforestation is the process of clearing the world's forests on a **massive** scale and converting the land to non-forest use. There are both direct and indirect, or **underlying**, causes of deforestation. Early efforts to mitigate deforestation and its damaging impact focused only on direct causes:

- The need for agricultural land causes much of the forest destruction. **Subsistence** farmers cut trees over a few acres and burn them, a process called "**slash** and burn." When the soil loses its **fertility**, the farmers then turn to cattle raising. After the land becomes so **severely degraded** that it is unusable, the farmers abandon the area.
- **Clearcut** logging (removing vast amounts of trees), **selective** logging, and construction of logging roads have caused catastrophic flooding in countries such as China, and have cleared over 90 percent of the primary forest in parts of Europe.
- Extensive migration and urbanization, which occurs often because of **population** pressures, consumes forest land and building materials. Construction and human **intrusion** due to tourism **deplete** and pollute forest resources.

▶ deforestation

- The **extraction** of oil and gas deposits in the tropical rain forest disturbs the ecosystem. Drilling or spillage can result in the release of contaminants into the atmosphere and water resources.

▲ slash and burn

▲ Extensive urbanization consumes forest land and building materials.

▲ Pollution produced by industrialization causes acid rain, which is a great threat to forests.

4 Some causes of deforestation are indirect, but their impact is at least as damaging as direct causes. Business and industry strategies encourage short-term profits from forests instead of long-term sustainability. Socioeconomic factors and political factors include inequalities in land **tenure**, and forced migration of indigenous peoples and subsistence farmers. **Overconsumption** by consumers in **high-income** countries creates an unbalanced demand for forest products. Also, industrialization contributes widespread pollution resulting in acid rain.

5 In the last 100 years, more than 80 percent of the world's natural forests have been destroyed, and the world's rain forests are disappearing quickly, with 90 percent of West Africa's coastline already gone. The global impact of deforestation is already being felt, but it could be catastrophic in the near future.

- Habitats will be totally lost for well over 50 percent of the Earth's animals and plants.

- Loss of genetic diversity will deprive the global population of food and medicinal sources.
- Global warming may increase as trees are not available to consume greenhouse gases.
- Rainfall patterns will be disrupted, causing extended droughts.

▲ Deforestation is a leading cause of global warming.

6 New **remote-sensing** technology developed and used by NASA can regularly monitor and assess trends in deforestation. Developed in the 1970s, satellites provide detailed images of changes in forests, particularly those in the tropics, over time. Global agencies also use the satellite information to **enforce** environmental policies.

7 Efforts to mitigate deforestation and its effects are already underway with such organizations as Consultative Group on International Agricultural Research, NASA, and the United Nations Environmental Program. Solutions to deforestation can begin, though, on the local level, with government and other agencies encouraging responsible habitation of forested areas. Farmers can employ **low-impact** agricultural practices, such as shade farming. Renewable forest products, such as timber, fruits, and medicinal plants can be sustainably produced and harvested. Ecotourism can stimulate economic and educational opportunities. National and global strategies might include incentives to reward developing countries and individual **landowners** who adopt forest conservation practices. International standards for forest conservation could be enacted and enforced. A combination of public awareness, sufficient public and private funding, and sustainable management practices is needed to preserve the future of forests.

▲ Several organizations are working to prevent deforestation.

TARGET WORD EXERCISES

A
Using the root word clues, identify the correct target word for each definition.

1. If **perpetual** means lasting or continuing indefinitely, then to cause something to exist continually, indefinitely, permanently is to _____
2. If **medicine** is an agent, such as a drug, used to treat disease or injury, then something having the properties of medicine is called _____
3. If **period** means the duration of one cycle of a regularly recurring action or event, then when something recurs or reappears from time to time, it is called _____
4. If **under** means beneath the surface of and **lying** means to be situated, then located beneath or below something is called _____
5. If **subsist** means to maintain or support with provisions, then the state of having minimal or marginal resources for subsisting is called _____
6. If **severe** means very bad in degree or extent, then to a severe or serious degree is called _____
7. If **grade** means a place on a scale of quality, rank, or size, then to fall below a normal state or deteriorate is called _____
8. If **select** means to choose something in preference to another or others, then characterized by very careful choice is called _____
9. If **intrude** means to thrust oneself in as if by force, then any entry into an area not previously occupied is called _____
10. If **extract** means to pull out or uproot by force, then the action of taking out something, especially by using effort or force, is called _____
11. If **populate** means to provide with inhabitants, then all the inhabitants of a place is called _____
12. If **mass** means a large quantity or number, then something that is large-scale, extensive, or of wide extent is called _____

B
Combine the following words to create compound words found in the article above, and match them with the correct definition. Some compound words are created using a hyphen.

clear	consumption	income	owner	rain	over	land
induced	low	spread	sensing	remote	impact	fall
house	human	green	wide	cut	high	

(_____) 1 having all of its trees cut down
(_____) 2 the amount of precipitation falling over a given area in a given period of time
(_____) 3 widely extended
(_____) 4 situations where consuming of available goods is so high that sustainability is not achieved.
(_____) 5 of or pertaining to those with a larger income than the average
(_____) 6 the technique or process of obtaining data or images from a distance, as from satellites or aircraft
(_____) 7 causing little or no damage to the surrounding environment
(_____) 8 an owner or proprietor of land
(_____) 9 relating to or contributing to the greenhouse effect
(_____) 10 brought on; brought about; caused by human actions

C Each of the following groups of words contains a target word and three words, two of them related to the target word. Choose the word which isn't related to the target word.

(____) 1 canopy
   a. cover
   b. opening
   c. sunshade

(____) 2 indigenous
   a. alien
   b. native
   c. original

(____) 3 exceed
   a. surpass
   b. deduct
   c. eclipse

(____) 4 massive
   a. tiny
   b. imposing
   c. monolithic

(____) 5 deplete
   a. reduce
   b. exhaust
   c. increase

(____) 6 tenure
   a. occupation
   b. residency
   c. vacancy

(____) 7 subsistence
   a. lack
   b. support
   c. maintenance

(____) 8 intrusion
   a. invasion
   b. imposition
   c. exit

(____) 9 extraction
   a. removal
   b. insertion
   c. withdrawal

(____) 10 degrade
   a. promote
   b. reduce
   c. worsen

Unit 13 Chapter 36 Forests and Their Threats

common recycling materials

▲ Non-ferrous materials can be recycled most efficiently.

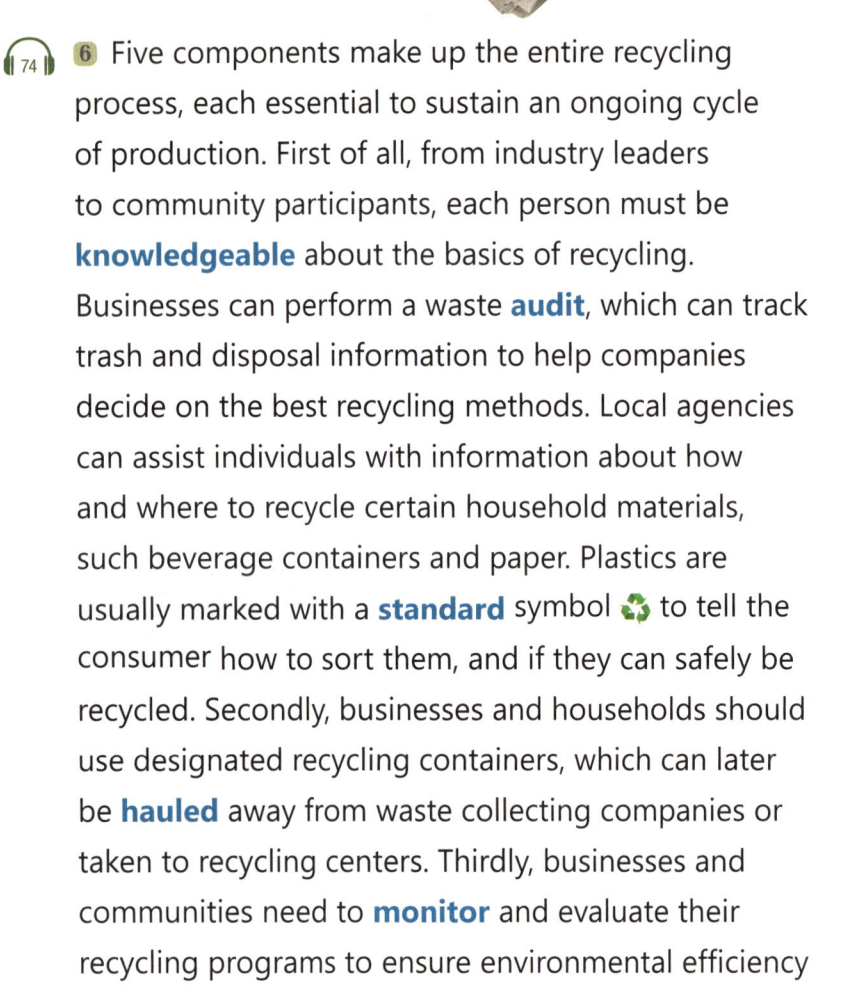

▲ Iron and steel are the most common recycled material.

6 Five components make up the entire recycling process, each essential to sustain an ongoing cycle of production. First of all, from industry leaders to community participants, each person must be **knowledgeable** about the basics of recycling. Businesses can perform a waste **audit**, which can track trash and disposal information to help companies decide on the best recycling methods. Local agencies can assist individuals with information about how and where to recycle certain household materials, such beverage containers and paper. Plastics are usually marked with a **standard** symbol ♻ to tell the consumer how to sort them, and if they can safely be recycled. Secondly, businesses and households should use designated recycling containers, which can later be **hauled** away from waste collecting companies or taken to recycling centers. Thirdly, businesses and communities need to **monitor** and evaluate their recycling programs to ensure environmental efficiency and economic **feasibility**.

▲ recycling center

▲ recycle bins

▲ the universal symbol for recycling

234

7 Fourth, companies are being created to purchase recyclable materials and manufacture them into new consumer products. Cost and quality of materials are primary considerations for these companies, including costs of adapting manufacturing processes to use recycled materials, the higher costs of high quality recyclable materials, and the cost of transporting recyclables. Lastly, businesses must also be available to purchase recycled products, or what is called closing the **loop** of the recycling process. Implementation of this step lags behind the other components; many more businesses recycle their materials than purchase recycled materials for their own operations. Developing the capacity to utilize recycled-content materials can be costly, so businesses have been slow to institute these capabilities.

8 Although recycling effectively reduces waste, it does not eliminate it entirely. However, a more recent effort to eliminate waste incorporates the design principle of zero waste. Developed in the 21st century, this philosophy combines the 3R approach with industrial design principles that require products to be free from toxic elements and produced to be reused or recycled.

9 Recycling also has its critics, particularly in regard to economics. For some communities, recycling programs are an economic **burden**. Additionally, when recyclable material is of lower quality, its value is lessened, making the recyclable process less economically viable. Furthermore, there is some evidence that government **mandated** recycling is more expensive than garbage disposal in landfills.

10 The benefits of recycling do, for the most part, outweigh its drawbacks. Some communities hold that they benefit from the jobs and tax revenue of local landfills. Recycling and waste management overall protects land, conserves energy and natural resources, and most importantly, will help protect the environment for future generations.

TARGET WORD EXERCISES

A Match the target words with the correct definitions.

monitor	destine	donate	mandate	contemporary
indefinitely	preferable	hierarchy	content	source
burden	incineration	knowledgeable	haul	ferrous
loop	delay	standard	audit	lag

(_____) 1 current; modern
(_____) 2 the origin or starting point
(_____) 3 give to a charity or good cause
(_____) 4 slowing down or falling behind
(_____) 5 to postpone until a later time; defer
(_____) 6 the act of burning something completely
(_____) 7 more desirable or suitable
(_____) 8 to assign or intend for a specific end, use, or purpose
(_____) 9 the proportion of a specified substance
(_____) 10 of or relating to or containing iron
(_____) 11 lacking precise time limits
(_____) 12 intelligent or well-informed
(_____) 13 any thoroughgoing assessment or review
(_____) 14 generally accepted as reliable or authoritative
(_____) 15 the act of transporting or carting
(_____) 16 something having a shape, order, or path of motion that is circular or curved over on itself
(_____) 17 to keep track of systematically with a view to collecting information
(_____) 18 a source of great worry or stress; weight; hardship
(_____) 19 an official or authoritative command to carry out a particular task
(_____) 20 a series in which each element is graded or ranked

B Many words related to the recycling process contain the prefix re-, which means again or anew. Circle the root words and match them to the correct definitions of these root words.

| a recycle | c recapture | e redeem | g return | i reuse |
| b reclaim | d regain | f reprocess | h recover |

236

(_____) 1 a complete series of recurring events
(_____) 2 be sufficient to meet, defray, or offset the charge or cost of
(_____) 3 a series of operations performed in the making or treatment of a product
(_____) 4 to demand as a right or as one's property
(_____) 5 to get an increase, profit, or advantage
(_____) 6 a change of direction or position
(_____) 7 to judge or consider worthy
(_____) 8 to take by force; seize
(_____) 9 to put into service or apply for a purpose; employ

C Replace the italicized word in each sentence with the target word that is its synonym.

1 A key component of the company's recycling plan will be to _____ (keep track of) container usage.

2 The student set a goal to _____ (give to charity) clothes at the end of every semester.

3 Many community governments _____ (require by law) recycling paper and plastic.

4 Zero waste is a _____ (modern) philosophy that addresses waste issues at the point of initial production.

5 Truck drivers who _____ (transport) waste products must obtain a special license.

6 Poor countries often _____ (develop more slowly) behind developed nations in recycling programs.

7 It is critical that consumers become more _____ (intelligent) about the benefits of recycling.

8 Recycling glass helps to _____ (postpone) its entry into a landfill almost indefinitely.

9 Reduction of waste is _____ (superior) to recycling.

10 The disposal of landfill waste through _____ (burning completely) creates additional atmospheric pollution.

11 The order of reduce, reuse, and recycle is a _____ (ranking) based on the most efficient and effective conservation methods.

12 Asphalt can be broken up and used again _____ (continually) in many products, such as more asphalt or roofing materials.

Unit 13
Chapter 38

Human Stress
on the Environment

[1] **H**umans have throughout history affected the environment. For instance, at times **overpopulation** has caused **localized** desertification or depletion of water supplies. However, the rapidly expanding human population over the last century, coupled with extensive improvements in standards of living, is causing devastating **stress** on the global environment. Nearly one half of the Earth's

▲ Overpopulation has caused the depletion of water supplies.

vegetated land area has been disturbed by humans, who are consuming natural resources exceeding what the Earth can replenish. As the world's population has quadrupled in the past 30 years and the world's economic **output** has increased nearly 20 times, the environment has not been able to keep **pace** with demand.

[2] Many human activities, whether industrial, agricultural, or even recreational, are having an **adverse** impact on the environment. Energy demands and policies have **endangered** fossil fuels, and have contributed to air and water pollution. Agricultural practices have encouraged deforestation and desertification with devastating impact on biodiversity and climate change. Even human use of land and water resources for recreation and tourism contributes pollution and diminishes the amount of available land for food supply.

▲ Human activities have contributed to air and water pollution.

3 Agriculture and land use have placed the greatest stress on the environment. About 10 percent of the global **landscape** is currently cropland, but the ratio of cropland available per person continues to diminish. More intensive land use activities are necessary to increase crop production, but without proper education and **oversight** in developing countries, these activities may lead to soil erosion and desertification. Within the past 50 years, over 30 percent of the world's cropland has been abandoned because it is no longer **productive**; it will take hundreds of years for the soil to become fertile again. In the meantime, new crop land is created by deforestation, a process of clearing

▲ soil erosion

▼ desertification

human-caused forest fire

away entire areas of forest. Improved crop production also increases energy resource consumption for **mechanization** and transportation needs. Political unrest, unstable economies, and **disproportionate** distribution of food often lead to world food shortages. Such shortages, in turn, heighten concerns about food security and lead to unsustainable demands for additional crop land.

4 Human overconsumption adversely affects global biodiversity in many ways.

- Overharvesting animal or fish populations can have devastating effects on their habitats, and on predator populations dependent on the target species as food sources.
- Waste and pollution come from industry, intensive agricultural practices, and carbon emissions generated from transportation sources.
- Currently about 50 percent of the world's population lives in cities, and the numbers continue to increase. **Urbanization** clears forests and grasslands, destroying habitats and diminishing water quality.
- Human-induced fires destroy hundreds of acres of land each year.
- Deforestation can cause fragmentation, a growing cause of habitat loss. When trees are clearcut, or cut in large swathes, then the ecosystem is fragmented into smaller, sometimes **nonadjacent** parcels of land, changing or destroying habitats for some of the **indigenous** species.

5 When human activity disrupts biodiversity, it also invites harmful **invasive** species into various habitats. With increased urban development, human trade and travel activities, **alien** species can readily enter and spread into new settings.

- Invasive species, such as small mammals, can infect indigenous species or decrease their yield.
- Alien species can foul water sources, changing the nutrient cycle of the habitat and destroying fisheries.
- Weeds can reduce crop yield by as much as 25 percent and degrade soil quality.
- Invasive species also can have an extensive economic impact, as they adversely affect agriculture and industry. The costs caused by invasive species tops $400 billion each year, and that estimate does not include losses due to unemployment, food and water **shortages**, human health issues, and the impact of increased number and intensity of natural disasters.

▲ Urbanization brings convenience to people, but it also destroys the habitats of other living things and diminishes the quality of the area's water.

▲ Weeds can reduce crop yield and degrade soil quality.

6 Changes in the global landscape can now be photographed and recorded by satellites. Satellite imagery is capable of precise and routine monitoring of large areas on the Earth. Information obtained by satellites is used for sustained **assessments** of environmental patterns. Satellites can also be employed for planning infrastructure changes and development. These remote sensors may soon aid in the enforcement of growing global environmental policies.

▲ satellite imagery

TARGET WORD EXERCISES

A Match the target words with the correct definitions below.

shortage	nonadjacent	productive	mechanization
landscape	localized	output	distribution
stress	invasive	endanger	
assessment	oversight	alien	
disproportionate	pace	vegetated	

(_____) 1 an extensive area of land regarded as being visually distinct

(_____) 2 to advance at the same speed as

(_____) 3 something that does not belong in the environment in which it is found

(_____) 4 not next to something; separated by space

(_____) 5 characterized by plant life

(_____) 6 a deficiency in amount; an insufficiency

(_____) 7 an applied force or system of forces that tends to strain or deform

(_____) 8 the act of implementing the control of equipment with advanced technology

(_____) 9 confined or restricted to a particular place

(_____) 10 not native to and spreading widely in a habitat or environment

(_____) 11 the act or process of producing; production

(_____) 12 the act of judging or analyzing a situation or event

(_____) 13 watchful care or management; supervision

(_____) 14 the sharing out of something among a particular group

(_____) 15 marked by great fruitfulness or fertility

(_____) 16 to expose to harm or danger; imperil

(_____) 17 not corresponding in size or degree or extent

B Underline the **root word** in each of the target words listed below. Then, using the **prefixes** and **suffixes** in the table, create new words that match the definitions.

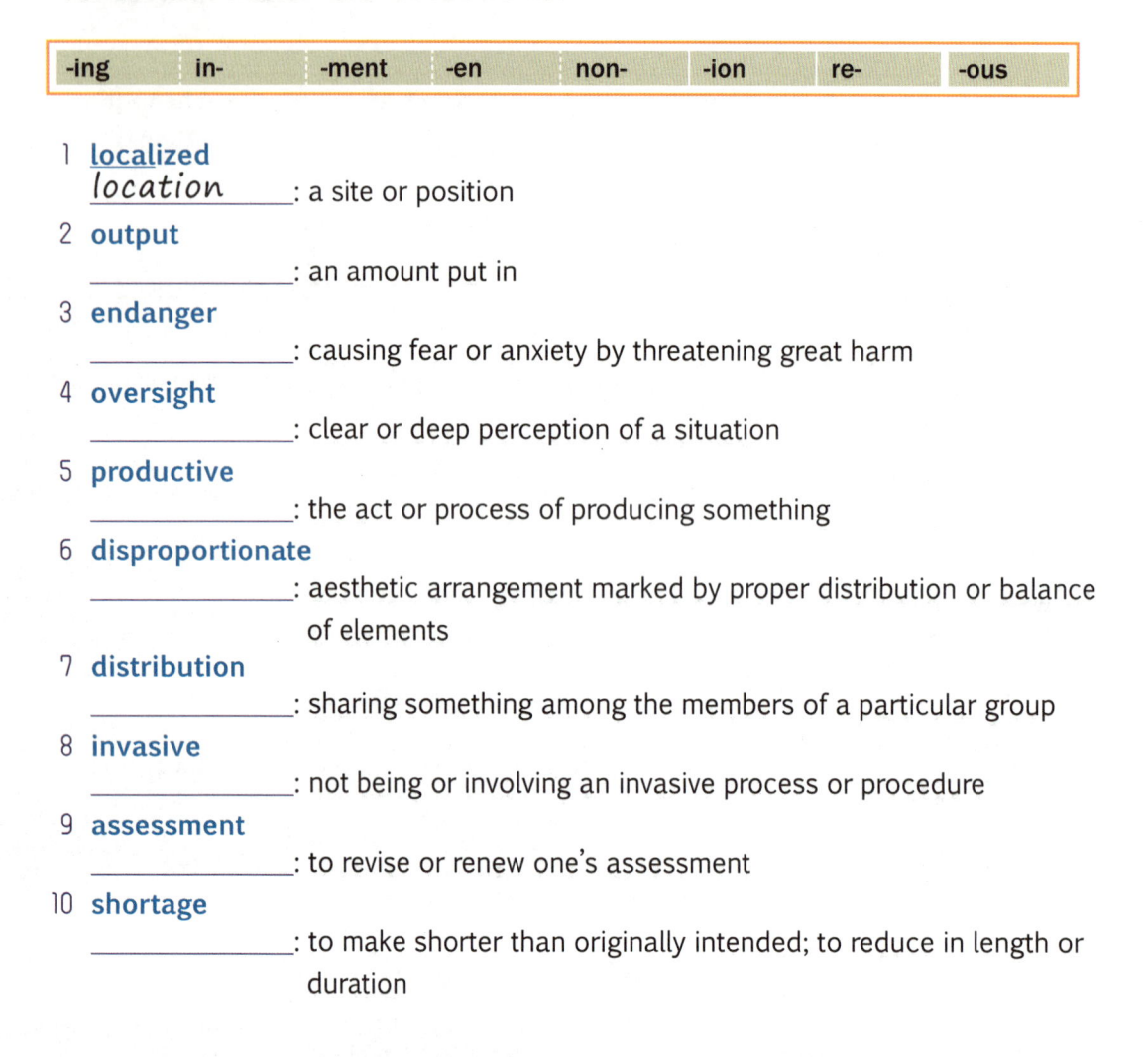

| -ing | in- | -ment | -en | non- | -ion | re- | -ous |

1. **localized**
   location : a site or position
2. **output**
   _____ : an amount put in
3. **endanger**
   _____ : causing fear or anxiety by threatening great harm
4. **oversight**
   _____ : clear or deep perception of a situation
5. **productive**
   _____ : the act or process of producing something
6. **disproportionate**
   _____ : aesthetic arrangement marked by proper distribution or balance of elements
7. **distribution**
   _____ : sharing something among the members of a particular group
8. **invasive**
   _____ : not being or involving an invasive process or procedure
9. **assessment**
   _____ : to revise or renew one's assessment
10. **shortage**
    _____ : to make shorter than originally intended; to reduce in length or duration

C Unscramble the anagram to make the correct target word. Use the given synonym as a clue.

ANAGRAM	TARGET WORD	SYNONYM
1 den anger	*endanger*	threaten
2 give short	_____	management
3 lilac doze	_____	regional
4 masses nest	_____	evaluation
5 age vetted	_____	wooded

6 cape	_____	rate
7 tidbit iron us	_____	allotment
8 putout	_____	production
9 horse tag	_____	deficit
10 canal sped	_____	terrain
11 a line	_____	foreign
12 curve dip to	_____	fertile
13 via veins	_____	intrusive

D Human stress on the environment is sometimes described with words that have the **prefix over-**. Combine over- with the root words in the table, and match each word with the correct definition.

| crop | grow | crowding | exploit | fertilize |
| graze | hunt | produce | tax | use |

(_____) 1 produce in excess

(_____) 2 to graze land too intensively so that it is damaged and no longer provides nourishment

(_____) 3 to exhaust the fertility of land by continuous cultivation of crops

(_____) 4 to hunt to an excessive degree

(_____) 5 the cramming of too many people into too small a space

(_____) 6 to become grown over, as with unwanted vegetation or weeds

(_____) 7 excessive use

(_____) 8 to exploit to the point of diminishing returns

(_____) 9 to make excessive demands on; to exhaust

(_____) 10 excessive application of nutrients that can weaken or kill plants

Unit 14

Chapter 39

Telescopes

① Hans Lippershey, Dutch scientist and eyeglass maker, is credited with creating the first telescope in 1608. He placed two glass lenses in a tube in order to **magnify** objects up to three times their normal size. The next year Galileo Galilei improved the telescope design, creating a telescope that could magnify up to 20 times, and he became the first person to use a telescope to study objects in the sky.

◀ Hans Lippershey is commonly associated with the invention of the telescope.

◀ Galileo Galilei was the first person to use a telescope to study objects in the sky.

246

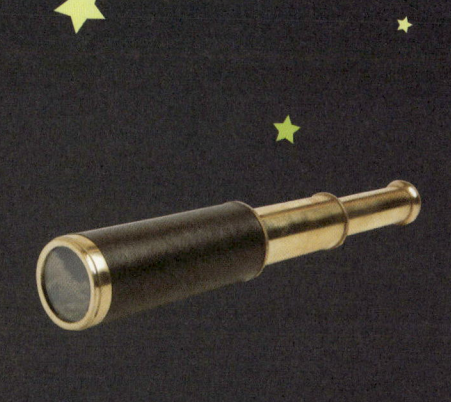

▲ telescope

▶ Optical telescopes are the most common type of telescopes.

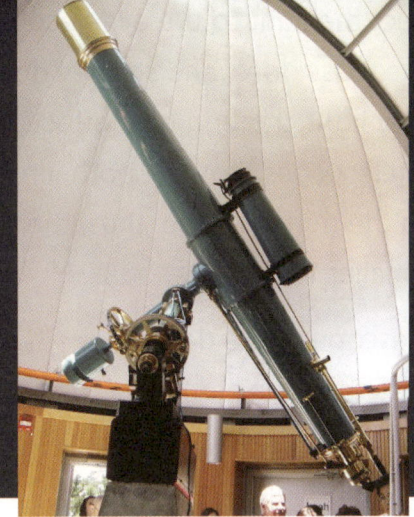

Unit 14 Chapter 39

Telescopes

2 Telescopes are used to observe and magnify objects that are too distant to be seen with the human eye. In an **optical** telescope, either a lens or a mirror collects the light, and an **eyepiece** lens magnifies the light. For scientists, the image must be recorded in order to complete the observation. Originally, observations were **recorded** by hand, but with the advent of photography, astronomers could take photographs through telescopes. In the 1980s, new technology enabled telescopic images to be recorded digitally. Digital cameras can be mounted on any type of telescope, and this type of digital photography is called astrophotography.

3 There are currently three types of telescopes in use—optical, radio, and X-ray and Gamma Ray. The most common type, the optical, can be **refracting**, **reflecting**, or **catadioptric**, differentiated by the types of lenses and mirrors they use. Refracting telescopes use a **convex** lens to bend light and bring it into focus. The lens is thicker in the center and thinner on the edges, so that light at the edges is bent more than the light coming through the center. All of the light **converges** at a focus point where the image is projected. The **concave** eyepiece lens, or **diverging** lens, curves inward and magnifies the image so that it spreads across the human retina to create a larger image than possible with just the human eye. Reflecting telescopes were developed by Isaac Newton. They use a

▲ replica of Newton's second reflecting telescope

247

concave mirror to reflect the light to the eyepiece lens. Mirrors do not split the light into colors like glass does, and so they do not have the problem of different wavelengths of light creating halo effects around images. Catadiotropic telescopes are hybrid telescopes that use both lenses and mirrors. A lens corrects any defects in the mirror image; thus, the mirror can be smaller, which allows for an overall smaller telescope.

4 Radio and X-ray telescopes were developed to observe objects that don't emit or reflect enough light to be captured by an optical telescope. These telescopes pick up invisible waves which are not **distorted** by the Earth's atmosphere, as light can be. Currently, researchers are working to move beyond using different kinds of radiation for imaging. For instance, telescopes may be able to search for gravitational waves.

▲ Radio telescopes were developed to observe non-light emitting or reflecting objects.

5 Another type of telescope that escapes the distorting effects of the Earth's atmosphere is the space telescope. These telescopes were first proposed in the 1940s, but the technology and funding to develop them was not available until decades later. From the early 1960s to the early 1980s, NASA launched **orbiting** observatories to study the sun, discover new sources of infrared radiation, and detect other space objects such as comets. In the mid-1980s, NASA developed the Great Observatories plan, which has so far placed four space telescopes into orbit. The Compton Gamma Ray Observatory was de-orbited in 2000, but the others—Hubble, the Chandra X-ray observatory, and the Spitzer Space Telescope—are still in orbit.

6 The most famous of the Great Observatories telescopes is the Hubble Telescope, named for 1920s American astronomer Edwin P. Hubble. The Hubble, launched in 1990, is a reflecting telescope with a mirror 240 centimeters in diameter; it can observe objects 100 times **faint**er than any telescopes located on Earth. For example, the Hubble telescope has revealed numerous **galaxies**, some over 10 billion light-years away. Because the Hubble is not looking through the Earth's atmosphere, it can observe **ultraviolet** light and infrared light—ultraviolet light emits from the formation of disks around black holes and exploding stars, while infrared light emits from events such as dust clouds forming around new stars. The Hubble is operated cooperatively by NASA and the European Space Agency (ESA), and is guided to points of observation by radio commands from NASA. Computer-driven instruments on the Hubble record the observations, which are transmitted by radio to researchers on the ground.

The Great Observatories

◀ The Hubble Space Telescope: the most famous

◀ The Compton Gamma Ray Observatory: deorbited in 2000

◀ The Chandra X-Ray Observatory

◀ The Spitzer Space Telescope: launched in 2003

7 In the second decade of the 21st century, NASA expects to launch the James Webb Space Telescope (JWST), which will contain a mirror 6.4 meters in diameter, over seven times the light-collecting area of the Hubble. Scientists hope that with future telescopes, the resolution of the images will be fine enough to observe extrasolar planets, black holes, and stars in the **arms** of galaxies with enough distinction to determine how the galaxies evolved.

TARGET WORD EXERCISES

A Match the target words with the correct definitions below.

reflect	concave	arm	eyepiece	orbit
galaxies	distort	magnify	convex	record
optical	faint	diverging	refract	

(_____) 1 relating to or using visible light

(_____) 2 to set down for preservation in writing or other permanent form

(_____) 3 to alter the shape of something

(_____) 4 the lens in a microscope, telescope, etc., into which the person using it looks

(_____) 5 curving outward, like the outer boundary of a circle or sphere

(_____) 6 to turn or bend any wave, such as a light or sound wave, when it passes from one medium into another of different optical density

(_____) 7 lacking brightness, clarity or distinctness

(_____) 8 tending to move apart in different directions

(_____) 9 to increase the apparent size of, especially by means of a lens

(_____) 10 numerous large-scale collections of stars, gas, and dust that make up the visible universe

(_____) 11 curved inward, like the inside of a circle or sphere

(_____) 12 to throw or bend back (light, heat, sound) from a surface

(_____) 13 the path of a celestial body or an artificial satellite as it revolves around another body

(_____) 14 something resembling a human limb in appearance or function

B Telescope is made from **tele** (*distance*) + **scope** (*to see*). Tele- has been paired with many words to name technological devices and processes. Match the root words listed below with tele- to create such words.

-photo	-graph	-gram	-conference
-phone	-vision	-thermometer	-metry

(_____) 1 a system for transmitting speech or computerized information over distances with a transmitter, receiver, and dialing mechanism

(_____) 2 the system or process of producing a moving image with accompanying sound on a distant screen

(_____) 3 an apparatus or system that converts a coded message into electric impulses and sends it to a distant receiver, originally in Morse code signals but now computers, radio and microwave signals, satellites, and lasers are used

(_____) 4 a message transmitted by telegraph

(_____) 5 of or relating to an instrument that electrically transmits photographs

(_____) 6 an apparatus for determining the temperature of a distant point, as by a thermoelectric circuit or otherwise

(_____) 7 a conference between persons remote from one another but linked by a telecommunications system

(_____) 8 the automatic measurement and transmission of data by wire, radio, or other means from remote sources, such as from space vehicles, to receiving stations for recording and analysis

C Replace the **synonym** with the correct target word and identify what part of speech it is.

1 Researchers **write down** observations.
   ↳ [_____] part of speech: [_____]

2 Militaries **supply** their soldiers with weapons.
   ↳ [_____] part of speech: [_____]

3 Earth follows a(n) **flight path** around the sun.
   ↳ [_____] part of speech: [_____]

4 The astronomer saw a **dim** light of a distant galaxy.
   ↳ [_____] part of speech: [_____]

5 New space telescopes are equipped with an outer layer than can **throw back** the sun's rays without being heated.
   ↳ [_____] part of speech: [_____]

Unit 14
Chapter 40
Spacecraft Systems

🎧 79 ❶ Since the mid-20th century, nearly 7,000 **spacecraft** have been launched for scientific, commercial, and military purposes. The majority of all spacecraft were sponsored and launched by either Russia or the United States, although other countries, such as Japan, China, and Israel, have also launched spacecraft in the 21st century. Nearly half of all spacecraft are communication or surveillance satellites, with only about 10 percent used for scientific purposes. Less than 10 percent of spacecraft have been piloted craft.

❷ The term spacecraft is applied to any vehicle designed for space travel. Various terms are used to describe spacecraft according to their specific missions, such as **probes** that explore other planets and bodies, and satellites, which may orbit **celestial** bodies for research or communication. Spacecraft demand **precise** engineering in order to survive and endure in the harsh environment of space. Also, once a spacecraft is in orbit, engineers have very few ways to carry out repairs.

▲ More than 100 Russian Soyuz manned spacecraft have flown since 1967.

▲ space probes on display in a museum

▲ space satellite

252

▲ Dr. Robert Hutchings Goddard (1882-1945), known as "Father of the Space Age"

3 Spacecraft are **propelled** into space by reaction engines. Liquid fuel is combined with an oxidizer, such as liquid oxygen, in a combustion chamber and burned into a high-pressure gas. The reaction engines then force this gas out the back of the spacecraft, at speeds of 5,000 to 10,000 miles per hour, forcing or **thrusting** the vehicle forward.

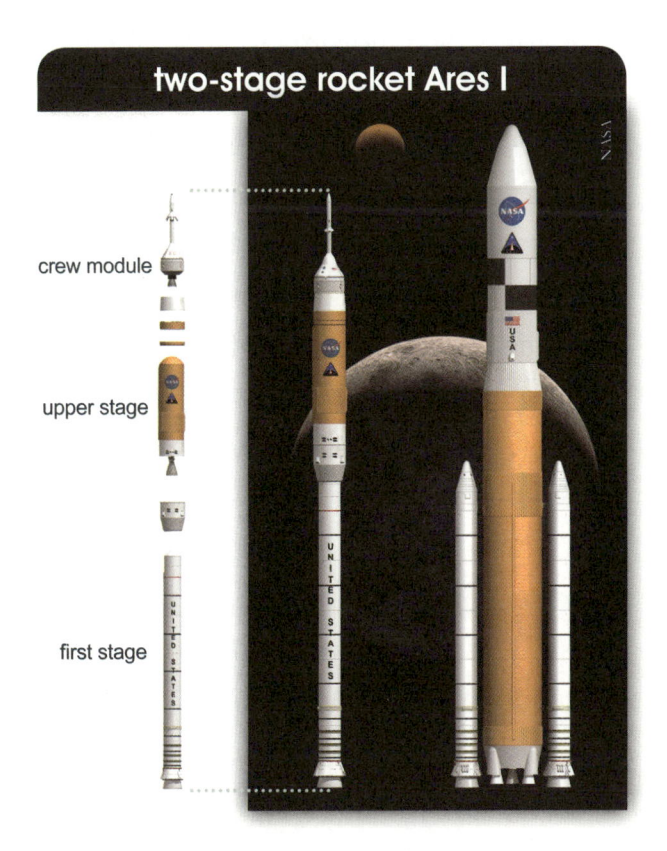

4 Spacecraft must be propelled by enough thrust to escape the gravitational pull of the Earth. One problem that scientists face is the weight of the vehicle itself, because the heavier the vehicle is, the more fuel is needed to thrust the vehicle out of the Earth's atmosphere, but this makes the vehicle even heavier. Robert Goddard, known as the "Father of the Space Age," provided a solution to this problem with his suggestion of multi-**stage** rockets. A spacecraft could be made with several rockets that are discarded once the fuel is finished in each one, requiring less and less fuel throughout the spacecraft's journey. Modern rockets usually have two or three rockets or stages.

two-stage rocket Ares I

- crew module
- upper stage
- first stage

1

▲ rover spacecraft *Sojourner* examining a Martian rock

2

▲ *Voyager 1* is a flyby spacecraft.

3

Galileo arriving at Jupiter

Galileo launching

Galileo with its main antenna open

▲ *Galileo* is an orbiter spacecraft.

4

◀ Apollo 13 is a piloted spacecraft.

5 The systems and instruments a spacecraft must carry depend upon the data it will gather and the functions it will carry out.

- **Atmospheric** probes or balloon packages are sent into an object's atmosphere to study gasses and winds.
- Lander, surface penetrators, and rovers are **deployed** to study the surface of a celestial body to **retrieve** information. Some craft take images and do soil analysis, while others **penetrate** below the surface to study terrestrial properties.
- Flyby spacecraft carry instruments that capture images and information while passing by a **target**, allowing for the target's own movement. An example of a flyby spacecraft is *Voyager 1* or *2*.
- Orbiter spacecraft decelerate at precisely the right moment so that they are pulled into an object's orbit, a process called retroburning or aerobraking, in order to gather information. The *Magellan* and *Galileo* craft are examples of orbiters.
- **Piloted** spacecraft are designed to carry humans, and they contain **crew** compartments and life support systems. They might also contain lander modules. Many of NASA's Apollo missions were piloted spacecraft.

6 All spacecraft consist of a number of subsystems which are necessary for their power, data gathering, and transmission. Power systems, such as batteries, fuel cells, and **Radioisotope** Thermoelectric Generators (RTG) or nuclear reactors, produce electricity for other systems and instruments. **Propulsion** systems are engines for thrust into orbit, for **stability** in orbit, and for **maneuvering** through space. Environmental systems protect the vehicle from the harsh environment of space. Passive systems, such as paint and reflectors, assist cooling processes, and active heating systems maintain minimum temperatures. **Shielding** protects the craft from dangerous particles.

7 In addition, **orientation** (compass position) or **attitude** (position relative to other objects) systems stabilize and control the movement of the spacecraft for accurate collection and interpretation of data. Thrusters or wheels can be used to move or rotate the vehicle, and computers manage the tracking and sensing of planets and other bodies. Science instruments detect and measure data from objects. Direct-sensing instruments measure composition or energy of objects, and remote-sensing instruments gather images or radiation information from objects. Data and telecommunications systems collect, process, and format data, which is then transmitted to Earth through computers or antennae.

8 Improved engine designs, along with radical changes such as the use of solar sails and nuclear power, will soon make space flight more feasible, perhaps even as a commercial **venture**. Space tourism, including space hotels and space sports, may soon exist. Humans may even be able to live in space for extended periods of time. Space vehicles will be designed to transport goods and passengers, as well as carrying out scientific and educational research. Future spacecraft may also be able to tap into additional energy resources, particularly solar energy.

> **Note**
> The accepted plural of spacecraft is "spacecraft." However, in the past few years, the use of "spacecrafts" has become more common, but not in research or scientific communication.

TARGET WORD EXERCISES

A Match the target words with the correct definitions.

a probe	e thrust	i retrieve
b target	f pilot	j attitude
c precise	g stage	
d crew	h stability	

(_____) 1 one of two or more successive propulsion units of a rocket vehicle that fires after the preceding one has been cast off

(_____) 2 something aimed or fired at

(_____) 3 the orientation of a spacecraft relative to other objects

(_____) 4 the forward-directed force developed in a jet or rocket engine as a reaction to the high-velocity rearward ejection of exhaust gases

(_____) 5 a spacecraft carrying instruments intended for use in exploration of the physical properties of outer space or celestial bodies other than Earth

(_____) 6 to find and carry or send back

(_____) 7 exact, as in performance, execution, or amount; accurate or correct

(_____) 8 to steer or control the course of

(_____) 9 a group of people working together on a project or task

(_____) 10 the ability of an object, such as a ship or aircraft, to maintain equilibrium or resume its original, upright position after displacement

B Place the correct target word in each sentence, using the italicized synonyms as clues.

1. The vehicle was *pushed into* space because the engines _____ the vehicle forward.
2. Each *part* of the rocket came off when the fuel was depleted, and this left one less _____ of the rocket each time.
3. Engineers have to be very *exact* about how they build a spacecraft, because _____ calculations prevent any vehicle defects or damages.
4. Some spacecraft *put* a lander craft *into* use to analyze soil on a planet, and some spacecraft _____ probes to take images of an object in space.
5. Surface rovers do not *break through* the soil to get information, but other types of spacecraft are designed to _____ the surface to get sub-surface information.
6. Scientists carefully calculate the *aim* of a spacecraft well before its launch so that it has the greatest chance to reach and study its _____.
7. Computers often *guide* a spacecraft, but sometimes humans can _____ a craft to specific points of observation.
8. Some materials are designed to *protect* a spacecraft from debris, and other materials help to _____ the craft from radiation.
9. New NASA spacecraft have *drills* that investigate the dust of the moon and _____ to search the moon's surface for hidden water ice.

C Match the target words with the descriptions.

| celestial | atmospheric | attitude | propulsion | orientation |

(_____) 1 I am the driving force that thrusts a spacecraft into space.
(_____) 2 My pressure can cause human fluids to boil.
(_____) 3 I am the position of a spacecraft relative to the points of a compass.
(_____) 4 My bodies are heavenly.
(_____) 5 Space such as gravity

Unit 14
Chapter 41

Emerging Space Technologies

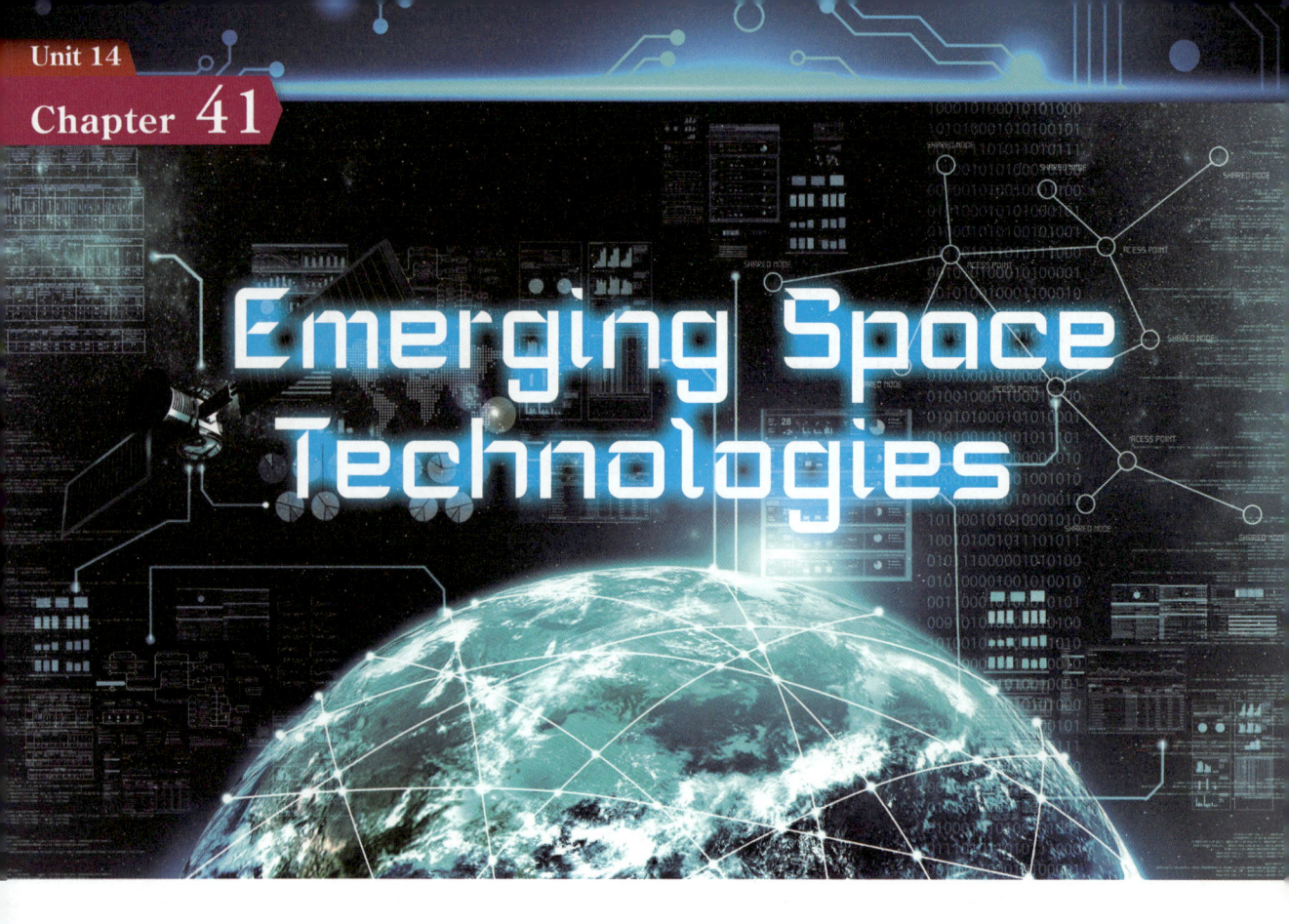

① For over 50 years, humans have been exploring space, deriving many benefits. In the 21st century, cutting edge, or emerging space technologies make space exploration more relevant and available to the global community than ever before.

② Experiments with **inflatable spacecraft** began in the 1960s, and inflatable craft launched in the 21st century are proving to be cheaper and more efficient than their conventional materials **counterparts**. Inflatable craft are **stored** in small containers on a rocket, which is equipped with **canisters** of inert gas. Once in space, the gas is deployed into the inflatable craft, inflating it to a full size of over 100 cubic meters. If the inflatable craft demonstrate long-term durability and a sustainable environment, they will open opportunities for private space stations and commercial space travel.

▲ inflatable space habitat

3 Commercial space travel might also take place on space planes. Over one hundred X-planes, planes built specifically for research purposes, have flown in the U.S. space program. New planes are being developed that can carry their own fuel, eliminating the need for rocket **boosters**.

▲ space plane (cc by D. Ramey Logan)

Also, they will be able to achieve speeds up to MACH 25, the speed necessary to orbit Earth. These planes also are equipped with reusable **launch** vehicle (RLV) technology, which makes them more cost efficient and capable of replacing the space **shuttle**. Ultimately, space planes will carry both **payloads** and tourists. In addition, both Japan and the European Space Agency have created space trucks, which will carry supplies and **dock** with international space stations.

4 New advanced spacecraft materials, made of **polymer** composites (such as carbon or Kevlar) and bubbles of a healing agent, can heal themselves. When the materials suffer tiny cracks in the harsh space environment, a **catalyst** is released that prompts the healing agent into action, **sealing** the microcracks. The internal wiring of a spacecraft will also be **self-repairing**; maintenance and management computer systems will detect, diagnose, and correct abnormalities in spacecraft systems.

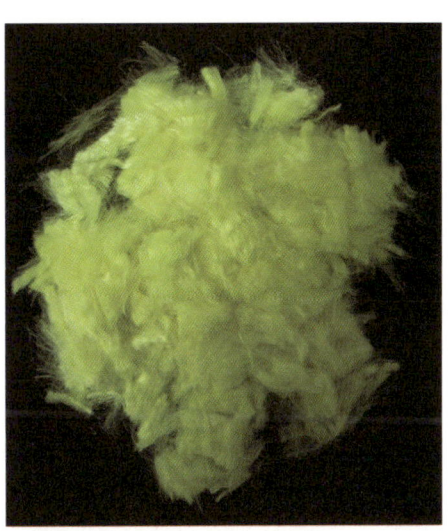

▲ Kevlar is a popular spacecraft shielding material. (cc by Cjp24)

5 Space **sail**s have the potential for **propellant**-free space flight. Using solar power, space sails will accelerate craft at several times the speed of conventional spacecraft. Sails made of carbon fibers seem most able to withstand intense heat from the sun.

▲ space sail

Unit 14 Chapter 41 Emerging Space Technologies

🎧 82 ⑥ Space elevators are being designed that would use a nanotube composite **ribbon**. Mechanical lifters or laser beams would move a spacecraft into and back down from space using the ribbon. Space elevators could move cargo and humans at a fraction of the cost of conventional spacecraft.

⑦ Spacecraft currently is powered by propulsion systems that have changed relatively little in the history of space flight. However, in the future, several different types of **propulsion** will be possible.

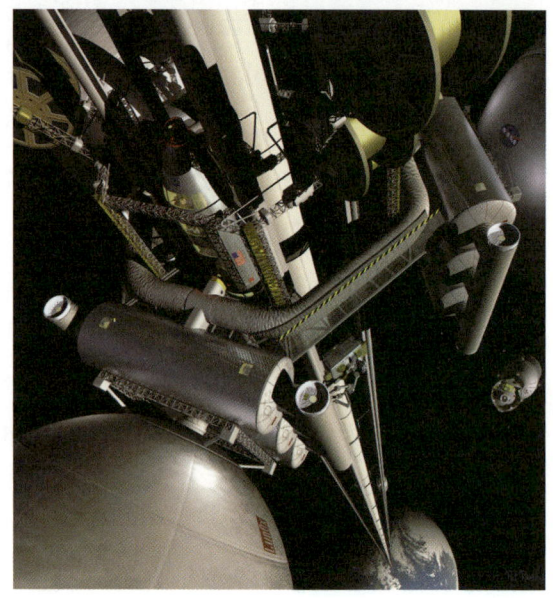

▲ artist's drawing of a space elevator from a space station to Earth

- Electric systems use electric power sources to produce an ionized gas or **plasma** into fuel. **Electrostatic**, electromagnetic, and electrothermal mechanisms produce a higher specific impulse than chemical mechanisms, which means that they thrust more fuel faster from the back of a rocket engine, increasing spacecraft speed and fuel efficiency.
- Light propulsion uses mirrors to focus laser beams that heat air until it **explodes** and propels the spacecraft forward. **Lightcraft** will weigh much less than conventional craft, travel many times faster, use significantly less fuel, and produce zero emissions.
- **Air-breathing** rockets take air from the atmosphere and combine it with hydrogen fuel in order to propel the flight into orbit. Air cannot provide enough thrust, so **air-augmented** rockets would thrust the spacecraft forward, and then the air-breathing rockets would take over and propel the craft into space. To achieve orbit, conventional engines would still be used to provide the necessary power.
- Antimatter spacecraft may be just decades from use. When antimatter and matter collide, 100 percent of the mass of both is converted into

260

energy, which is billions of times more powerful than any type of chemical combustion. Because antimatter is not available in amounts equal to matter, it must be created. When scientists can create enough antimatter, it will be the most efficient propulsion system available, even more powerful than nuclear fusion or fission.

8 Human life sciences will continue to benefit from space exploration. Future space technology will inform improvements in biotechnology, including more precise diagnostic and monitoring techniques for patients. Human implants, such as cochlea and heart devices will be **self-healing**. Transportation benefits include improved energy efficiency and navigation technologies such as global positioning systems. Space technology continues to shape effective management of the Earth's resources, such as forests and water. And, from improved athletic shoes to more aerodynamic golf balls, recreation also benefits from space technology. The **investment** in space science has been quite **minute** in relation to its global benefits, and the future investments promise only greater **returns**.

▶ GPS navigation device

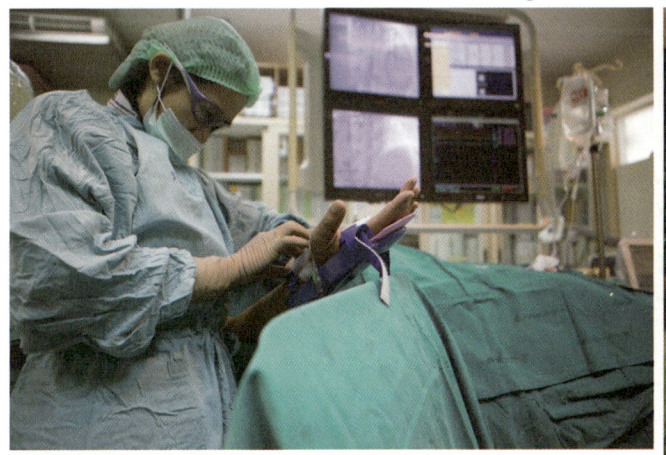

▲ Future space technology will inform improvements in biotechnology, including more precise diagnostic and monitoring techniques for patients.

▲ From improved athletic shoes to more aerodynamic golf balls, recreation also benefits from space technology.

TARGET WORD EXERCISES

A
Use the words and definitions below to create the compound target words. Be sure to include hyphens when necessary.

breathing	pay	light	self
craft	air	repairing	craft
load	healing	augmented	part
self	counter	air	space

1. region beyond Earth's atmosphere + vehicle = _____
2. the atmosphere + act of respiration = _____
3. one's own being + restoring to health = _____
4. revenue + cargo = _____
5. the atmosphere + to make greater in size, extent, or quantity = _____
6. electromagnetic radiation of any wavelength + vehicle = _____
7. one's own being + restoring to sound condition after damage or injury; fixing = _____
8. one that is an opposite + a piece, component, or segment of a whole = _____

B
Match the target word to its definition.

canister	booster	launch	dock	sail
explode	seal	store	minute	

(_____) 1. to reserve or put away for future use
(_____) 2. very small; tiny
(_____) 3. to close or secure tightly so as to make airtight or watertight
(_____) 4. a large piece of strong material used to catch the wind and propel a vessel
(_____) 5. a usually cylindrical storage container
(_____) 6. to set or thrust (a self-propelled craft or projectile) in motion
(_____) 7. a device for increasing power or effectiveness
(_____) 8. to join vehicles together in outer space
(_____) 9. to burst with great violence; blow up

C. Add at least one of the prefixes, suffixes, and/or combining words listed below to the following root words to create a target word. Then use each target word correctly in the following sentences.

Prefixes/Suffixes	Root Words
-ble	a. flatus (to blow into)
poly-	b. canne (reed, cane)
-ment	c. meros (a part)
in-	d. plassien (to form)
-ster	e. riban (ring or band)
-on	f. augere (to increase)
re-	g. vestire (to clothe)
-a	h. turnen (to spin or turn on a lathe)

1. The use of ionized gas or _____ in spacecraft means that about 99 percent of the matter of the universe could be used for spacecraft propulsion.

2. Advances in health and medicine are just a few examples of the high yield _____ on the investment into space science.

3. Composites of high molecular weight or _____ have enough strength to survive many of the harsh elements of space.

4. Besides spacecraft that can be filled with air, someday there will be _____ space hotels.

5. Space exploration is a worthwhile _____ for the global community because it has yielded many discoveries as well as international cooperation.

6. As the spacecraft thrust forward, a broad _____ of smoke curled out from the back of the engines.

7. Virtual technology is now added to the training of astronauts to _____ conventional techniques.

8. Space stations have _____s for storing energy, oxygen, and other supplies.

263

Chapter 42

Humans are naturally **diurnal** beings, meaning that we are active during the day and sleep during the darkness of night. Because human beings rely heavily on the sense of sight, we have difficulty functioning in the darkness, unlike other animals that can **navigate** by hearing or smell. In order to **maneuver** at night, then, human beings have utilized various forms of light, ranging from the natural light of fire to various artificial forms of illumination. As industrial civilization advanced, so the need for artificial light increased, and sources were created for both exterior and interior lighting. Beyond the light that humans needed for work and safe movement, lighting was developed for streetlights, advertising, commercial areas, such as restaurants and parks, and even sports. Much of this lighting is excessive and **obtrusive** in the natural environment, and over the past few decades it has come to be considered a form of pollution called light pollution.

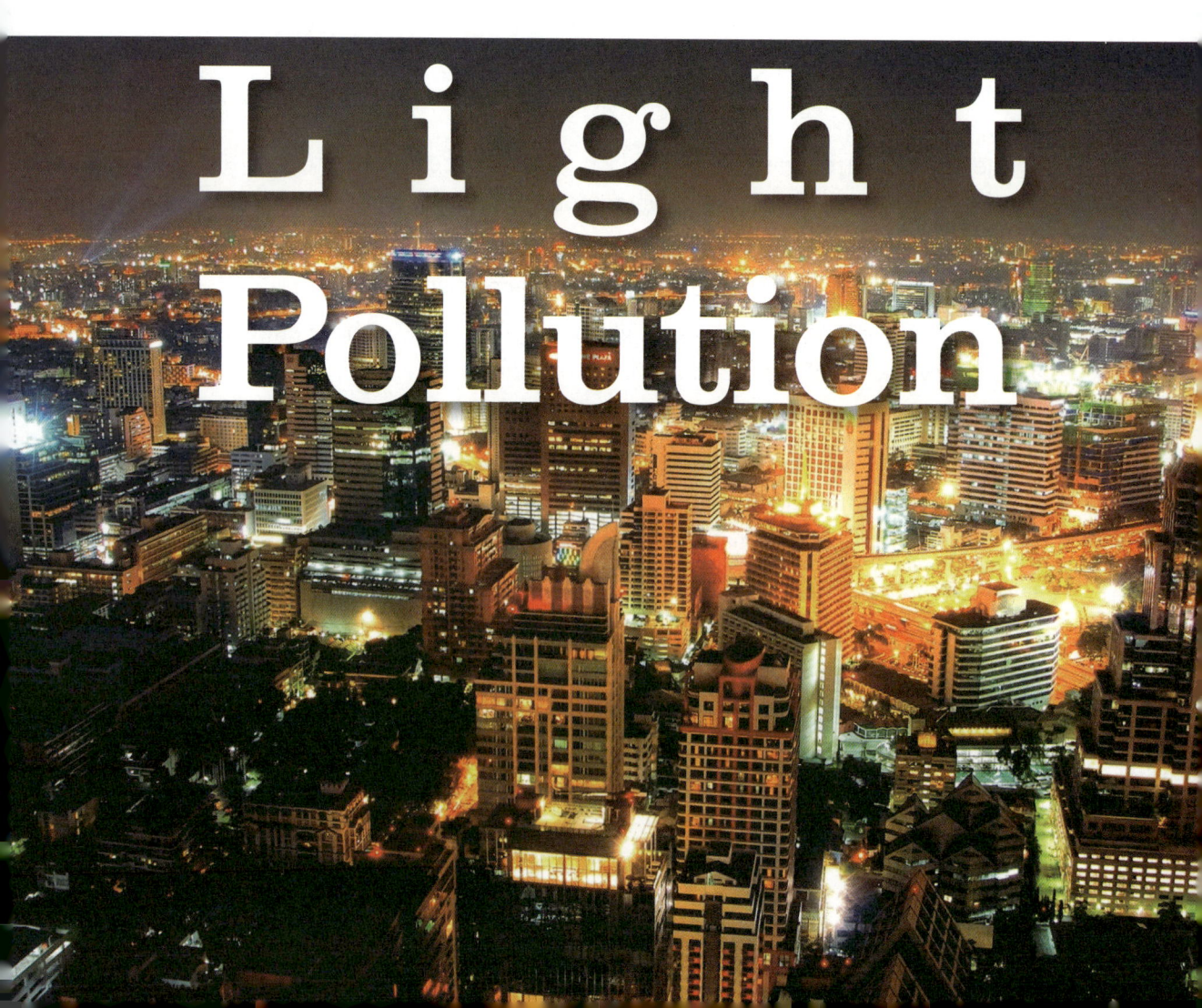

Light Pollution

2. Light pollution is also known as **luminous** pollution or photopollution, and is generally characterized in two ways:
- **excessive** light, which is generally indoor light that produces **discomfort** and possibly adverse health effects, especially in the workplace. Effects on the human body include fatigue, headaches, physical stresses that can lead to increased cancer risks, and psychological stresses that can lead to depression.
- stray light that **intrudes** into natural settings. Much of this light is emitted from poorly designed lighting sources, such as security or streetlights. Some of the stray light is reflected light from illuminated areas, but much of it is light that shines beyond its intended area. Stray lighting causes direct **glare**, light-**trespass** and skyglow. Not only does stray light dim the night sky and **obscures** other planets or stars, it also wastes energy and contributes to greenhouse emissions in several ways.
  - Direct glare is the visual discomfort caused by excessive or insufficiently shielded light sources. There are two types of direct glare: disability glare, caused by intense light sources, reduces visibility in the immediate field of view; discomfort glare, which is a **nuisance** or even painful adverse effect of intense light. Sensitivity to light varies greatly, although it generally affects more often

▲ aerial view of Paris at night

▲ A comparison of the night sky in a rural are (top) and a metropolitan area (bottom). Light pollution reduces the visibility of stars. (cc by Jeremy Stanley)

▲ Light trespass occurs when unwanted light enters one's property.

▲ In pristine areas clouds appear black and blot out the stars. In urban areas skyglow is strongly enhanced by clouds. (cc by Christopher Kyba and Ray Stinson)

265

older people who experience aging characteristics of the eye.
- ▸ Light trespass occurs when light spills into areas that don't need or want the light. For example, a streetlight might flood a neighboring home with light, illuminating an unintended indoor area.
- ▸ **Skyglow** results from both natural and human created sources. An example of natural skyglow is sunlight reflected off of Earth and its Moon. Human created skyglow comes most commonly from streetlights, outdoor advertising lights, and home security lighting. Skyglow varies depending upon weather condition; in **inclement** weather conditions, increased atmospheric particles **scatter** the light so that the wasted light and energy create a brighter glow.

▲ One example of human created skyglow is outdoor advertising lights.

3 Because light is a significant biological force, all species are affected by it to a certain degree.
- Seabirds attracted by search lights or oil rig platform lights sometimes circle the lights until they die from exhaustion.
- Insects that are drawn in clusters to streetlights become easy prey for animals such as bats.

▲ The migration and breeding cycles of birds and sea turtles are greatly affected by light pullution.

- Some birds have **fatal**ly **collided** with structures that emit bright lights.
- Various cycles of some birds' lives have been disrupted or altered by artificial light. Singing birds sing at unnatural hours; migration and breeding cycles occur too early, so that nesting conditions are adversely affected.

- Breeding and **nesting** of sea turtles, frogs, and toads are affected by artificial beach lighting, leading to increased hatchling losses.

④ A variety of responses to light pollution are now underway. In the United States, many states have passed legislation limiting light levels, placing **curfews** on public and private outdoor lighting, and requiring high efficiency lighting sources. In 2009, the International Year of Astronomy, one of the 11 Global Cornerstone Projects is called "Dark Skies Awareness." The project includes various international programs planned to better educate the public about light pollution and its adverse effects. "Dark Skies Awareness" also involves global citizens who participate in various activities to measure light pollution, count visible **celestial** bodies, and promote dark skies awareness in their communities. Some of the permanent contributions of the program are the establishment of dark sky parks and reserves. Also, dark locations will be designed for public education about light pollution.

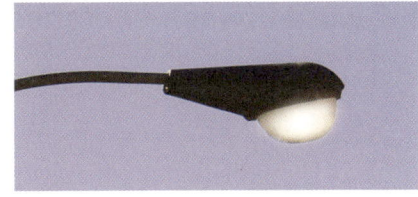

▲ Less efficient lighting allows light into unintended areas.

▲ high efficiency lighting with a full lamp shade

⑤ Many solutions to light pollution are relatively simple, such as using high efficiency lighting or redirecting light sources. However, only through **heightened** public awareness will the problem of light pollution be permanently mitigated.

TARGET WORD EXERCISES

A Choose the correct target word that is a synonym for the bolded word in each sentence below.

(____) 1 The haze caused the plane difficulty as it tried to **find its way** through the night sky.
   a. navigate   b. scatter   c. intrude

(____) 2 Humans find it difficult to **move** through neighborhood streets in complete darkness.
   a. trespass   b. collide   c. maneuver

(____) 3 Poor weather conditions can **distribute** the particles of light from overly bright advertising signs.
   a. heighten   b. scatter   c. maneuver

(____) 4 Street lights that shine into a house are often a **bother** to the occupants.
   a. nuisance   b. nesting   c. curfew

(____) 5 Overly bright light sources often disorient birds and have **deadly** consequences.
   a. nuisance   b. excessive   c. fatal

(____) 6 Light pollution has been known to cause marine birds to **strike** (with) lighthouses.
   a. scatter   b. maneuver   c. collide

(____) 7 Some states have set **legal order** start times for street lights in order to prevent light pollution.
   a. curfew   b. trespass   c. inclement

(____) 8 Light pollution can alter how sea turtles choose **breeding ground** sites.
   a. diurnal   b. obtrusive   c. nesting

(____) 9 One of the main goals of the Dark Skies Awareness project is to **increase** citizens' understanding of the causes of light pollution.
   a. navigate   b. heighten   c. intrude

(____) 10 **Too much** light pollution can affect human sleep and immune systems.
   a. Excessive   b. Luminous   c. Fatal

(____) 11 In some urban areas, the night sky is barely visible during periods of **poor** weather.
   a. excessive   b. obtrusive   c. inclement

(____) 12 Misdirected light can **encroach** into houses and disturb occupants' sleeping patterns.
   a. maneuver   b. intrude   c. navigate

(____) 13 Direct glare can disrupt a person's work and cause psychological **distress**.
   a. discomfort   b. trespass   c. nesting

(____) 14 Light pollution adversely affects the **daytime** activities of human beings, causing health and emotional distress.
   a. inclement   b. diurnal   c. curfew

B Match the target words (in bold) to their correct meanings. Then, add a **prefix** and/or **suffix** to the root words in the target words to make a new word. Use the definitions given as clues.

noct-	in-	pro-
having to do with night	into, within	located in front of, projecting

un-	il-	-able	com-
not	more	capable of	with, together, jointly

a. active during the day
b. reflecting or giving off light
c. to put or force in inappropriately
d. undesirably noticeable
e. entry to another's property without right or permission
f. the state of being tense and feeling pain

( ) 1 **diurnal** ➡ _____urnal: most active at night
( ) 2 **obtrusive** ➡ _____trusive: thrusting inward
( ) 3 **luminous** ➡ _____lumine: to brighten
( ) 4 **discomfort** ➡ _____comfort_____: causing irritation or pain
( ) 5 **trespass** ➡ _____pass: to encircle, to travel around
( ) 6 **intrude** ➡ _____trude: to stick out or project

C With the following words, correctly form **compound words** found in the article, and match them with their definitions.

sea	stone
light	glow
pollution	
street	under
bird	way
sky	photo
trespass	
light	corner

(_____) 1 fundamental basis, premise, key
(_____) 2 the spill of unwanted light into another space
(_____) 3 glowing effect seen in the skies, produced by overly bright outdoor light sources
(_____) 4 a bird that frequents coastal waters and the open ocean
(_____) 5 artificial light that has adverse effects on various life forms
(_____) 6 a lamp supported on a lamppost and used for illuminating a street
(_____) 7 currently in progress

Unit 15
Chapter 43

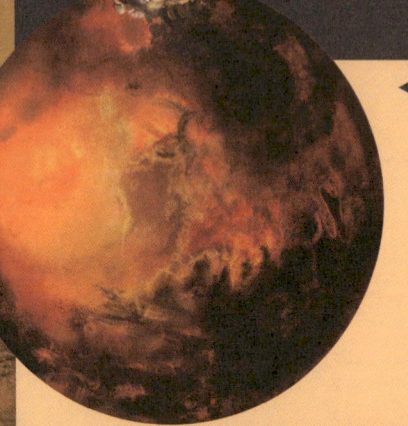

MARS

◀ Mars is commonly called the Red Planet.

▲ Mars compared to Earth

▲ Mars is the fourth planet from the sun; Earth is the third.

▲ the rocky surface of Mars

Mars is a neighboring planet of Earth, the fourth planet from the Sun, and the first planet explored by humans. It was given its name by the Romans to honor their god of war. Mars is also commonly called the Red Planet, because when viewed from the Earth, its soil and sky have a reddish-orange **hue**. Early observations of Mars revealed an **uneven** surface, polar **cap**s that undergo seasonal changes, and a dense enough atmosphere to support clouds and winds, all aspects that led some to believe intelligent beings existed on the planet. Although this belief **spawned** volumes of science fiction, it has not yet been supported by scientific evidence.

270

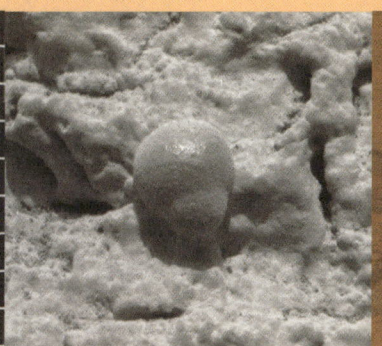

▲ picture of a crater on Mars taken by Mariner 4

▲ photomicrograph taken by *Opportunity* showing a gray hematite concretion, indicative of the past presence of liquid water

▲ silica-rich dust on Mars

2 In 1965, the U.S. sent the **flyby** spacecraft, Mariner 4, to capture close range photos of Mars, which revealed only naturally occurring surface **formations**, such as **craters**. Within the next decade, the U.S. launched several **orbiter** spacecraft to photograph and map Mars, and they revealed dry **riverbeds**, volcanoes, and **canyons**. More recent missions to Mars, undertaken by several countries, involved **landers** and **probes** that analyzed rock and soil samples, which indicate the presence of liquid water at some point in Mars' evolution; these missions have also discovered a vast amount of water ice.

3 Mars formed approximately 4 and a half billion years ago. Because space probes have been unable to return rock and soil samples to Earth, scientists can only estimate the evolutionary periods of Mars and their relative length of time. Mars most likely has undergone three evolutionary periods: the Noachian, the Hesperian, and the Amazonian, each named for surface characteristics that developed in the particular period. In the Noachian period, **valley** networks were created by water erosion, and

▲ the Martian north polar cap (1999)

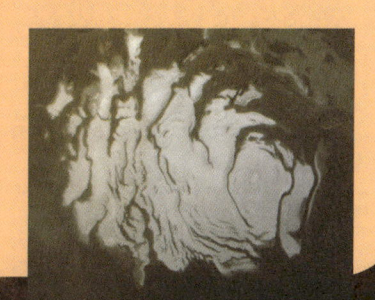

▲ the south polar cap of Mars (2000)

Unit 15 Chapter 43 Mars

there is evidence of extensive volcanic activity. In the Hesperian period, volcanic activity formed most of the **channels** on the planet. In the Amazonian period, the largest volcanoes were formed, as well as the polar ice caps.

4   Unlike Earth, Mars' atmosphere has a relatively small amount of oxygen, less than 1 percent, and over 95 percent carbon dioxide. Very little water exists in the atmosphere of Mars, but enough moisture is present to **condense** into clouds or **fog**. Some clouds at the poles, formed from carbon dioxide ice crystals, influence the general circulation of air on Mars. CO_2 flows toward the poles in winter, and when the CO_2 **evaporates** in the spring, the gases move away from the poles. Surface winds on Mars are seldom forceful, because the atmosphere is much less dense than Earth's. Typical temperatures on Mars range from 20°C to -140°C, depending on the season.

▲ the atmosphere of Mars

5   Although no probe has gone very deep below the surface of Mars, scientists believe that the planet consists of three basic layers—crust, **mantle**, and core. The crust is about 30 miles thick; the mantle consists of rock very similar to Earth's, and is probably heated similarly by radioactive decay; the core, differing from Earth's partially molten center, is most likely solid. Mars is also only about 70 percent of the density of Earth, and therefore only has less than 40 percent of Earth's gravitational force.

6   Much of Mars' surface resembles that of Earth, except for **impact craters**, evidence of many **meteorites** that have struck Mars over the years. Impact **basins** are also prevalent on Mars in the form of valley networks, channels, and small **gullies**. These geographic features indicate that at some point Mars must have had a more moderate temperature that allowed for the presence of liquid

water. Mars also has the largest volcanoes in the solar system, probably formed by extensive lava eruptions. Some regions of Mars were most likely formed by **sediment** from flowing water, and these regions may be the flattest and smoothest in the solar system. Polar caps on Mars consist of water ice and dust, most likely deposited from the atmosphere over long periods of time. The water ice remains many miles thick throughout the year.

▲ glacial-like deposit on Mars

7 Mars has two minor satellites or moon, Phobos and Deimos, characterized by many craters. Phobos has a diameter of 27 kilometers and Deimos is roughly 15 kilometers across. The moons may have formed with the planet itself, or they may have been **asteroids** that Mars pulled into its orbit at some point.

8 Future missions to Mars will use subsurface explorers in order to gather and bring back atmospheric, rock

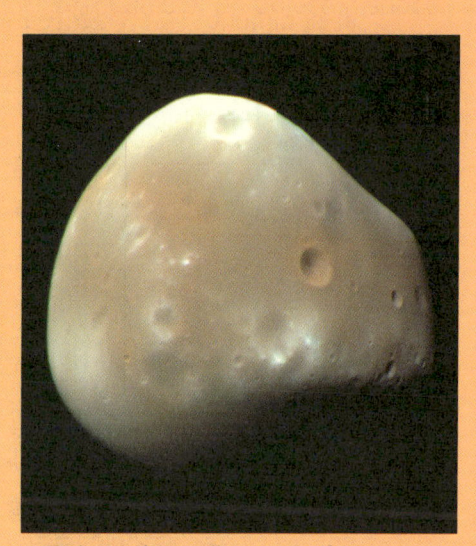

▲ Deimos, the smaller moon of Mars

and soil samples. Within the next decade, researchers plan to launch airplane and balloon flights in Mars atmosphere; these flights could access sharper images for longer periods of time than previous spacecraft. Also planned for the future are human spacecraft flights to Mars; NASA recently announced that it would try to put a human on Mars in 2035.

TARGET WORD EXERCISES

A Many of the target words describe geographic formations. Choose the correct answer for each question about geographic formations below.

(____) 1 Which of these is a bowl-shaped depression made by an explosion or the impact of a body, such as a meteoroid?
  a. mantle   b. crater   c. fog   d. uneven

(____) 2 Which of these is a channel occupied (or formerly occupied) by a river?
  a. riverbed   b. crater   c. hue   d. basin

(____) 3 Which of these is a long, deep, narrow valley with steep cliff walls, cut into the surface by running water?
  a. sediment   b. canyon   c. caps   d. channel

(____) 4 Which of these is a long, narrow region of low land between ranges of mountains, hills, or other high areas?
  a. crater   b. fog   c. basin   d. valley

(____) 5 Which of these is the bed of a stream or other way through which liquid can flow?
  a. channel   b. mantle   c. valley   d. circulation

(____) 6 Which of these is the layer of a planetary body between the crust and the core?
  a. basin   b. crater   c. mantle   d. gully

(____) 7 Which of these is a low-lying area, often bowl-shaped, on the surface in which thick layers of sediment have accumulated?
  a. basin   b. canyon   c. caps   d. impact

(____) 8 Which of these is a deep ditch or small valley originally worn away by running water?
  a. crater   b. caps   c. valley   d. gully

(____) 9 Which of these is material that has been deposited by water, ice, or wind?
  a. caps   b. fog   c. sediment   d. mantle

(____) 10 Which of these is a summit or top, as of a mountain?
  a. valley   b. cap   c. channel   d. riverbed

(____) 11 Which of these is a series of rocks or clouds of a particular structure or shape?
  a. canyon   b. gully   c. basin   d. formation

B **Place each target word in the correct sentence below.**

| spawn | uneven | condense | hue | impact | fog |

1. Gases _____ *(liquefy)* at the poles and influence the circulation of air on Mars.
2. Rumors of life on Mars helped to _____ *(produce)* a generation of science fiction movies about Martian aliens.
3. When the ice began to melt, it caused a thick _____ *(haze)* to hang over the highway.
4. The force of the _____ *(collision)* of meteorites on Mars may have thrown out debris to form a double crater.
5. The night sky before the storm had a reddish _____ *(color)*.
6. The flatter northern hemisphere of Mars stands in stark contrast to the _____ *(bumpy)* surfaces of its southern hemisphere.

C **Different types of space vehicles take their names from the task they perform. Match the type of vehicle with the description of its task.**

- probe
- orbiter
- flyby
- lander

(_____) 1 it *moves past* a planet or moon
(_____) 2 it *sets down or alights* on a planet or moon
(_____) 3 it *investigates or explores* a planet or moon
(_____) 4 it *moves in a trajectory or flight path* around a planet or moon

High Speed Penetrators

Space exploration since the 20th century has included numerous types of vehicles designed for observation tasks. Early missions employed space vehicles that captured photographs of moons and planets, and later missions involved spacecraft that engaged in surface exploration. Most recently, advances in space exploration technology are making possible the use of hard landing probes, or **surface penetrators**, to gather information about subsurface (**regolith**) **lunar** and planetary characteristics. Penetrators are missile-like **projectiles** which can be launched from rockets into the surface of various solar system bodies at a very high impact speed of 200-700 m/s. Some penetrators are referred to as micro-penetrators, because they are small and light, with a mass of only two to 13 kilograms.

All high speed penetrators can carry limited scientific instruments, including data-collecting systems and **sensors**. These technologies will be targeted to the specific celestial body under exploration:

- **Seismometer**: measures seismic waves that travel through the interior of a planetary body; it is used to detect presence of various elements and levels of **magnetism**.

- **Chemical Sensors**: detect water and organic chemistry with a micro-**sampling** tool (cameras).
  - *Descent Camera*: studies impact site
  - *Ground Camera/Microscope*: detects and **images** minerals and biological materials
  - *Wireless Camera Penetrators*: images surface or horizon characteristics; uses battery or solar power
- **Thermal Sensing**: detects surface and subsurface temperatures as well as how subsurface materials conduct heat. It may provide information about the interior composition of a celestial body.
- **Beeping transmitter and Magnetometer**: **detect** horizontal **crust**al shifts.
- **Radiation Monitor**: studies the subsurface radiation environment to determine possible placement of human bases and the **feasibility** of life.

3. A specific mission **architecture** (flight plan) is necessary to ensure that the penetrator precisely impacts its target and that the instrumentation remains intact.

- **Cruise Phase**: Penetrators are carried aboard a spacecraft that provides power and communications support.

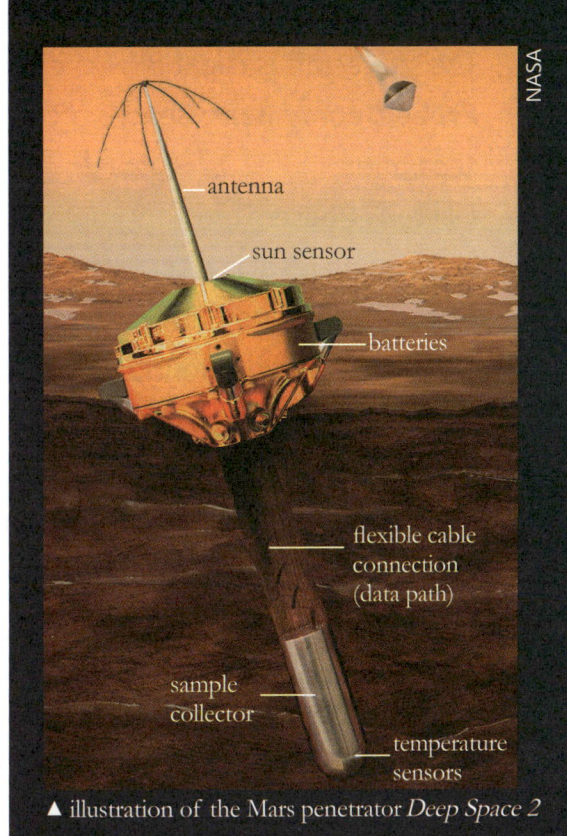

▲ illustration of the Mars penetrator *Deep Space 2*

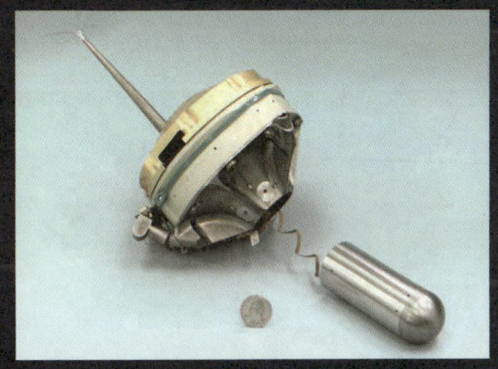

▲ *Deep Space 2* penetrator

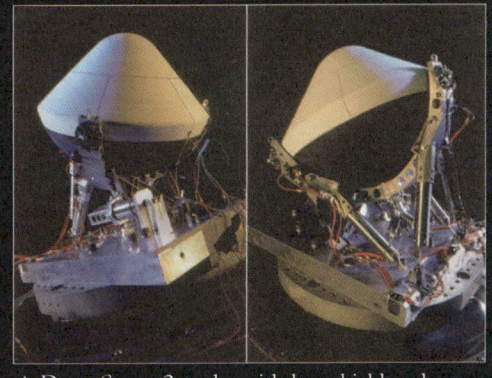

▲ *Deep Space 2* probe with heatshield and mounting

Unit 15 Chapter 44 High Speed Penetrators

277

The spacecraft is capable of checking the status of the penetrator.
- **Probe Deployment**: Spacecraft ejects the penetrator and confirms separation.
- **Descent Phase**: Thrusters control the velocity and attitude of the penetrator, allowing an ideal impact **velocity** of 200-300 m/s.
- **Impact**: Penetrator breaks the surface and strikes the regolith, penetrating to a few meters under the surface.
- **Subsurface Operation**: Battery powered penetrators observe with instruments such as chemical sensors, seismometers, and thermal sensing devices. Continued communications are controlled by the original spacecraft.

4 Penetrators may provide numerous benefits. They are capable of more successful impacts into hard or rough surfaces than soft landers, as well as being more cost efficient. Also, penetrators are capable of maintaining full operation upon impact and in very cold environments. Additionally, penetrators provide broad scientific data for later, more extensive investigations through soft-landed instrumentation. Penetrators are especially beneficial in that they provide in situ (natural or original) and near real-time data.

5 Currently, the United Kingdom Lunar Penetrator Consortium and the Mullard Space Science Laboratory Planetary Science Group are running penetrator

◀▼ The Japanese spacecraft *Lunar-A* (below) was scheduled to carry two 13 kg surface penetrators on a lunar mission. However, the mission was canceled in 2007 due to lack of financial resources. The illustration on the left is an imaginary depiction of the penetrator's landing process.

trials. To date they have conducted studies, **simulations**, and impact trials into sand targets resembling the sandy regolith of the Moon. The main objectives of the current trials include testing the ability of penetrators to survive high speed impacts, assess impact on scientific instruments, and test relationship between various penetrator materials and impact. Studies have so far concluded that penetrator missions will be at least as successful, if not more so, than soft lander missions.

6 The United Kingdom has proposed a penetrator lunar launch for 2013. Four battery-powered penetrators will be carried by an orbiter, which will launch them across the Moon's surface, with at least one targeted for the far side of the Moon and one at the Moon's polar region. Spacing the penetrators will allow for the study of a seismic and heat flow network across the lunar surface. The penetrators may also be able to determine the Moon's origin and explore the far side of the Moon for water. The mission will last at least one year, if not several, in order to study effects of the lunar cycles. The orbiter will remain to provide power, check on the status of the penetrators, and provide communications.

7 Plans are also underway for other specific penetrator missions. One mission will be to one of Jupiter's satellites, Europa, where penetrators equipped with **seismometers** can study under-ice oceans, and chemical sensors will detect organic chemicals and the possibility of **habitation**. Penetrators may also be launched into Near Earth Objects for geographical study.

▲ Europa

TARGET WORD EXERCISES

A Match the target words to their definitions.

a lunar	e sensor	i feasibility	m habitation	q crust
b regolith	f descent	j architecture	n simulation	r deployment
c surface	g image	k cruise	o magnetism	
d penetrator	h detect	l trial	p sampling	

(___) 1 the outer or the topmost boundary of an object
(___) 2 something that passes into or through (often by overcoming resistance)
(___) 3 the outermost solid layer of a planet or moon
(___) 4 a suitable sample for study
(___) 5 the act or process of testing, trying, or putting to the proof
(___) 6 a device that receives and responds to a signal or stimulus
(___) 7 to put into use or action
(___) 8 a downward incline or passage
(___) 9 to make or produce a likeness of
(___) 10 the layer of loose rock resting on bedrock, constituting the surface of most land. Also called *mantle rock*
(___) 11 capable of being accomplished or brought about; possible
(___) 12 the force exerted by a magnetic field
(___) 13 of, involving, caused by, or affecting the moon
(___) 14 the structure or design of anything
(___) 15 to travel at a constant speed or at a speed providing maximum operating efficiency for a sustained period
(___) 16 the act of dwelling in or living permanently in a place
(___) 17 to discover the existence or presence of something
(___) 18 imitation, representation, or reproduction

B Match the root words listed below to one of the suffixes in the boxes to create the correct words, and match tem to the examples below.

-ent	-ism
-or	-ment
-ing	-ity
-ure	-ion

a feasible	f deploy
b penetrate	g simulate
c descend	h magnet
d architect	i sense
e habit	j sample

280

(_____) 1   launching a missile, for example
(_____) 2   the possibility of a mission, for example
(_____) 3   a section of rock, for example
(_____) 4   the place where animals might live on a planet, for example
(_____) 5   the design of a flight to Mars, for example
(_____) 6   the downward flight of a penetrator, for example
(_____) 7   an instrument that detects radiation, for example
(_____) 8   a probe that impacts the surface of the Moon, for example
(_____) 9   a computer recreation of a penetrator impact, for example
(_____) 10 a field of force in a planet, for example

C

The target words below have several meanings. Use each target word correctly in the following sentences.

crust   image   sampling

1 _____ of bread
2 a camera takes an _____ of a planet
3 a _____ of rock and soil
4 TV _____ of Mars
5 _____ of the planet
6 the cook indulged in _____ the soup

D

Circle the correct antonym for each target word:

1 penetrator   a. withdrawal   b. infiltrator   c. invader
2 descent   a. plunge   b. ascent   c. fall
3 detect   a. overlook   b. identify   c. discover
4 feasibility   a. likelihood   b. possibility   c. impossibility
5 surface   a. exterior   b. core   c. test
6 habitation   a. desertion   b. occupancy   c. environment
7 simulation   a. imitation   b. reproduction   c. reality
8 sampling   a. part   b. whole   c. model
9 crust   a. exterior   b. covering   c. center
10 deployment   a. withholding   b. distribution   c. positioning

Unit 16
Chapter 45

Types of U.S. Patents

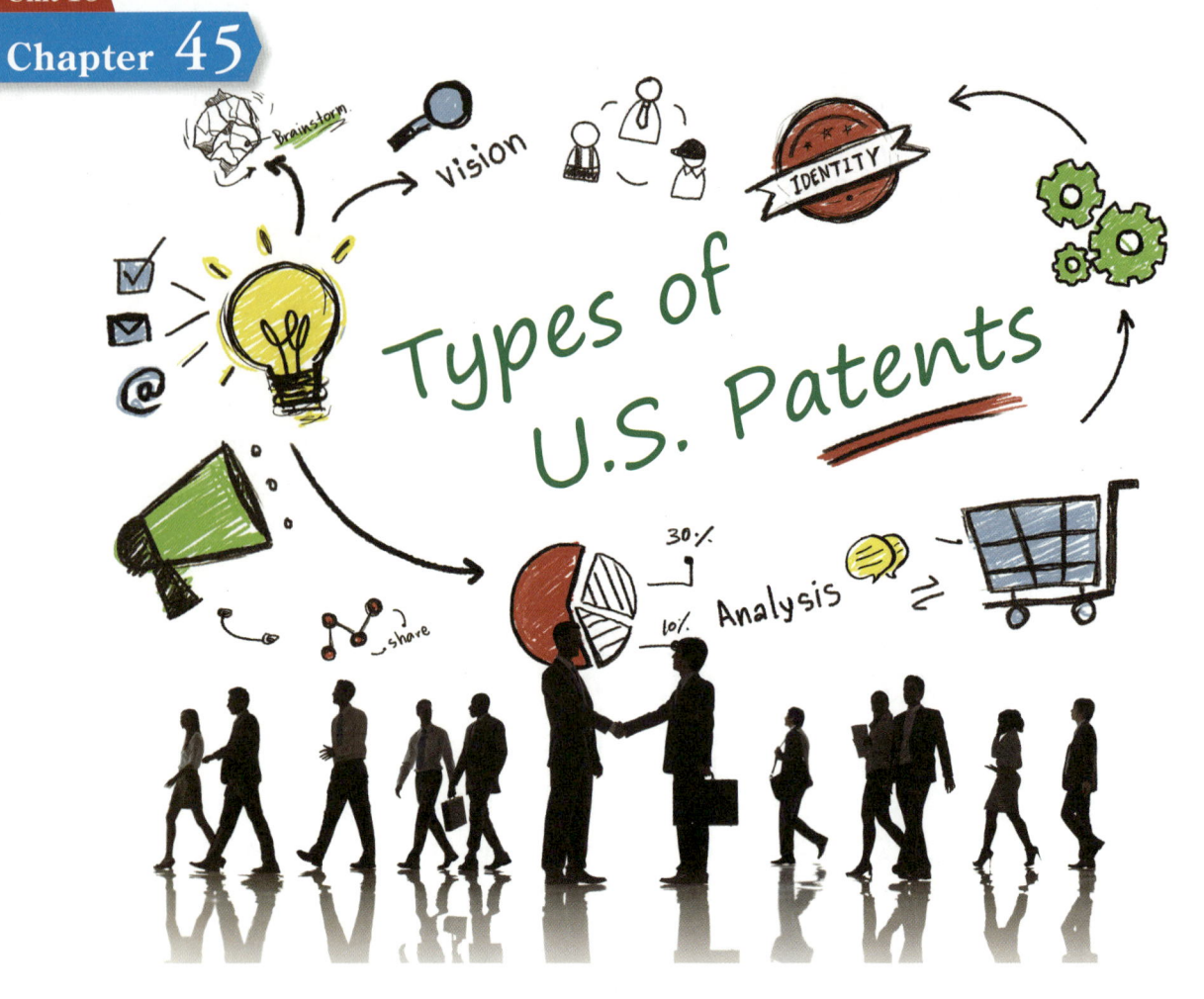

A **patent** is an exclusive government-granted property right. It is an intellectual property right issue, but a patent is different from a copyright or **trademark** in that it is granted basically for a process or product: process generally refers to an industrial or technical act or method, and products include machines, manufactured **articles**, chemical compositions, and **asexual**ly reproduced plants. The first patent was granted in the early 15th

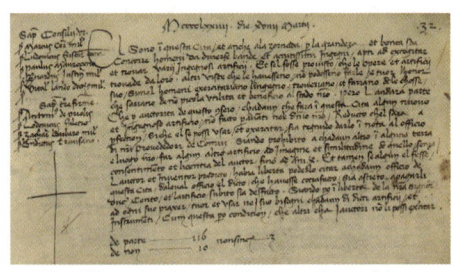

▲ The Venetian Patent Statute, issued by the Senate of Venice in 1474, is one of the earliest statutory patent systems in the world.

▶ James Puckle's 1718 early autocannon was one of the first inventions required to provide a specification for a patent.

century, and until the late 20th century, countries established individual patent terms, including the length of time for which a patent was granted. In the 1990s, the World Trade Organization (WTO) developed a uniform set of patent rights to be granted by governments.

2 To receive a patent, an **invention** must minimally meet three specific **criteria**. First of all, the invention, whether process, machine, or matter, must serve a **useful** purpose, and must be fully operational. Also, a knowledgeable peer should be able to replicate the process or product. Secondly, an invention cannot have been previously described in a printed publication or patented more than one year prior to the patent application. Thirdly, the invention to be patented must be sufficiently different from previous inventions in a significant or surprising way. For instance, changes in size or color may not be **eligible** for a patent.

3 Based on the criteria, patents fall into three basic categories or types: **utility**, **design**, and plant. An inventor applies for a specific type of patent according to the function and type of process or product. Ninety percent of all U.S.-origin patents granted are utility patents. These patents are granted for any new and useful processes, machines, manufactured articles, and compositions of matter, or improvements to previous inventions. A utility patentee must regularly pay fees for patent maintenance, which ensures that the inventor has legal protections for the **exclusivity** of the invention. The term of a utility patent is twenty years from the time of the application filing, but the term can be extended.

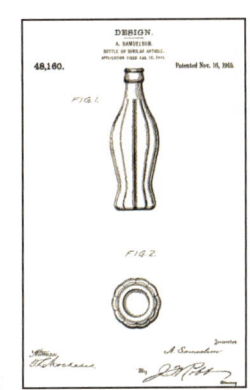

▶ certificates of U.S. patents

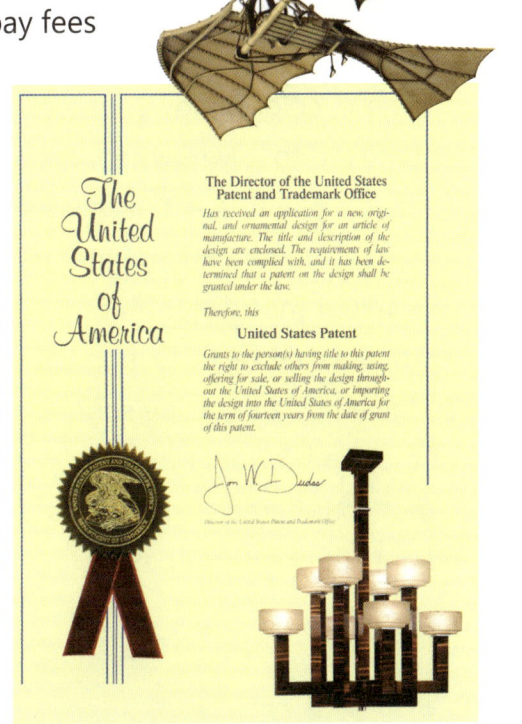

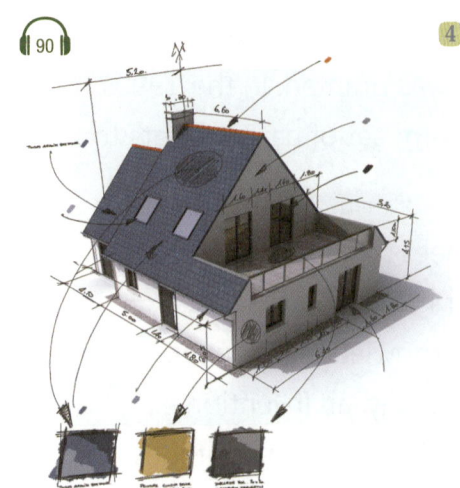

4 The next largest category of patents is the design patent. This type of patent is granted for a new, original, ornamental design. The design may consist of any type of **ornament**al characteristics intrinsic to or applied to an article of manufacture. Design **patentees** are not required to pay patent maintenance fees, and they may be granted a trademark along with a design patent. A design patent term is for a period of 14 years from the date the patent is granted.

5 The third patent category is the plant patent. This patent is granted for the discovery or invention of a living plant organism which can be replicated through asexual reproduction. Discovered plants may only be newly found **seedlings**, not for **tuber propagated** plants or plants found in an uncultivated state. Cultivated plants or plant varieties include **bud** variations, seedling variations by self-**pollination**, and hybrid variations. Various characteristics may distinguish a new plant, including resistance to extreme temperatures or conditions, color of flower or leaf, flavor, fragrance, or form. Plant patentees are not required to pay maintenance fees, and a plant patent term lasts 20 years. Unique to plant patents, the inventor may direct that the step of **asexual** reproduction be conducted by an outside source, but those performing the service are not considered co-inventors and are not granted a patent.

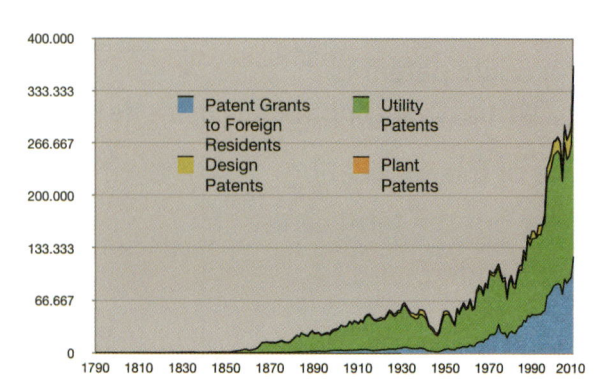

▲ U.S. patents granted, 1790–2010

▲ In the U.S. there are three types of patents: utility patents, design patents, and plant patents.

❻ Once an inventor has been granted a patent, there are other actions that he or she can take to ensure protection of the invention. To correct errors, the patent owner may request a certificate of correction or file for a reissue application. A reissue patent might also be used to either narrow or broaden the claims of a patent to preserve the **validity** of the invention. In some cases, additional information about a patent or competing patent claim becomes available after a patent is issued. When that happens, the patent owner or a third party may file a request for reexamination of the patent. Also, a patent owner may **disclaim** or dedicate to the public the entire term or remaining portion of the term of a patent. At the end of a patent's term, the invention is available for public use. Temporary exclusivity is important, though, to promote public research activity while providing the patent owner the best opportunity to initially profit from the invention.

TARGET WORD EXERCISES

A

Replace the synonyms (in italics) in each sentence with the correct target word.

ornament	design	exclusivity	useful
tuber	article	bud	patents
propagate	invention	utility	pollination
eligible	validity	seedlings	asexual

1. The phonograph is a(n) *newly created device* attributed to Thomas Edison.
 → _____

2. Design patents are for ornamental designs only, but sometimes are granted in conjunction with utility patents because the invention also is *able to be used advantageously or for several purpose*. → _____

3. Patent infringement is an issue that arises when the *credibility* of a patent is in question. → _____

4. Stems are the most common parts of plants used for *without the union of male and female gametes* reproduction. → _____

5. Certain inventors who pay maintenance fees are *qualified* for legal protection services. → _____

6. Some patents are granted for products that provide a *functional* service.
 → _____

7. Other patents are granted for the *decoration* on a product.
 → _____

8. A potato is a typical *swollen, fleshy, usually underground stem of a plant*, out of which new plant shoots arise. → _____

9. The architect created a unique *graphic representation* above the entry door.
 → _____

10. The botanist held many *government-granted property rights* for cultivating plant mutations. ↳ _____

11. Low cost tree and shrub *young plants produced from seeds* can be cultivated for use in conservation planting. → _____

12. New plant varieties sometimes exhibit unique *small protuberance on a stem or branch* colors. → _____

13. The *not shared or divided with others* of the plant patent allowed the biologist time to copyright all of his research. → _____

14 *The process by which plant pollen is transferred from the male reproductive organs to the female reproductive organs to form seeds* is a prerequisite to fertilization. → _____

15 Rose cuttings can be gathered and rooted in order to *reproduce or breed* additional plants. → _____

16 An *object or item* of manufacture must be useful in order to be eligible for a utility patent. ↳ _____

B Circle the prefix or suffix on the target words listed below. Then, using the table of additional prefix and suffix choices, create new words from the target root words (you may create more than one). For example, the word **resistance** includes the suffix **-ance** and the root word **resist**. The word **resisting** can be created by combining **resist** with **-ing**.

bi-	-less
in-	-ly
-s	-ed

1 asexual: _____
2 exclusivity: _____
3 seedling: _____
4 useful: _____
5 invention: _____
6 validity: _____
7 pollination: _____

C Placing certain **suffixes** at the end of a root word will change verbs to nouns that describe a person or thing that does a job. Add -ee, -or, or -er to the end of the following target words and match them with their correct definitions.

| -ee | -or | -er |

a invent
b patent
c design
d pollinat
e propagat
f us

(___) 1 an insect that carries pollen from one flower to another
(___) 2 the party that possesses or has been granted a patent
(___) 3 someone who specializes in creating graphics or plans
(___) 4 someone who is the first to think of or make something
(___) 5 someone who causes plants to multiply
(___) 6 someone who employs or consumes something

287

Unit 16
Chapter 46

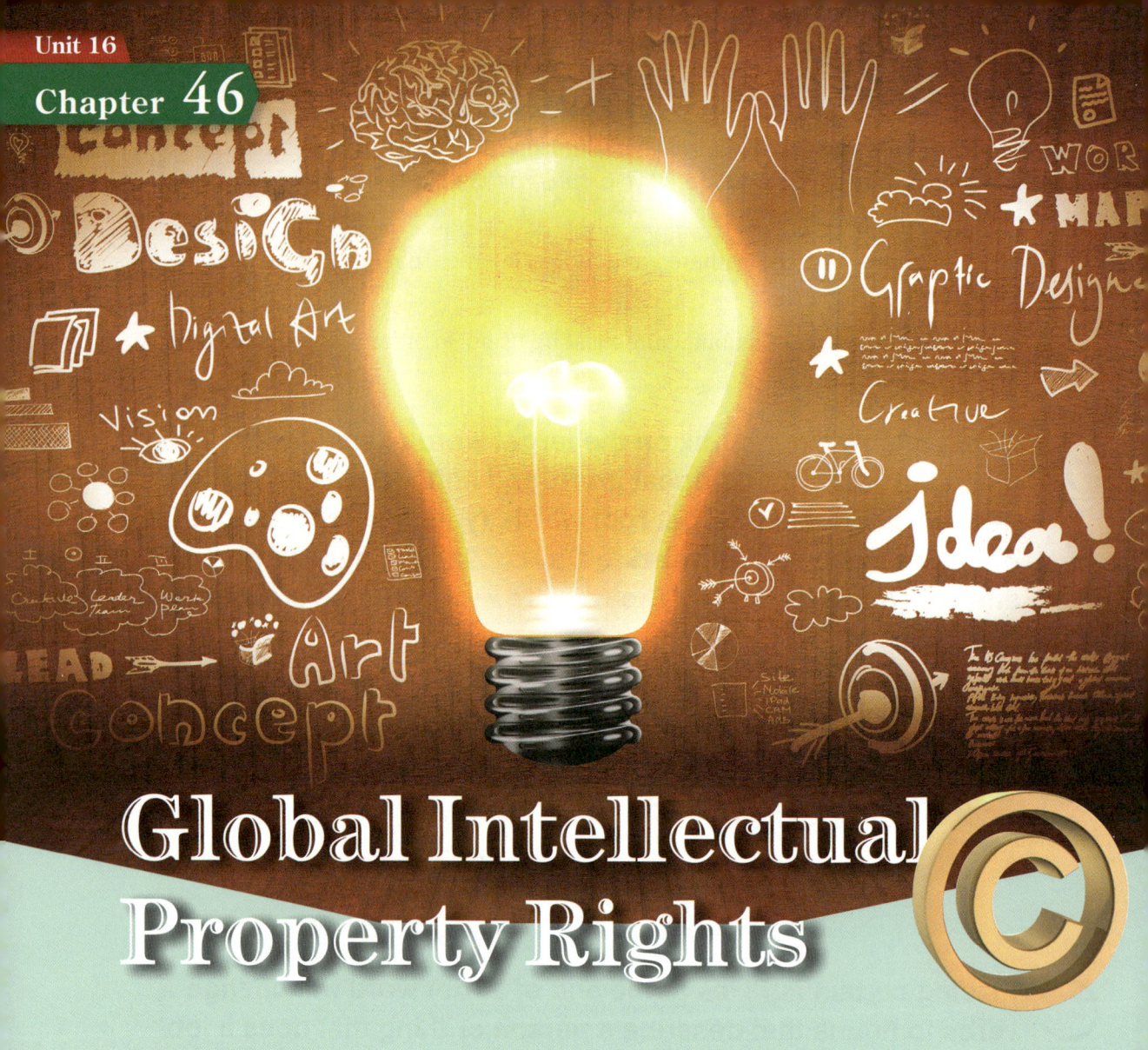

Global Intellectual Property Rights

1. Intellectual property refers to creations of the mind: inventions, literary and artistic works, and symbols, names, images, and designs used in commerce. Specifically, intellectual property does not refer to the actual property itself; instead, it refers to the ideas and creative expression of ideas through the property. To be granted **exclusive** rights to intellectual property means that one obtains the legal rights to specific and unique intellectual activity in the industrial, scientific, literary and artistic fields. The purpose

▲ Intellectual property refers to creations of the mind.

288

of intellectual property rights is two-fold: **protection** and **promotion**. First, intellectual property rights (IPR) help to protect the moral and economic rights of creators, and the right of the public to access **intellection** creations. Second, intellectual property rights help promote creative activity and the sharing of the results of creative work. Finally, they help encourage fair trade of innovation and invention that will contribute to economic and social development.

2 In the 19th century, with the **burgeoning** of the industrial revolution, arose the concern of how to protect the rights of intellectual creations. The first response came in 1883 with the establishment of the Paris Convention for the Protection of Industrial Property. This **treaty** afforded people protection of their intellectual creations in their own countries and those of the treaty members. Nearly 100 years later, the World Intellectual Property Organization was established to develop a more **accessible** international intellectual property system. This system, which oversees how various countries grant exclusive intellectual property rights, is designed to reward creativity, encourage innovation and invention, and contribute to global economic development. The WIPO works in a mutually supportive relationship with the World Trade Organization (WTO) to provide a broad system of assistance to both developed and developing nations.

▲ The World Intellectual Property Organization headquarters in Geneva

3 Even with the oversight of the WIPO and the World Trade Organization (WTO), the **extent** of protection and enforcement of intellectual property rights still varied around the world, and the differences created tension in international relations. To counter the legal **disparities**, the WTO, at the conclusion of a round of global trade negotiations lasting from 1986 to 1994, reached the TRIPS (Agreement on Trade Related Aspects of Intellectual Property Rights agreement).

This agreement introduced global minimum standards of protection for the intellectual property of fellow WTO members. Additionally, TRIPS established through the WTO a **settlement** system for trade **disputes**. TRIPS affords flexibility for countries to **accommodate** their own intellectual property systems while providing comprehensive standards for five broad issues:

- application of basic principles of the trading system and other international intellectual property agreements
- protection of intellectual property rights
- **enforcement** of intellectual property rights by individual countries in their own territories
- settlement of disputes over intellectual property between members of the WTO
- **transitional** arrangements during the period when TRIPS is introduced into member countries—number of years **allotted** for **compliance** depends upon the level of the country's development

Among the TRIPS standards for IPR are the types of legal protections or **paradigms** for intellectual property. Each paradigm involves a limited time period for which the owner is granted a temporary **monopoly** to **derive** financial rewards from the property and to take actions to preserve the temporary monopoly.

- **Patent:** granted for a unique product or process. Patents fall into three basic categories or types: utility, design, and plant. (Specific information regarding patents may be found in Chapter 45.)

▲ Coca Cola is a trademark.

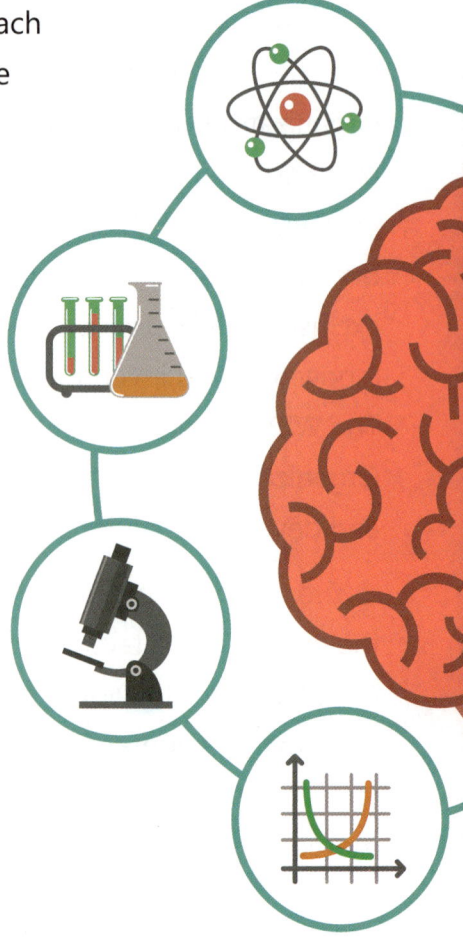

- **Trademark:** granted for a sign that demonstrates authentic or distinctive services or products. For example, Coca Cola is a trademark that can only be used on goods manufactured by the Coca Cola Company.
- **Copyright:** granted for literary and artistic works, including computer programs and databases. Examples of copyrights would be those given for books, film scripts, plays, music compositions, paintings, sculpture, maps, photographic works, movies, and interviews.
- **Geographical Indications and Appellations:** granted for specific characteristic of a good that is attributed to a specific geographic origin. Examples are French wines or certain perfumes.

5 All of these IPR paradigms are subject to change in light of rapid scientific and technological advances in the 21st century. For instance, countries have the right to enact laws to protect very specific types of intellectual property that do not fit under the existing types of protection. Also, international treaties can be negotiated to adopt protections for shared scientific or technological innovations. Ultimately, global agreements on intellectual property rights are needed to protect both the economic interests of intellectual property owners and intellectual property users.

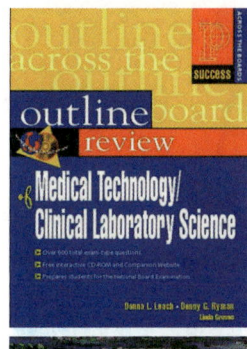

▲ Copyrights protect creative works such as books, paintings, and movies.

291

TARGET WORD EXERCISES

A
Replace the italicized word or phrase with the target word synonym.

derive	disparities	paradigms	appellation	extent
treaty	monopoly	burgeon	disputes	

1. There is almost global agreement on the *limit* of time intellectual property rights for patents can be granted. → _____
2. New developments in nanotechnology continue to *grow rapidly* annually. → _____
3. Computer software designers may seek patents in order to *get or receive something from a source* financial reward from their programs. → _____
4. Even with global minimum standards for intellectual property rights, *differences* still exist between countries in regard to accessibility to intellectual property. → _____
5. A(n) *agreement* with developed nations is crucial for developing nations to ensure food security for their poorest citizens. → _____
6. The WIPO offers arbitration for international intellectual property *arguments*. → _____
7. New developments in science and technology may soon call for additional *overall concepts accepted by most people in an intellectual community*, because they don't fall into established categories of protection. → _____
8. The artist was granted a copyright, which gave him a fourteen-year *exclusive control* over his sculpture. → _____
9. Champagne is a protected *name* of wine from the Champagne region of France. → _____

B
Circle the prefix and/or suffix on each of the following target words. Beside each word, write its part of speech and its correct root word. Then, match the root word with its correct meaning. You will need to use the context of each word as it is found in the article.

a. exclusive:
part of speech: _____
root word: _____

b. protection:
part of speech: _____
root word: _____

c promotion:
part of speech: _____
root word: _____

d accessible:
part of speech: _____
root word: _____

e settlement:
part of speech: _____
root word: _____

f enforcement:
part of speech: _____
root word: _____

g transitional:
part of speech: _____
root word: _____

(____) 1 to make a passage through or across
(____) 2 to refuse to admit, consider, include
(____) 3 to resolve a legal dispute by agreement between the parties
(____) 4 to help bring about or further the growth or establishment of
(____) 5 to gain entrance or admittance to
(____) 6 to shield from injury, danger, or loss
(____) 7 the power to control, persuade, influence

C Find the most similar or opposite word for the target words.

(____) 1 Choose the word most opposite in meaning to: **exclusive**
   a. selective   b. restricted   c. inclusive

(____) 2 Choose the word most opposite in meaning to: **burgeon**
   a. expand   b. contract   c. dispute

(____) 3 Choose the word most similar in meaning to: **accessible**
   a. convenient   b. restricted   c. dangerous

(____) 4 Choose the word most similar in meaning to: **derive**
   a. admit   b. receive   c. persuade

(____) 5 Choose the word most opposite in meaning to: **protection**
   a. influence   b. endangerment   c. oversight

(____) 6 Choose the word most similar in meaning to: **disparities**
   a. disputes   b. differences   c. dangers

(____) 7 Choose the word most similar in meaning to: **extent**
   a. degree   b. characteristic   c. category

(____) 8 Choose the word most opposite in meaning to: **disputes**
   a. dangers   b. treaties   c. agreements

(____) 9 Choose the word most opposite in meaning to: **transitional**
   a. inclusive   b. growing   c. stable

(____) 10 Choose the word most similar in meaning to: **monopoly**
   a. dispute   b. control   c. agreement

Translation

導讀 深入理解科技英語文章的策略

每一位讀者在閱讀英語時都會遇到不認識的單字，而他們的第一反應很可能是查閱字典，但閱讀的時候未必隨時有機會查字典，這也不是學習最好的方法。其實很多時候，文句章節裡已經具備充分的資訊，讀者能從上下文找到理解內容的提示，進而分析這些字句，找出生字的定義。

策略一

推敲上下文：讀者透過分析單字的上下文來判斷字義，這些提示的線索會出現在許多不同的位置：可能就在單字出現的那一個句子裡，也可能要到上一句或下一句話裡找線索。

❶ 尋找定義

有時作者會在同一句話或同一個段落中，清楚地定義出單字的意義：❶ 像是在使用一個未知的單字之後，立刻簡要說明它的定義，而單字與定義之間則以<u>逗號</u>、<u>括號</u>或<u>破折號</u>等標點符號區隔。❷ 如果緊接在單字後採用的是be動詞（是……）的句型，則更清楚顯示單字後面的說明其實就是它的定義。

▶ **Archaeologists**, anthropologists who study prehistoric people and their culture, search ancient sites for artifacts.
考古學家，研究史前人物及其文化的人類學家，會去探索遠古遺跡，尋找工藝品。

▶ **A chemical bond** is a strong force that holds two or more atoms together.
化學鍵是把兩種或兩種以上原子結合起來的強大力量。

❷ 範例或摘要

作者可能會運用一些讀者熟悉的範例，藉以說明一個全新而讀者不熟悉的概念或專業術語。說明範例或許會用在文章的重要篇幅或某個段落，而判斷文章內容是否為範例的關鍵字包括：

▶ 例如（such as、for example、for instance）
▶ 就此說明（to illustrate）
▶ 具體而言（specifically）

■ Hurricane **hazards**, such as strong winds and high water levels, can cause extensive damage to people and property along coastlines.
颶風導致的災害，例如強風與潮水升高，會造成沿海民眾生命財產的重大損失。

❸ 細節描述

有時候，幾個片語或句子，就能讓讀者在腦中描繪出單字的意義。

■ Lula was at her grandmother's farm when a yellow fever <u>epidemic</u> broke out in West Tennessee and Mississippi, only a few miles from the farm. An infectious disease of warm regions, yellow fever is carried by mosquitoes. The humid summer air provided the perfect climate for breeding the many mosquitoes that quickly spread the infection to thousands of residents.
露拉待在祖母的農場時，田納西州的西部和密西西比州正爆發黃熱病，距離農場不過幾哩。黃熱病是發生於溫暖地區的傳染病，透過蚊子傳播，當地夏季的潮濕空氣為蚊子了提供可大量繁殖的完美氣候，他們迅速將傳染病散播給數千位居民。→這一段以散播的過程說明傳染病（epidemic）的意義，由疾病的源起再提到居民間的迅速感染。

❹ 說明

「說明」其實很類似指出單字的「定義」。在同一個段落裡，作者通常會用簡單的字詞解釋比較難懂的單字，好讓字義更加清楚，而說明用到的篇幅通常會比定義更長。

- People with macular degeneration may soon be able to be fitted with a bionic eye. This artificial eye will contain a battery-powered videoprocessing unit that sends signals to an electronic unit behind the eye. The unit then sends signals to the brain, and the brain will interpret the signals as images.
  受黃斑部退化所苦的人們也許很快就能裝置人工眼球，這種人造的眼睛內有一種以電池驅動的影像處理系統，能將訊號傳遞至眼球後方的電子裝置，而電子裝置再將訊號內容傳至大腦，接著大腦便將這些訊號轉換成影像。

❺ 同義詞

有時作者會使用意義相同或相近的單字或片語取代較難理解的字詞，而判斷文字內容是否為單字同義詞的關鍵字包括：

- ▶ 換句話說（in other words）
- ▶ 又名（also known as）
- ▶ 也就是說（that is）
- ▶ 有時也被稱為（sometimes called）
- ▶ 或是（or）

- Patients with fibromyalgia sometimes suffer a sudden onset of acute pain, that is, severe pain that lasts a short time.
  患有纖維肌痛症的病人有時會突然感到一陣猛烈的疼痛，也就是一種暫時性的劇烈痛楚。

❻ 重述

類似指出同義詞的做法，不同之處在於重述是將困難的字詞用更簡單的形式再敘述一遍，且兩者間通常會以逗號區隔。

- After the long drought, the village was depopulated, most of the residents dead or moved, but the livestock remained untouched.

在長期的乾旱之後，村莊的人口減少，大多數居民不是死亡就是遷移，但牲畜則未受影響。

❼ 對比

有時一句話當中的片語或文字恰好與重點字彙的意義相反，而從文章中判斷字詞是否具對比意義的關鍵字包括：

- ▶ 但是（but） ▶ 相較之下（in contrast）
- ▶ 然而（however） ▶ 反面來說（in stead of）
- ▶ 不同的是（unlike） ▶ 不過（yet）

- Cultivated plants are purposefully grown for their products, unlike uncultivated plants that thrive in the wild without standard agricultural methods.
  栽培植物是刻意栽種長成的，和非栽培植物不同，後者在野外繁衍，沒有採用標準的種植方法。

❽ 因果關係

一項活動的成因可能會以不常見的詞彙說明，但造成的結果通常會用讀者熟悉的詞句闡述，讀者即可據此推斷前者意義。判斷文章是否說明因果關係的關鍵字包括：

- ▶ 結果（as a result of） ▶ 於是（accordingly）
- ▶ 因為（because） ▶ 因此（consequently）
- ▶ 因為如此（for this reason） ▶ 故（hence）
- ▶ 若是……，則……（if . . . then）

- The weeds in the garden are so profuse, that the neighbors can no longer see the flowers.
  庭園裡的雜草是如此茂盛，鄰居根本看不見花朵。

❾ 從文章整體推斷

有些作者能讓你透過推理與獲得背景知識找出單字的意義，這一類的線索比較難從上下文看出來。

- Sonny refused to accept that his wife's dementia, until she didn't recognize the grandchildren when they came to visit.
  索尼原本不肯相信妻子智力退化，直到他們去看孫子們時,她卻認不出孫子來,他這才相信。→ 例句後半段的子句說明智力退化造成的影響,點出 dementia 的字義。

⑩ 實驗結果或常識

單字的意義可以從讀者做的實驗和背景知識得出,亦即從「常識」與邏輯中得出,在此情況下文章內容會涵蓋讀者熟悉的資訊。

■ You can usually <u>cure</u> a cold by drinking lots of orange juice and getting lots of sleep. If you do that, you should <u>feel better</u>.
喝大量的柳橙汁、多補充睡眠往往可以治癒感冒,如果你照著做,身體會感到比較舒服。

策略二

字義分析:讀者分析寫作模式的修辭內容找出生字的字義。

字詞是由各種元素所組成—亦即字綴,包括字首和字尾、複合字和字根。事實上 prefix 和 suffix 這兩個英文字,就是指明單字元素的範例:pre 意指「之前」,fix 的意義則是「固定」或「附加」,所以 prefix 指的就是「附加的東西」;suf 是 sub 的變體,sub 原意為「在……之下」,所以 suffix 就是指「附加物」,以單字而言,便是指附加在後的成分。

字首	是放在單字前的一個字母或一組字母,會改變單字原本的意義,可能創造出與原單字完全相反的意義。	• un(非)+ science(科學)→ unscientific(不科學的)
字尾	是加在單字後的一個或一組字母,會構成字詞的另一種形式,例如將動詞轉換為名詞。	• -ion(某事的結果)+ infect(感染)= infection(感染)
複合字	是一個單字的某一部分,它只是複合字的元素之一。	• electro(源自 electric 電的)+ magnetic(磁性的)= electromagnetic(電磁的)
字根	一個單字在拿掉字首和字尾之後,所剩下的元素就是字根。	• act • complete
字彙群	很多字根都屬於同一組字彙群,亦即源自同一個字根,但在結合不同的字首字尾後,就成為意義相異但互相關聯的單字。	• action, acting, acted, react, inaction • completion, completing, completely, incomplete

增加英語字彙量,特別是為了要理解比較困難的科技類文章而增進字彙,是屬於記憶的簡單過程,但要理解單字真實的意義,絕不能只查字典—想要完整理解閱讀的主題內容,讀者必須理解這些詞彙所代表的概念。

運用多種學習字彙的技巧,能夠幫助讀者將不認識的生字串,連至原本通曉的字詞與觀念,藉以理解艱深的字義,並應用實例,區隔類似的詞彙與概念。運用學習字彙的策略,能讓讀者多方面思考字詞的意義與概念,同時在閱讀理解的過程中,充分運用認知與創意能力。

Chapter 1　台北 101 大樓

❶ 從遠古時期的埃及金字塔,到最近期的杜拜塔,這類雄偉的建築總是不斷吸引世人的目光,引發建築工程師之間的角力競爭。各種建築類型都曾為世界最高建築寫下定義,從觀景台(如加拿大的西恩塔),到玻璃帷幕(如哈里發塔),到尖塔(如台北 101)。台北 101(因整棟樓高 101 層而得名)於 2004 年完工後,便號稱為世界最高的建築,然而,2009 年哈里發塔新竣工後,便奪下第一的美名,哈里發塔總共有 169 層樓,超越台北 101 的整體高度。

❷ 台北 101(原名台北國際金融中心)的建築成就,是多位建築師與工程師合作的成果,他們的合作計畫造就了一座強化鋼筋混凝土高塔,嶄新的設計能防範強震與颱風的衝擊。台北 101 高度 508 公尺,座落在主要的斷層地形上,卻能抵擋每小時風

速100英里的強風。建築師李祖原及其合作伙伴，運用現行最佳的設計技巧防範大自然力量的侵襲，並加以結合傳統的中國意象與文化概念。

3 台北101建築的創新，始於深入地底30公尺、埋進岩床的380根1.5公尺基樁。上層結構以剪力釘附著於基座，同時有8根巨型鋼柱支撐，這是整棟建築最主要的直立結構；結構四個外側各由2根鋼柱支撐，至26樓則另有輔助結構的鋼柱與置於角落的支柱所形成的箱型空間，共同分散地心引力。所有鋼柱皆由鋼板與10000 psi（磅／平方英寸）混凝土混合，以防範大樓出現金屬疲勞的危機。從四面支撐的直立鋼柱，則形成整棟建築的中心結構。

4 在中心部分，四個對角的鋼柱使大樓的中心結構更為強化，倒V或V形骨架為電梯提供行進的通道，也讓候梯室的空間更為寬敞。大樓中心結構的巨柱間，有4x4大小的混凝土耐震壁，增加1-8樓的勁度。至於8樓以上的樓層，鋼架與撐起玻璃帷幕牆的抗彎矩格紋形骨架，全都與後方的巨大鋼柱緊密接合，以阻擋強風與地震的危害。整棟大樓是以8層樓為一單位，結合為一完整的結構；每8層有1層鋼鐵桁架，將地表的重力轉移由巨柱承受。

5 台北101最為不凡的一項設計，在於它架設了三座調質阻尼器，最主要的重達730噸，外觀似球體，位於88樓與92樓之間，是由41層的鋼板組合而成，並以8條鋼纜懸掛於此。8個環繞於大樓四周的粘滯性阻尼設計，能夠吸收調質阻尼器轉換時產生的能量（熱能），外層的緩衝環，則讓球體的擺動幅度不致於過大。由於重量過重，最主要的阻尼器無法用起重機吊起，而必須在現場架設製作。另外兩座體積較小、重量7噸的阻尼器，則裝置於塔頂的尖端，以降低大樓對渦漩引發擺動（VIO）的結構反應，這是強風導致塔頂內力矩彎曲的常見情況。

6 台北101的另一特色，是它擁有全世界速度最快的雙層增壓電梯。電梯遊走於入口大廳與89樓的觀景台間，以每小時60公里的速度上升、每小時36.6公里的速度下降，這表示遊客可以在40秒內抵達觀景台；另一座觀景台位在91樓。大樓的最高層則是一間私人俱樂部：Summit 101。身為一座綜合大樓，台北101內部也有購物商店、餐廳、辦公室和電信公司。此外，大樓下方的捷運站，也於2013年台北捷運信義線完工時啟用。

7 台北101不僅使用最先進的建築技術，也同時融入了傳統的中國風意象。台北無論在科技、藝術、創新、人文、環境與獨特性的表現，都讓人難以忘懷，而台北101，則傳遞出嶄新世紀的概念：101超越完美，比傳統象徵完美的數字100多出了1。至於大樓多方使用「8」的設計概念，則是因為8是中國傳統的吉祥數字—象徵著豐饒、繁盛與好運。這些重複以8層樓為一組的建築單位，讓人聯想到傳統的中式寶塔與竹節植物，是堅韌、適應力以及高雅的形象表現。

8 台北101位在信義計畫區的中心位置，這座台北唯一完善規劃的都市區，已經成為台北市的發展中心。雖然台北101大樓的領先優勢已被哈里發塔的高度遮蔽，但它持續穩定引領台北商業區的繁榮發展。

Chapter 2　反恐的建築設計

1 後911時代，世界上許多國家都成為恐怖攻擊的受害者。加強居住環境的安全性，已成為公眾的主要顧慮。安全且設計完善的居住環境，不僅能保障居民和住宅免受各種危險威脅，也能維持社會的高度生產力。目前世界各地有許多專門委員會與機構在檢測現有的建築設備，確認其是否禁得起恐怖分子的攻擊。部分國家甚至已發展出固定的規範、設計模式和建築技術，以保護老舊和新設計的建築免於恐怖攻擊的侵害。

2 能夠防爆或抗爆裂物的建築，是抵禦恐怖攻擊的第一道防線。雖然無法事先預知各種爆炸使用的手法和材料，但還是能夠設計出得以抵擋來自爆炸災害的建築物，包括內部及外部災害。建築的材質不但要能阻隔爆裂物使空氣猛烈衝擊牆壁和窗戶所產生的熱氣，還必須要能抵擋爆炸本身引發的震動波。爆裂物質在爆炸時迅速轉化為熱氣，此時會在建築物的各點施加極大壓力，削弱其抑阻爆炸威力的能力，因而導致建築物崩塌。雖然說部分爆炸是源於汽油彈或核子物質，但恐怖攻擊的炸彈往往比較可能由黃色炸藥（三硝基甲苯）製成，有時還會在成分中添加其他爆裂物質如RDX（也稱旋風炸藥，cyclonite），這類炸藥最常以車輛運送，但也有可能透過人或包裹傳遞。

❸ 每一棟建築物最初的反恐措施都採被動的抵禦方法，像是使用混凝土材質的屏障和景觀設施，包括擺放於屋內的花盆，以及用來抵禦車輛入侵的雕像或水泥座椅。但建築工程師不能單憑這些物品制止攻擊，他們必須為建築物規劃能夠防禦因爆炸造成損傷的設計，而最主要的目標就是使建築物所受毀壞程度降到最低，並防止其坍塌──至少在完成撤離工作前不能倒塌；另一項建築目標則是在撤離人員的過程中，維持緊急設備的運作。

❹ 反恐的設計必須超越傳統建築物所能承受的壓力指標，外層結構如牆壁和樑柱，都最容易收到氣爆的損害。強化延展性水泥牆，在面臨突然的爆炸時，會隨之彎曲而不會因此碎裂，特別是承重牆，它透過質量作用承受爆炸的威力。大量的質量會對爆裂產生的壓力與波壓做出反應，使建築物破裂和牆垣變形的機會降到最低。拿掉樑柱，只使用延展性水泥牆的建築最能夠抵禦爆炸，但樑柱若以混凝土完全包覆，且無法由建築物外層結構接近，也都能有效地產生防禦作用。

❺ 空氣中發生的爆炸對窗戶的損害最大，因此窗戶的設計必須能抵禦爆炸的威力，並使碎裂時的危害減到最小。鑲嵌玻璃或窗戶的設計與裝置，也能藉由減少窗戶的數量與尺寸、裝設第二層窗戶，或使用膠合玻璃以預防或降低窗戶破碎，來防範玻璃粉碎造成的危險。使用膠合玻璃或退火玻璃是較為可取的做法，退火玻璃一般來說較薄，玻璃上的薄膜因此才得以不讓玻璃碎片飛散，或縮小其飛散的面積，至於窗架內的窗戶或玻璃片，則應該以結構密封膠固定。窗戶抵擋爆炸的威力不及牆壁，通常是窗戶最先損壞，否則爆裂的威力會直接侵襲支撐的牆垣，反而摧毀建築物的整體結構。

❻ 門往往不是建築考量的重點，因為使用的時間較少，但還是應該考慮裝設鋼製的大門，門窗側柱旁也該考慮使用鋼筋混凝土。增強延展性的水泥柱比較適合用於支撐屋頂，建築物深入地表的部分，則可以在周圍設置地基較深的圍牆保護，土壤則為地基牆提供保護屏障。

❼ 現時的各種工具和建築規則，都為反恐的建築設計提供相關的技術資訊和公定方法，美國國防部即發展出一套統一設施標準（UFC），提供最基本的反恐建築準則。全面建築設計指南（WBDG），是由非營利組織結合美國政府和私人機構組成的部門，在網路上提供有關防衛性建築設計的整合方法。在國際間，美國產業安全學會（ASIS International）為許許多多的國家提供安全管理資訊，目前也提供會員資產保護的指導手冊（POA）。至於國際合作安全中心（CICS）也已經開始針對建築安全進行國際性研究，特別是這項研究的成果會對貧窮國家產生影響。

Chapter 3　環保建築

❶ 自然建築，亦即取用天然、當地的材料，以發揮建材最大功效的建築方法，非常具有環保意識，此種建築方法的發展，和建構居住環境的過程一樣久遠。應用土石作為建築材料，可以追溯到一萬年前，至於其他天然建材，例如稻草與木材，則在數百年前已有效地被使用。進入二十一世紀，在科技發展的協助下，人類轉而建造具有環保意識的永續建築或綠建築，這類型建築對人體的健康、自然環境、經濟和整體社會皆有益處，還能減少、甚至是預防自然資源的浪費。

❷ 興建住宅對全球的環境都產生巨大衝擊，根據美國綠建築委員會表示（其網址為www.usgbc.org），人類的住宅環境造成17%的淡水耗水量、25%的木材砍伐、33%的二氧化碳排放、40%的物料和能源使用（在中國大陸則是45%）。為了減少自然資源的浪費，國際建築規範委員會（ICC）發展出一套名為「國際節能規章」的建築標準，這是全球各地最常被採用的節能建築規範，至於「國際排水設施規章」則保障水資源的有效使用。無論是美國綠建築委員會或國際建築規範委員會，都提供了一些建築

的標準規範，同時改善居住及工作環境的住民健康，並促進生產。

❸ 有效的建材管理，或是在建築物整修完成後妥善處理剩餘建材（通常指建築廢料─C&D materials），其實是綠建築的首要重點。以往，剩下的建材往往被視為廢棄物，而廢棄材料的處理則是建築過程中典型的環節之一，然而，多達95%被丟棄的建材，都能再生製造為新材料或以新方法應用，這種做法能使建築業與整體環境都受益。

◆ 圖表1：由廢棄建材再生發展的新產品

建築廢料	再生製品
光潔、未經防腐處理的木材	木材、厚光面紙、甚至是燃料
混凝土	從房屋到核能電廠等各類建築工事
路面的瀝青和屋瓦	再生瀝青鋪路；美國目前就有一項名為「屋頂再生成道路」的建築計畫
各種金屬	同類金屬製品；金屬可以無限期回收再生，僅需製成原產品5%的能源，再生製品仍會保有本身的金屬特性
瓦楞紙板	硬紙板、厚紙板（即裝麥片的紙盒）、紙巾、面紙、印刷用紙和書寫用紙
石膏板	石膏板90%的成分都是石膏，可以再生製成新的石膏板、水泥或化學肥料

綠建築的設計，也是為了能更積極達到美國環境保護署與國際建築規範委員會所提出的能源使用目標，達到這些目標，能使溫室氣體的排放量降至最低，甚至完全消除。在美國，環保署的能源利用評估系統訂有各項標準，若建築的設計能達到或超越這些標準，就會獲得一顆能源之星（Energy star）建築標章；加拿大的綠建築有聰明建築（BuildSmart）的標章認證；在澳洲，綠建築協會（GBC）則提出一套自發的評估方案，名為綠色之星（Green Stars）。

❹ 建築要做到環保，得將注意力有效放在所需能源或建築過程中會使用到的一切能源上。所需能源包括在建材製造與運輸、建築過程，或在必要拆毀建築物時必須使用的各種能源。針對完整建築過程所涵蓋的能源使用規劃，包括下列幾點：

▶ 評估建築所需能源的多寡
▶ 考慮建材該如何運輸
▶ 盡可能減少材料的使用、多回收資源
▶ 考慮現有建築再利用和翻新的可能

❺ 澳洲的綠建築協會率先開啟了無碳建築的構想，亦即將二氧化碳的排放淨值降為零，做法包括：

▶ **誘導式設計**：以非機械方式進行通風與溫度調節
▶ **就地使用可再生能源**：使用太陽能板、太陽能熱水集水系統或風力、水力發電機
▶ **節能電器及照明設備**：裝設LED燈、智慧型控制系統、以及擁有「能源之星」標章的設備
▶ **選購環保能源**：購買使用再生資源的廠商所供應的產品
▶ **改善或移除HVAC空調系統**：加入金屬、塑膠或其他廢棄資源的節能再生應用

❻ 今日，全世界都致力於創造出綠建築的規範標準。2008年，ICC成立了永續建築技術委員會，為許多興建中的環保建築、永續建築和安全建築計畫提供監督與指導，至於美國的能源與環境設計指標（LEED）則替從香港到印度、瑞典等建築委員會，在發展綠建築的官方標準奠定了基礎。環保建築發展的最終意義，絕不僅止於緩衝環境所受的衝擊，而是要讓居住環境成為重建人類健康與自然環境的來源。

美國綠建築委員會為國際綠建築政策的發展提供許多資訊，因此不少有關綠建築的專有詞彙都以美式英語呈現，前文有兩個單字在美語和英語中擁有不同的拼法：

美式英語	英式英語
optimize, aluminum	optimise, aluminium

Chapter 4　機車引擎

❶1860年代，人們開始認真研究利用燃油發動機使腳踏車電動化。以下是19世紀以來，人們努力不懈所作的嘗試。

❷**1867**年：來自麻薩諸塞州洛斯柏里鎮的西維斯特‧霍華‧洛普從1867年起，即在各博覽會上示範以蒸汽發動的雙輪自行車。他的設計是在燃煤汽鍋中裝置替代的汽缸，藉此驅動機車後輪的曲柄行進。

❸**1892**年：法國的菲利斯‧米勒在1892年設計出一款由他自行命名為「motocyclette」的機車。他將腳踏車裝上氣胎，並在後輪內裝置一個五缸轉子引擎。

❹**1894**年：史上第一台大量生產的機車，出現在慕尼黑的希爾德布蘭和沃爾夫穆勒在1894年的發明（事實上僅製造了兩百台左右）。他們替腳踏車裝配了一台擁有2.5馬力、雙汽缸和四衝程的引擎。

❺**1895**年：接著，到了1895年，一家法國公司DeDion-Buton開始製造內建四衝程循環引擎的三輪機車，重量較過去的機車更輕，動力也更為強大。

❻二十世紀以來，以燃料驅動的機車普遍以二衝程循環引擎或汽缸內的活塞運轉為發動的力量。

❼**第一次動力衝程**：機車發動後即產生第一個動力衝程（或排氣衝程）。該力量使活塞下降，當活塞頂端通過排氣孔上方，大部分廢氣會因受壓而排出；而活塞持續下降，會將曲軸箱內空氣、燃料和汽油的混合體擠壓到汽缸中，取代汽缸內剩餘的廢氣，讓汽缸充滿新鮮的燃料。

❽**第二次動力衝程**：在新鮮空氣、燃料、汽油等混合體進入汽缸後，活塞開始上升，啟動第二次動力衝程，稱為進氣衝程（或壓縮衝程）。活塞上升會擠壓汽缸內的燃料，使曲軸箱轉為真空；真空導致簧片閥開啟，使來自化油器的空氣、燃料與汽油混合體進入，受到擠壓的燃料由火星塞點燃，再一次啟動同樣的發動步驟。

❾在2004年以後，機車的內燃機開始普遍應用四衝程循環，它的動力稍遜於二衝程循環，但耗油量較低。四衝程循環的過程包括進氣衝程、壓縮衝程、動力衝程以及排氣衝程。

- **進氣衝程**是在進氣閥開啟、汽缸內活塞下降時產生。這時空氣和燃料進入燃燒室，接著進氣閥關閉，迫使活塞上升，整個過程中都是隔熱的，在空氣與燃料的混合體受到擠壓時並沒有熱的傳導。

- 當壓縮衝程開始時，電接點開啟，但是當壓力達到最高點，電接點即關閉。

- 當電接點再度打開，動力衝程啟動，點燃汽缸裡空氣與燃料混合體，引發強力的爆炸，製造出炙熱的廢氣，迫使活塞再度下降。活塞降到最低點時，排氣閥開啟。

- 廢氣擠壓通過閥門，排出引擎，此一排氣衝程的功能在於清淨汽缸，再次重複循環步驟。

❿2008年5月，石川秀男發明的機車發動設備取得專利權，該設置採用以皮帶驅動的無段自動變速系統結合內燃機。石川設計該發動設備是為了簡化以較短的配線組合電動馬達和啟動馬達的程序，使配線和組合工作變得更簡便，也讓整個引擎顯得更輕巧。

⓫石川設計出一種箱型容器，能夠做為樞軸，支撐位在同一側的電動馬達和啟動裝置。這樣的結構配置，可以縮短馬達接線，以降低成本，同時還能讓線路和機組安裝的工作更周延。而由於箱子的體積小，騎車時造成的震動也能因此降低或減緩。

⓬除此之外，輕巧的設計能避免機身各部分結構，如後輪，跟引擎外觀的設計規劃產生衝突；箱型容器還能保護電動馬達及啟動馬達不受水和泥巴的汙染，延長使用期限。至於小巧且結構安全的發動裝置使得裝配更為輕鬆，同時增加機車最大可靠性。

Chapter 5　生物醫學工程

① 雖然歷史上曾出現為數可觀的先例，生物與工程科學間逐漸頻繁的跨領域合作卻是在近十年內才順勢而起。亞里斯多德即曾寫下有關「模仿」的論述；李奧納多·達文西在自己發明中模仿自然現象；伽利略則在探究機械與生物領域的關係上居領航地位。但一直到二十世紀，工程師與科學家之間的合作才在生物醫學的研究和應用上取得迅速的進展。

② 仿生學的研究開發出許多新材料作為應用，從骨板到奈米科技，類型眾多。在1900年代早期，植入人體的骨板是為了幫助固定並治癒骨折。當骨折的部位癒合、骨頭能再次承受外來壓力時，通常會將植入的骨板拆除。到了50年代，置換人工血管不再是不可能的手術，而到了60年代，許多人體器官與身體部位也都能動手術更換。

③ 同時應用流體力學與固體力學解決生物醫學上的難題是專業科技整合的其中一例，目前研究人員正在努力設計計算模式，希望能更加準確計算並修正血液動力學（決定血流的物理因素）工程方面的問題、物質的耐久性，與心瓣膜植入手術所產生的生物反應。生物學家與物理學家的研究合作還改善了成人護理墊的設計，同時間這些科學家們研究出尿液在纖維布料上的延展方式。

④ 固體力學與生命科學的整合啟動生物醫學的創新，舉例來說，在光學的領域中，研究人員設計出一套機械設備，研究眼球水晶體的各種組成成分與畸形狀態。藉由研究黏彈性的模型，以及透過理論模擬水晶體結構，研究人員正在開發人類視覺中水晶體調節的新技術。

⑤ 固體力學的研究對於判斷人工關節所能承受的壓力和磨損程度，以及該如何預防壓力與磨損問題也至為關鍵。在置換人工關節的手術中，患病的關節部位會以人工製造的關節取代，材質可能是金屬（例如鈦或鈷鉻合金）、陶（如鋁氧化物或氧化鋯）、塑膠（如超高分子量聚乙烯），也可能是前述三種材質的結合。在人體植入人工關節是為了恢復受損的生理機能，但骨頭與人工關節接合處產生的壓力是無可避免的，正因如此，固體力學的研究對摩擦學（研究磨損、摩擦力、潤滑作用的科學）的貢獻極為重要，尤其是針對研發更具耐壓性與生物相容性的義肢材質而言。在改善義肢的材質與固定性後，植入體內的人工關節得以延長近兩倍的使用壽命。

⑥ 植入人體後會引起組織反應的生物材料主要有三種：惰性物質、生物可吸收性物質及生物活性物質。

▶ 惰性物質和周遭組織所產生的化學作用有限；鈦和礬土都是使用在整形與植牙手術的惰性材料。雖然惰性物質能增加生物相容性，但近期研究顯示，為了增進植入物的黏著性和療癒性，部分的細胞反應仍是必須的。

▶ 生物可吸收性的材質，如磷酸三鈣，會慢慢地被身體組織再吸收和替代。使用具有生物可吸收性材質的一項實例就是以支架引導組織再生的牙科手術，近來成為效果看好的先進治療方式。用受與者細胞製造的生物可吸收性支架是為了仿造自然的人體組織，這些支架一旦植入病人體內，就會被自身的組織吸收取代。整個過程可能只需要進行一項微創手術，而且它不僅能應用於人工器官移植手術，還能藉此治療其他退化性疾病、發炎性或感染性疾病。

▶ 某些生物材料，例如生物活性玻璃和生物活性陶瓷，會與接合的骨頭或軟組織形成化學鍵。鍵合的骨頭會減少植入物接合處活動與摩擦而導致剝離、鬆脫與磨損的可能性。介面力學的應用原理，持續改進了使用生物活性材料的研究成果。

⑦ 工程學的專業知識與生物研究的結合還增進了醫療診斷器材的開發，同時改良獲取人體內部構造細部資訊的程序：

▶ 核磁共振造影：使用有效的磁場與無線電波技術
▶ 放射線攝影：利用X光照射創造精細的影像
▶ 斷層攝影：利用電腦斷層（CT）掃瞄身體部位，有時會在掃瞄時使用染劑
▶ 超音波：使用高頻率的聲波

⑧ 工程師與科學家依然持續擴展科技合作的發展領域，例如醫學成像與醫療器材、人工器官植入手術、仿生學、衛生保健技術、以及分子生物工程皆涵蓋在內。而許多國際性與各國國內的研討會議，每年都會提供科學家與工程師交流的場合，分享他們的研究成果，合力提升生物醫學工程的技術與應用。

Chapter 6　油電混合動力車

❶雖然油電混合動力車在近二十年左右才受到汽車產業的矚目，但它其實早在一百多年前即已首次亮相。二十世紀初期，費南迪‧保時捷博士開發出首部混合動力車，一台由油電共同驅動的車輛。這輛車是利用內燃機轉動使發電機充電，再供給電力到位在前輪輪軸的電動馬達。但不巧的是，生產一輛混合動力車比生產汽油車要昂貴許多，因此在開發出運轉時更安靜、更平穩的汽油引擎和電動啟動裝置後，多數混合動力車即被迫停產。

❷1960年代，基於對環境汙染的顧慮，美國又興起對混合動力車的興趣，沒過多久即再度生產，但一直到1990年代時才開始量產。1990年代晚期，豐田汽車的 Prius 混合車款引進日本市場，緊接著奧迪汽車在歐洲推出混合動力車款；1999年，本田汽車在美國發表 Insight 車款，美國亦加入混合動力車的市場。

❸混合動力車是由兩種甚至更多種能源驅動的車輛，最主要的驅動能源是汽油和電力，但並不是每一輛混合動力車的構造或驅動方式都相同：

並聯式

油箱 → 電池／電動馬達 → 傳動系統 → 車輪

串聯式

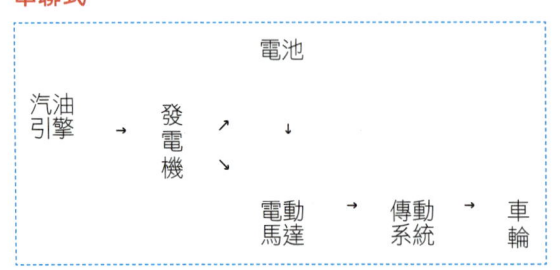

汽油引擎 → 發電機 → 電池／電動馬達 → 傳動系統 → 車輪

❹無論是前述何種動力系統，都是由汽油引擎提供車輪正常行駛所需的動力，而當車輛要穿越坡道、開上山坡或加速時，電動馬達負責提供動力，保留原本多餘的能量負載；此外，電動馬達也會在車輛空轉時提供動能，待汽車發動時汽油引擎才重新啟動。結合這兩種動力系統，車輛二氧化碳的排放量顯著降低，汽車里程數則大量增加，在過程中駕駛人甚至不會注意到動力供給系統的轉移。

❺混合動力車另一項節省能源的特徵就是再生煞車系統（再生制動）。傳統煞車系統是藉由摩擦以反轉車子的推進力，此一過程會產生過量的熱能，占整輛車將近30％的電力，這些電力單純地被浪費掉；至於再生煞車系統在減速或煞車時會將電動馬達轉為一台發電機，將動能傳導回電池內，以後再使用。

❻整體而言，混合動力車的效能歸功於它使用更小、更輕巧的組件。較小型的燃料引擎減少廢氣的排放，不過產生的電力也較少，但透過有效的外部設計，亦即結合鋁、碳纖維等輕量材料，混合動力車克服此電力不足的問題。這些輕量材料再搭配低滾動阻力的輪胎、輪軸軸承和煞車，也降低了行車時的空氣阻力。其他降低行車阻力的設計元素，還包括齊平的窗戶、嵌入式的擋風玻璃雨刷系統、流線型車頭和狹長的車尾、凹式車門把手、半隱藏式後輪，以及最細的車身接縫。對車輛未來的建議設計還包括以監視錄影器取代現有的後照鏡。

❼並非所有的動力混合車都是結合汽油和電力發動，其他類型的引擎技術也可以用於製造混合動力車：

▶ **天然氣引擎**：汽油引擎可以轉換為壓縮天然氣（CNG）、液化石油氣（LPG）或是氫等燃料；而電子控制單元（ECU）則能夠從無數的感應器中接收傳達訊息，以調節使用最適量的燃料，以及找出正確的燃燒時機。這種引擎能表現最完美的效能，同時降低車輛二氧化碳的排放。

▶ **甲烷引擎**：甲烷引擎內所使用的生物物質可以經由天然資源的厭氧分解過程獲得——取自從木材到動物排泄物等種種資源類型，過程類似廢水處理廠數十年來進行的程序：有機物質透過低氧和高溫的處理過程，使生物質氣化，生物甲烷引擎再結合電動引擎的功能，進一步減少二氧化碳的排放量。

▶ **生質燃料引擎**：生物物質在精煉後能夠生產引擎燃料。乙醇燃料源自玉米作物，再添加少量石油，即可用於 E 85 引擎；也可以改良引擎，讓它使用85%的乙醇與15%的一般燃料運轉。目前正在進行的研究是要從其他來源取得乙醇燃料，包括青草和一般的家庭廢棄物。生質燃料引擎能供給電動馬達電力，而非直接發動傳動系統，如此一來便能進一步減少二氧化碳的排放。

❽ 今日的混合動力車在傳統車輛以外，提供人們一個有效且負擔得起的選擇。相較於一般車輛，部分混合動力車能減少高達90%的汙染源，且由於耗油量減少，也更富經濟效益；它的折舊率持續維持比傳統車款更低。許多國家的政府已經開始或正在考慮實施減稅，增加消費者購買混合動力車的誘因，這項投資就經濟面而言顯然也很有保障。混合動力車對全球的經濟與環境，已經產生可觀的衝擊，而隨著公眾對節能車輛的需求增加，也將有更多以替代能源做為驅動燃料的混合動力車上市。

英式英語及美式英語拼字的差異：	
美式英語	英式英語
aluminum, fiber, fueled	aluminium, fibre, fuelled

Chapter 7　致命的傳染病

❶ 儘管醫學研究、疾病診斷和治療的效果在二十世紀期間迅速發展，傳染性疾病仍然是全球的致命威脅，僅2007年，傳染性疾病即占全世界死亡案例的26%。研究人員歸納出各種導致致命傳染疾病發生與傳遞的原因類型：

▶ 新出現的病原體，例如細菌、病毒或黴菌
▶ 最近才被先進醫療診斷儀器和看診程序發現的病原
▶ 現有致命傳染疾病的比例增加
▶ 人類行為改變，如人口稠密區的轉移、旅遊習慣的改變以及科技與產業的重心變動
▶ 抗生素的使用增加
▶ 施打規定接種疫苗或現有疫苗的比例減少

❷ 二十世紀晚期出現最重大的疾病之一當屬 HIV 和 AIDS（愛滋病），長久以來都位居全球人口死亡的首要因素，也是歷史上最具毀滅性的流行病，與淋巴腺鼠疫和1918年爆發的流感並列。HIV 是人類免疫缺乏病毒（human immunodeficiency virus）的縮寫，在感染的最後階段即成為愛滋病（AIDS），也稱後天免疫缺乏症候群（acquired immunodeficiency syndrome）。HIV 病毒的特異之處在於它會直接攻擊T細胞或CD 4細胞。它們屬於白血球細胞的一種，是人體免疫系統抵抗疾病不可或缺的一環。HIV 並不會經由一般的接觸傳染，只有體液的直接接觸才會感染，通常是因為性行為或共用針頭所導致。在一診斷出感染HIV病毒時，即可立即採取幾種抗逆轉錄病毒療法（因為HIV是一種逆轉濾過性病毒），以抑制病毒的發展，但即使不採取任何療程，HIV病毒也可能在多年以後才會轉變為愛滋病。愛滋病的死亡率很高，但疾病本身並不是直接致死的原因，而是導因於一些由愛滋病引發的疾病，最為人知的包括肺炎、流行性感冒與肺結核。邁入二十一世紀後的初步調查雖然顯示，美國境內因HIV、愛滋病及相關疾病導致的死亡案例數量下滑，但新的醫療診斷技術卻指出自2006年起，因前述三種因素致死的情況有增加的趨勢。在國際間，診斷出HIV與愛滋病的比例也令人憂心，尤其是非洲，目前當地有關愛滋病的教育、治療和預防都在廣泛地推展中。

❸ 二十一世紀出現最具破壞性的疾病之一要屬SARS，或稱嚴重急性呼吸道症候群，是一種由冠狀病毒（一種具有套模的冠狀單股RNA基因組）所引起的病毒性呼吸道病變。2002年SARS在中國的廣東省爆發，但直到2003年研究人員才終於確認病症，當時全球29個國家已出現近八千起病例，包括774起死亡案例。然而，感染SARS冠狀病毒的案例又迅速接連發生，各種像是隔離病患等有關公眾健康的政策也緊急制訂，因此疾病的傳播在幾個月內即獲得控制。

❹ 部分再發疾病，如肺炎和瘧疾，其感染率在世界各種流行病中一直高居不下。由結核分枝桿菌引起的肺炎（TB），在美國的感染案例自1980年起增加了20%，且全球新增的病例每年約為九百萬

起，其中近兩百萬的患者死亡。肺炎的再次流行主要肇因於病菌對抗生素的抗藥性增加，然而貧窮也是原因之一。絕大多數肺炎引發的死亡案例都發生在非洲及亞洲最貧窮且營養缺乏的區域。至於每年感染瘧疾的案例則將近有五億起，其中超過一百萬名病患死亡，多數是住在撒哈拉沙漠以南非洲地區的幼童。瘧疾一般是經由瘧蚊叮咬感染，傳播迅速主要是因為寄生於瘧蚊的病菌首先會感染人體的肝細胞，接著是紅血球，如果不立刻治療很可能會致命。肺炎和瘧疾都是可以治療、預防的疾病，而全球性的預防措施也已經透過美國的疾病管制局和世界衛生組織著手制訂進行。

5 除了生物自然演化過程之外，致命的傳染病也可能透過刻意的生化恐怖攻擊而傳播。生化恐怖攻擊是利用具危險性的有毒生物試劑做為威脅性武器，散布至人體、動物或植物上，全球預備及應變網絡即是眾多對付生化恐怖攻擊的國際合作組織之一。

6 即使全球對於疾病的偵測、治療及預防的措施不斷進步，但要完全消滅持續威脅全人類、特別是兒童性命的致命傳染病，仍有一大段路要走。近期相關的醫學研究進展包括以3D影像呈現病毒蛋白質和細菌蛋白質，以及自全球各地最新的資料庫取得傳染病的相關資訊。生物科技為疾病的診斷、藥物研發和運輸提供了新的方法，雖然要完全消除致命疾病並不可能，許多研究人員仍相信，只要全球持續努力籌措資金、進行研究和溝通，還是得以應付並控制這些病毒和細菌所帶來的威脅。

Chapter 8　肥胖危機

1 二十世紀中期，肥胖症首度成為國際疾病分類的病症之一，經過五十年後，肥胖症已可以算是全球最大的健康危機，國際肥胖專案小組將它取名為「千禧病症」。雖然部分醫學專家不斷拒絕承認肥胖症可以被歸類為一種疾病，但全球各地的機構，從聯合國到世界衛生組織，至美國公共衛生期刊，全都提出警告，肥胖症可能成為下一個全球流行病。

▶ 聯合國的報告指出，到了下一個千禧年，全球體重過重的人數將多過遭遇飢荒的人口。
▶ 世界衛生組織的研究發現，2005年，全世界體重過重的成人數量為16億，到了2014年，全球有19億的過重成人人口，而研究人員預測，至2030年時，肥胖症可能會成為世界貧窮人口面臨的頭號殺手。
▶ 美國公共衛生學會報告指出，美國過重兒童的人數比過去20年多出一倍，美國每五名兒童當中就有一名過胖。

2 跟過去相比，顯然有越來越多的人面臨各種健康問題，包括心血管疾病、糖尿病，甚至是某些癌症。但經由教育、餐飲業的行動、市場改革以及政府的支持，肥胖症其實可以預防的。

3 肥胖症被定義為體內脂肪異常且不健康地累積，產生體重相對身高超過比例的情況。肥胖症，也就是體重過重，是以身體質量指數（BMI）為衡量準據，這是一種以體重除以身高平方的間接測量值，適用於各個性別與年齡層。全球的衛生組織一致同意，若BMI值大於或等於25即代表過重，若BMI值大於或等於30即屬於肥胖症。前述標準只是一般的測量基準，未必能說明個別情況的差異，部分研究也顯示，BMI值高於21時，發生慢性疾病的機率亦普遍增加。

4 肥胖症的成因眾多，但它們最終導致能量攝取與消耗的不平衡。就多數情況而言，原因來自攝取高脂肪和高熱量的飲食習慣，而在各地取得日漸便利的加工食品則和全球肥胖症病例增加有直接的關連性。全球現代化，包括擁有汽車的人數激增、現代化用品使用便利，加上隨處可得的科技產品，如電視與電腦，導致更多人過著久坐的生活型態，是罹患肥胖症比率升高的另一因素。其他形成肥胖症的原因還包括荷爾蒙的影響、環境因素、文化因素，以及遺傳基因。

5 過剩脂肪可能引起為數眾多的健康問題，心血管疾病已經成為世界級的頭號殺手，每年將近一千七百萬人因心臟病發作和中風而死亡。證據顯示，肥胖症會使血膽固醇和三酸甘油酯的指數上升、減少高密度脂蛋白（「好的」膽固醇）的含量、使血壓升高——全都是導致心臟病發作和中風的主要原因。肥胖症還可能引發糖尿病，雖然兩種病症之間的關聯尚未明朗界定，但過多的脂肪顯然會增加胰島素抗阻，進而導致血糖濃度增加。糖尿病會強化這些引發心血管疾病的成因，進一步增加心臟病發作的危機。肥胖症患者體內的胰島素改變也可能增加罹患某些癌症的機率，如乳癌與結腸癌；此外，研究還發現因肥胖症導致性激素變化和癌症之間的關聯性。

❻ 世界各地有許多組織都採行各種策略，對抗及預防肥胖症問題。

▶ 「健康人民2010」是美國衛生及公共服務部於2000年1月開始推展的計畫，結合健康推廣與疾病的預防活動，專注於28項活動要點，其中的一項便是營養與過重問題。

▶ HOPE（歐洲預防肥胖、推廣健康計畫）是歐盟跨領域合作網絡進行的一項計畫，監督管理肥胖症成因及其控制預防相關的知識整合和政策發展。

▶ 在2004年，世界衛生組織採行一項推廣健康飲食與身體活動的政策，讓國際間的公私成員都致力做到：
  - 降低肥胖症引發慢性病的危險
  - 增加與健康飲食和身體活動相關的教育
  - 發展改善飲食習慣和身體活動的長期全球政策
  - 監督並推廣健康飲食習慣和身體活動的研究

❼ 遵行上述或其他國際組織所提供的建議與指導，對於杜絕罹患肥胖症的危機具有決定性影響，無論是私人餐飲業開發出更健康的飲食選擇，或是由公共組織推廣更健康的飲食習慣與身體活動，都必須結合全球的力量，始能逆轉肥胖症的趨勢及不良影響。

Chapter 9　健康生活的秘訣

❶ 現代科學與醫藥的發展顯著延長了二十世紀人類的平均壽命，也消除許多傳染病的致命威脅，但在此同時，不斷邁向工業化的社會卻經歷各種生活習慣疾病迅速而普遍的襲擊。這些慢性疾病——主要是心血管疾病、癌症、糖尿病、阿茲海默症，以及憂鬱症——迥異於其他類型的疾病，因為這些病症是由個人的生活習慣所造成，但同樣地，它們也可以藉由改變生活習慣來預防。

❷ 首先，我們可以改變平日的習慣，進行健康的活動：

▶ 戒煙
▶ 維持健康的體重
▶ 適量飲酒或完全不飲酒
▶ 選擇積極的生活型態，例如每日健行，進行體力活動
▶ 用健康的態度面對壓力，如做瑜伽或寫日記
▶ 每晚充足睡眠八小時

❸ 第二，我們可以做些聰明的決定，選擇能夠增進身心整體健康與延長壽命的食物、飲料、身體活動與保健方式。

▶ 食物
  - 水果和蔬菜的熱量低，富含纖維質，含有大量維他命與礦物質，能降低罹患慢性病的機率，還能維持認知功能。
  - 精益蛋白質會激發肌肉蛋白質合成，促進肌肉生長。
  - 每天攝取20%至25%的健康脂肪，也就是多元不飽和脂肪酸與單元不飽和脂肪酸，促進脂溶性維生素如維生素A、D、E的吸收；健康的脂肪，例如某些魚類體內富含的omega-3多元不飽合脂肪酸，亦顯示能降低因心血管疾病引發的死亡。

▶ 飲料
  - 適量飲酒（每天一或兩杯）可以帶來減少罹患心臟病、糖尿病與中風機率的益處。
  - 高糖分的飲料可能導致蛀牙與肥胖，應該盡量避免飲用。
  - 每天飲用兩公升的水可以補充身體的水分、預防脫水。
  - 適量攝取咖啡因（每天兩或三杯）可避免罹患第二型糖尿病和結腸癌。

▶ 規律的身體活動
  - 固定做有氧運動，每天約三十分鐘，強化心血管系統、保持健康的體重。運動也能改善睡眠模式、增加心智的敏銳度、激發性慾並增進性功能表現。
  - 身體的親密接觸會釋出荷爾蒙，使血壓降

低、製造出美好的感受。
- 保持身體活動與平衡的能力能改善日常的身體機能，尤其是老年人，能夠避免跌倒造成骨頭斷裂或其他傷害。

4 根據年齡與性別的差異，也必須採行不同的保健方法：

▶ 兒童與青少年
- 需要多補充熱量促進發育，但他們也需要均衡的飲食，以吸收適當的養分，避免過度肥胖。
- 需要從事健康的身體活動。

▶ 成人
- 需要攝取的熱量較少，因為新陳代謝會隨著時間逐漸趨緩。
- 必須有均衡的飲食習慣，食用養分高的食物以維持體重。
- 每天至少做三十分鐘的運動。

▶ 老年人
- 必須每天做安全的運動，不能壓迫關節，但要讓關節活動舒展以保持彈性。
- 需要攝取的熱量低但飲食要均衡，老年人因咀嚼受限與胃口不佳，必須補充適當的養分。
- 必須從事有挑戰性的動腦活動，讓腦袋保持活躍、反應機警。

5 雖然絕大部分有關各年齡層的健康生活資訊，都是由美國各家組織和機構發表，但其他許多國家也已經制訂相關計畫，欲增進人民的身心健康。

▶ 加拿大已開始採行一項泛加拿大健康生活策略；2005年，歐盟執行委員會推行飲食、身體活動與健康交流平台；OneWorld South Asia則是由數洲共同成立的組織，從許多方面推動亞洲的永續發展，包括健康議題。

6 沒有任何一個組織擁有確保人類長壽健康的知識或能力，世界上也沒有萬靈丹或青春之泉，但一個持續成長的研究組織結合全球對健康生活的關注與努力，會讓健康而長壽的生活在世界各地實現。

Chapter 10　幹細胞

1 西元1998年，威斯康辛大學麥迪遜分校的生物學家，詹姆士·湯普森博士所帶領的研究團隊，首度成功分離出人類胚胎幹細胞（hESCs）。既然是身體組成的源頭，又形成人體的基本骨架，因此針對身體如何生長、維持，甚至在某些情況下，如何自我修復的研究，幹細胞即成為首要研究對象。了解幹細胞的功能並加以利用，可以獲得最新且更為有效的醫療方法，處理身體傷害、疾病與失調的問題。

2 幹細胞是一種未分化或未特化細胞，有發展為兩百種以上人體細胞的潛力。未分化細胞並不具有特定組織能力，無法在人體內進行特定功能，但這些未分化細胞屬於複能性細胞，亦即具有分化的可能性。與存在於肌肉或血液內、不會自行複製新生的多數細胞不同，幹細胞可以重複自我更新多次，最後複製出來的數量有時高達數百萬。對幹細胞增生的了解可以幫助研究人員判定並應付不正常的細胞分裂，讓他們能夠在實驗室裡成功地培養出幹細胞。

3 現存的幹細胞主要有兩種類型：胚胎幹細胞與成體幹細胞，但兩種幹細胞皆有各種變體。

▶ 胚胎幹細胞來自從試管培養的胚胎。
- 當胚胎發育成長數天後，胚胎內即存在一種複能性細胞，這些細胞會形成一種中空的球體細胞，稱作囊胚，該球體為一三層結構的細胞：
  (1) 構成外膜的滋養層細胞
  (2) 囊胚腔，位於囊胚內的中空腔
  (3) 內細胞團是在囊胚腔一端的一個細胞群，最後將發展成胚胎
- 在實驗室裡也能成功培養出胚胎幹細胞，囊胚腔裡的內細胞團發展成熟後移到培養皿內，只要供給適當的養分，就會在培養皿內分裂並形成胚胎幹細胞株。截至目前為止，多數胚胎細胞都來自老鼠胚胎，但試管培養的人體胚胎細胞以及來自治療性複製的胚胎幹細胞，都是進行幹細胞研究的潛在資源。

▶ 成體幹細胞是容易讓人被誤導的專業術語，

因為嬰兒與兒童體內也有成體幹細胞，它屬於一種未分化細胞，存在於已發展成熟身體組織的分化細胞中。科學家已經知道成體幹細胞的主要功能是生長或修復身體組織，但尚未能找出該細胞的根源。

- 成體幹細胞可以在其所存在的身體組織內分化為特化細胞，但有時候也有能力分化成其他組織的細胞類型，此一過程稱為轉分化或可塑能力。若科學家能鑑別並控制幹細胞的轉分化機制，或許就能用這種新細胞來測試細胞對新藥物的反應，也可以將細胞注射至異常的身體組織內進行修復與更新，這種過程稱為細胞療法。

❹研究人員以幹細胞鑑別及預防重大疾病根本病因的發展頗受看好，未來，幹細胞療法能夠提供可再生細胞與組織，以修復並治療脊髓的損傷、燒傷、糖尿病與關節炎。使用複能性細胞進行治療具有修復取代受損器官的可能性，例如因罹患帕金森氏症、阿茲海默症或因中風而受損的心臟或腦部細胞。至今為止，以幹細胞療法治療白血病等血液疾病的成功率有限，但對於治療其他血液相關病症如鐮刀性細胞症，仍具有相當的潛力。

❺關於幹細胞研究最受限制的問題就在於相關的道德爭議。

❻**反對者**：人類的生命在卵子受精的那一刻即已開始，因此，改變或摧毀人體胚胎在道德上是站不住腳的。

❼**支持者**：許多在試管內受精的卵子，並沒有移植到子宮繼續生長，可以利用這些本來要丟棄的多餘受精卵進行研究、拯救生命。

❽**反對者**：成體幹細胞也可以用於相同的研究與治療。

❾**支持者**：雖然相較於過去的看法，研究人員不斷在成體幹細胞中發現更強的適應性，但成體幹細胞的多能性比起胚胎幹細胞的複能性，仍然受限較多。

❿即使許多政府嚴格限制有關幹細胞的研究與經費籌措，科學家仍持續發展對幹細胞功用與潛能的知識。雖然許多政府與經濟政策已獲得解除，有關幹細胞潛力的完整研究成果，還是要數年後才能得以實現。

Chapter 11　基因療法

❶透過先進的基因改造科技，科學家為了治療或預防疾病，已發展出改造人類基因物質的技術。基因治療是一項實驗流程，將受到控制的基因注入受損的細胞內，以修復基因或預防有缺陷的基因導致疾病發生。醫師在使用藥物或手術治療疾病之前，可以先採行基因療法。

❷多數基因治療的研究是將正常的基因送入有缺陷的細胞中，取代異常或會引發疾病的基因，最常見的技術就是將治療性基因，又稱介質分子或載體，以基因工程進行改造，接著再導入病人體內的目標細胞。最為常見的載體就是基因改造病毒，它在動物體內會產生極大的作用，因為它會侵入細胞，迫使細胞複製病毒，這就是它在體內傳播的方式。研究人員可以利用病毒這種毀滅性的威力，以改造或摧毀異常的細胞，但前提是，改造的病毒只會以體內的異常細胞作為攻擊目標。非病毒載體也不斷在進行研發中，但一直到最近才發現一些基因修復的成功案例。

❸載體必須進行基因工程改造，主要是為了達到兩種特定的功能：

▶ **基因傳遞**：將病毒DNA或非病毒DNA引入受損的細胞內，以治療疾病或身體的異常。

▶ **基因表現**：DNA指令傳達至目標細胞，進而產生蛋白質，藉此改變了目標細胞的基因組成。

❹此一程序可舉一例說明：

> 當病人的肺部細胞被注入病毒載體→
> 載體將含有治療效果的人類基因留置在目標細胞內→
> 治療基因產生一種功能性蛋白質，使目標細胞回復原本正常的狀態。

❺基因治療有兩種主要的類型：

▶ **體細胞基因治療**：用於人類身體的基因療法，特別是針對人體組織的治療，使用的治療技巧包括：

- **基因抑制療法**：遏止或介入運作失常的基因活動。治療方式是引入載體，以抑制基因表現或是會導致傳染病、癌症和遺傳性疾病

307

的致病基因、異常基因活動。

- **基因消除**：特別針對目標基因所進行的治療程序，主要是為了迫使這些基因釋放出有毒物質，即一般為人所知的自殺基因。此療程必須特別針對自殺基因進行，否則將導致大範圍的細胞死亡。

- **基因增補**用於治療導致遺傳性疾病的無功能性基因，是將具備正常功能的複製基因，重新注入原本缺乏的身體基因內，以複製必須的蛋白質。

▶ **生殖細胞基因治療**：在胚胎仍處於成長期間即針對卵子或精子進行基因改造，該療法具有藉由後代基因來修正遺傳性疾病的可能性。

❻ 由於生殖細胞基因療法是由人類做出改變基因物質的決定，因而引起不少道德顧慮。無論科學家或一般大眾對此都感到憂心，包括長期所帶來的影響、社會觀感以及貧富差距可能導致無法公平獲得生殖細胞基因治療的機會，但最主要的顧慮，還是圍繞在生殖細胞基因治療本身的做法：

▶ **不可預期性**：進行生殖細胞基因治療時，基因改造的效果無法預測，即使病症得到治癒，還是有可能導致胚胎發生其他問題或產生變異。

▶ **主控權**：受到生殖細胞基因治療的病人子女完全無法表達個人看法，主張自己的基因是否應該進行改造。

▶ **濫用**：生殖細胞基因療法能夠增加個人身上值得擁有的特質、減少較差的特質，如此做法可能導致未來的世代成為所謂的「改造小孩」，由父母選擇個人的特性，甚至刻意製造出符合優生學的後代，這完全是對整體人類基因特質的刻意操弄。

❼ 在基因療法成為實用的治療疾病方法之前，研究人員還必須克服許多技術上的挑戰。將治療性基因與細胞結合的難題以及許多細胞迅速分裂的特性，都讓基因療法無法達到長期的效果。病毒載體也為病患帶來許多潛在的問題，包括產生發炎反應、毒性問題、基因的控制，病毒甚至可能突變，導致病人罹患其他疾病的風險。除此之外，基因療法特別難以有效治癒因多重基因缺陷所導致的病症。

❽ 然而，有幾項基因治療實驗已經出現令人期待的成果，成功治癒老鼠身上的鐮刀細胞型貧血，為將來人體治療應用先行鋪路。目前研究顯示基因療法有可能治癒地中海貧血症、囊胞性纖維症、帕金森氏症、還有包括黑色素瘤、肺癌等癌症。研究人員還發現，基因療法有可能治療耳聾和眼盲。雖然這些成功案例持續緩慢地增加，但就其為許多疾病提供根本或長期的治療而言，基因療法無論是作為唯一的治療方法或結合其他藥物治療，未來的發展都極具可觀性。

Chapter 12　罕見疾病藥物

❶ 相較於那些較為普遍的疾病，罕見疾病的研究在歷史上所受到的關注較少。這些罕見疾病，在美國的定義是少於二十萬人所罹患的疾病，在歐洲則是指每一萬人中不到五人罹患的病症，意味著要研發治療的新藥，亦即罕見疾病藥物，市場開發的潛力較小。直到今日，市面上有250種研發成功的罕見疾病藥品，然而，全世界卻存在五千種以上的罕見疾病。製造和取得罕見疾病藥物存在許多難題，這是因為藥品製造的不確定性（僅有少數分子測試顯示藥物具有療效）、發現新藥物分子到核准藥物上市的時間長度（通常是十年），以及經費問題（生產罕見疾病藥物的費用是一般藥品的數倍）。

❷ 基於公眾需求而非經濟誘因所生產的藥物，常被認定為罕見疾病藥物。有些藥物雖然是用於治療較為普遍的疾病，當發現它同時具有應付罕見疾病徵候的療效，也會重新被指定為罕見疾病藥物。最後，罕見疾病藥物也有可能是無法上市販賣的產品，原因也許是藥物在研發過程中無法取得專利，又或者是因為藥品的目標市場無法負擔購買藥物的費用（這是替第三世界國家開發罕見疾病藥物的獨特難題）。

❸ 絕大多數的罕見疾病藥品，接近80％，皆為生技製藥—以生物科技製造出的藥品，其中一個實例就是ATryn，是萃取基因轉殖山羊乳所生產出人類重組抗凝血物質的藥品。ATryn的功效是當人體缺少通常存在於血漿內的抗凝血酵素時，適度調節凝血作用，常使用在風險高的手術療程中。另一

項研發中的藥物則與介白素有關，這是一種因基因內冷凝比林（CIAS1）變異而過度產生的蛋白質。當數量過盛時，介白素會引起發炎反應，導致一些如冷凝比林相關週期症候群等罕見疾病發生，然而當介白素與藥物接觸，就不會再附著於細胞表面受體，反而可以從體內被沖走。另一種在研發中的藥物也很類似，能抑制人體免疫系統內造成發炎反應的蛋白質，這類蛋白質可能會使體內多重器官發炎或受損。

4 過去二十年來，許多政府都採行相關措施，確保能研發出適當的醫療與生物製品，治療各種罕見疾病。自80年代初期，全球各地即開始實施激勵措施，鼓勵開發罕見藥品。為了應付藥物研究缺乏與經濟誘因不足的問題，美國在1983年通過罕見疾病藥品法案，針對鼓勵臨床研究、提供罕見藥品獎金、租稅優惠以及經藥物管理局核准藥品享有七年的獨家販賣權等獎勵措施，提供經濟補助。在法案通過前的十年間，所生產販賣的罕見疾病藥物只有10種，但是自1983年起，超過230種罕見藥品在美國上市。歐洲議會在1999年也通過了類似的規定，提供藥品財務補助，給予歐洲醫藥評估局核准藥品十年獨家銷售的專利。日本在1993年開始實施罕見疾病藥物條例，為厚生勞動省核准的藥物提供市場販售的獎勵，以及五年的市場專屬權以茲發展。

5 後基因時代的一項獨特挑戰，將是對罕見疾病藥物的重新定義。診斷學與科學研究的持續進展，會影響常見疾病中次要族群的定義，因而導致罕見疾病及其治療轉而被定義為超級罕見的性質。罕見疾病認定範圍的擴張必然會加深治療藥物與產品的道德辯論，例如科學界對於是否該為特殊疾病和治療爭取資金補助仍持分歧意見。成本效益一直以來都是研發罕見疾病藥物的重大問題，而公平分配的問題—在健康效益與資源使用間取得平衡—也是擴大研發其他罕見疾病藥品的重要課題。分子醫學的進步讓多數利害關係雙方相信，罕見疾病藥物的研究與製造，將在二十一世紀持續發燒。除了道德爭議與可能發生的安全問題，許多人發現，罕見疾病藥物其實也為全球合作創造出一個正面的契機。

Chapter 13　發光半導體

1 過去兩個世紀以來，由於科技的創新，天然光源的替代品種類迅速擴增。對白熾燈的實驗從十九世紀初期開始，發電時，電子沿著燈泡裡的鎢絲線移動會產生高溫，白熾光即是從高溫的原子（約攝氏2200度）內所釋放出的光子，在此過程中，將近90%的熱能會流失，故製造的光線很微弱，實際上也不具有能源效率。緊接著發明了日光燈，燈管上塗抹的一層磷粉使日光燈製造的光線更為明亮。當加熱後的水銀原子與磷相互碰撞，磷原子的溫度會升高，因而發出光亮。使用日光燈時只有微量的能源和熱源損失，因此比白熾燈更能節省能源。

2 節能效率遠超過白熾燈與日光燈的是固態照明，係使用發光二極體（LED）做為光線來源。LED在60年代首度開發，但直到80年代才普遍為人使用。LED光是固態半導體所發出的光線，並不是從鎢絲線或燈管產生。儘管可以使用其他的化學元素或是化合物作為半導體，但最常見的材料還是矽，而導電方式是攙入其他雜質，無論是增加電子創造更多能量（N型半導體）或製造出缺乏電子的空洞（P型半導體），兩種方式都會創造更多電子活動，因而產生更多能源。

3 用於製造光線的固態半導體稱為二極真空管，由N型半導體和P型半導體共同組成，使電子從一個電極流到另一個電極，但不能夠反向流動。當半導體二極管內產生電流（密封在連接至電源的套膜裡），即產生可見光。初期LED僅能發出微弱的光線，大部分照明設備使用LED的價格也過於昂貴，因此早期對LED的應用，往往是當作工具儀表板、儀器設備和汽車儀表板等裝置的固態指示燈。LED的照明亮度在二十一世紀已有相當的進步，得以廣泛運用在消耗性個人電子產品、交通號誌和戶外展示等外部照明上，甚至能應用於生化檢測過程及醫療器材。

4 根據光源的演色性指數（CRI），即測量以白光照明時重現物體外觀色彩的清晰程度，LED燈的顯色品質尚無法與陽光或其他光源相提並論。

自然光和白熾燈	100 CRI
日光燈	85 CRI
未來的LED燈	80 CRI
目前的LED燈	70 CRI

能源效率是以輸入電力和產生的光線量（流明）比例做為測量基準，未來LED燈的節能效率與使用年限，很可能高於白熾燈或日光燈的10倍。

未來的LED燈	150到200流明	10萬小時
日光燈	85流明	1萬小時
目前的LED燈	30流明	2萬小時
白熾燈泡	16流明	1千小時

LED燈擁有更佳的節能效率與更長的使用壽命，可為消費者節省近90%的照明成本，此外，LED照明尚有顯著減少能源排放的潛能。隨著LED技術的進步，全世界用在照明的電力可以減少一半，節省的電力將可應用於其他層面，且全球的碳排放量也可能大幅降低。

❺ 多數LED照明使用的是無機半導體，但使用有機發光二極體（OLED）的數量亦在成長中。OLED所使用的有機半導體材料—碳基小分子或聚合物，擁有分明的層次，在供應電力後會發出冷光。OLED材料使半導體更具彈性，應用上也更趨多元，且OLED照明比一般LED燈的光線更明亮、更快、也更清晰。目前OLED照明的價格已經比LED燈更低，若再增加使用上的可靠性，很可會能取代以往的各種照明設備。

❻ 未來LED照明將廣泛使用於公私領域。許多研究人員預測，LED燈很快會以更經濟的方式生產，取代白熾燈和日光燈等家用照明設備，且LED燈的亮度、維修容易／使用期限長、節省能源等優點，將會遠超過其他照明。日本已經開始使用LED燈取代傳統的路燈，除了節省能源和成本之外，LED燈製造出的光線投射更為均勻，刺眼的程度也達到最低。未來幾年內，博物館內可能會改用LED燈，除了能節省成本，還能降低館裡的溫度、消除紫外線；這兩項功能都能增加參觀者的舒適感，讓藝術作品保存更完好。而在接下來的數年間，傳統照明極有可能隨著LED燈和OLED燈的廣泛使用而遭到淘汰。

Chapter 14　半導體與環境安全

❶ 在二十一世紀，半導體設備的製造是一項全球性的事業，40年代末期開發出全球第一個電晶體後，世界各地的企業都迅速挺進半導體產業。1970年代，「半導體產業協會」創立，很快即著手研擬產業的指導方針，希望此一迅速蓬勃的行業能健全而成功的發展。隨著半導體事業在歐洲、日本、韓國、台灣等地的成長，產業也趨於全球性的發展規模。這些國家聯合發起「國際半導體技術藍圖」這項計畫，希望在面對創新且瞬息萬變的環境挑戰下，仍能保證產品品質，同時確保整體產業的健全經濟與完善環境。

❷ 雖然健全的世界經濟仍是各半導體產業組織目前關注的核心問題，但環境健康也已經成為他們留心的重點。許多組織為改善半導體產業的整體環境、健康與安全狀態，訂出各項標準和實用的指導守則，其中受到關切的特殊議題包括環境管理，特別是有毒廢棄物的處理問題、職業健康與安全，以及消防與建築安全等問題。

❸ 在80年代初期，全世界的半導體產業都在尋找有毒化學材料的替代品。半導體的製造過程會產生大量有害工作和整體環境的廢棄物，在生產半導體的過程中，會釋出好幾種具毒性的化學物質，它們也會擴散流進工業廢水中。這些有毒物質包括二氧化矽、銅和氟化物，毒性最強也最具危險性的廢棄物是砷。砷和鎵合成的化合物（砷化鎵）其電子速度較矽更快，擁有更高的電子移動率，因而在電子產品中得以產生更高的頻率和更快的速度，但是，以鎵作為半導體材料時，砷的功能是拿來當作摻雜劑（摻質）；在製造程序中砷被釋出成為廢料，這些廢料被運送到掩埋場後很可能會汙染地下水。即使許多政府對砷廢棄物的排放都訂下規範標準進行管制，美國北部卻發現大量的砷廢棄物，而在東

南亞各地都有暴露高度砷汙染的情形。美國國家環境保護局（EPA）現正努力帶領全球減少砷廢棄物的排放，同時盡力找出具有經濟利益又能兼顧安全的鎵再利用方法。畢竟鎵是一種數量稀少、價格又昂貴的金屬元素。

4 1995年，美國的半導體產業和環境保護局達成一項協議，雙方約定要大幅減少排放造成高度全球暖化潛勢（GWP）的氣體，尤其是全氟碳化物（PFCs）。全氟碳化物在大氣中的生命期很長，很可能導致環境、氣候改變，對經濟造成破壞性的影響。美國環境保護局的這項協議為全球政府與產業間的類似協議立下準據，1999年，「世界半導體委員會」開始採行一項保護氣候的方案，計畫在2010年底之前減少全氟碳化物的排放量，至少必須比產業在1995年的標準再減少10%。

5 有毒化學物質也讓半導體產業的員工暴露在具有風險的工作環境中：

- **急性曝露**：會導致各種呼吸、消化和皮膚疾病
- **長期曝露**：導致各種疾病，從皮膚病至數種癌症類型都有可能

6 很多國家的政府組織，如「美國國家職業安全衛生研究所」，即針對工作環境的有毒化學物設定容許暴露濃度值（PEL）的指標，當管理與工程控制做得不夠完善時，可能會要求工作人員穿上個人保護裝備。如果工作人員曾經曝露在具有毒性的化學汙染物下，即必須進行消毒工作，保障衣物和個人的衛生。

7 消防與建築安全同樣也是保障員工健康安全的重點。一般的建築消防法規並沒有針對半導體製造過程中所使用的多種化學物質和無塵室（在製造過程中使用的無汙染室）物理環境的要求提供適當的安全保障。為了滿足這項安全需求，半導體產業協會成立了「消防建築安全委員會」（FABS），為整體產業提供指導準則，同時結合應用地區性的消防建築法規，這些準則就化學原料的儲存、工作站的化學含量、建築使用的材料都訂下嚴格的標準，而消防建築安全委員會的成立，也為所有參與半導體產業協會的國家帶來重大的衝擊。

8 在90年代晚期，世界半導體委員會成立環境、安全與健康小組，欲就下列事項推動全球一致的行事準據及成果評鑑標準：

- ▶ 資源保護
- ▶ 汙染防制
- ▶ 降低全氟碳化物排放量
- ▶ 廢棄物處理
- ▶ 具有環保、安全、健康（ESH）意識的產品設計
- ▶ 創造安全而健康的工作環境
- ▶ 達到全球性的「最佳實踐」

9 上述有關全球環境、安全與健康問題等目標的可行性與執行績效，則會在年度國際半導體環境安全健康研討會中，根據各項制訂標準進行一年一次的評量。

Chapter 15　半導體與能源效率

1 每年半導體元件售出的數量超過五千億，而使用半導體元件的產品類型從攜帶型電子產品到人造衛星，為社會貢獻全面的效率與便利。半導體元件同時也領導潔淨能源，應用於取代汙染能源、減少自然資源的使用，並降低有毒氣體與廢棄物的排放。

2 半導體是積體電路（IC）的基本材料，而今日大多數的電子器材都是靠積體電路驅動。IC，或一般俗稱的晶片，是單晶結構的半導體材料，例如矽，結合電子電路與同一晶體製造的零件組合而成。積體電路可能由數百萬種元件組成，當簡短的訊號通過電路時，能夠以更快的速度、使用更低的電量傳遞。大量生產這些小型電路的價格相對而言並不昂貴，且製造的小型電路還具備高度可靠、高效節能、高速處理等特性。

3 積體電路的發展成果包括高效率壓縮機與除霜功能，使冰箱與冷凍庫的能源效率提升20%；安裝節能馬達的洗碗機所使用的能源比傳統洗碗機減少近40%，水的用量也同樣較少；類似的節能方法用在洗衣機上也一樣可行，洗衣機內的先進電路系統可以降低能源使用量，故每年能夠省下好幾千加

命的水；至於數位訊號處理器則讓高畫質電視與其他數位電器用品擁有高能量轉換效率（能源輸入轉換為有用的能源輸出過程中，只損失很少的能量）。

❹數位電子設備組件也會裝配半導體照明，又稱固態照明（SSL），其節能減碳的表現凌駕過去所有的照明設備。一般消費者或企業若使用固態照明，可以節省超過50%的電力，除此之外，固態照明還能降低全球30%的總體能源消耗量，若將其與電池和太陽能技術的直接相容性考慮進去，能源節省的總量甚至能增加更多。

❺太陽能科技的應用必須仰賴光電（PV）電池，雖然太陽能板的電力為可再生能源的使用提供另一項選擇，但目前太陽能板的運作僅有15%的能源轉換效率。以半導體材料製成的光電電池會吸收太陽光，來自太陽光的熱能使電子得以在半導體材料內流通，因而產生電力。由於只有部分太陽光能源能夠驅動電子，且半導體材料也會反射陽光，因此實際發電的能源大約僅占太陽光的15%。光電製造業目前仍努力研擬方案，欲增進太陽能電池的使用效率。

❻晶片科技的其他發展還包括適應性電壓調節（AVS），一項先進的能源處理程序，經調節後，能在不增加能源用量或縮減組件使用壽命的情況下增加電壓，加快處理效率。事實上，使用AVS可以減少高達70%的數位處理器能源用量。LCD（液晶顯示器）技術是由亮光穿過液晶極化偏光鏡後，在平面上創造出影像，將LCD技術應用在攜帶型電子產品、電視和電腦上，能夠節省30%以上的能源使用量。由於許多攜帶型電子產品都以驅動太陽能系統的晶片技術充電，因此要省下更多能源的目標將可以迅速達成。

❼晶片啟動的特性能降低車輛的能源用量，同時增加車輛的性能與可靠度。積體電路的應用則在許多方面都能節省汽車燃料用量，包括使用計時與燃燒控制，以及燃油直接噴射引擎，而晶片啟動的蒸發排放控制系統則增進車輛節省燃油和減少汙染的可能性。將IC技術應用於遠距辦公和電話會議上，甚至能減少實際駕駛車輛的需求。

❽若產業使用變速驅動器（VSD）和變頻驅動器（VFD）來調節馬達驅動系統的速度以配合系統負載量，即可以達到節省能源的效果。定速驅動器在車輛發動後通常會使系統負載量達到高峰，導致負載量或流量下降時的能源使用無效率，而晶片啟動的變速驅動器能使馬達速度符合系統負載要求，此一程序能夠節省75%以上的使用能源。

❾全球無數機構都盡力採用先進的半導體技術，希望達到節省能源的目標。「能源效率公會（CEE）」是位於北美的非營利機構，致力推廣節能產品，同時鼓勵能源市場在整體結構與行動上進行變革；美國能源部的「高效能源及再生能源辦公室（EERE）」則進行國際性的宣導，推動使用可再生能源，包括那些利用迅速開發的半導體技術所創造的資源；至於「世界半導體委員會」，2008年在台北所舉辦的會議中做出一項聲明，承諾半導體產業將繼續努力貢獻，維持更潔淨的生態環境。

Chapter 16　奈米科技簡介

❶奈米科技最基本的定義就是對奈米尺寸物質進行組合及操作運用的過程。奈米尺寸能夠測量比微小物質更小的物體，測量的尺寸約從1奈米（nm）至100奈米不等。1奈米是1毫米的100萬分之1，若以更具體的方式表達，一張紙的厚度是10萬奈米。事實上，原子的尺寸比奈米尺寸還小（1奈米粗估為3或4個原子的大小），但奈米尺寸才是物質能夠合成的最小基礎單位。奈米科學就是要研究奈米尺寸物質的性質與作用，研發出使用這些物質最有利的方式。

❷當物質為奈米尺寸大小時，其作用狀態與大體積物質相當不同。奈米材料具有較大的表面積與體積比，這表示相對於大型材料，奈米材料暴露在外的表面積更多，也因此，它與周圍環境能產生交互作用的範圍較大，加強奈米材料對外部作用產生某些特殊反應的能力，例如導熱或反射光線。至於碳奈米結構，當它被結合應用在單車或棒球等產品上，其結構體不但比傳統的木材或鋁等材料更加堅固，就實際情況而言，它其實算是目前所知最穩固的結構。奈米碳管同樣也有新穎的超導電特性，此

一特性讓它未來極可能超越矽、鎵等元素的活動速度與生產力,而兩者正是目前半導體產業所使用的元素。

❸奈米科技原本是指由原子開始堆疊建立的架構,亦即由下往上的建構方式。早在1959年,諾貝爾獎得主物理學家理查‧費曼即提出此一技術願景;1980年代,艾瑞克‧卓斯勒繼續發展費曼的理念,將「奈米科技」一詞變得普及化,但艾瑞克是特別針對生產分子尺寸機械裝置的可能性而言,即所謂分子製造。此後奈米科技的定義即擴展為研發從奈米科學到奈米製程等技術的跨學科領域。

❹奈米科技源自大自然中渾然天成的一切事物發展,天然奈米工程的實例之一,就是光合作用的基本程序,目前科學家正在發展人造光合作用,創造乾淨的能源;另一個例子是運用蓮花葉的奈米結構,製造出天然的防水界線。蓮花葉的結構已被模仿製造出各式各樣能夠防水的材料;而蜘蛛絲因含有奈米微晶,自然強化結構,能夠延展40%的長度、比鋼多吸收一百倍的能量卻不斷裂。研究人員相信他們不僅能以人工方法複製蜘蛛絲,還能將微晶體重置於更強韌的絲纖維內。由於蜘蛛絲的主要成分為蛋白質和水,因此這項環保的複製流程可以取代目前生產如克維拉(Kevlar)等耐久性人造纖維所使用的刺激性化學原料。

❺由美國政府創立,負責監督奈米科技整體研究與發展計畫的國家奈米科技啟動計畫(NNI),提出發展奈米科技至少要規劃四個階段,而目前完成的只有前兩個階段。

▶ **被動式奈米結構**:具有穩定的結構與功能,應用在改進各種產品的組成零件。
  - 使高爾夫球飛出去的角度更直
  - 製作抗化學性的戰鬥軍服
  - 隔離有害光線,增加對皮膚保護的保養品

▶ **主動式奈米結構**:在運作時會產生變動的奈米結構。
  - 應用於雷射裝置
  - 會在輸送過程中改變藥物化學成分的藥物輸送粒子

▶ **系統化奈米系統**:生物集合或自我組合所創造的系統。
  - 為組織工程架設結構

▶ **分子奈米系統**:各分子皆有自己獨特的結構及角色功能的異質分子系統。
  - 能夠控制光線與物質間相互作用以保存能源的分子集合

❻將奈米科技應用在商業的好處包括:能濾淨全球的水資源、製造出潔淨的效率能源並分配使用,同時利用精密農業創造更健康的環境,從而燃料的使用量降低、對汙染的監測也減少。但隨著奈米科技的研發與應用,風險也隨之增加。奈米材料也有可能受到濫用,例如被使用在侵入性的監視系統、被恐怖分子用於大規模的毀滅性武器,且低成本奈米材料的激增還會造成經濟的崩解。「前瞻奈米中心」、「奈米科技全球議題工作小組」,以及其他相關的全球性組織,都在盡其努力確保奈米科技的正面發展,而對奈米科技目前所面臨的挑戰及風險,也提供基本的指導,並且協助改進全球奈米科技的相關政策。

Chapter 17 破壞性科技

❶「破壞性科技」一詞最早由哈佛商學院教授克雷頓‧克里斯汀生於1977年提出,他以此描述顛覆已開發技術,最終革新消費者使用習慣、產品價值及經濟競爭的科技,它改變了某些科學技術的現狀與特定技術的市場結構。二十一世紀,破壞性科技的實例包括取代其他儲存個人資料方式的快閃式記憶體,以及在專業市場外大量取代傳統底片攝影的數位攝影。奈米科技的創新發明,如奈米管、奈米球、奈米線,都是基於商業化所發展出來的最新破壞性科技。

❷生醫科技、能源效率與生物恐怖攻擊,是目前在製造及傳播面都因奈米科技發展而受到破壞的三個重要領域。對生醫科技而言,奈米科技正迅速成為其診斷與治療癌症的顛覆性技術。

- 量子點（奈米晶體半導體）可就基因和蛋白質做光學檢測，也有使腫瘤與淋巴結顯影化的可能。
- 奈米殼層（核心為氧化矽，外殼為金屬）將很快能應用在針對深層組織內癌細胞所進行的熱消融術（熱摧毀療法）與腫瘤成像顯影。
- 奈米線和碳奈米管可使用在進行疾病的蛋白質生物標記檢查、DNA突變檢測與基因表現檢測。
- 樹狀高分子（含有分子的圓形奈米結構）能透過顯像劑診斷出是否罹患癌症，同時還能控制藥物遞送時釋出的劑量協助治療。
- 對於可溶性低的藥物，奈米晶體能改善其配方。
- 奈米分子能應用在多功能治療與標的性給藥。

❸ 透過更敏銳與精密的程序，包括增加癌症細胞的局部檢測，這些破壞性科技將大幅改善偵測癌症細胞的速度與可靠性。目前雖然進行癌症研究治療的成本與發病率都有持續上升的趨勢，但未來在生產奈米設備更經濟的情況下，癌症預防可能性增加，再加上檢測與治療成本減少，將大幅減低癌症相關治療的費用。

❹ 二十一世紀初，節能科技與能源儲存設備，可能會讓以化石燃料作為能源的做法大轉彎：

- **奈米電池**：矽電池能與其他電子組件合成為單一裝置，奈米尺寸的體積即可發電，同時只製造出需要的電力大小。這兩項進步的功能會大量減少電力浪費，如此一來就能延長電池壽命、減少電力的輸出。
- **太陽能**：開發以奈米晶體製造的超薄不定型太陽能電池，奈米晶體具有較高的太陽光電電力轉換效率，這類有機電池與無機電池的電力較強、彈性較大，而生產的成本也不貴。
- **風能**：奈米鍍膜，包括除冰與自潔技術，會減少風力發電的障礙。

❺ 破壞性科技還包括能夠偵測出生物危機並提出警示的產品，或許也能應用於預防生化恐怖攻擊。

- 感應科技能迅速感測到微量的化學與生物元素，對傳染性疾病如SARS做出防護。
- 探測器能追蹤阿茲海默症的病人，或身處危險環境的工人，或是偵察到他們所在的位置。
- 警告系統可能很快能應用在警示農業面臨的威脅，如狂牛症或禽流感。

❻ 破壞性科技很快也將對全球安全形成更多的影響，讓維安系統能順應即將面臨的威脅做出調整，提供前瞻性而非反應性的技術。

- 生物辨識提供進行臉部識別與多重特徵識別（如虹膜掃瞄與指紋造影）的可能性。
- 可搜尋監視保全系統，能夠預防政府資訊與基礎結構遭受網路攻擊。
- 奈米衛星能蒐集恐怖活動的相關情報，舉例來說，這種衛星能夠在監測化學或生物戰劑時，將有犯罪嫌疑的實驗室拍攝下來。

❼ 即使破壞性科技擁有這些重大的優勢，但潛在的風險同樣也存在著。

- **健康風險**：有毒物質與材料、生化危機、超細微奈米分子、奈米製造食物導致不明的安全危機，例如抗營養素與過敏原。環境保護局即指出，目前的化學特性識別功能尚不足以使用在奈米材料上。
- **環境風險**：奈米材料在大氣層、土壤、水源裡的反應作用尚未得知；生物分解的潛在機制不明。
- **安全風險**：生物攻擊，如廣泛散布病原體，以及如放射性炸彈等生化武器。
- **經濟風險**：破壞貿易關係、取代現存的商品市場，便宜產品充斥導致經濟混亂，與經濟、社會政策的不平等。

❽ 奈米科技是一般預測將在數年內對全球市場造成重大衝擊的破壞性科技，雖然它對部分現存產業，如生醫設備與汽車零件的生產，造成反面的破壞，但就長期而言，它將為能源、健康與環境等產業帶來降低成本與改善效率等益處。

英式英語及美式英語拼字的差異：	
美式英語	英式英語
labeled, tumor	labelled, tumour
behavior, realize	behaviour, realise
visualization	visualisation

Chapter 18　奈米製造技術

❶ 隨著奈米技術進步，最有可能崛起的應用領域之一當屬製造業。部分研究人員預測，在未來的十年內，多達半數生產及應用材料的創新都會以奈米尺寸呈現。奈米製造的內容同時包括使用奈米材料及應用奈米技術生產更大規模的產品。現今奈米製造的研究與發展如此迅速，許多行業的領導者都相信，此一技術會引發二十一世紀全球性的產業革命。

❷ 奈米製造的目標是將奈米科學的研究發現，有效地轉換成創新、適合使用且富應用責任的科技。奈米製造術正蓄勢待發，將起而革新全球的生產力、能源效率和經濟，目前應用在處理奈米材料的做法有許多種，實例如下：

▶ **奈米鍍膜、薄膜及奈米合成材料**：奈米材料，如奈米晶體，被應用在大規模的產品上，作為耐高溫、耐磨損、耐腐蝕及耐刮痕之用。採用這些技術有許多好處，從強化儀器的切割功能到耐刮光學儀器的製造，以及生產多種耐用且節能的各種汽車類型。

▶ **奈米觸媒**：為使大規模製造產品產生化學反應所使用的奈米分子或一群奈米材料。奈米觸媒能增強化學物質、石油、紙漿與紙張，以及能源的生產。使用奈米觸媒的好處包括降低生產成本及減少環境汙染源。

❸ 奈米製造過程包括5個主要階段：合成、分解、淨化、穩定、組成，在每一個階段材料的性質都會改變，因此必須進行檢查以保障品質。

▶ **合成**：特定性質反應產生後，改變奈米材料的特性作為應用。

▶ **分解**：在不影響奈米材料特性，即品質和結構的條件下，剔除無用的成分。至於最常必須進行的分解過程，是對奈米材料分子的解構。

▶ **淨化**：部分奈米產品需要做進一步的分離，但需要與否取決於技術的應用目的，例如是作為電子或光學的運用。

▶ **穩定**：為配合儲存、運送或特殊使用，可能需要進行修正工作。奈米製造的挑戰之一，就是在變更產品表面材質時，仍須維持奈米材料本身的特性，如導熱或磁性。

▶ **組成**：直接組合成產品，或是另作修正調整後再合成奈米產品。

❹ 奈米製造面臨一些非常特殊的挑戰。目前，在未證實奈米製造方法能夠增加生產績效前，僅能產出數量有限的產品，且以舊有方法生產所製造出的大量廢棄物，目前也不會因此減少。奈米製造技術的研發部門，正積極地找出在不影響奈米材料特性並大量減少有毒廢料的情況下，能夠大規模生產奈米產品的方法。負責任的技術開發是奈米製造的一大重點，風險管理研究必須要找出經工程改造和天然奈米材料可能造成的潛在影響，並加以處置、解決製造過程中可能產生有毒物質的問題，同時還必須能夠處理奈米製造所引發的其他社會問題，如法律及道德議題。

❺ 另外，奈米製造也採用最新技術，保障產品能維持最佳品質。舉例來說，要控制奈米結構與奈米合成材料的組合過程，革新的技術不可或缺，而為了精確測量奈米材料，要求對量測科學（計量學）的創新運用與儀器或其他電腦工具的進步發展。

❻ 奈米製造技術最後將與所有類型的生產形式結合，開發出無數供日常生活使用的產品，並增加將來研發製造出創新產品的可能性，最終將引發製造業在健康、安全與環境方面的革命。奈米科技使低成本與節能的製造過程變成可能，從而將促成大量革命性產品的出現，如：

▶ 進步的能源儲藏技術
▶ 價格能夠負擔的太陽能
▶ 輕型節能車
▶ 潔淨煤工廠
▶ 淨水設備與處理程序
▶ 藥物輸送設備
▶ 檢測疾病的奈米尺寸生物感測器

❼ 雖然奈米製造對經濟及環境能源的節省效果頗大，但目前仍需負擔相當的成本與投資風險。要同時使大企業與剛起步的小公司降低風險，需要全球共同合作，研擬策略與激勵的誘因；政府可藉由

推動計畫幫助清楚定義智慧財產權的範圍，維護奈米科技的發展；而私人組織及公民組織也能對奈米製造的發展有所貢獻，方式包括擬訂各種有利政策，類型從經濟獎勵到政府贊助創新研究的成果發布；至於科際整合與全球攜手合作則是可以提供共享資訊的工具，協助奈米製造廠商使用新興的奈米技術，建立學術研究與商業應用間的聯繫。

英式英語及美式英語拼字的差異：

美式英語	英式英語
stabilize, oxidize, fiber	stablise, oxidize, fibre

Chapter 19　無線網路

❶雖然無線科技看似近期才剛興起的通訊科技，然而事實上，無線通訊服務已存在超過一個世紀。1896年，古利耶莫·馬可尼在成功研究出遠距無線電波後，即創立了無線電訊有限公司。1901年，無線電訊號穿越大西洋，二十世紀中，無線通訊技術證實為不可或缺的軍事工具，儼然已成為一項兩用科技。無線電訊號能夠將計畫和指示內容轉換為傳送和接收的密碼，無須冒資料未經授權被取得的風險。

❷1970年代，企業與機構開始對無線技術進行變革，過去用電線連結以分享資訊的電腦和其他電子設備，此時則是被無線電頻率（RF）取代。供應交流電連至天線後創造出電磁場，有時候被稱為無線電波，會透過空間傳播。

❸無線網路的範圍可能只涵蓋一個相對小型的區域，如住家或辦公室，也可能廣泛至跨越國際。在某個區域範圍內的電腦網路稱為區域網路（LAN），區域網路連結範圍內的各個電腦結點，或中央處理器，使網路系統內的每一部電腦都可以互相取得設備與資料。兩個以上的區域網路能夠結合為廣域網路（WAN），廣域網路通常涵蓋大型的地理範圍，各結點間則通常透過公用網路如電話系統或衛星結合，而目前存在最大的廣域網路就是網際網路。

❹沒有任何一種網路是完全無線的，至少有一項設備會使用到線路。舉例來說，在家庭電腦網路系統中，可能會有一台電腦經電線與路由器連結。路由器是作為網路存取器（AP）之用，將無線訊號播送出去，家中其他台電腦在偵測到訊號後，即調整至相當的頻率。路由器會連接有線網路的可得資源，尤其是網路連線，而擁有無線網路的電腦則是透過無線網卡與路由器或網路存取器連上網路。無線網卡可能內建在個人電腦的硬體設備裡，也可以插入擴充槽、隨身碟接口，筆記型電腦的無線網卡可能內建，也可以插入PC卡插槽後使用。

❺「電機電子工程師學會」（IEEE）建立了一套無線網路標準，各項網路設備必須嚴格遵守。符合IEEE的驗證標準即被稱作WiFi（也稱無線相容性認證）。WiFi無線網路的傳輸效果比手機和電視更強大，其設備是利用無線電頻譜，以2千4百兆赫或5千兆赫頻寬傳送，且傳送資料的速度介於每秒1千1百萬位元（11 Mbps）和2億7千萬位元（270 Mbps）間。WiFi無線網路的類型有好幾種：

▶ 802.11b傳送的頻率為2千4百兆赫，它的傳輸速度是最慢的11 Mbps，也是價格最低的無線網路標準。它使用互補碼鍵控（CCK）的調變方式，一種將有限的資料序列搭配在一起，以增加傳輸速度的過程。

▶ 802.11a以5千兆赫的頻率傳輸，速率最高可達每秒5千4百萬位元。此種無線網路使用的是效率更佳的調變方法，稱為正交分頻多工系統（OFDM），在無線電訊號傳送至接收器前，將其分解成數個子訊號的編碼過程，因而增加傳輸的速度，同時能減少干擾。

▶ 802.11g以2千4百兆赫的頻率傳輸，由於使用的是正交分頻多工系統，傳輸速率每秒可高達5千4百萬位元。

▶ 802.11n是目前可用的最新無線網路標準，據說傳輸速率每秒高達1億4千萬位元，IEEE已在2009年正式核准。

❻無線網路的訊號容易受到干擾，通常是因為建築物的各式建材影響，如混凝土或玻璃，可能會使無線電波轉向或吸收電波。有時建築物中的其他電器產品，如無線電話或微波爐，都可能因為使用

相同的頻率波段而干擾訊號；利用特殊天線更正無線電波傳送的方向或改變無線網路硬體的擺放位置，都可以修正訊號的干擾。

❼如果沒有加密的功能，未經授權的使用者很可能連上任何一家無線網路。無線網路加密系統會擾亂資料頻率，惟有持正確密碼的使用者才能取得資訊。幾種標準的加密機制包括：

▶ **有線等效保密（WEP）:** 基地台與電腦兩端都需進行使用者認證，但加密的過程卻證實不夠周延，這是因為被鎖碼的資料，可能只透過一組數有限字的金鑰串傳送，或是共享一組不常更換的密碼，讓駭客有機可趁查到密碼。

▶ **無線網絡安全存取（WPA）:** 要求每一位無線網路的使用者輸入通行碼，產生個人專屬的加密金鑰。加密金鑰的數值會經常改變，提供更安全的防護措施。

▶ **無線網絡安全存取進階版（WPA 2）:** 使用進階加密標準（AES）為資料加密。進階加密標準的加密與解密都是使用專用晶片處理，因此升級至WPA 2系統可能需要更新或購買額外的硬體設備。

❽無線網路持續迅速地發展，目前研究的重心已從網路的覆蓋範圍轉變為實際的負載量，使用者傳送資料的速度幾乎每年增加一倍。為了面對發展而生的挑戰，如今研究人員已經將研究重點放在能夠整合行動通訊和電腦網路系統的跨層設計與混合型網路上。

Chapter 20 ｜ USB 技術

❶通用序列匯流排（USB）是一種電腦的通用界面，也就是互相連結的系統。USB的設計目的在於解決對介面卡及輔助界面如並列埠、串列埠的需求。USB接口內建在電腦中（有超過90%的電腦都配備USB接口），以搭配連結其他外接設備的USB連接線。USB使電腦更為多樣化，因為它讓電腦或主機運作時可以增加或是移除額外的功能設備，事實上，USB控制器能夠支援目前所有類型的電腦周邊設備：

▶ 鍵盤 ▶ 印表機 ▶ 控制桿 ▶ 滑鼠 ▶ 遊戲遙控器
▶ 外接硬碟 ▶ 外接光碟機 ▶ 大容量資料儲存裝置
▶ 攝影機 ▶ 行動電話 ▶ 影音裝置
▶ 各種小電器，像是烤麵包機、空氣濕潤器和鬧鐘

❷有好幾家公司，包括康柏電腦、IBM（國際商業機器股份有限公司）、英特爾和微軟公司，都投入流行的趨勢，在90年代初期創造了第一代的USB。這些公司共同建立了名為USB應用廠商論壇（USB-IF）的非營利機構，負責監控USB的銷售市場、規格標準和搭配的應用程式。至1997年，USB已經和許多家出產個人電腦的公司結合，不久之後，Windows 98成為第一個配置USB的作業系統，同年，iMac亦成為蘋果電腦第一台搭配USB的產品。

❸USB技術是透過被稱作管線的聯絡管道，讓電腦與其周邊設備得以共享資訊。通常以USB連結一項設備到電腦上會使用32條管線，16條連接到主控制器，另外16條則由主控制器送出。每當主機的電力開啟，就會主動搜尋所有連結的周邊設備，並經由外接設備內裝的特定驅動器，為每一項配備指定名稱，接下來隨著機器的運轉，管線會持續記錄，檢查主控制器的狀況，確認是否需要提供額外或不同的共享資訊。

❹USB能支援的周邊設備多達127種，係因其應用的階層式星狀架構或星狀拓撲架構，是由配備USB插孔的多埠USB集線器所支援。

❺USB集線器：用於增加USB插孔數量的USB配備，以一台有三個接口的集線器為例，就是由一個連接至電腦USB的插口與兩個支援外接設備的插口所構成。

❻USB插孔：USB接頭是透過各種插孔類型與電腦連結：包括A型、B型、迷你插孔及微型插孔。

▶ **A型插孔:** 位於電腦或集線器上的長方形接口

▶ **B型插孔:** 位於集線器輸入端和電腦周邊設備上的正方形接口

▶ **迷你插孔:** 其設計與標準的A型插孔和B型插孔相同，但用於較小的電子產品，如PDA、行動電話與數位相機。

317

▶**微型插孔**：比迷你插孔更小，用於取代手機或較小型的攜帶式電子設備等插孔。

7 USB 技術已經歷經數個世代的演進，第一代產品是 USB 1.0 和 USB 1.1，資料傳輸的速率範圍從 1.5 Mbps（每秒百萬位元）到最高全速 12 Mbps；USB 2.0 傳送資料的速度增加為 480 Mbps，2001 年 USB-IF 將其定位為標準速率；至於 4.8 Gbps（每秒 10 億位元）的超高資料傳輸速率，比 USB 2.0 的標準還要快上 10 倍，目前 USB 3.0 已經達到此一速率標準。其他 USB 技術的形式還包括 USB OTG（USB on the go 的縮寫），一種兩用 USB 設備，能夠連結其他配備至電腦，也能在不經電腦作為媒介的情況下，連接兩種攜帶式電子設備。此外還有無線 USB（WUSB），無線 USB 推廣小組於 2004 年所開發的技術，在功能與架構上都與 USB 2.0 相同，但無須連接任何電子線路。

8 USB 技術的引進已增加了電腦及其周邊設備的運作速度、電力及便利性。

▶ USB 是一種「熱插拔」技術，這表示使用者在插上或移除接頭時不必關電腦，也不必使用特殊的軟體或驅動器。

▶ 使用 USB 的周邊設備都是「隨插即用」，也就是一插進 USB 接孔就立刻可以運作。

▶ USB 接線的長度不超過 5 公尺。接線可以使用多插孔的 USB 集線器延長，訊號即透過延展的 USB 接線傳輸，也可以使用 USB 橋接器，連接兩台個人電腦的設備。

9 USB 技術持續往前發展，能夠進行更大量的資料傳輸，如數位影像和音樂檔，傳輸的速度也加快。USB 技術從有線發展到無線，極可能使 USB 成為從電腦到行動通訊科技等電子產業用來傳輸資料的標準規格。

Chapter 21　行動計算技術

1 「行動計算」是指在移動時還能同時使用電腦設備的一種技術。但行動計算絕不僅止於攜帶型電子設備，無線通訊、高等微處理技術以及先進機器設備，如 PDA 和穿戴式電腦等，也都是構成行動計算的重要部分。行動計算科技的設計主要是為了因應人們日常生活的各種需求，從商業交易到政府運作再到人際往來，隨著無線科技進步和電腦設備微型化，行動計算正迅速地延伸其發展範圍，逐步改變全球人類的生活與互動模式。

2 世界各地基本的無線網路架構為行動計算提供了必要的應用技術。有些無線網路所能涵蓋的範圍有限，例如無線區域網路（wireless LANs）與藍芽技術，其他無線網路，像是無線廣域網路（wireless WANs），則涵蓋較廣的網路範圍。最普遍的廣域網路要屬蜂巢式行動電話技術，該技術於 80 年代中期首次被提出，部分廣域網路僅能進行非常有限且速度相對較慢的語音傳輸，而最新一代的廣域網路，則是能夠支援複雜的寬頻多媒體應用設備，以指數的倍率更迅速地進行傳輸。

3 行動計算環境的結構設計是由無線網路系統與行動裝置共同組成，網路系統無論涵蓋的區域範圍多大，必然包括一個基地台，配備無線介面供轉換編碼以及和行動裝置交換通訊信息之用，此外還配備位置記錄器，以追蹤行動裝置的位置。行動電腦或手機都是行動裝置或設備的一種，透過行動計算平台，即運作系統，網路系統和行動裝置間的溝通聯繫因而變得可行。行動計算平台可支援三種型態的工作：

▶ 網路傳輸服務：通常是由網際網路所提供，特別是為行動裝置提供移動式 IP（網際網路通訊協定）。移動式 IP 技術結合原始位址與暫時位址，再將暫時位址傳到新的主機，使網路連線持續不中斷。

▶ 中介軟體服務：中介軟體的開發是為了使連線網路和行動裝置的應用能夠互相作用，軟體的部分功能還包括資料格式轉換或壓縮、偵測設備特性以達數據輸出的最佳化、基於安全考量進行加密，以及進行設備和網路的疑難排解。

▶ 本地平台服務：特別為行動裝置所提供的作業系統和其他軟體服務。

4 安全是使用無線網路的一個重大問題，因為無線網路是透過一項公眾共享的基礎設施在運作，很容易遭到攔截或入侵。以下是幾個使用無線網路的安全原則，與行動計算有直接的關連：

- **機密性**：不要將秘密資料洩露給未經授權的人。
- **完整性**：保持資訊的完整不受破壞。
- **可得性**：只讓合法的使用者取得資訊。
- **不可否認性**：確認傳送者和接收者的身分
- **授權**：比對使用者特徵後才讓其取得資訊。
- **計費**：計算提供服務收取的費用。

5 很多預防性的技巧和措施都能用於保障無線網路通訊的安全性：

- **加密**：提供給特定使用者的演算數字或代碼
  - 對稱式金鑰加密：加密和解密的金鑰相同
  - 公開金鑰加密：解密的金鑰不同於加密的金鑰

- **密碼保護**：一串做為認證工具的符號，鑑別使用者身分或使用的裝置，同時能確認使用者的權限層級。

- **數位簽章**：用於證實資料傳送者身分、保障傳送文件真實性的電子簽名。

- **數位憑證**：由憑證管理中心（CA）核發的電子證明文件，認證中心制訂的憑證內容包括：
  - 名字 - 產品序號 - 到期日 - 數位簽章

- **審核記錄**：電腦系統存取和近期運作的記錄

6 行動計算未來幾乎擁有無限的發展潛力，然而目前仍有一些必須要克服的限制：

- 網路效能的變化，包括網路涵蓋範圍與頻寬的限制
- 無線網路的低度安全性
- 行動裝置的記憶體、電力與處理能力都有限
- 小型顯示螢幕
- 電池儲存的電力有限

7 儘管目前存在諸多限制，許多針對行動計算的革新技術已經蓄勢待發，例如雷射鍵盤、高等資料轉換技術與提升的顯示科技，再過不久，4G和5G無線網路也將使行動計算的速度增加到10 Mbps以上。未來，行動計算設備的儲存量將增加，處理器的速度也會更快，並具備更多功能，如視訊會議和資料處理軟體。其他創新的功能還包括電池容量、能源效率的增加，以及機動性的提升，穿戴式行動設備即為一例。電腦與通訊技術的典型正迅速轉型為更真實的行動計算環境，在此環境中充滿創新的技術，還有更多發明在未來幾年間即將嶄露頭角。

Chapter 22　網際網路

1 網際網路是一套全球性的網路系統，將超過100個國家中的數百萬台電腦連結在一起。網際網路的結構是將硬體與多種應用軟體做分立而錯綜複雜的結合，經由無數網路供應者，並能透過許多種方式取得使用的服務。

2 1969年，最早的網路是由美國國防部高等研究計畫署（ARPA）所架設，連接四台電腦，亦即介面訊息處理器（IMP），作為分享資訊之用。此一網路系統，即一般所知的阿帕網路（ARPANET），其設計是以路由器傳送切割成小包的資訊，或是能在網路系統內流動的每一組資訊片段，在抵達目的地後重新匯集，再結合為完整的訊息。

3 網際網路初期的使用是在開發靜態的網站和應用。早期網頁的內容包含使用者可以利用的資訊，但無法在網站上進行互動，也無法以任何方式更改網頁的資訊。此外，早期使用者可以下載網路軟體，但這些下載的軟體無法進行修改。基本上，網際網路的初始開發只是作為線上資訊儲存系統之用。

4 由於網路公司邁入二十一世紀後股價猛烈下跌，網際網路的經濟未來看似將會非常慘澹；然而，在2004年，提姆·歐萊禮及他的歐萊禮媒體公司，為2000年出現的新網路環境起了一個新名稱：Web 2.0。Web 2.0（這麼稱呼是為了與前一代的Web 1.0區隔）事實上是一組漸進式發展的習慣與原則，互動式的網路環境即據此建立。Web 2.0網路世界最重要的特徵，就是它屬於一種超媒體形式，一個動態的環境，無論多少外部資源使用者都能夠連接，甚至能修改現有的文字或內容。維基百科就是最受歡迎的超媒體網站之一。由網路使用者創造和修改內容所產生的線上百科全書，雖然實際

❺Web 2.0最重要的原則之一，就是協同運作。歐萊禮媒體公司指出，會參與發展網站內容的使用者最有可能繼續回到固定的網站。因此，在金錢數字與經濟的驅使下，網路研發人員迅速掌握這個創新的概念，讓使用者能同時與網站內容和其他使用者進行互動。個別網路使用者彼此合作的良好範例就是Flickr，這是一個線上整理與分享照片的應用軟體。Flickr是根據一種稱為分眾分類（folksonomy）的概念而來，是指讓眾多使用者自行選擇關鍵字來定義個人相片的一種合作式分類。這些關鍵字稱為標籤，標籤讓使用者之間產生重複的關聯。另外，網路應用程式，特別是開放源碼軟體（或共享軟體），乃是由同儕生產而發展，例如Linux和Python等軟體，任何使用者都能下載程式，針對個人目的進行修改，並將修改後的程式與其他使用者分享，以推動開放源碼軟體持續不斷的進步。

❻由於科技的改變迅速，加上軟體設計持續往增加使用者自訂內容的方向轉變，網路的發展即將超越目前的2.0環境。目前已經使用中的是語義網，這是分析比較各個資料庫、從分歧的資訊找出共通意義的詮釋資料庫。虛擬世界儼然已是電玩遊戲的主要內容架構，但為了配合一般性應用目的如引導路線、甚至是找出商店內各排商品項目等，相關內容也很快被修正以適應使用目的。

❼隨著各家公司為電視與行動電話開發更高的畫面與聲音品質，它們也將為客戶提供更多網路服務。電視已經開始邁向數位播放，而遠超過目前只能購買電視節目或廣告商品的互動式觀賞方式，或許很快將掀起電視革命。行動電話已使用過數以萬計的網路軟體，而隨著每一代行動網路電話的生產，軟體的可用性也不斷增強。

❽目前所有的網路產品在世界各地都能找到，但全世界卻只有不到20%的人能夠使用並且也在使用網路。網路使用的挑戰包括世代間的差異（年長者比較不上網）、個人形象（有些人覺得自己不夠「聰明」，無法使用網路）和財富。但很多人預測，由於國際間通訊的增加，加上如Google提供網路使用資訊和語言翻譯的服務，在未來的50年，使用網際網路的人數可能達到目前使用者的四倍。

Chapter 23　人工智慧

❶影印機能夠自動調整影印品質；電腦會根據股市的變動判斷買賣股票的時機；生產線上的自動機器能組裝和油漆汽車；自動化系統可以偵測信用卡盜刷；醫師能透過數位設備查看病歷，為病患進行適當的治療。這些工作和其他類似的活動都因為人工智慧（AI）的出現而成為可能。人工智慧是電腦科學的一個分支，研究機器取得與產出智慧的科學。事實上，在過去50年間，人工智慧的應用已經擴及許多其他的領域，促成無數科技的進步。

❷人工智慧的出現乃源自二十世紀時，人類對生產智慧機器的探求。事實上，這樣的想法並不算新奇，但二十世紀中電腦技術的發展，讓製造這類智慧型機器的可能性成為事實。人工智慧一詞最早出現於1956年，早期對人工智慧的發展與應用研究是透過模仿人類高度智慧行為的形式進行。運用人工智慧最出名的活動之一出現在60年代，以電腦程式控制機器下高難度的西洋棋。目前人工智慧的開發主要落在三個基本的研究範疇：

▶ **強人工智慧**：具備相當於人類甚至超越人類智能的機器。

▶ **應用人工智慧**：生產於商業層面具可行性的智慧型機器，從事生物辨識、醫學診斷和買賣股票等活動。

▶ **認知模擬（CS）**：對人類腦部運作理論如臉部辨識或解決抽象問題，進行驗證的機器。

❸人工智慧的進展其實取決於對「智慧」的定義。雖然時至今日，我們理解人類、動物和機器的智慧，也觀察出各種智慧的差異程度，但人工智慧卻只侷限定義人類的智慧，而甚至連這般定義都是具有疑問。目前可以為機器模仿的人類智慧包括：

▶ 學習　▶ 推論　▶ 解決問題

▶ 洞察力 ▶ 對語言的理解

❹以電腦再創人類智慧有兩種基本的方法，第一種方法是由下而上（bottom-up），模仿傳遞訊息到腦部的神經網路，正如人類的腦部運作一般，類神經網路會以電子訊號傳遞和儲存資訊。目前這種電腦組成的網路仍然受到尺寸的限制，模仿人類大腦需要比現有機器大上幾千倍的電腦才能進行，且發展類神經網路的成本也過於高昂。但是進入二十一世紀後，新的電腦結構與平行運算法（利用數台電腦進行同一種功能）很可能為類神經網路開發出新的研究成果。

❺以機器重新創造人類智慧的第二種方法，是模仿人腦的認知功能，這些電腦採用由上而下（top-down）的步驟，通常是根據累積的知識模仿人類做出決策。

- **專家系統**：以兩種根本方式模仿人類行為的電腦結構：知識表示（蒐集學科領域專家的知識）與知識工程管理（彙編整理取得的學科領域知識）。應用相關資訊與組織化的設計，專家系統得以解決問題同時進行決策。
- **人工智慧遊戲程式**：將人工智慧與娛樂結合，累積過去的資訊，配合新環境進行整合，使遊戲程式的發展更具智慧。
- **框架理論**：根據所面臨的狀況，取得一組一組的資訊，即框架下的資訊來配合運用。框架的應用也使電腦系統得以增加更多相關知識。

❻人工智慧的研究發展在某些智慧的應用上仍面臨重大的挑戰。生物系統能不斷地適應調整，但人工智慧系統之間卻幾乎無法溝通交流，當然也絕不可能自行重整，應用於不同的電腦組織架構（機器再加上軟體）。目前的語音辨識系統只能就正常的人類語言進行初步翻譯，且偏向逐字重述的做法，至於憑藉直覺做決定與實現創意的部分，人工智慧系統的能力也極為有限。但是應用電腦工具創新，從語言學到美術的範疇，都是人工智慧研究正在成長的領域。

❼人工智慧所造成的實質衝擊已非常深遠，人工智慧系統能監控周遭的環境、取得專門知識並加以處理、協助人類從設計規劃到輔助教學等類型廣泛的活動。發展中且即將興起功能的還包括擴展教育系統、家庭與車輛的精密安全設備，以及提供從購物到藝術創作等各種訊息的資訊處理系統，一旦能夠自動進步的人工智慧技術發展成功，這項科技的未來將會無可限量。

Chapter 24　保育農業

❶保育農業或保育耕種是一種保護自然資源、增加作物潛在收穫的農事經營方法。保育農業最主要的任務之一，就是農地管理，包括施行特殊的耕作方法，即保育耕作法，並實施適當的輪作模式；其他實踐保育農作的方法還有對水資源及蟲害的管理。

❷保育耕作法是指任何一種在種植作物後，土壤表面仍覆蓋至少30％的作物殘株—處理收成作物後留下的剩餘物質—的農作系統。覆蓋於土地上的作物殘餘能減少土壤侵蝕、控制雜草生長、還能增加土壤的養分。目前農夫能夠使用的保育耕作法有好以下幾種類型。

- **不整地栽培**：除了播種以外，不去翻動殘餘的土壤和作物殘株；以少量的除草劑控制雜草生長。
- **畦作**：耕耘時為控制雜草生長而翻動土地所形成約10到15公分的隆起地面，作物殘株會留在隆起的地脊間。
- **覆蓋物耕作**：在耕種前先翻整農地，耕種後留下的植物殘餘需覆蓋至少30％的耕地面積。
- **有限耕作**：播種前翻動整片農地，種植後留下的作物殘株會覆蓋15％到30％的土壤表面。

❸保育耕作法的另一個優點應該是減少滲入地下水的化學農藥，但要確認這樣的影響是否為真，仍須做進一步的研究。

❹實施輪作（輪流種植不同作物）或輪耕（依固定順序種植不同作物）也能夠達到土壤保育的作用。典型的輪作模式通常是2到3年更換一次作物：

- **行作作物／小型穀物輪作**：每隔三年輪流耕種行作作物與小顆穀類作物。

321

- **牧草作物輪作**：乾草、牧草與其他前一年或過去數年間使用的牧草作物輪作。
- **休耕輪作**：在過去一年或幾年沒有使用、改作其他用途或休耕的土地。

5 土地輪作能夠維持甚至是增加土壤的養分，而增加的養分能延長土地的耕種期。土地輪作也是預防雜草過度生長、對付植物病害與管制蟲害的方法之一；就經濟層面而言，實施輪作能做為經濟市場波動時的緩衝。

6 農作管理的執行，例如土地輪作、農作殘餘物管理（包括覆蓋作物）與保育耕作的實施，都必須與水資源管理共同進行，以達到控制土地侵蝕和保護土壤養分的最佳效果。農人也許會選擇在未開發的土地上設置緩衝區，這些區域讓水源能直接從土地表面取得，或沿著排水道或溝渠轉自耕地。農業用水管理還包括以更省水抗旱的方式種植作物，並使用低水量及水資源回收的灌溉系統。

7 此外，由於實施名為綜合蟲害管理（IPM）的專業工作，農作也才能順利地發展。農夫先檢查並監視作物受到蟲害的程度，使用機械設備和其他昆蟲來抑制蟲害後，利用其他物質控整昆蟲的生長、破壞昆蟲的交配，最後再搭配使用微量的殺蟲劑。

8 全世界各個地區的組織，如國際農村重建研究所、世界農林中心（ICRAF）、聯合國國際農業發展基金會與聯合國糧農組織，都針對保育農作在進行推廣、研究、發展，透過這些組織的努力，農民、私人企業、科學家、開發組織、贊助機構與決策者，能共同為保育農業發展新的實踐方法與策略。在二十一世紀，這些組織最主要的目的都是讓農產品的產量倍增，同時減少自然資源的耗損，尤以生物多樣性、土地和水資源為甚。除此之外，與保育農業息息相關的要角也能透過國際會議與全球各地的政府合作，發展世界共通的政策，提出讓農民改變生產模式、轉換為保育耕作的誘因；更甚者，全世界都已經投入努力，要讓全球農業能順應氣候變遷的挑戰持續發展。

英式英語及美式英語拼字的差異：

美式英語	英式英語
fiber, behaviors, center	fibre, behaviours, centre

Chapter 25　食品生物技術

1 幾個世紀以來，植物和動物都曾與不同的種類交配繁殖，生產出混合的品種，但是這樣的過程極費功夫，也需經歷了好幾個世代才告完成。二十世紀晚期，現代生物科技被引入農業與食品的混合品種生產，得以省下無數的時間與心力。現行的食品生物技術同時包括傳統的混種培育與現代的生物技術，如基因工程，以培育出味道更好、抗病能力更強、產量更高的食用植物和動物。農業基因改造歷年隨著技術的改變而出現過許多名稱：

- 農業生物科技　▶ 生技作物
- 基因改造食品（GM食品）
- 基因工程食品（GE食品）　▶ 植物生物科技
- 動物基因體學　▶ 選殖
- 新式食品（一般是指尚未證實人類或動物能安全食用的基因改造食品）

2 基因改造包含兩個步驟：首先，基因會被改變，接下來這些改變會隨之延續到生物體的下一代。基因的改變是為了要刻意製造出特定的結果或特性，例如增加作物產量或讓食物變得更美味。根據刻意提升的特性劃分，基因改造作物被分為三種類型，即三個世代的產品。

- **第一代基因改造作物或增進輸入的特性（刻意設計輸入特性以提高產量）**：耐除草劑、抗蟲害、抗病毒、抵抗環境壓力，如乾旱。
- **第二代基因改造作物或增加價值輸出或使用特性**：提高營養成分，例如增加Omega-3脂肪酸或動物飼料中離氨基酸的分量。
- **第三代基因改造作物**：針對藥品生產或改進生質燃料的處理。

❸ 至於動物生物科技，透過多種生物技術的應用，對環境與健康也能發揮潛在的助益。

▶ **動物基因體學**：根據動物的基因型進行選擇性繁殖，找出持續生產高品質食品最理想的營養成分需求。

▶ **選殖**：對現有品質最佳的同卵雙生動物進行人工輔助複製生殖，以繁衍後代。

▶ **基因工程改造**：刻意以現代生物技術改變動物的基因組。

❹ 動物生物科技能製造出藥品、進行移植手術的組織和器官、外科手術縫線的材料、針對致病細菌的抗菌劑，還能生產更健康的食品；至於動物也能從改善動物健康的生技工具中獲益，而複製的技術則有助野生動物的保育。

❺ 無論是環保人士或宗教組織，當中都有人對基因改造食品提出批評。社會上對基因改造食品最主要的顧慮著重在三個範疇：對人類健康構成風險、環境問題以及經濟問題。對人類健康的不安，主要是擔心生技食品的安全性和導致過敏問題，包括對新食品產生過敏反應，以及產生新過敏原的可能危險。對環境的危害可能包括源自基因改造食品的有毒物質、對基因改造作物產生抗體的害蟲、因混種繁殖使殺蟲劑的抗藥性轉移至雜草上，還有複製動物對野生動物造成的威脅。就經濟面而言，食品生物技術涉及長時間且昂貴的製造過程，這可能導致開發中國家面臨經費不足的問題，專利侵害也可能對經濟形成威脅；除此以外，部分批評者也不斷要求對科技審查實行更嚴格的規範。

❻ 基因改造食品同時也激起了嚴重的道德議題。某些宗教與道德團體反對基因改造食品是基於他們的核心信仰：人類無權控制生命。對其他團體來說，基因工程對傳統定義的植物和動物分類造成了威脅；另一個道德爭議則是對能夠操控兩個不同物種基因的科技，社會是否擁有充足的知識管理控制。最後，人類行為的倫理問題也被提起，它點出了人性自私可能使基因改造產生意外後果以及研究成果遭濫用的可能性。

❼ 漸漸地，消費者變得越來越支持使用食品生物科技。在美國，很多消費者都會注意到商店內販賣的生技食品，也願意購買；多數消費者都預期食品生物科技能為他們帶來好處，包括食物的品質和安全。然而世界各地的消費者對食品生技的知識並不如美國消費者高，因此，對於食品生物技術的科學研究，以及其潛在利益及風險，有必要讓國際間進行更深入的了解。現階段除了美國以外，另有20幾個國家正積極以生物技術生產食品，再者，目前世界許多國家都設立了專門的機構，負責對農業生物科技進行管制監督。

❽ 食品生物科技具有幫助解決許多健康與環境問題的潛力，更多的食物產出與更健康的食品，也能夠對付飢餓和營養不量的問題，對有害的自然環境具高度抵抗力則能減少可能的汙染。只要相關研究與發展持續投入努力，繼續取得公眾的信任、提供經濟公平、維護生態環境的最佳狀態，食品生物科技將繼續對全球群體產生重大的影響。

英式英語及美式英語拼字的差異：	
美式英語	英式英語
favorable	favourable

Chapter 26　農業食品奈米科技

❶ 每一年，全世界投入研發奈米科技的經費將近1百億美元，而在2020年之前，奈米科技產品和服務在全球市場的產出將可能超過1兆美元。其中一個由奈米科技引導的創新專業領域就是農業食品，主要是食物及農產品的生產與加工處理。奈米技術極有可能取代現存的農業科技，包括從檢測、改變動植物的健康成分，到確保食品安全等技術。透過改變動植物生長、食物處理包裝及運輸系統的應用技術，食品產業的各個層面都可能為農業食品的奈米科技所改變。

❷ 奈米技術能從多方面應用於農業食品，例如能夠感應溫度與濕度變化的智慧型包裝系統，不僅具有抗細菌和抗真菌的性質，甚至能夠修補包裝的

裂縫或破洞。智慧型食物包裝會放進特殊材料，提醒消費者不要食用不安全的過期產品，至於其他用於裝瓶或飲料包裝的材料是由奈米合成的塑膠製成，讓食品在貨架上有更長的保存期限。

❸膳食補充品的發展是農業食品奈米技術的另一個主要的成長領域。奈米材料可以加進固態食品、液態食品中，也可用於製造食品外層的包膜，增加各種不同的營養成分，舉例來說：

- 類胡蘿蔔素（抗氧化劑）的奈米分子，可以添加於水果飲料中
- 添加於菜籽油內的奈米分子能提供健康的脂肪酸
- 奈米簇，由相當於沙粒十萬分之一大小的微小分子組成，與純可可粉一起添加，可以增加巧克力飲料的風味，無須添加任何糖分或其他人工甘味
- 裝置奈米感測器的聰明食品，可以偵測食品中缺乏的營養成分
- 奈米膠囊在經奈米感測器啟動前會保持安定

❹維他命和礦物質中的奈米分子也能夠與微胞（micelle）結合，這是一種奈米尺寸的水溶性分子串。微胞將脂溶性的營養素裝入膠囊，使其可溶於水，接著迅速將營養素輸送至消化系統，增進吸收與新陳代謝。微胞也能進行基因改造，以阻絕食物中的某些成分，如有害的膽固醇或食物過敏原，進入身體的特定部位；相反地，基因改造後的微胞也可以將有害的膽固醇傳送至指定部位，如腦部，以對抗特定的癌細胞。此外，奈米食品科技為健康帶來其他可能的益處還包括能增強體能、改善認知和免疫功能、同時減少老化的效用。

❺奈米科技也能為農業系統帶來好處，例如奈米尺寸設備可以發現或預防植物的健康問題。奈米技術現在也持續開發，用於製作奈米分子膠囊和控制奈米分子，這些技術能夠應用在許多類型的農業活動上：

- 減少蟲害
- 對繁殖畜產的生長激素進行用量管制
- 在運送至銷售市場前先檢測動物體內的病原體並進行中和作用
- 節省用水、殺蟲劑和化學肥料，以達減少汙染的目的
- 能夠配合環境變化如高溫和潮濕的化學肥料及除蟲劑供給系統

❻農業食品的奈米科技會為經濟帶來諸多利益：奈米元件能監控並追蹤食物供給，同時留下食物生產過程中各個步驟的歷史環境記錄；恢復食物新鮮度的感測系統可減少食物的浪費；確認食物供給的地點、報告並加以遙控，會讓食物的運送過程更有效率且更加安全。目前農業食品奈米科技的成本依然高昂，但隨著持續開發創新與越來越多的設備及食物產出，未來成本很可能大幅下降，低於使用傳統方式種植和處理的食物成本。

❼接下來的幾十年間，奈米技術應用在農業食品的機會應該會顯著增加，如此一來，自然農業系統能得以保存並持續進步；糧食產品的運輸會變得更可靠，零售市場也將成為更有吸引力、更安全、更具教育意義的環境。消費者比較不容易罹患食物引發的疾病；奈米科技能夠偵測食用後會導致疾病的食物，故消費者能從中受惠。

❽然而農業食品的奈米技術仍處於創發階段，對於人體健康和環境會造成的潛在影響，仍存在許多不確定分子，且截至目前為止，僅進行過少數的風險評估。至於人體對奈米分子的吸收、輸送和排泄能力，可得的資訊非常有限，而檢測計算食物、飼料或人體內奈米材料的程序，目前也仍在發展階段，更甚者，新的研究並未充分說明奈米材料可能造成的副作用，甚至可能產生有毒物質的問題。為了使農業食品奈米技術的發展成功，全球必須共同合作，協助並規範其研究發展，使這項技術能完整執行，建立一套健全的政策。

英式英語及美式英語拼字的差異：

美式英語	英式英語
agrifood, nanotechnology	agri-food, nano-technology

Chapter 27　能源回收系統

① 二十一世紀，由於全球都在努力減輕有害汙染物對環境的破壞，新的能源回收技術也因而出現。部分能源回收技術是利用可再生能源，也有部分技術循環利用已生產能源。能源經過工業、車輛或家庭使用後通常會製造出數量可觀的廢棄物，但透過新的技術，能夠重新取得這些能源廢料加以使用，使能源回到這些系統持續循環。以工業回收的熱能為例，這些資源能夠製造出供給丹麥全國總用電量50%的電力。回收能源占北歐其他國家電力供給的40%，在德國則占35%，但是在美國，只有不到10%的電力來自回收能源。

② 能源首度被循環利用是在一百多年前，第一次使用的是熱與電力結合系統（CHP），或稱汽電共生發電系統，能在同一時間產生電力與回收熱能。產出的電力會製造出熱能，而熱回收設備會保存這些熱能，用於調節空間溫度的高低、設備的運作，或製造出蒸汽或熱水。湯瑪斯‧愛迪生建造了全世界第一座熱電共生工廠，同樣的發電系統今日仍持續沿用。

③ 過去一個世紀以來，工業體系發展出其他能源回收系統。工廠製造出的廢棄熱能，多數仍可重新用於其他層面，舉例來說，高溫廢氣是爐灶和火爐在高氣壓中製造出來的，壓力必須下降氣體才能燃燒，而廢氣通常會被釋放或上升至大氣中，但是我們可以裝置渦輪機，當壓力下降時即開始旋轉，驅動發電機製造出數百萬瓦特的電力，廢氣所釋放的汙染物因此減少，甚至不再產生，而工廠也能在不使用燃料的情況下發電。

④ 此外，工業體系很可能即將採取另一種能源回收流程，稱作氣化。氣化的過程會將價值不高的含碳材料或工廠原料，例如煤，轉換為合成氣（也稱syngas）。氣化系統必須仰賴氣化爐供應熱能和壓力，以切斷原料中的化學鍵，製造出原始的合成氣。在去除雜質後，合成氣就可以當作燃料燃燒產出電力，或是經進一步處理後應用在石化和精煉產業。不會氣化的礦物質或其他從合成氣中剔除的雜質，也可能會成為無害的惰性物質；有時這些副產品會被轉換成固體，在市場上當作煤渣銷售，或是成為類似玻璃的無害產品，作為蓋屋頂或鋪路的材料。

⑤ 汽車也有回收能源、減少燃油用量與廢氣排放的潛力。油電混合動力車即已利用再生煞車系統回收能源：當混合動力車的速度變慢或引擎在倒車時，摩擦產生的能量會被保存下來而不被浪費，接著儲存在電池裡，待之後再使用。更輕且速度更快的是新的動能回收系統，在車輛減速時保留動能，系統接著會將保留的動能輸送至機械飛輪系統，此系統能更快速地產出電力並減少廢氣的排放。

⑥ 家裡也一樣可以配備能源回收系統，如能源和熱能回收通風系統。能源回收通風系統會保留一般經由通風設備排出的能源，將廢氣能源轉換流進室內的氣流中。能源回收通風系統能恢復溫度與濕度，而熱能回收通風系統只能回收熱能，兩種通風系統都能回收廢氣中高達85%的能源。

⑦ 廢水（或灰水）熱能回收系統能留住流入排水管的熱水，流出的熱水伴隨的多是家庭中用來加熱水溫的熱能。廢水熱能交換器能夠回收從蓮蓬頭、澡盆、水槽、洗碗機和洗衣機流出熱水中的熱能，有些熱交換器還備有空間，儲存回收的熱能待稍後利用，有些則是直接將熱能從還有餘溫的廢水傳導至冷的供給用水。至於供給熱能的方式可能是直接導入流出的冷水，也可能將熱能引導進熱水器內。

⑧ 能源回收的創新發明在全球以飛快的速度持續進行，透過能源回收的設備與方法，能源效率的改善程度可能近100%，至於未來增加能源回收的做法還包括強化氫燃料電池科技、增進生物製程技術，以及增加創新奈米技術的實際應用。

Chapter 28　核子能源

① 原子能量的研究和應用始於二十世紀。原子分裂，也就是核分裂的理論，於30年代出現在歐洲與美國，但直到40年代才實際成為可應用的技術。核子反應的能量迅速被拿來做為軍事用途，二次世界大戰結束沒多久，美國為發展核能的和

平與民生用途，成立了「原子能委員會（AEC）」。1951年，第一座核子反應爐成功發電，此後全世界不斷投入努力，將核能當作替代性能源使用。如同其他永續能源一般，核分裂也是一種低碳的發電方式。

❷核分裂的過程是來自鈾原子的核子分裂，分裂是因為自由中子高速撞擊鈾原子所引發，鈾的核子吸收中子後分裂，製造比原本多出2.5倍左右的中子與大量能量，這些中子會被其他的鈾原子吸收，成為自行持續的核反應，也就是一種連鎖反應。

❸為了控制核反應的狀態，會將體積小且質地堅硬的鈾燃料丸填充進長管內，再一批一批將這些管子插入核子反應爐後用水覆蓋。核反應所製造出的熱能會將周圍的水轉為蒸汽，蒸汽再驅動渦輪機使發電機轉動，接著製造出電力。

❹設計一座核子反應爐只有兩個目的，不是做研究就是發電。

▶ **研究用核子反應爐**：在大學和研究中心內操作，目的在進行研究、測試，並且製造非能源用途的放射性物質。

▶ **發電用反應爐**：通常存在於核能發電廠，作為生產電力之用，小型的反應爐則是可以用來發動船艦。

❺在所有發電技術中，核能發電是最省成本的，燃料成本低廉，設備所占的土地面積也很小，除此之外，核能所帶來的益處也能解決能源不足的問題，例如核能可以為氫燃料電池製造氫氣，也能為電力驅動車發電。核子能量還能產生高熱溫，幫助製造化學產品，並且使海水和地下水源的性質轉變成為淡水。

❻使用核能的另一項優點在於，核電廠製造出的廢料遠比傳統發電廠產生的廢棄物少。目前核廢料會先經處理變成固體形式，裝入密封的混凝土罐或填水的混凝土窖中，接著儲存在核電廠內。但科學家也考慮採用其他方式處理核廢料，包括排進海裡、太空中，或是埋藏在冰層底下。

❼現在國際間出現了科學上的共識，欲將核廢料埋入地底深層，也就是所謂的地下貯存場。其他相關研究也正在進行中，希望能發展出回收廢棄燃料大部分能源的技術，進一步減少核能發電過程所製造出必須處理的副產品。

❽核能發電的廢棄物可能意外流入工地或社區，是反對核能發電人士最大的顧慮。其他對核能的批評還包括核電廠的興建會破壞野生動植物的水陸棲息地，而且堆放過放射性廢料的土地將永遠無法恢復。雖然核電廠在關閉後必須進行除役，也就是除汙或清除放射性物質，但重新利用的這塊土地未來很可能有遭受放射性汙染的危險。

❾雖然核能發電具有潛在的危險，但也帶來許多好處。使用核能可以大量減少全球對煤、石油等化石燃料的依賴；小量的核輻射對於醫學和宇宙科學等各類學科的發展也有助益。放射性同位素可在醫療診斷過程中找出血液的流向或癌症的擴散，對很多種癌症還有治療效果；手錶和煙霧警報器會使用極少量的放射性物質製造光線或聲響，放射線還能消毒醫療產品和化妝用品；食品照射能夠在不改變食物性質或受到放射線汙染的情況下殺死致病的細菌、昆蟲和寄生蟲；此外，以放射性物質驅動的發電機，還能夠為無人駕駛的太空船提供電力。

❿目前核能是世界各地不斷成長的能源，約30座核能反應爐供應歐洲將近30%的電力。核能在美國供電的比例近20%，美國國內設有超過100座的核能發電設備；南韓及日本都已經有約30%的電力供應是透過核能發電，而目前亞洲境內也有14個國家支持研究核子反應爐的運作。

Chapter 29 | 可再生能源

❶動植物殘骸歷經數百年所形成的化石燃料（煤、石油、天然氣），提供全世界85%以上的能源。但是化石燃料並非可再生的能源，一旦供給使用的分量耗盡，這些資源也就永遠消失；另外，化石燃料燃燒後排放的氣體也對環境有害。由於全球

對能源的需要擴大，再加上對環境破壞的憂心，尋找其他替代性能源的需要勢不可當。

❷可循環利用的乾淨能源是化石燃料問題最為可行的解決之道，這些能源通常是自然產生，使用時也很少或是根本不會排放有害物質。

▶ 太陽能系統使用太陽輻射製造熱能與電力。
- 太陽能供熱系統：由太陽能集熱器吸收太陽輻射以增加水或空氣溫度，作為電暖氣和熱水系統之用。
- 太陽能集熱發電系統：太陽能集熱器利用太陽射線集中加熱流體，使其產生高溫；受到加熱的流體製造出蒸汽，用於驅動渦輪機，使其在發電機裡運作產生電力。
- 太陽光電發電系統：太陽能電池直接將太陽射線轉換成電力，可為手錶或甚至其他大型設備中數百種小型機械裝置供應電力。

▶ 風力發電機能捕捉風力，風能可以使轉輪上的葉片轉動，驅動連接在發電機上的轉軸旋轉，產生電力。全球75%以上的風力發電機設置集中在5個國家，其中光是歐洲就擁有超過三分之二的風力發電機。

▶ 流動的水也能夠用來供給機械設備發電或製造電力，當水壩或水庫裡的水導入渦輪機和發電機後，就能把水的能量轉換成電能。全世界20%的電力來自水力發電；挪威境內99%以上的電力都來自水力發電，而在紐西蘭，水力則占75%的電力供應。

▶ 水力發電的另一種形式則是來自海灣或河口的潮汐發電廠。這些發電廠內設有渦輪機，潮水流動時會驅動渦輪機旋轉而製造出電力。目前法國、俄羅斯、加拿大和中國大陸都有潮汐能發電廠。

▶ 地熱，地球內部產生的熱水和蒸汽，可透過探鑽岩石層的方式取得。地熱被用於加熱或發電等目的，目前已成為美國、冰島和歐洲其他區域使用的重要替代能源。但一般對利用地熱能的顧慮仍然存在，這是因為從地底釋出的化學物質可能會汙染空氣，破壞水生棲地。

▶ 非化石植物材料（生質能源），像是木材、都市廢棄物、甲烷氣以及生質燃料，都可以用來製造熱能；紙漿殘留物、燃燒的垃圾以及甲烷氣，都可以再生利用製造電力；生質燃料如乙醇，以及食用油和動物脂肪所製造的「生質柴油」，都被用來當作燃油加強劑、替代性燃料來源，並作為加熱之用。

▶ 把水分解為氫和氧的過程會產生氫氣，此一過程稱為電解作用。燃料電池是一種透過氫氣氧氣交互作用而產生電力的機械設備，這些都是供應汽車燃料、熱能和電力的潛在來源。

❸全世界現在有一系列鼓勵投資和使用可再生能源的措施，各個國家和國際組織都在研擬讓經濟永續發展的能源政策。部分國家，像是一些歐盟國家，便制訂提高能源供給安全性的計畫；而其他獎勵措施，如聯合國提出的可再生能源金融倡議，即在創造能源投資的經濟誘因。由於全世界都感受到開發替代性能源的急迫，解決方案也迅速由能源的研究轉為新能源的開發，例如現階段就針對攜帶式電子設備的發電器進行測試，要利用人體運動或血液循環發電；到了2020年，有翅膀的車可能真的會出現。另一個創新的概念則是以太陽能板重新鋪設道路和高速公路，吸收太陽能供家庭、企業，或是供在太陽能板路面上行駛的電力驅動車使用。無論是這些替代能源或其他新開發能源，都將能協助減少全球環境與經濟能源的負擔。

Chapter 30 ｜地震與海嘯

❶科學家自二十世紀初開始追蹤地底震動，迄今並未發現此類活動發生次數有明顯增減。然而，隨之而來的毀滅性地球物理現象如地震和海嘯，卻隨著人口膨脹與環境日益破壞而造成甚於以往的重大損失。

❷當地殼底下的岩塊漂移，釋放出能量波導致地面輕晃甚至天搖地動時，就發生了所謂的地震。世界各地都有可能發生地震，但是多半集中在斷層線上，也就是板塊（地殼的最外層）容易脆裂漂移之處。這些脆弱的板塊只要承受一點壓力，斷層就會破裂，因此九成的地震都沿著斷層發生。

❸以下要介紹相關地震能量波生成位置和種類的術語：

- **震源**：板塊始破裂處，能量由此釋放。
- **震央**：位於震源的正上方，通常是地震最劇烈的地點。
- **震波**：傳送地震的振動。
- **體波**：穿越地球內部的振動。
  - 初波（P波）：藉由岩石的膨脹壓縮來行進，最快可以每秒6.4公里的速度穿過地球內部。
  - 次波（S波）：藉由岩石的上下或兩側震動來前進，每秒速度約3.2公里。
- **餘震**：地震過後地表重整所產生的較微弱振動。

❹ 地震依其強度和影響，有兩套度量標準：

- **芮氏震級**：此法是測量地震的「震級」（地震規模），亦即地震所釋放的能量，並以小數編號，例如：芮氏規模6.0的地震。而地震規模的測量是利用地震儀來記錄震波強弱。
- **麥卡利地震度表**：此法是測量地震的「震度」（地震強度），或解釋為震動的程度，這種震度因地而異。震度的測量憑藉人工觀測感受，震度數值由1到12共十二度。

❺ 地震有時發生於海底。震源傳出的能量若是轉移到水裡，可能將海水抬升出正常海平面，產生「海嘯」這種波浪或連續波浪。tsunami這個字其實源於日文，在日文中tsu意指港口，nami則指波浪。海嘯有時會與「潮浪」混為一談，雖然海嘯衝擊海岸的力量確實依潮位而有所不同，但是海嘯的成因實在與潮汐沒有關聯。此外，海嘯也常被稱為「地震海波」，但海嘯的成因也不盡然是地震，諸如海底岩石崩塌或隕石撞擊都可能造成海嘯。

❻ 一道海嘯可能延綿數百英里，時速最快達480公里，並且持續一小時不退散。海嘯和風浪不同。風浪通常是短浪，時速至多90公里，行進數秒鐘就消失殆盡。海嘯動輒浪高100公里，待其抵達海岸線時，浪高早已超過水深，因此海嘯波被歸為淺水波。即使海嘯進入淺水區後速度減慢，它的浪高還是足以蘊含大部分能量。

❼ 海嘯所帶來的災害是無與倫比的。它往往能沖刷整片海岸線，將泥沙植被一掃而盡，造成生命財產的重大損失。現行的多種海嘯偵測器有助於減少海嘯引發的災難。

- **驗潮儀**：負責測量海平面及潮位，一旦水位提升即發出警報。
- **衛星測高計**：以雷達直接測量海面高度。
- **短期海嘯襲擊預報系統（SIFT）**：將地震、海平面數據與數值模式整合後，能預測海嘯發生的時間、高度和侵襲陸地的時間。
- **水海嘯偵測浮標系統（DART）**：運用浮標偵測海平面升降，將訊息傳回警報中心。

❽ 時至今日，人類預測地震和海嘯的能力依然有限。科學家雖然已能精確測出某斷層所承受的壓力，但究竟何地、何日、何時會發生地震仍屬未知。美國的「國家地震預測評估委員會」負責檢閱地震預報，截至目前為止也無法發展出任何能準確預報地震的系統。位於斷層附近的地區只能宣導民眾採取防震措施，並制訂建築抗震標準，才能使傷害減至最低。至於日本等海嘯高危險區，則一直在進行教育宣導，讓民眾認識海嘯警報系統以及疏散方式。

Chapter 31　衛星海洋學

❶ 地球表面超過70%為水。這些水域不停與大氣互動，進行熱與水的交換。熱隨著全球錯綜複雜的洋流系統從熱帶流向極區，再次返回熱帶時隨之釋放回大氣層。這些水流浩大湍急又緻密，因為經常處於流動狀態，很難進行細部研究。直到90年代初期，海洋學（海洋的科學化研究）利用船隻和浮標所蒐集的資訊進行研究，這些資料包含了水溫、海面高度、鹽度和洋流模式等。1992年，第一座用來繪製海洋地形的人造衛星 TOPEX/Poseidon 發射，人們得以觀測更精確細部的海洋動力型態。

❷ 衛星海洋學是一門採用衛星雷達測高計的學問。測高計能往海面發射微波脈衝，計算訊號返回的時間，藉此獲得海平面高度變化的數據。從反射回來的訊號長度和波形也能看出風速和浪高。科學家藉著這些數據來判斷洋流速度和流向，分辨其寒暖，繪製風速和海浪規模表。

❸衛星能夠偵測海裡的巨大能量和洋流模式，這兩者對於海洋生物及天氣現象影響甚鉅。舉例來說，衛星測高計能夠測得沿海（例如鄰接太平洋的美國西海岸）冷暖水團位置變化之數據。這些水團左右著噴流路徑，噴流又是決定陸上暴風生成位置的氣流。衛星海洋學協助預測與這類水團息息相關的季節性天氣活動，也協助地方為渦流或颶風等天氣現象做好防備。

▶ 渦流：一種可產生漩渦的環狀水流。一個渦流可延伸數百英里，持續數年不散，其龐大力量往往迫使該區域的生物外移，天氣型態連帶產生變化。衛星可觀測渦流取得一系列資訊：
  - 研究人員藉由研究渦流動力結構可預測天氣。
  - 科學家可找出如油溢（石油外漏）等汙染所引起的渦流，這類汙染會影響該區域之生態系統。
  - 船員仰賴渦流資訊來導航、安排航線，連舉辦快艇大賽都必須考慮渦流因素。
  - 許多近海工業掌握渦流資訊來保障工人安全和排定近海鑽探工程。

▶ 颶風與氣旋：定期參考衛星測高計所得之數據來預測整季的颶風數量和強度，該數據還可顯示海洋中可能生成並維持氣旋的熱儲量。

❹衛星數據還可用來追蹤廣大的海洋生產力。

▶ 生物學家觀察海色變化追蹤養分重新分布的情形，包括群集的浮游植物、浮游動物和蝦類。

▶ 海水溫度和顏色明顯改變的區域稱為鋒面區，在一片汪洋中是顯而易見的。如此突兀的變化通常代表有大量魚群聚集。此外，鋒面區水域的聲學特質比其他區域來得強烈，假設軍方可以精確偵測到這些區域，可能會發出警告，其中藏有監聽設備的可能性極高。

▶ 衛星科技可觀察海洋生物的遷徙模式，為漁民和漁業管理者提供重要資訊。河川湖泊（特別是偏遠地區）的水位也可以用衛星測高計測量，所得數據用來預測水患或乾旱，名且能夠規劃水資源。

❺好幾代的測高術已運用在衛星海洋學。第一代是美國太空總署於1978年發射的「海洋衛星」，用來測量海面地形。相隔近二十年後的1992年，美國太空總署與法國的國家太空研究中心（CNES）合作展開了TOPEX/Poseidon計畫，每十天對95％的地表非凍結水面進行一次測量。進入二十一世紀後，美國太空總署再次與法國國家太空研究中心合力推展兩項測高任務，分別是2002年的〈傑森一號〉和2008年的〈傑森二號〉，這兩項任務至今仍在進行中。〈傑森一號〉負責提供幾近即時與長期（數十年）的觀測報告，〈傑森二號〉則沿用〈傑森一號〉的記錄，唯獨正確性與精密度更加升等，最新的觀測衛星「傑森三號」已於2016年1月17日發射。

❻近期還有多項衛星發射計畫，各將裝載更先進的成像技術以及遙感性能，以取得海面高度、鹽度、溫度、向量風等資訊，未來的衛星將能窺得海洋全貌。在衛星海洋學持續改良海洋模式與資料同化技術之下，未來將能提供重要的地球動力資訊，尤其是氣候變遷相關資訊。

Chapter 32　火山

❶地球地表有90％由火山噴發所形成。數百萬年來，火山口噴出的氣體和水蒸氣構成海床和大氣。火山本身也是這些噴發物堆積的產物。volcano這個字有時指噴出熔岩和氣體的開口，也可以指噴發物於火山口周圍沉積出來的錐形山。

❷熔岩即俗稱的岩漿。地殼和下方的地函是由鬆動的板塊組成，這些板塊的交接處通常就是岩漿生成的地方。每當板塊互相摩擦，地函便會熔化產生岩漿。岩漿是液態，又比周圍岩石來得輕，因此會往上翻湧，部分聚積在所謂的岩漿庫。岩漿庫內壓力較低，使得岩漿內的氣體得以膨脹，將岩漿自地殼裂隙中擠出，就發生了火山爆發。等到這些板塊再度分離，炙熱的岩漿又將縫隙填塞。這個過程被稱為「擴張中心之火山作用」。另外還有一種非板塊交互作用的「熱點」火山，來自於上湧的炙熱地函物質所形成的「熱柱」，一旦有大陸板塊移到熱柱上方，熱柱就開始活動。

❸火山噴發依據噴發頻率和方式來分類。經常性噴發的稱為活火山；只在史上有噴發記錄的稱為休火山；從未噴發過的稱為死火山。火山噴發可呈現數種不同方式：

- **蒸氣式（蒸氣噴發）**：當岩漿接觸地下水或地表水而爆發，把蒸氣、水連同火山灰和岩屑（火山碎屑物）一起炸開，這種噴發作用僅止於地底。
- **夏威夷式**：此為非爆發型的火山噴發。起因於釋放氣體將噴發柱推出火山口，可達1公里高。噴發物以熔岩為主，少有火山碎屑物。
- **斯沖波利式**：屬於溫和爆發型的火山噴發，會產生熔岩流以及少許火山噴物（火山灰和火山塵）和火山彈（熔岩碎片）。
- **佛卡諾式**：屬於爆發威力強大的火山噴發，最大特色在於高達數公里的噴發柱，帶來的火山碎屑流相當可觀。
- **碧麗式**：猛烈爆發型的火山噴發，會產生火山碎屑流組成的白熱灰流。
- **普林尼式**：火山持續噴發45公里高的猛烈型噴發。噴發柱挾帶四射的火山碎裂流和灰雲，可在極短時間內籠罩地球。

❹至於火山的種類從完美的圓錐形到積水深坑都有，依其特色可分三類：

- **盾狀火山**：寬闊平坦的圓頂狀火山，源於流動緩慢的極稀熔岩流溢火山口。
- **複成火山（又叫層狀火山）**：由火山本身噴發的火山泥流—熔岩流、火山碎屑流、危險的泥流，挾帶之熔岩和岩屑層層交疊所形成的陡峭錐形山。
- **火山臼**：當岩漿爆發過於猛烈，淘空火山口使其底部失去支撐而崩塌，落在附近的火山碎屑物又不足以將之填平，便留下了直徑延綿數公里的坑洞。火山臼是最可怕的火山，爆發時可見大規模火山碎屑排山倒海而來，地面塌陷的震撼甚至可能引發海嘯。

❺火山噴發嚴重危害人身安全，可能造成窒息性死亡。火山噴發可能引起土石流、洪水和燎原大火等其他天災，同時也可能汙染飲用水，造成電力中斷。影響人身安危的部分還包括灼傷等傷害和呼吸系統疾病，甚至可能爆發傳染病。火山噴發時噴出的碎屑物對環境也是極大威脅，尤其是其中蘊含的有毒氣體，像二氧化碳屬於溫室氣體，它是構成酸雨的元兇；硫酸鹽氣膠則會破壞臭氧層。

❻世界各地有各種組織監測著火山活動，必要時發出警報。美國「地質勘探局（USUG）」和「國家海洋與大氣總署（NOAA）」，採用熱紅外光技術和氣象衛星等科技來預測火山爆發的時間和規模。世界各地的火山灰警告中心同樣使用衛星追蹤火山灰雲，其中一種最新研發的火山活動衛星偵測法稱為「穩定衛星技術」，能夠比對火山的過去資料與當前活動，更精確地辨識追蹤火山灰雲，同時偵測並監控各種危險性的熱變化。未來需要更靈敏的監控儀器為飛機與地方提供警報，以降低火山活動造成的災害。

Chapter 33　熱帶天氣擾動

❶熱帶天氣擾動特指熱帶地區的暴風雨和雷雨，地理位置介於南北緯23.5度之間的區域屬於熱帶地區，此區終年承受劇烈日照（陽光曝晒）。熱帶海洋受熱之後蒸發暖水氣，在赤道附近形成雨帶與低氣壓。熱帶地區的水氣、熱氣與風系輻合之後，就有機會生成雷雨—挾帶狂風暴雨的天氣擾動。

❷當潮濕的低氣壓周圍風力增強時，很容易生成連串雷雨。假如風力持續增強，最後維持在20到34節之間，這種擾動就被歸為熱帶低壓。每年有數百個熱帶低壓於世界各地生成，每一個都會加以編號。

❸一熱帶系統逐漸增強的同時，風會螺旋向內吹拂，將水氣往中心聚集。當這種風出現在低壓系統附近，在北半球呈逆時針旋轉，在南半球呈順時針旋轉，就稱為氣旋式氣流。這些風一邊往赤道外移動，一邊吸收地球自轉所造成的偏轉風（一種稱為科氏效應的現象）。待其吸收到足夠的風力，便可能形成熱帶風暴、氣旋、颱風或颶風。一個熱帶系統發展到持續風速超過34節（每小時39英里）的程度，以國際標準來看就構成了熱帶風暴，一旦超過63節則演變為熱帶氣旋。它們共同的特徵在於中心有暗點：風暴眼。風暴眼周圍的狂風和雨帶形

成眼牆。從風暴眼向外延伸數百公里的部分稱為螺旋雨帶,是充滿強風豪雨的狹長雲帶。

❹熱帶氣旋只是一個統稱。發生在西北太平洋海盆以及亞洲(日本)的熱帶氣旋稱為颱風,發生在中北美洲的熱帶氣旋稱為颶風。這些風暴以最大持續風速來分級。颱風強度有三種基本分級法,分別由世界氣象組織(WMO)、日本氣象廳(JMA),以及位於美國的聯合颱風警報中心(JTWC)所規範使用。

WMO	JMA	JTWC
颱風(64節以上)	颱風(34-63節)	一級颱風(64-82節)
	強烈颱風(64-84節)	二級颱風(83-95節)
	超強颱風(85-104節)	三級颱風(96-113節)
颱風(64節以上)	猛烈颱風(105節以上)	四級颱風(114-135節)
		五級颱風(135節以上)

❺颱風的名字五花八門,一有颱風生成,也就是風速達到颱風標準時,就會對其命名。颱風最大的特色之一,在於其生成和解除(或說其壽命)的判定。正因判定颱風的國際標準不一,各地所認定的颱風數量也有歧異。

❻颱風一年四季都有可能發生,但是多半集中在七月到十一月,二月到三月初最少。每年的颱風報告約有八十個,大部分、同時也是最劇烈的都發生於南海。颱風除了帶來風害,還會引發山崩和洪水。

❼至於生成於大西洋或東太平洋、中太平洋的64節以上熱帶風暴則稱為颶風。颶風依其風速,對照「薩非爾—辛普森風級表」可歸為一到五級,類似聯合颱風警報中心對颱風的分級。三至五級颶風又稱主要颶風。目前每年約有八個颶風生成,幾乎是一百年前的三倍。

❽颶風會隨著信風進入加勒比海,接著可能轉北登陸美國,甚至有機會侵襲加拿大。每年有97%以上的颶風發生在6月1日到11月30日之間,活動量最密集在九月初。颶風所到之處往往狂風暴雨,海面波濤洶湧,造成地方損失慘重。

❾現在氣象學家利用精密的人造衛星和雷達來預測及追蹤熱帶天氣擾動,各地氣象單位也定期發送氣象公報給地方政府和大眾媒體。這些對於當前天氣狀況的預測、報告或警報,可以確保各方在災害發生之前採取適當預防措施。雖然氣象學家仍無法準確預測某熱帶氣旋的登陸地點和登陸強度,但是發出預警仍有助於社會大眾及早準備。

Chapter 34　水管理

❶水約占地球70%與人體65%的成分,這樣的數據顯示水是人體與地球保健的關鍵。地球整體的水資源十分豐沛,藉由蒸發再降下的循環過程,水可以源源不絕地補充。即便如此,仍有將近七億人口的居地面臨水荒。氣候、乾旱、洪水等自然現象往往影響水供給,但是水資源分配不均、水源汙染以及可用水開發取得上的困難,才是二十一世紀水危機節節升高的主因。最有效的危機處理方式是改善全球水資源的開發與管理。

❷隨著全世界越來越富裕,耗水量也越來越大。然而,全球大約只有3%的水是淡水,其餘都是不能飲用的海水。這3%當中又有80%是結冰的無效水。剩下的0.5%,要同時供應農業(約占70%)、工業(約占20%)還有含飲用水的家用水(約占10%)。全世界有40%左右的地區缺乏乾淨的飲用水或衛生設備。每年約有150萬人死於不安全的用水(water)、個人衛生(hygiene)和公共衛生(sanitation,三者合稱WSH),其中九成是兒童。WSH的問題經由改善或許已經趨向安全,但是隨著氣候變遷和水土品質每況愈下,供水只能勉強持平甚至減少,使用者之間的爭奪越演越烈。

❸商業和工業擴張加上快速都市化,也會提高用水需求,然而供水卻是有限。所謂的商業活動需求,涵蓋了生產用水和消耗用水。

▶ **能源生產**:例如在熱能產生的過程中,需要有水作為冷卻劑。

- **商品製造**：從食品到藥品等加工成品都需要用水。

- **消耗用水**：工業汙水使得潔淨的給水也受限。

❹ 全球人口膨脹以及飲食習慣改變，連帶對於新鮮糧食的需求也提高，農業用水消耗量更大。如何有效給水、開發生產成為重要議題。灌溉用水占去全球供水的70%，在某些開發中國家更達近全國用水的90%。畜產、魚產也皆需要用水。

❺ 為解決當前水危機，有三點必須納入全球考量：首先，大環境必須改變。譬如說減少總用量，灌溉或工業盡量重複使用未處理水資源。灌溉利用離峰水（供給高於需求時之水資源）可以降低輸水系統的負擔。各國還必須研擬缺水權變，以防乾旱或枯水期的發生。

❻ 水危機也可以透過政治和社會變革而獲得改善。政府要確保水資源公平分配，致力提升水品質，除了保障水權，還可以提出經濟誘因鼓勵優良水管理。地方政府機構應該設法灌輸民眾用水常識，同時採納傳統知識以建立更全面的社區策略，來對抗地方缺水問題。此外，跨社區合作可以促進地區經濟發展、推動文化保存，減少缺水所引起的衝突。

❼ 政府要對抗供水問題，制訂整體經濟政策也是一條可行之路。社區或個體農民可取得的資金來源有多種，例如政府津貼（尤其牽涉到季節性需求問題）、小額貸款（提供給貧民與低收入戶的貸款）、私人投資以及社區合資。政府與投資人雙方都應該以公平為原則開放水市場、從事公平交易，保障水的取得與運輸。雙方還可以共同商討最為可行的水規費。再者，全球水資源管理可為各社區用水規範合適的測量、監控與回報系統。

❽ 許多組織如聯合國、世界水資源協會、全球水資源合作夥伴，都已經著手並持續資助全球論壇和倡議組織，這些論壇和倡議組織旨在永續發展全面性的水管理方法。透過整合已廣泛施行於全世界的水資源管理法，將能夠結合金融、科技和人類資源，一同面對永續水管理這項重要議題。

Chapter 35　氣候變遷

❶ 天氣是短期的大氣變化，每天影響著地球上的生物。長期的大氣平均狀態則稱為氣候。氣候深受自然因素以及人為活動所影響。當全球的天氣型態產生長期性的巨變，例如溫度、降雨降雪或風產生變化，一般歸之為氣候變遷。

❷ 當來自太陽的電磁輻射能與地球本身的輻射熱之間因種種外力而失去平衡，地球的氣候便會產生變化。基本的氣候變遷進程有二：

- 外部進程發生於地球之外，像是地球公轉軌道的細微轉變，或是日照強度的增減。

- 內部進程則是地球自身氣候系統的改變。像海洋環流或火山爆發異常，還有地球大氣結構的變化都是。過去五十年來，氣候變遷的唯一關鍵，可能在於汙染以及地球大氣成分改變。

❸ 人類消耗化石燃料、砍伐森林，都市化發展等諸如此類的人為因素，顯然是造成大氣成分改變的元凶。這些環境摧殘行為會產生有害氣體，加速地球自然暖化週期。當二氧化碳或甲烷之類的氣體過度累積，原本能夠自然釋出大氣層的紅外線熱能被困在大氣內，使得大氣有如一座巨型溫室。受困的熱能對大氣底層及地表產生增溫效果，結果就是眾所周知的全球暖化。

❹ 自1750年以來，氣候就有暖化的趨勢，然而真正產生巨變卻是過去五十年左右的事，最高溫落在1995年之後，也就是從1850年人類首次測量地表溫度的後幾年。氣候變遷所帶來的衝擊是相當驚人的，例如：

- 大氣與海洋溫度上升，阻礙農業發展和森林經營，也為海洋生物帶來危機。以拉丁美洲為例，熱帶林可能被莽原取代，可耕地也可能變成荒漠（沙漠化）。

- 地表與海洋溫度上升也會造成棲地消失。目前瀕臨絕種的動物中，有多達25%的哺乳類動物和12%的鳥類即將滅絕。

- 南北半球的覆冰量正在逐漸減少，隨之而來的則是全球海平面上升。光是格林蘭冰層融化就可以使海平面上升七公尺之多。

▶ 世界各地雨雪量的改變,可能提高洪水氾濫或水土流失的機會,也會造成地下水汙染。

▶ 兩極的海洋鹽度被稀釋,加上低緯地區海洋鹽度上升,將直接反應在洋流的變化上,進而可能引發更多氣候變遷。

▶ 海洋酸度提高可能破壞珊瑚礁,威脅海洋生物。

▶ 諸如乾旱與熱帶氣旋這類的極端天氣事件會降低農產量,對地方造成生命財產的損失。

▶ 洪水或乾旱過後可能緊接著爆發傳染病。糧食短缺或食物生產轉移可能造成營養不良的現象;天氣過熱或過冷都會造成死傷。

▶ 旅遊稅收減少、農漁產量縮減,再加上水資源匱乏,許多國家經濟可能因此蒙受莫大損失。

5 為了因應氣候變遷,初期各界著重的防治政策展現出無比決心。政策目標放在減少甚至消除所有溫室氣體排放源、保護水資源與能源。其中一些有效政策已經付諸實行,範圍可能小至地方大至全球性,並且還會持續下去。許多民眾開始少用化石燃料,地方則投入經費改善建築和道路等公共建設,加強其使用效率。同時地方或國家立法機關也陸續通過諸多能源提案。

6 更近期的因應措施延伸到應變策略。以往社會大眾能夠適應自然的氣候變遷,但是當今氣候變遷的速度與強度已非同以往,我們需要更新穎的對策。政府可以資助一些公共衛生計畫,確保水資源公平分配、保障水權。各級政府機關和私人機構也早已著手拯救海岸線和濕地,改善農業操作與防治病蟲害。地方可以擴展預警系統及緊急應變系統。民眾可能需要調整衣著和活動層次。舉例來說,天氣越來越熱,民眾可以選擇包覆性佳的輕裝以防曬傷。此外也要避免在一天最熱的時段從事戶外活動。最終還有國際在全方位考查、調整和擬定防治政策上所做的努力,都將協助地球氣候回歸自然變遷週期。

Chapter 36 森林與森林危機

1 地球將近三分之一的土地為森林所覆蓋。界定森林的標準有很多,一般而言,一塊土地覆有10％林冠,也就是樹木覆蓋,就可稱做森林。地球上超過60％的生物多樣性存在於森林內,是很重要的生態、文化、經濟資源。舉例來說,樹木使水不停循環,可促進降雨;樹木吸收二氧化碳,有助於調節自然與人為引發的溫室效應。此外,森林可以預防洪水和土壤流失,提供休閒旅遊的好場所。很多經濟資源如藥用植物、水果、肉品、柴木與木材都來自森林。對原住民來說,森林代表文化認同,是各大儀式或習俗舉行的地方。

2 森林必須承受來自自然力的週期性威脅,例如:天氣擾動、森林大火或火山活動。這些天然事件或許橫掃範圍大,卻不至於徹底摧毀森林。森林之生物多樣性擁有絕佳的快速再生力(通常不到150年),能夠自我恢復甚至超越往昔的規模。

3 森林最大的損失,或者說「森林砍伐」,主要來自人為。「森林砍伐」是大規模清空地球上的森林,把土地轉為他用。森林砍伐有直接肇因也有間接(隱性)肇因。早期為了減緩森林砍伐與其帶來的破壞性衝擊,多半只針對直接肇因行動:

▶ 農地需求造成許多森林被摧毀。糊口農民砍倒數公頃的林木後焚燒,這個過程稱為「燒墾」。當土壤肥沃不再,農民就轉而牧牛。直到土地降為不毛之地,農民只好棄地。

▶ 原木「皆伐」(大量砍伐)、「選伐」以及林道建設已於中國等國引發暴洪,歐洲部分地區也有超過90％的原始林因此消失殆盡。

▶ 主要源於人口壓力的大規模人口聚居和都市化,一直在消耗林地和建材。人類以旅遊為目的而建設、入主森林,則會消耗和汙染森林資源。

▶ 熱帶雨林區的油氣開採行為會干擾生態系統。油氣鑽探或漏溢可能導致汙染物進入大氣和水資源。

4 有些森林砍伐來自間接肇因,但是衝擊並不亞於直接肇因。商業和工業政策著重短期獲利,缺乏永續經營。屬於社會經濟因素和政治因素的現象有：土地分配不均、強制驅離原住民和糊口農民。高收入國家消費者的過度消費，造成林產供需失衡。而工業化產生的大片汙染形成了酸雨。

5 過去一百年來，全世界超過80％的天然林地被摧毀、全球雨林快速消失、西非沿海90％的森林已被夷為平地。濫砍濫伐所引發的全球效應已經浮出檯面，未來恐怕更為嚴重。

▶ 地球一半以上的動植物即將面臨棲地消失的命運。

▶ 基因多元化喪失將使全球人口失去糧食和醫療資源。

▶ 樹木不再吸收溫室氣體，全球暖化現象可能日趨嚴重。

▶ 降雨型態被破壞，導致乾旱擴大。

6 美國太空總署所研發採用的新式遙感技術，能夠定期監控並評估森林砍伐的趨向。1970年代研發的人造衛星能夠長期捕捉森林變化的細部影像，尤其針對熱帶地區。世界各地其他機構，則利用這些人造衛星資訊來施行環保政策。

7 為了舒緩森林砍伐的現象並降低其衝擊性，一些組織如「國際農業研究諮商組織」、「美國太空總署」、「聯合國環境規劃署」已經採取行動。但是拯救森林計畫還是可以從基層做起，由政府和一些組織發起林區居住責任。農民可以運用「庇蔭耕作」這類的低衝擊農耕法。可再生林產品如木材、水果和藥用植物可以永續生產、收成。舉辦生態旅遊可以提高經濟及教育機會。全國或全球性策略則有：獎勵採納森林保育措施的開發中國家及私人土地擁有者，也能制訂並執行國際森林保育準則。森林的未來需要倚賴大眾意識覺醒、政府與私人提撥經費，也不能缺少永續經營管理。

Chapter 37 ｜廢棄物減量與管理

1 隨著全球工業化高漲，尤其是二十世紀，連帶消費與生產也雙雙暴增。結果就是，每人製造的垃圾量不斷攀升，在過去五十年來幾乎成長兩倍，諷刺的是，工業對於廢棄物減量、重複使用和資源回收的現代措施又功不可沒。所謂的現代廢棄物管理，指的是廢棄物處理層級，或稱為廢棄物的三個R：reduce（減量）、reuse（重複使用）和recycle（資源回收）。

2 廢棄物減量又稱為源頭減量，指改進製造過程來減少有毒或固態廢棄物。產品以大容量包裝或者採用可重複使用的包裝材料，都算是源頭減量。最簡單的方法是減少用料，同樣要製造容量兩公升的塑膠瓶，可以減少塑膠用量。另外也可選用無毒的原料，清潔用品的製造常運用此法。

3 廢棄物重複使用是另一種環保作法。消費者可以捐獻物品供重複使用，例如：有些市立中心接受電子設備，有些商店如Goodwill專門販售民眾捐贈的二手衣。物品經過重複使用至少可以延長壽命，避免垃圾在收集、掩埋或焚化過程中所產生的處理成本和環境傷害。

4 雖然保護地球資源還是以不製造垃圾為上策，資源回收也不失為一種有效的環保措施。資源回收意指將原本要丟棄的物品回收，並且用它們製造再生產品。將近75％的地球垃圾都是可以回收的。資源回收不僅可以節省原料、降低能源使用，還可以減少汙染物。

5 可回收的材質很多，但是大多數都需要加工處理，方式視材質而定。紙類看似最普遍的回收材質，但實際上鐵、鋼等鐵金屬才是最多的。鋁這類非鐵金屬最容易有效回收，玻璃則幾乎可以再三壓碎重新使用。塑膠、電池和木材也都是常見的回收材質。

6 完整的資源回收流程包含五個環節，每一環節對於永續維繫產品週期都是舉足輕重。首先，從工業領導人到社區參與者，都必須瞭解資源回收的基本原理。企業可以進行廢棄物稽查，藉由追蹤廢棄物及其處理方式，選擇最適合的回收方法。地方機構可以提供個人諮詢，指示一些特定家庭廢棄物（如飲料罐和紙類）的回收方法或地點。塑膠類通常會標示標準回收符號，告訴消費者該如何分類，以及它們是否為安全的可回收材質。第二，企業和家庭都應該使用專門的回收容器，以便後續垃圾清運公司的搬運，或直接送往回收中心。第三，企業和社區必須審視評估回收系統，以確保在經濟負擔許可下能有效做環保。

7 第四，一些專門收購回收料的公司已經成立，將材料回收製造新的消費品。這類公司的主要關注在於回收料的成本和品質。這裡說的成本，包含調整製造流程以處理回收料的經費，還有收購高級回收料相對要付出的高價，以及搬運回收料的運費。最後，還要有人願意購買再生產品，才算完成了這個「封閉式回收系統」，但是最後一個步驟卻往往被忽略。許多企業做了回收，自己內部的營運生產卻沒有意願使用再生材料。要能使用再生材料需要投注一定的經費，在這一點上各企業還需加快腳步。

8 資源回收再怎麼有效減少廢棄物，都不可能百分之百完全消除。新一波的廢棄物減量計畫則開始結合「零廢棄」的設計理念。「零廢棄」是二十一世紀的新興概念，它的訴求是將三個R融入工業設計理念，強調產品要無毒、可重複使用、可資源回收。

9 資源回收也有其爭議之處，特別是牽涉到經濟問題的時候。對某些地方來說，資源回收是一項沉重的負擔。除此之外，有些回收料品質堪慮，降低回收價值，相對於回收成本根本不划算。再者，有證據顯示政府進行的資源回收竟比垃圾掩埋來得昂貴。

10 大致來說，資源回收還是利多於弊。有些地方聲稱當地的垃圾掩埋場為他們帶來工作機會和收入。然而整體看來，資源回收和廢棄物管理不但可以保護土地、節約能源和自然資源，最重要的是留給後代子孫一片更美好的環境。

Chapter 38　人為的環境壓迫

1 人類活動自有史以來就一直牽動著環境變化，不時的人口過剩造成局部地區沙漠化或水資源耗竭即為一例。過去一世紀來人口快速擴張，生活水準大幅提昇，卻對全球環境帶來莫大浩劫。地球上將近一半以上的植栽地被人類占據，消耗天然資源的速度讓地球措手不及。過去30年世界人口暴增四倍，商品產量增加近20倍，環境難以應其需求。

2 人類不論工業、農業甚至娛樂活動經常對環境產生負面影響。化石燃料消耗殆盡，空氣被汙染，水也被汙染，歸咎到底都是人類能源需求和能源政策釀禍。農業開發致使森林消失、土地沙漠化，對生物多樣性及氣候變遷帶來巨大衝擊。即使人類利用水陸資源從事休閒旅遊都會造成汙染，減少可生產糧食的土地。

3 農業土地利用對環境的壓力最大。目前地球景觀約10%是農地，不過換算成個人土地分配率卻是持續下降。為了提高農產量，土地使用密集度勢必增加，如果開發中國家欠缺妥善教育和監督，就會造成水土流失和沙漠化。近五十年內，全球超過30%的農地因失去生產力而被廢置，這些土壤需要等到數百年後才能重燃生機。在此同時，人類藉由「森林砍伐」——清空一整片森林的過程，繼續開墾新農地。農產改良也帶來機械與運輸需求上的高能源損耗。政治動盪不安、經濟不穩定、食物分配不均，都會導致全球糧食短缺。糧食短缺反向提高全球對糧食保障的重視，結果又見土地所無法負擔的新墾農地。

4 人類的過度消費，可能為地球生物多樣性帶來幾個方面的負面影響。

▶ 對動物或魚類濫捕濫殺可能會連帶影響棲地。以這些物種為食物來源的掠食性動物也會因食物短缺而銳減。

▶ 工業活動和密集耕作不停製造廢棄汙染物，交通工具的碳排放也在其中。

▶ 目前世界人口有一半集中在都會區，數量還在持續攀升。都市化踏平森林和草原、摧毀生物棲地，同時也降低水質。

▶ 每年，人為引發的大火燒毀數百英畝土地。

▶ 森林砍伐會造成土地分割，此舉逐漸成為棲地消失的原因。林木若採「皆伐」，也就是大面積帶狀砍伐，生態系統會被切割得支離破碎，一些在地物種面臨棲地改變或消失的命運。

❺ 人類活動破壞生物多樣性的同時，也給了有害物種入侵各棲地的機會。當都市日益發展、貿易繁榮，交通流量增加，外來物種要進入、分布到新環境不再是難事。

- 類似小型哺乳動物這樣的物種入侵，可能給在地物種帶來傳染病，或者減少牠們的生產量。
- 外來物種可能汙染水源，影響棲地的營養循環，也可能破壞漁場。
- 野草增生可能將農產量縮減達25%，土壤肥沃度也會下降。
- 外來物種阻礙農工業發展，也等於給了經濟重重一擊。人類每年為此付出的代價高達四億，還不包含失業、糧食飲水短缺、人體健康因素，還有日漸頻仍、破壞力更勝以往的天災所造成的損失。

❻ 現在我們能利用人造衛星拍攝記錄地表景觀的變化。人造衛星能定期取得地表大範圍的清晰影像。自人造衛星所獲之資訊，有助於環境型態的長期評估，人造衛星也可以用來規劃基礎建設之改善或發展。不久，這些遙感裝置將成為更多全球環境政策執行上的好幫手。

Chapter 39　望遠鏡

❶ 一般認為荷蘭的科學家也是眼鏡商漢斯‧李普錫於1608年發明了世界上第一座望遠鏡。他把兩片玻璃透鏡裝在管子裡，以便把物體放大最多至三倍。隔年伽利略改良這個原型，創造出放大倍率達20倍的望遠鏡，成為首位利用望遠鏡觀測天體的人。

❷ 望遠鏡的作用在於觀測和放大肉眼所不及的遙遠物體。光學望遠鏡利用透鏡或面鏡聚光，再由目鏡放大光線。然而，科學家還必須記錄影像才算完成觀測。最初天文學家全憑手繪記錄，直到攝影術出現才得以透過望遠鏡拍照。1980年代開始採用新技術，以數位方式保存望遠鏡取得之影像。任何一種望遠鏡都可以架設數位相機，這種數位攝影被稱為天文攝影。

❸ 現今使用中的望遠鏡有三種：光學望遠鏡、電波望遠鏡、X射線和伽瑪射線望遠鏡。其中最普遍的光學望遠鏡，又可分為折射、反射或折反射，視其配置的透鏡和面鏡來區隔。折射望遠鏡使用凸透鏡曲光聚焦，透鏡內厚外薄，通過外側的光線折射角度較大，所有光線匯集的焦點即為成像之處。凹目鏡又叫發散透鏡，其表面面向內彎曲，因此可以放大影像使之延展於人類視網膜，獲得比肉眼所見更大的影像。反射望遠鏡則是牛頓所發明，使用一片凹面鏡把光線反射到目鏡上。由於面鏡不會像玻璃一樣對光分色，所以影像周圍不會出現因光波長短而產生的月暈效應。折反射望遠鏡是同時運用透鏡和面鏡的混合型望遠鏡，由一片透鏡校正面鏡成像的缺陷，因此面鏡不需要大，望遠鏡的整體體積也能越做越小。

❹ 當遇到不發光或者不太反光的物體，光學望遠鏡變得毫無用武之地，因此促成電波望遠鏡和X射線望遠鏡的研發。這兩種望遠鏡專門接收穿過大氣層而未變形的不可見波，和接收光的道理一樣。近來研究人員更在各種輻射之外致力於尋求新的成像來源，嘗試用望遠鏡搜尋重力波即為一例。

❺ 另一種不受地球大氣層扭曲效應影響的望遠鏡是太空望遠鏡。太空望遠鏡雖早在1940年代問世，卻歷經數十年才發展出足夠的技術和經費進行研發。從1960年代初到1980年代初，美國太空總署陸續發射軌道天文台，用它們研究太陽，尋找紅外輻射新來源，以及偵察慧星等天體的活動。1980年代中期，美國太空總署推動「大天文台」計畫，迄今已發射四座天文望遠鏡進入軌道。康卜吞伽瑪射線天文台已於2000年除役，但是其他三座─哈柏太空望遠鏡、錢德拉X射線天文台、史匹哲太空望遠鏡仍在軌道上運行。

❻ 「大天文台」望遠鏡裡最赫赫有名的莫過於哈柏太空望遠鏡，是為了紀念1920年代的美國太空人愛德恩‧包威爾‧哈柏而命名。哈柏太空望遠鏡發射於1990年，是一座架設了直徑240公分面鏡的反射望遠鏡。它能觀測到比任何架設於地球的

望遠鏡所測再暗一百倍的物體。舉例來說，就是靠著哈柏太空望遠鏡發現了無數星系，有的甚至遠達一千萬光年。哈柏太空望遠鏡無須經過地球大氣層，所以能夠收到紫外光和紅外光——當黑洞附近有星系盤形成，或者恆星爆炸時，會放射紫外光；新星附近若有塵雲生成，則放射紅外光。哈柏太空望遠鏡由美國太空總署和歐洲太空總署（ESA）共同操作，美國太空總署負責發射無線電波引導哈柏轉向。哈柏上配有電腦驅動設備記錄觀測結果，同樣以無線電波回報地面研究人員。

7 待邁入二十一世紀的第二十年，美國太空總署計畫發射韋伯太空望遠鏡（JWST），上面會裝置一面直徑6.4公尺的主鏡，集光面積是哈柏的七倍。科學家們盼望未來的望遠鏡能達到足夠的高解析成像，協助他們研究太陽系外行星、黑洞和位於星系旋臂的恆星，取得充分的特徵來推斷這些星系的演化過程。

Chapter 40　太空船系統

1 自二十世紀中葉以來，以科學、商業或軍事目的而發射的太空船約有7,000架。大部分的太空船由美、俄主導發射，而日本、中國和以色列也曾在二十一世紀發射太空船。其中將近半數是通訊衛星或監視衛星，只有10％左右用於科學研究。另外，不到10％的太空船有人駕駛。

2 太空船（spacecraft）泛指任何設計於太空中航行的交通工具。若以個別任務做區分，則有各式各樣的名稱。「探測器」專門探索行星或星體；「人造衛星」可以環繞天體運行，發揮研究或通訊功能。為了在險惡的太空環境中耐久生存，太空船工程極要求精密。況且一旦太空船進入軌道，便難以仰賴工程師進行維修。

3 太空船靠反應引擎送進太空。液態燃料與液氧之類的氧化劑於一燃燒室中混合，燃燒產生高壓氣體。接著，反應引擎將此氣體自太空船尾端噴發，以時速五千到一萬英里推進太空船。

4 太空船必須擁有足夠的推力來擺脫地心引力。令科學家最頭痛的是太空船本身的重量問題。太空船越重，需要攜帶越多燃料才足以脫離大氣層，這無疑是雪上加霜。「太空時代之父」羅伯・高達德曾提出一個解決之道，他建議使用「多級火箭」。一艘太空船同時裝配好幾節火箭，每當一節火箭的燃料用罄，就脫離丟棄，如此一來，路上所需的燃料只會越來越少。現代火箭一般都擁有二至三節火箭，或者說二至三級。

5 太空船該配備哪些系統、哪些儀器，視其功能與所要蒐集的資訊而定。

▶ 大氣探測器或氣球探測包受遣進入某星體之大氣層，分析氣體和風。

▶ 登陸器、地表穿透機和漫遊車探索天體表面並取回資訊。其中有些負責攝影、分析土壤，有些負責穿透地表之下研究地面屬性。

▶ 近天體探測器能飛掠目標物上空取得畫面和資訊，將目標物的移動因素也考慮進去。〈航海家一號〉和〈航海家二號〉即屬於此類太空船。

▶ 軌道太空船能判斷減速時機，以便被導入天體軌道蒐集資訊。此一過程稱作制動火箭燃燒或氣阻減速。〈麥哲倫號〉和〈伽利略號〉屬於此類太空船。

▶ 駕駛式太空船用來搭載太空人，備有組員艙和維生系統，也可能攜帶登陸艙。美國太空總署的阿波羅計畫多屬此類。

6 所有太空船均配備多套子系統，用來提供動力、蒐集資訊、或傳輸訊號。電力系統如電池、燃料電池、放射性同位素熱電產生器或核子反應器，作用是為其他系統或儀器供電。推進系統由多座引擎分別負責將太空船推進軌道、維持穩定繞軌，甚至賦予太空船游移宇宙之機動性。環境系統保護太空船歷險而不受損；被動系統如漆料和反射器用來輔助冷卻；主動式加熱系統負責維持最低溫度；而屏蔽裝置隔絕有害粒子。

7 除此之外，太空船仰賴定向（羅盤方位）系統或航姿（太空船與其他天體的相對位置）系統維持行進穩定、調整移動方向，以求能準確蒐集、分析資訊。推進器或機輪控制太空船移動或旋轉，電腦系統負責追蹤感應行星或其他天體。科學儀器探測星體資料。直測儀器測量天體成分及能量，遙測儀器收集影像並偵測輻射線。數據通訊系統蒐集、處理、排列資料，透過電腦或天線傳回地球。

❽改良引擎設計，再加上採用太陽光帆和核能等重大革新，太空飛航將不再遙不可及，甚至可能帶來商機。太空旅遊像是下榻宇宙飯店、從事太空運動，不久後都有機會實現。人類將能在太空中長時間生活。宇宙交通工具不但可載客運貨，從事科學或教育研究也不是問題。未來太空船也可能利用以太陽能為主的其他能源。

（註解：spacecraft 這個字公認之複數形為 spacecraft。即使過去幾年內 spacecrafts 的寫法越來越普遍，學術研究或科學交流上仍沿用 spacecraft。）

Chapter 41　新興太空技術

❶人類從事太空探索已有超過五十年歷史，並且從中獲益無數。二十一世紀多了尖端（或者說新興的）太空技術的輔助，全球地方社群比以往更有機會直接參與太空探索。

❷充氣式太空船之研發始於1960年代，直到二十一世紀發射的充氣式太空船，證實比傳統材質更能達到低成本高效率。充氣式太空船裝配在數個小型容器中後以火箭載運，火箭另外備有筒裝惰性氣體。一旦進入太空，惰性氣體會被填充至充氣式太空船內，使之還原到超過100立方公尺的大小。假設這種充氣式太空船能夠達到一定的耐久性，還能維持內部狀態的穩定，就可能為私有太空站或商務太空之旅打開契機。

❸太空飛機也有可能成為商務太空之旅採用的載具。美國的太空計畫至今已發射一百多架實驗機（用來進行學術研究的機種）。目前研發中的新機種能夠自行攜帶燃料，無須倚賴火箭助推器，其飛行速度可達25馬赫─足以繞地球運行的速度。這些飛機都配備「可再使用發射載具」（RLV）技術，可提高成本效益，甚至取代太空梭。最終太空飛機將會是客貨兩用的太空船。此外，日本及歐洲太空總署都已成功研發太空貨運船，將用來運送補給品，停靠各個國際太空站。

❹最先進的太空船材質採用碳或克維拉（Kevlar）纖維等聚合物以及泡狀癒合劑，具有自我修復能力。當這類材質遭遇險惡的太空環境，產生輕微裂痕時，會釋放催化劑刺激癒合劑發揮作用，修補這些細微傷痕。太空船的內部線路也具有自癒能力。負責維修和管理的電腦系統將自動偵測、診斷，然後修正太空船的系統異常。

❺太空帆的出現為無推進劑太空飛行留下伏筆。太空帆吸收太陽能，能提升飛行速度數倍於傳統太空船。面對劇烈日照的耐熱度似乎以碳纖維表現最佳。

❻目前仍在設計中的還有運用奈米管複合材料輸送帶的太空升降機。機械式升降機或雷射光束能透過這條輸送帶讓太空船往返太空。太空升降機運貨載人的成本相較於傳統太空船節省許多。

❼自太空飛行問世一直到今日，太空船的推進系統未有太大革新，但未來將出現更多樣化的推進方式。

▶「電力系統」運用電源產生游離氣體，即電漿，再轉換為燃料。採用靜電、電磁、電熱的機械裝置可產生強於化學燃料裝置的特殊高脈衝，代表它們可以自火箭引擎尾端更快速地注入大量燃料，加速推進太空船，提高燃料效能。

▶「光束推進」利用面鏡聚集雷射光束，使空氣受熱爆發後推動太空船。光束飛行器的重量遠輕於傳統飛行器，行進速度可達數倍之快，耗燃量相當少，且廢棄物排放量等於零。

▶吸氣式火箭吸取大氣氣體，混和氫燃料以便將飛行器送進軌道。然而光靠空氣不足以產生足夠推力，因此先由吸氣增強式火箭驅動太空船，再由吸氣式火箭接手航向太空。此時仍須仰賴傳統引擎才能提供太空船進入軌道的必需動力。

▶ 實現反物質太空船大概距離我們只剩數十年之遙。當物質和反物質相互碰撞，雙方質量都會完全轉換為能量，此比任何化學燃燒產生的能量強上數百萬倍。但是現存之反物質數量難與物質相當，必須仰賴人為製造。一旦科學家能夠製造出足夠的反物質，前所未有的高效推進系統即將誕生，核融合或核分裂產生的能量亦無法與之匹敵。

❽ 人類生命科學將持續受益於太空探索活動。未來太空技術將左右生物技術的改良，患者病情之精準診斷和監控技術都能獲得提升。人體植入物如耳蝸與心臟裝置將具有自癒能力。運輸系統也將因改良式高效能源及諸如全球定位系統的導航技術問世而受益。太空科技將持續對地球資源如森林和水建立有效管理。此外，從改良式運動鞋到氣動式高爾夫球，連休閒娛樂都是太空技術的受益範圍。人類投入太空科學的成本與其為全球帶來的利益已不足以相提並論，我們可以期待未來的投資將獲得更多回報。

Chapter 42　光害

❶ 人類原本就屬於白晝生物，我們白天活動、晚上睡覺。人類不像其他動物能靠聽覺或嗅覺導航，而是靠視覺，因此一旦進入黑暗中便感到窒礙難行。為了能夠在夜間活動自如，人類開始利用從天然火光到各種人工照明等各式各樣的光源。隨著工業文明演進，人類對於人工照明的需求也越來越高，進而開發出許多室內外照明光源。除了用於工作和安全考量的照明之外，還有專為路燈、廣告、商圈（如餐廳或公園），或者運動場所設計的照明設備。這類照明多數對於自然環境是過度而且刺眼的，過去幾十年來已被視為一種汙染，稱為「光害」。

❷ 光害（light pollution）在英文裡又稱做 luminous pollution 或 photopollution，一般可分為兩種：

▶ 「過度照明」通常發生於室內，當光線造成人體不適甚至可能危害健康時，就構成了過度照明。此種光害尤以工作場合為甚。對人體產生的影響有疲勞或頭痛，造成的生理壓力可能提高罹癌機率，而心理壓力可能導致沮喪。

▶ 第二種是流入自然環境中的「雜散光」，大多來自於設計不良的光源，如：感應燈或路燈。有些雜散光是燈光投射在目標物的反光，更嚴重的是燈光流溢出預定照射範圍。雜散光會造成直射眩光、光侵擾或天空輝光。它不僅讓夜空迷濛、星光黯淡，同時也浪費能源，可能在數方面會導致溫室氣體排放。

- 直射眩光是由過量或遮罩不足的光源所引起的眼部不適，可分為兩種：「礙視眩光」，因強光照射降低眼前視野能見度；「不適眩光」，由強光造成之干擾甚至極度不適感。人眼的光敏性差異極大，但普遍來說，視力已開始退化的老人家對光較為敏感。
- 當光線流入不需要照明的地方，就構成了光侵擾。舉例來說，路燈可能照進一旁的住家，而這些室內範圍並非原本設定的照明目標。
- 天空輝光可能出於天然或人為光源。自然界的天空輝光像是地球或月球反射的太陽光。人為的天空輝光主要來自路燈、戶外廣告燈或是居家保全照明。天空輝光的程度依天候而異，天候不佳時，大氣懸浮粒子增加，光線散射下產生的多餘光和能源使天空散發著耀眼的輝光。

❸ 光具有一種強大的生物支配力，所有物種都或多或少受其影響。

▶ 被探照燈或鑽油平台燈所吸引的海鳥，有時會圍繞燈光飛翔，直到力竭而死。

▶ 群集在路燈周圍的昆蟲很容易成為蝙蝠等動物的獵物。

▶ 有些鳥類因為撞上發光物而送命。

▶ 人工照明擾亂或改變部分鳥類的生命週期。鳴鳥異常時間鳴叫、候鳥遷徙、繁殖週期提前，連帶築巢行為也失常。

▶ 海灘設置人工照明的情況下，海龜、青蛙、蟾蜍的繁殖和築巢行為都受到影響，致使卵的孵化量逐漸減少。

❹ 針對光害問題的因應措施已陸續上路。美國許多州已經通過法規限制光度，為公私場合的戶外照明立下宵禁，同時要求各方使用高效率的照明系統。2009年被訂為「全球天文年」，11項《全球基

石計畫》之一的「星空保育」舉辦了許多國際性的活動，旨在教育大眾認識光害問題。星空保育鼓勵全球民眾參與，讓民眾親自測量光害、計算可視天體數量，然後親自深入社區宣導星空保育的概念。星空保育同時也促成一些永久建設，例如：暗天公園和星空保育區。該計畫還將設計無光害空間，作為充實大眾光害知識之用。

5 其實只要利用一些簡單的小方法往往就能免除光害，像是採用高效照明或者修正光源。然而，唯有社會大眾的意識覺醒才能永續改善光害問題。

Chapter 43 　火星

1 比鄰地球的火星是距離太陽的第四顆行星，也是人類首次探索的行星。羅馬人為了紀念他們的戰神，用戰神的名字Mars來為這顆行星命名。火星俗稱「紅色星球」，因為從地球看過去，火星的土壤和天空呈現一片橘紅色。早期的觀測發現火星上地表崎嶇，極冠會隨季節而變化，大氣濃度足以成雲起風。所有跡象都顯示火星上應該曾有高等生物存在。雖然這個說法尚未獲得任何科學證據支持，市面上已經不乏以火星人為題材的科幻小說。

2 1965年，美國派遣近天體探測太空船〈水手四號〉近距離拍攝火星照片，然而從照片中僅能看出火星表面如隕坑等自然力造成的地形。此後的十年中，美國又陸續發射軌道太空船捕捉火星畫面，繪製火星地表構造。他們發現火星上面有枯河床、火山，還有峽谷。近期，跨國合作的火星探測任務則運用登陸器和探測器來分析岩石、土壤的取樣，得到了火星演進過程中應該曾有液態水存在的結論，他們也在火星上發現了大量水冰。

3 火星約起源於45億年前。關於火星的演化年代和各年代的長短，因為太空探測器無法將岩石土壤取樣送回地球，科學家們也只能臆測。火星極有可能經歷過三次演化：諾亞紀、赫斯伯利亞紀和亞馬遜紀，分別以最具該時期地表特徵的地理名稱命名。在諾亞紀，水流侵蝕出錯綜複雜的山谷，證實也顯時當時的火山活動頻仍。到了赫斯伯利亞紀，火山爆發刻鑿出火星上大部分的水道。亞馬遜紀生成了最大的一座火山，兩極也出現冰冠。

4 和地球不同的是，火星的大氣層含氧量不到1%，95%以上都是二氧化碳。大氣的水氣雖然低，還是足夠凝結成雲霧。二氧化碳冰晶於兩極附近所組成的雲氣左右了火星的大氣環流。冬天時，二氧化碳向兩極聚集，到了春天蒸發，往兩極之外消散。火星的大氣層不如地球般濃密，其地表鮮有強風吹拂。氣溫視季節從攝氏20到140度不等。

5 雖然太空探測器還無法深入火星地底進行探測，科學家認為火星內部應該分為三層基本構造：地殼、地函和地核。地殼厚約30英里；地函由近似地球的岩石組成，因放射性衰變的受熱型態也與地球類似。火星地核則異於半熔融狀態的地球地核，幾乎呈現完全的固態。火星的密度只有地球的70%，相對的地心引力也不到地球的40%。

6 火星的地表大部分與地球相似，但是火星多了許多隕坑，不難想像其經年累月所承受之隕石撞擊。外力造成的凹陷也常以山谷、水道或小峽谷的姿態出現，可見火星曾經氣候溫和、適合水流活動。全太陽系最大的火山都位於火星，可能是大規模的熔岩噴發沉積出來的。還有一些區域極有可能由水流沖積而成，這些區域說不定是全太陽系最平坦、光滑的地表。大氣層落下的水冰和塵土的長期堆積，應該是火星極冠的成因，這些水冰終年都能維持好幾英里的厚度。

7 火星擁有兩顆小衛星，分別是佛勃斯（火衛一）和狄莫司（火衛二），兩者表面都是坑坑洞洞。佛勃斯的直徑27公里，狄莫司大概15公里。這兩顆衛星若非與火星同時生成，就是突然被火星拉進軌道的小行星。

8 未來的火星任務將採用地下探測器蒐集甚至帶回大氣、岩石和土壤樣本。研究人員還打算在未來十年內，發射飛機或熱氣球進入火星大氣層，進行比現在更清晰、持久的拍攝任務。未來也可能派遣太空人前往火星，美國太空總署近期宣布將於2035年讓人類登上火星。

Chapter 44　高速穿透機

❶自二十世紀以來，星際探索行動運用過各式各樣專門執行觀察任務的飛行器。早期的飛行器僅執行拍攝月球或行星照片之任務；後期的太空任務開始採用能夠探測地表的飛行器。時至今日，先進的太空探索技術逐漸成功發射重落地探測器（或稱地表穿透機）來蒐集月球或行星的地下（表岩屑）資訊。所謂的穿透機是一種類似飛彈的投射物，能自火箭上發射，以每秒 200 到 700 公尺的超高撞擊速度衝擊太陽系各種天體的地表。另外還有一種微型穿透機，非常輕薄短小，重量只有 2 至 13 公斤而已。

❷所有的高速穿透機都能攜帶少量的科學儀器，如：資料收集系統或感應器。這些科技儀器將被投射至科學家們欲探索的特定天體上。

▶ **地震儀**：測量穿過星體內部的地震波，如此可探知星體內部所存在的化學元素以及各種磁力。

▶ **化學感測器**：利用一些顯微取樣工具（攝影機）來偵測水和有機化學反應。
 - 下降攝影機：負責撞擊點之影像蒐集。
 - 地面攝影機／顯微鏡：負責礦物或生物的偵測與成像。
 - 無線攝影穿透機：負責拍攝地表或地平線特徵，動力來源為電池或太陽能。

▶ **熱感測器**：用以測量地表或地下溫度，偵測地底物質如何導熱。熱感測器能提供關於天體內部組成的資訊。

▶ **訊號發送器與磁力計**：感應水平方向的地殼漂移。

▶ **輻射監測器**：研究地下輻射分布，來決定何處適合架設人類基地，並判斷生物存在的可能性。

❸為了確保穿透機正中目標的同時，各種儀器能夠毫無損傷，科學家必須規劃出一套具體的任務架構（飛航計畫）。

▶ **巡航階段**：穿透機由太空船搭載。太空船要負責提供動力、維持穿透機與地球之聯繫，也要隨時掌握穿透機的狀態。

▶ **部署探測器**：太空船發射穿透機，確認穿透機完全脫離母船。

▶ **下降階段**：此時由推進器來調整穿透機的速率和姿態，將最後的理想撞擊速度控制在每秒 200 到 300 公尺之間。

▶ **撞擊地面**：穿透機穿破地面進入表岩屑，向下穿透數公尺。

▶ **地下作業**：穿透機所攜帶的觀測儀如化學感測器、地震儀、熱感測器等開始運作。此時的穿透機仰賴電池發電，母船則持續傳輸訊號。

❹穿透機可以帶來許許多多的好處。它們比輕落地式登陸器更擅於衝撞堅硬粗糙地表，成本效益也較高。就算經過強力碰撞或置身嚴寒環境，也不必擔心功能失常。此外，穿透機先行收集豐富的科學數據，可供後續輕落地式儀器在做大範圍調查時參考使用。穿透機最為人稱道之處，在於它提供了即地（最真實或原始的）、而且幾近即時的第一手資料。

❺目前英國月球穿透機協會與 Mullard 太空科學實驗室的行星科學團隊，展開了一系列的穿透機實驗計畫。他們仿製月球的砂質表岩屑，迄今已經完成從研究、模擬到實體撞擊試驗。這項試驗的目的在於檢驗穿透機承受高速撞擊的能力、評估科學儀器所受的影響，並測試各種材質的耐撞程度。截至目前為止的研究顯示，採用穿透機來進行太空探索所獲得的成就，就算未能超越輕落地式登陸器，至少也能與其並駕齊驅。

❻英國公布了一項 2013 年的月球穿透機發射計畫，由一繞軌人造衛星攜帶四座電池發電的穿透機，將它們分送至月球各地，其中兩座將分別落在月球背面和極區。將四座穿透機分散配置有助於研究月球表面的震波和熱流分布。穿透機甚至有可能判定月球的起源，並搜尋月球背面是否有水存在。這項太空任務如果無法拉長至數年，預計也至少會維持一年，以利於觀測月週期所引發的效應。人造衛星則會持續提供其動力、觀察穿透機的狀況，維繫穿透機與地球之間的資料傳輸。

❼目前還有其他的穿透機任務正在規劃之中。其中一座被派往木星之衛星歐羅巴（木衛二）的穿

透機，將配備地震儀潛入冰層下方海域進行勘查，附載之化學感測器負責偵測有機化學物質或生物棲息的可能性。穿透機也可以發射到任何近地物體從事地理分析。

Chapter 45　美國專利類型

❶「專利」是由政府核發的特定財產權。它屬於智慧財產權的一種，與著作權或商標不同的是，專利權授予的對象以產品或製程為主：一般而言，製程意指工業或技術行為、方法；產品則包含機器、商品、化合物或無性生殖的植物。首項專利於十五世紀初發出，直到二十世紀末各國制訂了個別專利條目，於其中載明專利核准之年限。1990年代，世界貿易組織（WTO）發展出一套制式的專利權，交由政府來授權。

❷一項發明要獲得專利至少必須符合三大條件：第一，這項發明，不管是製程、機械或物質，都必須具實用性並能操作使用，而此製程或產品還能夠再次被執行或製造。第二，這項發明不得事先刊載於任何出版物，或者在提出申請之一年前已獲得專利。第三，這項發明必須與過去的發明物有所區隔，足以令人耳目一新，諸如顏色或尺寸的變化並不符合專利的申請資格。

❸根據以上三大條件，專利又可分為三種類型：發明專利、設計專利和植物專利。發明人將依據該製程或產品的功能和類型來申請專利。美國所核准的專利權中，90％屬於發明專利。任何嶄新而實用的技術、機器、商品、合成物，甚至對過去發明物的改良，都在發明專利的核發之列。發明專利權之所有人必須定期繳納規費，才能保有專利資格，確保法律保障發明人對該發明物之獨有權。發明專利之專利年限為申請人提出申請起20年，有必要可延長年限。

❹專利權之第二大類型為「設計專利」，這項專利是核發給新的、原創的設計式樣。商品本身或外加的任何裝飾性特徵，都算是式樣。設計專利權的所有人不需繳納維持專利權之規費，同時商標權通常會連同設計專利權一併核發。設計專利權的年限為自發證日起14年。

❺第三種專利類型為「植物專利」。當發現或培植出一種可存活、無性繁殖的植物有機體，便可申請植物專利權，但是僅限於新發現的種子植物，不能是塊莖植物或發現自非耕地的植物。人工栽種的植物或植物變異包含芽變、自花傳粉的種子植物變異，以及混種變異。用來判定是否為新植物的特徵有很多：特別耐寒耐熱、可存活於險惡之環境、花瓣或樹葉之顏色、氣味、香氛或外型皆在考慮之內。植物專利權為期20年，所有申請人不需繳納規費。此外，獨見於植物專利權之特色在於，發明人在整個無性繁殖植物的過程中可處於指揮者的角色，外發給他人來執行，然而執行者並不能分享此專利權。

❻一旦發明者已獲得某項專利，還有一些方式可以保障他的發明物。如欲修正專利瑕疵，專利權所有人得以提出修正證明，或者申請重發專利。重發專利亦可擴大或縮小專利範圍，來維持發明物的有效性。有些案例在專利審查核准之後，卻出現更多關於該專利或其競爭專利的資訊，則專利權所有人或第三人得以要求對該專利重新檢驗。當然，專利權所有人隨時可以放棄專利權，或將所有或部分剩餘之專利期限轉讓給社會大眾。當專利期限屆滿，該發明物即歸於公有。不過，在鼓勵公共研究之同時，又要讓專利權所有人占有優先獲利的絕對優勢，暫時的獨有權依然有其必要性。

Chapter 46　全球智慧財產權

❶智慧財產指的是透過智力所創造的東西：舉凡各種發明、文學藝術作品，乃至商業用途之符號、品名、圖像或式樣，都屬於智慧財產。明確來講，智慧財產指的並非實際的財產本身，而是一種概念，或者是透過財產所表現的創意思維。一個人若獲得智慧財產的獨享權，代表法律賦予他在工業、科學、文學或藝術領域內從事特定智慧活動的權利。設立智慧財產權的目的不僅在於保護，亦在

於提倡。一來，智慧財產權（IPR）使創作者在道德上獲得尊重，在利益上受到保障；同時，也保障大眾欣賞或使用這些智慧創作的權利；再者，智慧財產權鼓勵創作並分享創作。最後，智慧財產權有助於推動新事物和新發明的公平交易，可促進經濟及社會發展。

❷十九世紀時，隨著工業革命急遽發展，各界開始注意智慧創作品的保護問題。首次因應這項議題而生的是1883年制訂的《保護工業財產權之巴黎公約》。此公約用以保障人們的智慧創作品在其祖國與各會員國內的智慧財產權。近百年後，「世界智慧財產權組織」成立，並且建構出一套更可親的全球智慧財產系統。這套用來監督各國核發特定智慧財產權的系統，目的是為了獎勵創意、鼓勵創新與發明，對於全球經濟發展功不可沒。世界智慧財產權組織（WIPO）與世界貿易組織（WTO）相互支援，為已開發國家及開發中國家提供更廣泛的協助。

❸即便在世界智慧財產權組織以及世界貿易組織雙重監督之下，各地對於智慧財產權的保護尺度及執行程度依然迥異，各國尺度的差異亦引發國際間的緊張關係。為了消弭各國立法之間的差異，世界貿易組織在1986到1994年間一連串的全球貿易協商之後，依照決議制訂了TRIPS（《與貿易有關之智慧財產權協定》）。該協定提出了各會員國對於智慧財產權保護的國際低標，此外，《與貿易有關之智慧財產權協定》也透過世界貿易組織，擬出一套裁決貿易糾紛的系統。《與貿易有關之智慧財產權協定》允許各國制訂自己的智慧財產系統，但對於五大議題提出全面性的準則：

- ▶ 對於貿易體系之基本原則以及其他國際智慧財產協定的施用
- ▶ 智慧財產權的保護
- ▶ 各國於境內對於智慧財產權的執行
- ▶ 世界貿易組織會員國之間與智慧財產相關之糾紛協調
- ▶《與貿易有關之智慧財產權協定》被完全引進各會員國之前的各項過渡期協定；寬限年限視各國的開發程度而定。

❹TRIPS針對智慧財產權的規範中有舉出智慧財產的法律保障類型或範例。每一則範例中，智慧財產所有人可獲得特定年限的暫時獨占權，意味著智慧財產所有人可以透過此智慧財產取得經濟利益，並且有權採取行動來維護此暫時獨占權。

- ▶ **專利權**：對於某獨特產品或製程可以賦予「專利」。專利有三種基本類型：發明專利、設計專利與植物專利。（關於專利的具體說明請見Chapter 45。）
- ▶ **商標權**：有些符號象徵某種真實或特殊的服務或產品，對於這些符號可以註冊「商標」。例如：Coca Cola是一個商標，只能用於可口可樂公司所生產的商品上。
- ▶ **著作權**：對於文學或藝術作品可賦予「著作權」，電腦程式或資料庫亦在此列。舉凡書籍、電影劇本、戲劇、音樂作曲、繪畫、雕刻、地圖、攝影作品、電影、訪談都屬於著作權保護的對象。
- ▶ **地理標示權**：對於一樣產品沿自特定產地的特色，可以給予「地理標示」之保護。法國酒品或一些香水常採用此法。

❺隨著二十一世紀科技的突飛猛進，這些智慧財產的類型隨時可能產生變化。舉例來說，各國有權制訂法令來保護特例、不適用現行法令的智慧財產類型。同時，各項國際協定也並非不可動搖，對於某些經由合作研發的創新科技可以採用共享智慧財產權的方式。最終，必須建立國際性的智慧財產權協定，以保障智慧財產所有人與使用者雙方的經濟利益。

Subject-related words in each article

Chapter 1>

1.	structural	(a.)	建築上的
2.	collaborative	(a.)	合作的
3.	reinforced	(a.)	強化的
4.	seismic	(a.)	地震的
5.	column	(n.)	圓柱
6.	perimeter	(n.)	周邊；周圍
7.	composite	(n.)	複合材料
8.	fatigue	(n.)	疲勞
9.	core	(n.)	中心部分
10.	stiffness	(n.)	勁度；硬度
11.	truss	(n.)	桁架
12.	lattice	(n.)	格子
13.	module	(n.)	模數（建築部件等的度量單位）
14.	damper	(n.)	阻尼器
15.	sling	(n.)	吊索；吊鏈
16.	viscous	(a.)	黏滯性的
17.	dissipate	(v.)	消除
18.	pressurized	(a.)	增壓的；加壓的
19.	observatory	(n.)	瞭望臺
20.	mnemonic	(a.)	有助於記憶的
21.	pluperfect	(a.)	非常完善的
22.	resilience	(n.)	彈性

Chapter 2>

1.	terrorist	(n.)	恐怖分子
2.	technique	(n.)	技術
3.	blast	(n.)	爆炸
4.	protected	(a.)	受保護的
5.	explosive	(n.)	爆裂物
6.	resistant	(a.)	抗……的
7.	restraining	(a.)	遏阻的
8.	deterrence	(n.)	制止
9.	barricade	(n.)	障礙物
10.	intrusion	(n.)	侵入
11.	evacuation	(n.)	撤離
12.	ductile	(a.)	可延展的
13.	flexure	(n.)	彎曲
14.	fracture	(n.)	斷裂
15.	deformation	(n.)	毀壞
16.	hazardous	(a.)	有危險的
17.	glazing	(n.)	鑲嵌玻璃
18.	lamination	(n.)	層壓（物）
19.	annealed	(a.)	退火的
20.	sealant	(n.)	密封材料
21.	transitory	(a.)	短暫的
22.	perimeter	(n.)	周圍

Chapter 3>

1.	environment	(n.)	環境
2.	sustainable	(a.)	永續的
3.	green	(a.)	綠色的；環保的
4.	impact	(n.)	衝擊
5.	withdrawal	(n.)	收回
6.	emission	(n.)	散發
7.	occupant	(n.)	居住者
8.	productivity	(n.)	生產力
9.	renovation	(n.)	翻修
10.	construction	(n.)	建設
11.	demolition	(n.)	拆除
12.	disposal	(n.)	處置
13.	discarded	(a.)	被丟棄的
14.	recycle	(v.)	回收
15.	minimize	(v.)	最小化
16.	eliminate	(v.)	消除

17.	embodied	(a.)	具體的
18.	furbish	(v.)	恢復；更新
19.	ventilation	(n.)	通風
20.	negate	(v.)	否定
21.	restorative	(n.)	有助恢復健康的東西

Chapter 4>

1.	alternating	(a.)	交替的
2.	cylinder	(n.)	汽缸
3.	pneumatic	(a.)	充氣的
4.	power	(v.)	提供電力
5.	piston	(n.)	活塞
6.	exhaust	(n.)	排氣
7.	ignition	(n.)	點火
8.	intake	(n.)	吸入
9.	compression	(n.)	壓縮
10.	compress	(v.)	壓縮
11.	vacuum	(n.)	真空
12.	crankcase	(n.)	曲軸箱
13.	carburetor	(n.)	汽化器
14.	ignite	(v.)	點燃
15.	combustion	(n.)	燃燒
16.	adiabatic	(a.)	隔熱的
17.	facilitate	(v.)	促進
18.	pivot	(n.)	樞軸
19.	configuration	(n.)	結構
20.	alleviate	(v.)	減輕；緩和
21.	interference	(n.)	干擾
22.	constituent	(a.)	組成的
23.	durability	(n.)	耐久性

Chapter 5>

1.	interdisciplinary	(a.)	跨學科的
2.	bionic	(a.)	仿生學的
3.	implant	(v.)	移植
4.	vessel	(n.)	血管
5.	computational	(a.)	計算的
6.	hemodynamics	(n.)	血液動力學
7.	incontinence	(n.)	大小便失禁
8.	innovation	(n.)	創新
9.	deform	(v.)	使變形
10.	viscoelasticity	(n.)	黏彈性
11.	articular	(a.)	關節的
12.	synthetic	(a.)	合成的；人造的
13.	impaired	(a.)	受損的
14.	fixation	(n.)	固定（法）
15.	inert	(a.)	惰性的
16.	resorb	(v.)	再吸收
17.	adhesion	(n.)	黏著
18.	therapeutic	(a.)	治療的
19.	ceramic	(n.)	陶瓷
20.	bond	(n.)	結合

Chapter 6>

1.	hybrid	(a.)	混合的
2.	gasoline	(n.)	汽油
3.	hub	(n.)	輪軸
4.	accelerate	(v.)	加速
5.	idling	(a.)	空轉的
6.	engage	(v.)	發動（引擎）
7.	emission	(n.)	排放物
8.	transition	(n.)	轉變
9.	regenerative	(a.)	再生的
10.	momentum	(n.)	動能
11.	friction	(n.)	摩擦
12.	dissipate	(v.)	消散
13.	reverse	(v.)	使倒轉
14.	kinetic	(a.)	動力的
15.	aerodynamic	(a.)	空氣動力的
16.	drag	(n.)	阻力；摩擦力

#	word	pos	meaning
17.	flush	(a.)	齊平的；緊接的
18.	recessed	(a.)	凹進的；嵌壁的
19.	streamlined	(a.)	流線型的
20.	tapered	(a.)	錐形的
21.	ethanol	(n.)	乙醇；酒精
22.	petroleum	(n.)	石油
23.	incentive	(n.)	優惠

Chapter 7>

#	word	pos	meaning
1.	infectious	(a.)	傳染性的
2.	mortality	(n.)	死亡率
3.	transmission	(n.)	傳染
4.	compliance	(n.)	依從
5.	morbidity	(n.)	發病率；發病
6.	catastrophic	(a.)	災難性的
7.	pandemic	(n.)	（疾病）大流行
8.	outbreak	(n.)	爆發
9.	immunodeficiency	(n.)	免疫不全
10.	retrovirus	(n.)	逆轉濾過性病毒
11.	tuberculosis	(n.)	結核病
12.	acute	(a.)	急性的
13.	coronavirus	(n.)	冠狀病毒
14.	contain	(v.)	控制；遏制
15.	resurgence	(n.)	死灰復燃；再現
16.	parasite	(n.)	寄生蟲
17.	deposit	(v.)	放置
18.	mitigate	(v.)	減輕
19.	eradicate	(v.)	根絕；消滅

Chapter 8>

#	word	pos	meaning
1.	obesity	(n.)	肥胖
2.	millennium	(n.)	千禧年
3.	risk	(n.)	風險
4.	cardiovascular	(a.)	心血管的
5.	diabetes	(n.)	糖尿病
6.	reform	(n.)	改革
7.	accumulation	(n.)	積累
8.	excessive	(a.)	超量的；過度的
9.	indirect	(a.)	間接的
10.	calculation	(n.)	計算
11.	assessment	(n.)	評估
12.	benchmark	(n.)	基準
13.	chronic	(a.)	（病）慢性的
14.	prevalence	(n.)	流行
15.	imbalance	(n.)	失衡
16.	accessible	(a.)	可得到的
17.	sedentary	(a.)	久坐不動的
18.	cholesterol	(n.)	膽固醇
19.	triglyceride	(n.)	三酸甘油酯
20.	induce	(v.)	引起；導致
21.	monitor	(v.)	監控

Chapter 9>

#	word	pos	meaning
1.	expectancy	(n.)	預期
2.	infectious	(a.)	傳染性的
3.	cessation	(n.)	停止
4.	moderate	(a.)	適度的
5.	cope	(v.)	處理
6.	holistic	(a.)	整體的
7.	wellness	(n.)	健康
8.	longevity	(n.)	壽命
9.	stimulate	(v.)	刺激
10.	polyunsaturated	(a.)	多元未飽和的
11.	monounsaturated	(a.)	單不飽和的
12.	absorption	(n.)	吸收
13.	soluble	(a.)	可溶性的
14.	dehydration	(n.)	脫水
15.	mobility	(n.)	移動性；機動性
16.	metabolism	(n.)	新陳代謝
17.	preponderance	(n.)	優勢
18.	panacea	(n.)	萬靈丹

Chapter 10>

1. embryonic (a.) 胚胎的
2. undifferentiated (a.) 無差別的
3. potential (n.) 潛力
4. unspecialized (a.) 未專門化的
5. pluripotent (a.) 複能性的
6. differentiation (n.) 分化
7. replicate (v.) 複製
8. proliferation (n.) 增殖
9. adult (a.) 成年的
10. in vitro 在試管內
11. blastocyst (n.) 囊胚
12. tripartite (a.) 由三部分構成的
13. cavity (n.) 腔
14. fetus (n.) 胎
15. cloning (n.) 複製
16. specialized (a.) 專門化的
17. transdifferentiation (n.) 分化轉移
18. plasticity (n.) 可塑性
19. spinal (a.) 脊髓的
20. inhibitive (a.) 抑制的
21. fertilize (v.) 使受精
22. discard (v.) 丟棄
23. flexibility (n.) 靈活性

Chapter 11>

1. modification (n.) 改造;改變
2. alter (v.) 改變
3. therapeutic (a.) 治療的
4. molecule (n.) 分子
5. vector (n.) 載體
6. functional (a.) 功能性的
7. somatic (a.) 細胞體的
8. inhibition (n.) 抑制
9. pathogenic (a.) 致病的
10. toxic (a.) 有毒的
11. augmentation (n.) 增加
12. inherited (a.) 遺傳性的
13. sperm (n.) 精液
14. germline (n.) 生殖系
15. repercussion (n.) 間接後果
16. mutation (n.) 突變
17. suppress (v.) 抑制
18. eugenics (n.) 優生學
19. integrate (v.) 整合;結合
20. inflammatory (a.) 炎症性的
21. thalassaemia (n.) 地中海型貧血
22. melanoma (n.) 黑色素瘤

Chapter 12>

1. orphan (a.) 罕見的
2. molecule (n.) 分子
3. therapeutic (a.) 治療的
4. indication (n.) 徵兆;病徵
5. development (n.) 發展
6. recombinant (a.) 重組的
7. antithrombin (n.) 抗凝血酶
8. transgenic (a.) 基因轉換的
9. clotting (n.) 凝血
10. plasma (n.) 血漿
11. inflammatory (a.) 炎症性的
12. receptor (n.) 感覺器官
13. protein (n.) 蛋白質
14. immune (a.) 免疫的
15. adequate (a.) 充足的
16. scant (a.) 不足的
17. grant (n.) 授予(權利等)
18. post-genomic (a.) 後基因的
19. diagnostics (n.) 診斷法
20. proliferation (n.) 增殖;擴散
21. designation (n.) 指定;命名

| 22. | equity | (n.) | 公平性 |
| 23. | cooperation | (n.) | 合作 |

Chapter 13>

1.	innovation	(n.)	改革
2.	proliferate	(v.)	激增；擴散
3.	incandescent	(a.)	白熱的
4.	photon	(n.)	光子
5.	emit	(v.)	排放
6.	atom	(n.)	原子
7.	electron	(n.)	電子
8.	filament	(n.)	燈絲
9.	fluorescent	(a.)	螢光的
10.	phosphor	(n.)	磷光體
11.	mercury	(n.)	汞；水銀
12.	solid	(a.)	固體的
13.	illumination	(n.)	照明
14.	semiconductor	(n.)	半導體
15.	silicon	(n.)	矽
16.	impurity	(n.)	雜質
17.	diode	(n.)	兩極真空管
18.	reverse	(n.)	反向
19.	current	(n.)	電流
20.	detection	(n.)	檢測
21.	equivalent	(a.)	相當於
22.	render	(v.)	表現；表演
23.	lumen	(n.)	流明（光束的能量單位）
24.	generation	(n.)	產生
25.	versatile	(a.)	多功能的
26.	ultraviolet	(a.)	紫外的
27.	obsolete	(a.)	過時的

Chapter 14>

1.	device	(n.)	設備
2.	transistor	(n.)	電晶體
3.	burgeoning	(a.)	蓬勃發展的
4.	proportions	(n.)	[複]面積
5.	quality	(n.)	品質
6.	assurance	(n.)	保證
7.	hazardous	(a.)	危險的
8.	occupational	(a.)	職業的
9.	alternative	(n.)	供選擇之物
10.	fabrication	(n.)	製造
11.	toxic	(a.)	有毒的
12.	disperse	(v.)	散布
13.	wastewater	(n.)	廢水
14.	fluoride	(n.)	氟化物
15.	arsenic	(n.)	砷
16.	velocity	(n.)	速度；速率
17.	impurity	(n.)	雜質
18.	dopant	(n.)	摻雜物
19.	advantageous	(n.)	有利的
20.	baseline	(n.)	基線
21.	exposure	(n.)	暴露
22.	affliction	(n.)	疾病
23.	dermatitis	(n.)	皮膚炎
24.	decontamination	(n.)	消毒
25.	contaminant	(n.)	汙染物
26.	restrictive	(a.)	限制的
27.	feasible	(a.)	可行的

Chapter 15>

1.	conductor	(n.)	導體
2.	convenience	(n.)	便利
3.	integrated	(a.)	整合的
4.	circuit	(n.)	電路
5.	crystal	(n.)	晶體
6.	component	(n.)	組件
7.	trace	(n.)	痕跡；訊號
8.	miniature	(a.)	微型的

9.	defrost	(v.)	解凍
10.	eclipse	(v.)	使失色
11.	consumer	(n.)	消費者
12.	conversion	(n.)	轉換
13.	voltage	(n.)	電壓
14.	computer	(n.)	電腦
15.	combustion	(n.)	燃燒
16.	variable	(a.)	可變的
17.	consortium	(n.)	聯合；國際財團

Chapter 16>

1.	assemble	(v.)	裝配
2.	microscopic	(a.)	顯微鏡的
3.	behave	(v.)	表現
4.	interact	(v.)	互動
5.	react	(v.)	反應；起作用
6.	incorporate	(v.)	組成
7.	novel	(a.)	新穎的
8.	eclipse	(v.)	遮蔽；使失色
9.	envision	(v.)	想像；展望
10.	multidisciplinary	(a.)	有關各種學問的
11.	photosynthesis	(n.)	光合作用
12.	repellent	(a.)	防水的
13.	artificial	(a.)	人工的
14.	rearrange	(v.)	重新排列
15.	comprehensive	(a.)	廣泛的
16.	passive	(a.)	被動的
17.	steady	(a.)	穩定的
18.	fatigue	(n.)	疲勞
19.	fluctuate	(v.)	波動
20.	heterogeneous	(a.)	由不同成分形成的
21.	filtration	(n.)	過濾
22.	intrusive	(a.)	侵入的
23.	surveillance	(n.)	監視

Chapter 17>

1.	disruptive	(a.)	破壞性的
2.	displace	(v.)	取代
3.	revolutionize	(v.)	革新
4.	competition	(n.)	競爭
5.	critical	(a.)	關鍵的
6.	visualization	(n.)	形象化；成像
7.	thermal	(a.)	熱的
8.	ablation	(n.)	消融
9.	image	(n.)	影像
10.	contrast	(n.)	對比
11.	soluble	(a.)	可溶性的
12.	sensitized	(a.)	敏感的
13.	trend	(v.)	趨向
14.	amorphous	(a.)	無定形的
15.	capacity	(n.)	容量
16.	impediment	(n.)	阻礙
17.	proactive	(a.)	積極主動的
18.	authentication	(n.)	鑑定
19.	iris	(n.)	虹膜
20.	surveillance	(n.)	監視

Chapter 18>

1.	predict	(v.)	預測
2.	innovation	(n.)	革新
3.	scale	(n.)	規模
4.	revolution	(n.)	大變革
5.	poise	(v.)	作好準備
6.	wear	(n.)	磨損
7.	corrosion	(n.)	腐蝕
8.	optical	(a.)	眼睛的；光學的
9.	cluster	(n.)	群；組
10.	pulp	(n.)	紙漿
11.	synthesis	(n.)	合成
12.	purification	(n.)	淨化；精鍊

13.	stabilization	(n.)	穩定
14.	assembly	(n.)	裝配
15.	specific	(a.)	特定的
16.	aggregation	(n.)	聚集
17.	yield	(v.)	生產
18.	precursor	(n.)	先驅
19.	accurate	(a.)	精確的
20.	array	(n.)	一系列；大量
21.	mitigate	(v.)	減輕
22.	bridge	(v.)	連結起來

Chapter 19>

1.	communication	(n.)	傳播
2.	wireless	(a.)	無線的
3.	dual	(a.)	雙重的
4.	encrypted	(a.)	加密的
5.	unauthorized	(a.)	未經授權的
6.	frequency	(n.)	頻率
7.	antenna	(n.)	天線
8.	electromagnetic	(a.)	電磁的
9.	radio wave		無線電波
10.	broadcast	(v.)	廣播
11.	network	(n.)	電腦網絡
12.	span	(v.)	橫跨
13.	access	(n.)	進入；使用
14.	router	(n.)	路由器
15.	cast	(v.)	投擲；投射
16.	adapter	(n.)	轉接器
17.	ware	(n.)	……製品
18.	expansion	(n.)	擴大
19.	adhere	(v.)	遵守
20.	spectrum	(n.)	頻譜
21.	modulation	(n.)	調整；變調
22.	interference	(n.)	干擾
23.	deflect	(v.)	使轉向
24.	encryption	(n.)	加密
25.	stream	(n.)	流
26.	decipher	(v.)	破解密碼
27.	phrase	(n.)	詞組

Chapter 20>

1.	universal	(a.)	通用的
2.	adapter	(n.)	配接器
3.	peripheral	(a.)	周邊的
4.	port	(n.)	埠；接口
5.	host	(n.)	主機
6.	cellular	(a.)	蜂巢式的
7.	gadget	(n.)	器具
8.	humidifier	(n.)	增濕器
9.	implement	(v.)	執行
10.	query	(v.)	查詢
11.	address	(n.)	位址
12.	driver	(n.)	驅動器
13.	poll	(v.)	記錄；民調
14.	tier	(v.)	層層排列
15.	topology	(n.)	拓撲
16.	socket	(n.)	插座
17.	portable	(a.)	手提式的
18.	mediation	(n.)	媒介；斡旋

Chapter 21>

1.	miniaturization	(n.)	微型化
2.	infrastructure	(n.)	公共建設
3.	broadband	(a.)	寬頻的
4.	range	(n.)	範圍
5.	equip	(v.)	裝備
6.	register	(n.)	登錄器
7.	platform	(n.)	平台
8.	temporary	(a.)	臨時的
9.	constant	(a.)	持續的
10.	optimize	(v.)	最佳化

11.	interception	(n.)	竊聽
12.	legitimate	(a.)	合法的
13.	repudiation	(n.)	拒絕
14.	property	(n.)	屬性
15.	render	(v.)	提供
16.	algorithm	(n.)	演算法
17.	encryption	(n.)	加密
18.	authentication	(n.)	驗證
19.	certificate	(n.)	憑證
20.	credential	(a.)	憑據
21.	expiration	(n.)	到期
22.	variation	(n.)	變化
23.	bandwidth	(n.)	頻寬
24.	conservation	(n.)	保存
25.	transcriber	(n.)	資料轉譯

Chapter 22>

1.	decentralize	(v.)	使分散
2.	available	(a.)	可得到的
3.	route	(v.)	按路線發送
4.	packet	(n.)	數據包
5.	reassemble	(v.)	再集合
6.	destination	(n.)	目的地
7.	static	(a.)	靜態的
8.	drastic	(a.)	猛烈的
9.	predecessor	(n.)	（被取代的）原有事物
10.	hypermedia	(n.)	超媒體
11.	modify	(v.)	修改
12.	content	(n.)	內容
13.	interactivity	(n.)	互動
14.	collaboration	(n.)	協同運作
15.	tag	(n.)	標籤
16.	domain	(n.)	網域
17.	propagate	(v.)	傳播
18.	semantic	(a.)	語義的

19.	disparate	(a.)	不同的
20.	quadruple	(v.)	成為四倍
21.	translation	(n.)	翻譯

Chapter 23>

1.	automated	(a.)	自動化的
2.	access	(v.)	取出資料
3.	task	(n.)	任務
4.	artificial	(a.)	人工的
5.	possess	(v.)	擁有
6.	advancement	(n.)	進展
7.	quest	(n.)	探索
8.	application	(n.)	應用
9.	program	(v.)	設計程式
10.	biometrics	(n.)	生物測定學
11.	simulation	(n.)	模擬
12.	vary	(v.)	變化
13.	replicate	(v.)	複製
14.	perception	(n.)	知覺
15.	neuron	(n.)	神經元
16.	prohibitive	(a.)	（價格等）過高的
17.	parallel	(a.)	平行的
18.	reconfigure	(v.)	重新裝配
19.	natural	(a.)	自然的
20.	intuit	(v.)	由直覺知道
21.	expert	(n.)	專家
22.	expansive	(a.)	擴張的

Chapter 24>

1.	husbandry	(n.)	耕種
2.	preserve	(v.)	維持
3.	tilling	(n.)	耕作
4.	rotation	(n.)	輪作
5.	nutrient	(n.)	營養的
6.	herbicide	(n.)	除草劑

#	word	pos	meaning
7.	ridge	(n.)	山脊
8.	cultivation	(n.)	耕作；栽培
9.	mulch	(n.)	護蓋物
10.	seepage	(n.)	滲流
11.	alternate	(v.)	使輪流
12.	sequencing	(n.)	按順序安排
13.	divert	(v.)	使轉向
14.	fallowed	(a.)	休耕的
15.	infestation	(n.)	蟲害
16.	via	(prep.)	透過
17.	degradation	(n.)	剝蝕
18.	stakeholder	(n.)	利害關係人

Chapter 25>

#	word	pos	meaning
1.	crossbred	(a.)	雜交的
2.	laborious	(a.)	費力的
3.	hybrid	(n.)	合成物
4.	yield	(n.)	產量
5.	alteration	(n.)	改變
6.	modified	(a.)	改造的
7.	genomics	(n.)	基因體學
8.	cloning	(n.)	複製
9.	novel	(a.)	新的
10.	trait	(n.)	特性
11.	boost	(v.)	增加
12.	herbicide	(n.)	除草劑
13.	drought	(n.)	乾旱
14.	feed	(n.)	飼料
15.	pharmaceutical	(a.)	製藥的
16.	selective	(a.)	選擇性的
17.	optimum	(a.)	最佳的
18.	deliberate	(a.)	蓄意的
19.	transplantation	(n.)	移植
20.	suture	(n.)	縫線
21.	allergic	(a.)	過敏的
22.	allergen	(n.)	過敏原
23.	toxin	(n.)	毒素
24.	pesticide	(n.)	殺蟲劑
25.	infringement	(n.)	侵權
26.	manipulate	(v.)	運用
27.	regulatory	(a.)	管理的
28.	malnutrition	(n.)	營養不良

Chapter 26>

#	word	pos	meaning
1.	smart	(a.)	智慧型的
2.	sense	(v.)	檢測出
3.	embed	(v.)	嵌入
4.	alert	(v.)	使警覺
5.	supplement	(n.)	補充
6.	coating	(n.)	外層包覆物
7.	nutrient	(n.)	養分
8.	suffuse	(v.)	充滿；遍布
9.	deficiency	(n.)	缺乏
10.	dormant	(a.)	靜止的
11.	activate	(v.)	使活化
12.	micelle	(n.)	膠束
13.	soluble	(a.)	可溶性的
14.	encapsulate	(v.)	封裝
15.	block	(v.)	阻斷
16.	conversely	(adv.)	相反地
17.	dosage	(n.)	劑量
18.	pathogen	(n.)	病原體
19.	fertilizer	(n.)	肥料
20.	distribute	(v.)	分配；散布
21.	excrete	(v.)	排泄

Chapter 27>

#	word	pos	meaning
1.	recovery	(n.)	重獲
2.	waste	(n.)	廢棄物
3.	recycle	(v.)	回收

#	Word	POS	中文
4.	generate	(v.)	生產
5.	thermal	(a.)	熱的
6.	capture	(v.)	獲得
7.	flare	(v.)	燃燒
8.	feedstock	(n.)	原料
9.	rely	(v.)	仰賴
10.	remove	(v.)	去除
11.	refine	(v.)	精鍊
12.	inert	(a.)	惰性的
13.	slag	(n.)	煤渣
14.	friction	(n.)	摩擦力
15.	kinetic	(a.)	運動的
16.	deceleration	(n.)	減速
17.	flywheel	(n.)	調速輪；飛輪
18.	boost	(v.)	提高
19.	ventilation	(n.)	通風
20.	incoming	(a.)	傳入的
21.	drain	(n.)	排水；流出
22.	exchange	(n.)	交換
23.	storage	(n.)	存儲

Chapter 28>

#	Word	POS	中文
1.	fission	(n.)	分裂
2.	harness	(v.)	利用
3.	split	(v.)	產生核分裂
4.	self-sustaining	(a.)	自立的
5.	chain	(n.)	鏈
6.	pellet	(n.)	顆粒狀物
7.	submerge	(v.)	浸入水中
8.	rod	(n.)	棒
9.	turbine	(n.)	渦輪
10.	non-energy	(a.)	非能源的
11.	canister	(n.)	罐
12.	disposal	(n.)	處理
13.	consensus	(n.)	一致
14.	geologic	(a.)	地質的
15.	repository	(n.)	貯藏處
16.	reuse	(n.)	再利用
17.	decommission	(v.)	退役
18.	decontamination	(n.)	去汙
19.	map	(v.)	繪製地圖
20.	detector	(n.)	探測器
21.	sterilize	(v.)	消毒
22.	irradiation	(n.)	輻照
23.	disease-causing	(a.)	致病的

Chapter 29>

#	Word	POS	中文
1.	fossil	(n.)	化石
2.	deplete	(v.)	用盡
3.	harmful	(a.)	有害的
4.	viable	(a.)	可行的
5.	radiation	(n.)	輻射
6.	power	(v.)	提供動力
7.	installation	(n.)	安裝
8.	blade	(n.)	葉翼
9.	shaft	(n.)	軸
10.	flow	(v.)	流動
11.	reservoir	(n.)	蓄水庫
12.	hydropower	(n.)	以水力所發的電力
13.	tidal	(a.)	潮汐的
14.	interior	(n.)	內部
15.	layer	(n.)	層
16.	municipal	(a.)	市的
17.	methane	(n.)	甲烷；沼氣
18.	residue	(n.)	殘留；渣滓
19.	rubbish	(n.)	垃圾
20.	panel	(n.)	嵌板

Chapter 30>

1.	geophysical	(a.)	地球物理學的
2.	phenomena	(n.)	[複] 現象 [單] phenomenon
3.	tsunami	(n.)	海嘯
4.	catastrophic	(a.)	災難的
5.	fault	(n.)	斷層
6.	tectonic	(a.)	地殼構造上的
7.	plate	(n.)	薄板
8.	brittle	(a.)	易碎的
9.	focus	(n.)	震源
10.	rupture	(n.)	破裂
11.	seismic	(a.)	因地震而引起的
12.	vibration	(n.)	震動
13.	magnitude	(n.)	震級
14.	intensity	(n.)	強度
15.	strike	(v.)	來襲
16.	meteorite	(n.)	隕石
17.	shallow	(a.)	淺的
18.	gauge	(n.)	測量儀器
19.	warn	(v.)	發出警告
20.	inundation	(n.)	泛濫；洪水
21.	buoy	(n.)	浮標

Chapter 31>

1.	atmosphere	(n.)	大氣
2.	circulate	(v.)	使流通；使循環
3.	turbulent	(a.)	洶湧的
4.	salinity	(n.)	鹽度
5.	current	(n.)	水流；流動
6.	pulse	(n.)	脈衝波
7.	shape	(n.)	形狀
8.	eddies	(n.)	渦流
9.	displace	(v.)	迫使離開
10.	navigation	(n.)	航海；航行
11.	yacht	(n.)	遊艇；快艇
12.	cause	(v.)	造成
13.	sustain	(v.)	支撐；維持
14.	abruptly	(adv.)	突然地
15.	acoustic	(a.)	聲學的
16.	migration	(n.)	遷徙
17.	satellite	(n.)	衛星
18.	remote	(a.)	遠處的
19.	altimetry	(n.)	高度測量術
20.	topography	(n.)	地形
21.	precision	(n.)	精確性；準確性
22.	holistic	(a.)	全部的
23.	assimilation	(n.)	同化

Chapter 32>

1.	eruption	(n.)	火山爆發
2.	vent	(n.)	噴口
3.	molten	(a.)	熔化的
4.	eject	(v.)	噴出
5.	mantle	(n.)	地幔
6.	magma	(n.)	岩漿
7.	reservoir	(n.)	儲藏所
8.	diverge	(v.)	偏離
9.	plume	(n.)	羽狀物
10.	frequency	(n.)	頻率
11.	dormant	(a.)	靜止的；休眠的
12.	explosive	(a.)	爆發性的
13.	discharge	(n.)	排出
14.	lava	(n.)	熔岩
15.	avalanche	(n.)	突然的大量事物
16.	dome	(n.)	圓頂
17.	basin	(n.)	盆地
18.	surge	(n.)	激增；洶湧
19.	suffocation	(n.)	窒息
20.	trigger	(v.)	觸發
21.	contaminate	(v.)	汙染

22.	respiratory	(a.)	呼吸的
23.	sulphur	(n.)	硫磺
24.	aerosol	(n.)	氣溶膠
25.	infrared	(n.)	紅外線

Chapter 33>

1.	disturbance	(n.)	擾動
2.	band	(n.)	帶
3.	convergence	(n.)	輻合
4.	gust	(v.)	一陣陣地勁吹
5.	constant	(a.)	持續的
6.	knot	(n.)	結
7.	spiral	(v.)	成螺旋形
8.	inward	(adv.)	向中心
9.	swirl	(v.)	旋轉
10.	deflect	(v.)	轉向
11.	rotation	(n.)	自轉；旋轉
12.	intensity	(n.)	強度
13.	hurricane	(n.)	颶風；暴風雨
14.	designate	(v.)	表明；定為
15.	cyclone	(n.)	氣旋
16.	generic	(a.)	總稱的
17.	maximum	(a.)	最大的
18.	determination	(n.)	判定
19.	span	(n.)	一段時間；全長
20.	peak	(a.)	高峰的
21.	trade	(n.)	信風
22.	surge	(n.)	大浪
23.	meteorologist	(n.)	氣象學者

Chapter 34>

1.	replenish	(v.)	補充
2.	evaporation	(n.)	蒸發
3.	scarcity	(n.)	缺乏
4.	misallocation	(n.)	分配不當
5.	affluence	(n.)	富裕
6.	undrinkable	(a.)	不能飲用的
7.	domestic	(a.)	家用的；家庭的
8.	consumption	(n.)	消耗；消耗量
9.	sanitation	(n.)	公共衛生
10.	hygiene	(n.)	衛生
11.	urbanization	(n.)	都市化
12.	accelerate	(v.)	使增速
13.	consumer	(n.)	消費者；消耗者
14.	dietary	(a.)	飲食的
15.	commodities	(n.)	[複] 貨物；商品
16.	irrigation	(n.)	灌溉
17.	incentive	(n.)	誘因；動機
18.	transboundary	(a.)	跨區的
19.	preservation	(n.)	保護；維護
20.	initiative	(n.)	倡議

Chapter 35>

1.	natural	(a.)	自然的
2.	factor	(n.)	因素
3.	balance	(n.)	平衡
4.	forcing	(a.)	推進的
5.	slight	(a.)	輕微的
6.	circulation	(n.)	環流
7.	substantial	(a.)	重要的
8.	intensify	(v.)	加強
9.	warming	(a.)	暖化的
10.	trap	(v.)	網羅住；捕捉住
11.	considerable	(a.)	可觀的
12.	extensive	(a.)	大規模的
13.	impact	(v.)	衝擊
14.	cover	(n.)	覆蓋物
15.	dilution	(n.)	稀釋；沖淡
16.	revenue	(n.)	收入；收益
17.	ambitious	(a.)	野心勃勃的

18.	mitigation	(n.)	緩和
19.	legislature	(n.)	立法機關
20.	rapidity	(n.)	迅速
21.	allocation	(n.)	配給
22.	equity	(n.)	公平
23.	forego	(v.)	放棄

Chapter 36>

1.	canopy	(n.)	篷形遮蓋物
2.	perpetuate	(v.)	使永存
3.	rainfall	(n.)	降雨量
4.	human-induced	(a.)	由人類引起的
5.	greenhouse	(n.)	溫室
6.	medicinal	(a.)	藥用的
7.	indigenous	(a.)	本地的
8.	periodically	(adv.)	週期性地
9.	widespread	(a.)	廣泛的
10.	exceed	(v.)	超出
11.	massive	(a.)	大規模的
12.	underlying	(a.)	潛在的
13.	subsistence	(n.)	自給自足
14.	slash	(v.)	砍
15.	fertility	(n.)	肥沃
16.	severely	(adv.)	嚴重地
17.	degrade	(v.)	剝蝕
18.	clearcut	(a.)	大片砍伐的
19.	selective	(a.)	選擇性的
20.	population	(n.)	人口
21.	intrusion	(n.)	入侵
22.	deplete	(v.)	耗盡資源
23.	extraction	(n.)	抽取；開採
24.	tenure	(n.)	占有；占有權
25.	overconsumption	(n.)	過度消費
26.	high-income	(a.)	高收入的
27.	remote-sensing	(a.)	遠距感測的
28.	enforce	(v.)	執行
29.	low-impact	(a.)	低衝擊的
30.	landowner	(n.)	地主

Chapter 37>

1.	contemporary	(a.)	當代的
2.	hierarchy	(n.)	層級
3.	source	(n.)	源頭
4.	donate	(v.)	捐出
5.	municipal	(a.)	市立的
6.	delay	(v.)	延遲
7.	disposal	(n.)	處理
8.	incineration	(n.)	焚化
9.	preferable	(a.)	更好的
10.	destine	(v.)	預定；注定
11.	content	(n.)	內容；含量
12.	ferrous	(a)	含鐵的
13.	indefinitely	(adv.)	無定限地
14.	timber	(n.)	木材
15.	knowledgeable	(a.)	有知識的
16.	audit	(n.)	稽查
17.	standard	(a.)	標準的
18.	haul	(v.)	拖運；搬運
19.	monitor	(v.)	監控
20.	feasibility	(n.)	可行性
21.	loop	(n.)	環路；環線
22.	burden	(n.)	負擔
23.	mandate	(v.)	委託

Chapter 38>

1.	overpopulation	(n.)	人口過剩
2.	localized	(a.)	局部的
3.	stress	(n.)	壓力；壓迫
4.	vegetated	(a.)	植栽的
5.	output	(n.)	生產
6.	pace	(n.)	步調

7. adverse (a.) 有害的
8. endanger (v.) 使遭到危險
9. landscape (n.) 地貌
10. oversight (n.) 失察;疏忽
11. productive (a.) 肥沃的
12. mechanization (n.) 機械化
13. disproportionate (a.) 不均衡的
14. urbanization (n.) 都市化
15. nonadjacent (a.) 非相鄰的
16. indigenous (a.) 土著的;本地的
17. invasive (a.) 入侵的
18. alien (a.) 外來的
19. shortage (n.) 短缺
20. assessment (n.) 評估

Chapter 39>

1. magnify (v.) 放大
2. optical (a.) 光學的
3. eyepiece (n.) 目鏡
4. record (v.) 記錄
5. refract (v.) 折射
6. reflect (v.) 反射
7. catadioptric (a.) 兼反射光及折射光的
8. convex (a.) 凸面的
9. converge (v.) 會合
10. concave (a.) 凹面的
11. diverging (a.) 分叉的;發散的
12. distort (v.) 扭曲;變形
13. orbit (v.) 繞軌道運行
14. faint (a.) 模糊的
15. galaxy (n.) 銀河系
16. ultraviolet (a.) 紫外線的
17. arm (n.) 臂狀物

Chapter 40>

1. spacecraft (n.) 太空船
2. probe (n.) 探測器
3. celestial (a.) 天空的
4. precise (a.) 精確的
5. propel (v.) 推進
6. thrust (v.) 用力推
7. stage (n.) 階段
8. atmospheric (a) 大氣的
9. deploy (v.) 部署
10. retrieve (v.) 擷取(資訊)
11. penetrate (v.) 穿入
12. target (n.) 目標
13. pilot (v.) 駕駛
14. crew (n.) 全體人員
15. radioisotope (n.) 放射性同位素
16. propulsion (n.) 推進
17. stability (n.) 穩定性
18. maneuver (v.) 機動動作
19. shield (v.) 防護
20. orientation (n.) 定位
21. attitude (n.) 航姿
22. venture (n.) 冒險

Chapter 41>

1. inflatable (a.) 膨脹的
2. spacecraft (n.) 太空船
3. counterpart (n.) 互應的人或物
4. store (v.) 貯存
5. canister (n.) 筒狀金屬容器
6. booster (n.) 推進器
7. launch (n.) 發射
8. shuttle (n.) 【空】太空梭
9. payload (n.) 火箭所載彈頭
10. dock (v.) 在外層空間對接

357

11.	polymer	(n.)	聚合物
12.	catalyst	(n.)	【化】催化劑
13.	seal	(v.)	封
14.	self-repairing	(a.)	自行修復
15.	sail	(n.)	帆
16.	propellant	(n.)	推進燃料
17.	ribbon	(n.)	帶狀物
18.	propulsion	(n.)	推進（力）
19.	plasma	(n.)	電漿
20.	electrostatic	(a.)	靜電的
21.	explode	(v.)	爆炸
22.	lightcraft	(n.)	輕型飛行器
23.	air-breathing	(a.)	吸氣式
24.	air-augmented	(a.)	增加氣體的
25.	self-healing	(a.)	自行療癒的
26.	investment	(n.)	投資
27.	minute	(a.)	微小的
28.	return	(n.)	收益

Chapter 42>

1.	diurnal	(a.)	白天的
2.	navigate	(v.)	導航
3.	maneuver	(v.)	機動
4.	obtrusive	(a.)	刺眼的
5.	luminous	(a.)	發光的
6.	excessive	(a.)	過度的
7.	discomfort	(n.)	不適
8.	intrude	(v.)	侵入
9.	glare	(n.)	刺眼的強光
10.	trespass	(n.)	侵害
11.	obscure	(v.)	使變暗
12.	nuisance	(n.)	有害物
13.	skyglow	(n.)	天空輝光
14.	inclement	(a.)	氣候嚴酷的
15.	scatter	(v.)	散布

16.	fatal	(a.)	致命的
17.	collide	(v.)	碰撞
18.	nesting	(n.)	築巢
19.	curfew	(n.)	宵禁
20.	celestial	(a.)	天空的
21.	heighten	(v.)	提高

Chapter 43>

1.	hue	(n.)	色調
2.	uneven	(a.)	不平坦的
3.	cap	(n.)	帽
4.	spawn	(v.)	造成；產生
5.	flyby	(n.)	近天體探測飛行
6.	formation	(n.)	形成
7.	crater	(n.)	火山口
8.	orbiter	(n.)	太空船
9.	riverbed	(n.)	河床
10.	canyon	(n.)	峽谷
11.	lander	(n.)	登陸器
12.	probe	(n.)	太空探測器
13.	valley	(n.)	谷
14.	channel	(n.)	水道
15.	condense	(v.)	凝結
16.	fog	(n.)	霧氣
17.	evaporate	(v.)	蒸發
18.	mantle	(n.)	地涵
19.	impact	(n.)	撞擊
20.	crater	(n.)	隕石坑
21.	meteorite	(n.)	隕石
22.	basin	(n.)	盆地
23.	gully	(n.)	小峽谷；沖溝
24.	sediment	(n.)	沉積物
25.	asteroid	(n.)	小行星

Chapter 44>

1. surface (n.) 表面
2. penetrator (n.) 穿透機
3. regolith (n.) 風化層；土被
4. lunar (a.) 月的
5. projectile (n.) 發射體
6. sensor (n.) 感應器
7. magnetism (n.) 磁性
8. sampling (n.) 抽樣；取樣
9. descent (a.) 下降的
10. image (v.) 成像
11. detect (v.) 監測
12. crust (n.) 地殼
13. feasibility (n.) 可行性
14. architecture (n.) 架構
15. cruise (n.) 航行；巡航
16. deployment (n.) 部署
17. velocity (n.) 速率
18. trial (n.) 試驗
19. simulation (n.) 模擬
20. seismometer (n.) 地震儀
21. habitation (n.) 居住

Chapter 45>

1. patent (n.) 專利
2. trademark (n.) 商標
3. article (n.) 商品
4. asexual (a.) 無性的
5. invention (n.) 發明
6. criteria (n.) (單數 criterion) 標準
7. useful (a.) 有用的
8. eligible (a.) 有資格的
9. utility (n.) 實用工具
10. design (n.) 設計
11. exclusivity (n.) 排他性；獨享
12. ornament (n.) 裝飾
13. patentee (n.) 專利權所有人
14. seedling (n.) 幼苗
15. tuber (n.) 塊莖
16. propagate (v.) 繁殖
17. bud (n.) 芽
18. pollination (n.) 授粉
19. validity (n.) 有效性
20. disclaim (v.) 放棄

Chapter 46>

1. exclusive (a.) 獨有的
2. protection (n.) 保護
3. promotion (n.) 促進
4. intellection (n.) 思考
5. burgeon (v.) 急速成長
6. treaty (n.) 條約
7. accessible (a.) 易使用的
8. extent (n.) 範圍
9. disparity (n.) 不同；不等
10. settlement (n.) 解決
11. dispute (n.) 爭端
12. accommodate (v.) 考慮到
13. enforcement (n.) 執行
14. transitional (a.) 過渡的
15. allot (v.) 分配
16. compliance (n.) 接受
17. paradigm (n.) 典範
18. monopoly (n.) 獨占權；專利權
19. derive (v.) 得到
20. appellation (n.) 名稱；稱號

Answer Key

Introduction Answer Key

A 1. b 2. a 3. c 4. a 5. b

B a) bio-; chemistry   b) -ic; aqua
    c) mal-; nutrition   d) de-, -ion; hydrate
    e) in-, -ion; flame   f) mal-; practice
    g) photo-, -is; synthesize   h) hemi-; sphere
    i) dis-; charge   j) im-; balance

1. g 2. j 3. c 4. b 5. e
6. a 7. i 8. d 9. h 10. f

Chapter 1 Answer Key

A 1. g 2. b 3. h 4. j 5. a
   6. e 7. c 8. d 9. i 10. f

B 1. fatigue 2. seismic 3. trusses
   4. Composite 5. pressurized 6. dampers
   7. slings

C 1. columns 2. structural 3. lattice, trusses
   4. reinforced, composite 5. resilience
   6. perimeter 7. core 8. seismic 9. dampers
   10. sling

D 1. collaborative 2. viscous 3. resilience
   4. fatigue 5. core 6. composite

E 1. T 2. F 3. T 4. F 5. F 6. T

Chapter 2 Answer Key

A 1. d 2. f 3. b 4. c 5. e 6. a

B 1. explosive, terrorist 2. fracture
   3. flexure 4. blast 5. ductile

C 1. b 2. h 3. f 4. a 5. j
   6. i 7. d 8. g 9. c 10. e

D 1. transitory 2. evacuate 3. deterrents
   4. flexure 5. resist 6. protect 7. restrain
   8. ductile

E 1. re 2. ex 3. trans 4. re

Chapter 3 Answer Key

A 1. c 2. d 3. b 4. a

B 1. impact 2. restorative 3. construction
   4. Renovation 5. embodied 6. recycle
   7. productivity

C 1. f 2. b 3. d 4. a 5. g 6. c 7. e

D 1. discard 2. demolition 3. negate
   4. eliminate 5. minimize 6. disposal

E 1. c 2. a 3. e 4. b 5. d 6. f

F 1. em 2. im 3. ing 4. re 5. dis 6. dis
   7. re, ive 8. able

Chapter 4 Answer Key

A 1. a 2. e 3. k 4. m 5. i 6. g
   7. f 8. p 9. l 10. h 11. o 12. n
   13. c 14. j 15. d 16. b

B 1. alternating 2. facilitate 3. interference
   4. compression 5. Adiabatic 6. ignition
   7. combustion 8. alleviated 9. pivot
   10. constituent

C 1. ex-haust 2. com-bustion 3. com-pression
   4. in-take 5. in-terfer-ence 6. al-levi-ate
   7. con-stitu-ent 8. al-ternat-ing 9. ad-iabat-ic
   10. durabil-ity

D a) non b) out c) ex d) de e) un
   1. c 2. e 3. b 4. d 5. a

E 1. noninterference 2. extinguish
   3. decompression 4. outtake 5. unpowered

Chapter 5 Answer Key

A 1. mimetics 2. logy 3. medical
   4. engineering 5. nics 6. compatible
   7. active 8. resorbable

B 1. ar 2. im 3. ad 4. ion 5. inter 6. syn
   7. im 8. de 9. al 10. in 11. in

C 1. impair 2. innovation 3. implanted
   4. Computational 5. interdisciplinary
   6. synthetic 7. articular 8. inert

D 1. a 2. e 3. f 4. b 5. d 6. c

Chapter 6 Answer Key

A 1. ac-celer-ate 2. en-gage 3. emis-sions 4. transit-ion 5. re-generat-ive 6. moment-um 7. frict-ion 8. kine-tics 9. re-verse 10. aero-dynamic 11. reces-s 12. stream-line

B 1. mogas 2. gas 3. petroleum 4. fuel 5. petroleum spirit 6. gasoline 7. petrol

C 1. c 2. b 3. a 4. d 5. b

Chapter 7 Answer Key

A 1. a 2. f 3. h 4. c 5. j 6. e 7. i 8. g 9. d 10. b

B a) out b) immuno c) a d) con e) in f) com g) pan h) re i) retro
1. contained 2. resurgence 3. compliance 4. acute 5. pandemic 6. retrovirus 7. outbreak 8. infectious 9. immunodeficiency

C 1. b 2. c 3. b 4. c 5. a 6. c

Chapter 8 Answer Key

A 1. b 2. d 3. a 4. b 5. c 6. d 7. c 8. a 9. d 10. b 11. a 12. b 13. d 14. b 15. c 16. a

B a) im b) re c) in d) pre e) in f) pre
1. f 2. e 3. d 4. a 5. b 6. c

C 1. ble, accessible 2. ion, calculation 3. ment, assessment 4. ion, accumulation 5. ive, excessive 6. ence, prevalence

Chapter 9 Answer Key

A 1. remedy 2. balm 3. curative 4. restorative 5. antitoxin, serum

B 1. g 2. m 3. a 4. c 5. k 6. d 7. e 8. h 9. l 10. i 11. j 12. b 13. f

C 1. wellness 2. cope 3. stimulate 4. absorption 5. moderate 6. cessation 7. holistic 8. preponderance

D 1. b 2. a 3. d 4. e 5. f 6. c 7. h 8. g

Chapter 10 Answer Key

A 1. tripartite 2. differentiation 3. potential 4. inhibitive 5. in vitro 6. proliferate 7. replicate 8. pluripotent 9. adult 10. plasticity 11. cavity 12. cloning

B 1. fertilized 2. tripartite 3. flexibility 4. in vitro 5. potential, differentiation 6. Adult, plasticity 7. specialized 8. inhibitive 9. replicate 10. cavity 11. pluripotent 12. undifferentiated 13. proliferation 14. embryonic, clones

C a) un-differentiated b) trans-genic c) un-specialized d) tri-partite e) pluri-potent, multi-potent
1. tripartite 2. undifferentiated 3. pluripotent, multipotent 4. transgenic

D 1. b 2. e 3. c 4. a 5. d

E 1. b 2. f 3. d 4. e 5. a 6. c

Chapter 11 Answer Key

A 1. e 2. g 3. i 4. h 5. m 6. p 7. f 8. d 9. b 10. l 11. a 12. c 13. j 14. k 15. n 16. o

B 1. therapeutic 2. toxic 3. pathogenic 4. inhibition 5. Integrating 6. functional 7. suppress 8. somatic 9. Inflammatory 10. molecules

C 1. alter 2. augmentation 3. inflammatory 4. molecules 5. inherited 6. vector 7. modification 8. eugenics 9. functional 10. toxic

Chapter 12 Answer Key

A 1. a 2. i 3. d 4. l 5. k 6. b 7. f 8. j 9. o 10. h 11. c 12. e 13. g 14. n 15. m

B a) dia   b) trans   c) ment   d) post
   e) auto   f) ing   g) co
  1. autobiography   2. transform   3. diagram
  4. movement; postoperative   5. redefining
  6. coworker

C 1. Antithrombin; plasma   2. diagnostics
  3. immune   4. adequate
  5. Transgenic; recombinant
  6. indications   7. post-genomic   8. orphan
  9. cooperation   10. designation
  11. equity   12. clotting

Chapter 13   Answer Key
A 1. i   2. b   3. e   4. a   5. g
  6. c   7. h   8. d   9. f
B 1. Fluorescent   2. current   3. filament
  4. generate (emit)   5. illuminate
  6. Incandescent   7. semiconductor
  8. solid   9. emit (generate)
C a) re   b) in   c) pro; ate   d) im; ity   e) de
  f) ent   g) able
  1. c   2. e   3. a   4. g   5. b   6. d   7. f
D 1. classic   2. forward   3. fragile
  4. concealment   5. darken   6. prevent
  7. hollow   8. absorb   9. dark   10. diminish
  11. decontaminant

Chapter 14   Answer Key
A 1. a   2. c   3. c   4. a   5. a
  6. b   7. c   8. b   9. b   10. b
B 1. F   2. T   3. F   4. T   5. F
  6. F   7. T   8. T   9. T
C 1. d   2. f   3. g   4. c   5. b   6. a   7. e

Chapter 15   Answer Key
A 1. conversion   2. contribute   3. conventional
  4. control   5. consumer   6. component
  7. continue   8. conductor
  9. consortium   10. consumption
  11. computer   12. convenience

B 1. Integrated   2. Circuit   3. Variable
  4. Crystal   5. Trace   6. Energy
C 1. a   2. a   3. b   4. b   5. a   6. a

Chapter 16   Answer Key
A 1. h   2. b   3. e   4. k   5. j   6. g   7. m
  8. f   9. d   10. a   11. i   12. c   13. n   14. l
B 1. eclipse   2. convert   3. object   4. conduct
  5. eclipse   6. harvest   7. convert
  8. measure   9. harvest   10. conduct
  11. novel   12. object   13. novel
  14. measure
C 1. incorporation   2. reaction
  3. comprehension   4. interaction
  5. fluctuation

Chapter 17   Answer Key
A 1. b   2. c   3. a   4. c   5. c
  6. a   7. c   8. a   9. a
  10. c   11. a   12. c
B 1. b   2. a   3. a   4. b   5. c
  6. b   7. a   8. b
C a) re-   b) -ary   c) -ive   d) repo-   e) -ism
  f) e-   g) du-   h) -ity   i) meta-   j) retro-
  k) inter-   l) -ion   m) -ize   n) -ic
  1. f   2. a   3. l   4. e   5. m
  6. b   7. h   8. n   9. i   10. g
  11. j   12. k   13. c   14. d

Chapter 18   Answer Key
A 1. c   2. b   3. f   4. g   5. j
  6. e   7. h   8. a   9. d   10. i
B 1. accurate   2. corrosion   3. stabilization
  4. predict   5. aggregate   6. wear   7. array
  8. specific   9. poised
C 1. pulp   2. aggregate   3. aggregate   4. scale
  5. yield   6. wear   7. yield   8. bridge
  9. bridge   10. scale   11. pulp   12. wear

362

Chapter 19 Answer Key

A a) wire-less b) key-stream c) pass-phrase
d) tele-communications e) broad-cast
f) net-work g) hard-ware
1. broadcast 2. hardware 3. passphrase
4. network 5. wireless
6. telecommunications 7. keystream

B a) re b) un c) ad d) en
e) ex f) de g) inter
1. c 2. f 3. b 4. g 5. a 6. e 7. d

C 1. singular 2. wires 3. limit 4. hide
5. monitor 6. interference

D 1. c 2. b 3. a 4. a

Chapter 20 Answer Key

A 1. e 2. l 3. m 4. a 5. f 6. g 7. d
8. b 9. c 10. i 11. j 12. h 13. k

B 1. port 2. host 3. driver 4. port
5. topology 6. adapter 7. host
8. peripheral 9. driver 10. adapter
11. topology 12. address 13. peripheral
14. address

C 1. universal, b 2. driver, a 3. mediation, a
4. peripheral, b 5. queries, a 6. adapter, a

Chapter 21 Answer Key

A 1. f 2. d 3. a 4. j 5. g 6. k 7. i 8. b
9. h 10. e 11. c

B 1. b 2. a 3. c 4. a 5. b 6. c 7. a

Chapter 22 Answer Key

A 1. c 2. k 3. n 4. f 5. h
6. a 7. p 8. b 9. i 10. d
11. m 12. j 13. e 14. g 15. o 16. l

B 1. decentralize 2. available 3. packet
4. destination 5. translation 6. content
7. static 8. collaboration

C 1. b 2. b 3. a 4. a 5. b 6. a 7. b
8. c 9. c 10. c

Chapter 23 Answer Key

A 1. natural 2. artificial 3. program
4. access 5. simulation 6. replica
7. perception 8. reconfigure 9. expansive
10. neural 11. vary

B 1. b 2. a 3. b 4. a 5. c
6. c 7. a 8. c

C 1. b 2. c 3. a 4. c 5. a
6. c 7. c 8. b

Chapter 24 Answer Key

A a) ry b) ing c) ion d) ion
e) ing f) ed g) ion
1. c 2. g 3. a 4. d 5. f 6. b 7. e

B 1. a 2. c 3. a 4. b 5. d 6. a 7. e
8. c 9. b 10. d

C 1. a 2. c 3. b 4. a 5. c 6. b 7. a 8. b

Chapter 25 Answer Key

A 1. p 2. f 3. d 4. a 5. e 6. n 7. o
8. g 9. c 10. h 11. j 12. b 13. k
14. i 15. l 16. m

B 1. pharmaceutical 2. boost 3. Cloning
4. deliberate 5. feed 6. modified
7. laborious 8. regulatory 9. drought
10. allergy 11. optimum 12. malnutrition
13. sutures 14. infringement 15. selective
16. traits

C 1. noun–noun–adjective
2. adjective/noun–adjective–noun
3. adjective–adverb 4. adjective–noun–verb
5. adjective–verb–noun
6. adjective–noun–verb
7. noun–noun 8. verb–adjective

Chapter 26 Answer Key

A 1. b 2. a 3. a 4. b 5. a 6. b
B 1. c 2. a 3. b 4. c 5. c 6. b
C a) -ent b) -ant c) -ate d) con-, -ly
e) -ent f) -ing g) em- h) -ble i) en-, -ate
j) dis- k) ex-
1. f 2. a 3. g 4. h 5. e 6. b 7. k
8. c 9. i 10. j 11. d
D 1. nutrition 2. active 3. contribute
4. solution 5. concrete 6. reverse
7. Supplemental

Chapter 27 Answer Key

A 1. a 2. c 3. f 4. b 5. d 6. e
B 1. covery 2. act 3. use 4. cycle
5. newable 6. lease 7. ly 8. moved
9. generative 10. verse 11. resulting
12. duce
C 1. recovery 2. deceleration 3. exchanger
4. generation 5. ventilation
D 1. flare 2. boost 3. waste 4. drain
5. exchange 6. waste 7. flare 8. drains
9. boost 10. exchange
E 1. flair 2. flare 3. waste
4. waist 5. flue 6. flu

Chapter 28 Answer Key

A 1. re-use 2. non-energy 3. ice-sheet
4. self-sustaining 5. by-product
6. disease-causing
B 1. e 2. c 3. h 4. f 5. a
6. g 7. d 8. b
C 1. b 2. c 3. a 4. c 5. a
D 1. c, geologic 2. b, repository 3. a, sterilize
4. a, decommission 5. b, decontamination
6. c, self-sustaining 7. b, by-product
8. a, re-use

Chapter 29 Answer Key

A 1. h 2. c 3. e 4. n 5. g
6. b 7. j 8. f 9. i 10. l 11. m
12. d 13. k 14. a 15. o 16. p
B a) installation b) flow c) harmful
d) municipal e) power f) rubbish
g) layer h) radiation i) fossil
j) security k) viable l) tidal
1. viable 2. rubbish 3. municipal
4. security 5. installations 6. radiation
7. layer 8. fossil 9. flow 10. Tidal
11. harmful 12. power
C 1. harmful 2. interior 3. power 4. security
5. viable

Chapter 30 Answer Key

A 1. geophysical 2. seismic 3. plates 4. brittle
5. fault 6. rupture 7. focus 8. tectonic
9. magnitude
B 1. earthquake 2. shallow-water
3. Wind-generated 4. rockslides
5. coastline 6. high-risk 7. Aftershocks
C 1. catastrophic 2. shallow 3. strike
4. phenomena 5. inundation
6. warn 7. buoy 8. gauge

Chapter 31 Answer Key

A 1. salinity 2. precision 3. shape 4. displace
5. current 6. remote 7. migration
8. turbulent 9. pulse 10. yacht 11. abruptly
12. acoustic 13. cause 14. navigation
15. circulate 16. sustain
B 1. verb 2. noun 3. noun 4. verb 5. verb
6. verb 7. verb 8. noun 9. noun
10. noun 11. noun 12. verb
C [Target Words] 1. -ate, circulate
2. -ent, turbulent 3. -ity, salinity
4. -ly, abruptly 5. -ion, navigation
6. -ion, migration 7. -ion, precision
[New Words] 1. -ed, circled (circling, circulation)

2. -ence, turbulence   3. -ed, salted (salting)
4. -ness, abruptness   5. -ed, navigated (navigating)   6. -ed, migrated (migrating)
7. -ly, precisely (preciseness)

C a) hydropower   b) hydrophobic
c) hydroelectricity   d) hydrologist
e) hydrography   f) hydrology
1. c   2. f   3. b   4. a   5. e   6. d

Chapter 32   Answer Key

A 1. c   2. b   3. a   4. c   5. a
6. b   7. b   8. a   9. a   10. c

B 1. b   2. c   3. a   4. c   5. a   6. b   7. b

C a) disruption   b) reject   c) nonexplosive
d) resurge   e) converge   f) prevent
g) recharge
1. c   2. f   3. g   4. a   5. e   6. b   7. d

Chapter 33   Answer Key

A a) designate   b) disturbance   c) spiral
d) constant   e) rotation
f) maximum   g) determination
h) intensity   i) generic   j) inward
1. i   2. d   3. c   4. j   5. a
6. e   7. h   8. b   9. g   10. f

B 1. thrust   2. crust   3. gust   4. sand
5. band   6. land   7. ran   8. plan   9. span
10. wade   11. trade   12. made   13. weak
14. wreak   15. peak

C 1. disturbance   2. convergence   3. constant
4. rotation   5. intensity   6. designate
7. generic   8. inward   9. maximum

Chapter 34   Answer Key

A a) consumption   b) evaporation
c) sanitation   d) urbanization
e) preservation   f) consumer
g) sustainable   h) dietary   i) transboundary
1. urbanization   2. dietary   3. consumption
4. consumer   5. preservation   6. evaporation
7. sustainable   8. sanitation
9. transboundary

B 1. b   2. c   3. d   4. f   5. g   6. a   7. e
8. h   9. i   10. j   11. k

Chapter 35   Answer Key

A 1. force; forcing   2. substance; substantial
3. warmth; warming   4. intense; intensify
5. consideration; considerable
6. extent; extensive   7. diluting; dilution
8. ambition; ambitious
9. legislative; legislature
10. rapid; rapidity

B 1. b   2. a   3. a   4. b   5. b   6. a   7. c
8. a   9. a   10. a   11. b   12. b   13. b

C (in any order)   1. short-term   2. long-term
3. makeup   4. greenhouse   5. Greenland
6. groundwater   7. cold-related   8. coastline
9. wetlands   10. coal-producing

Chapter 36   Answer Key

A 1. perpetuate   2. medicinal   3. periodically
4. underlying   5. subsistence   6. severely
7. degraded   8. selective   9. intrusion
10. extraction   11. population   12. massive

B 1. clearcut   2. rainfall   3. widespread
4. overconsumption   5. high-income
6. remote-sensing   7. low-impact
8. landowner   9. greenhouse
10. human-induced

C 1. b   2. a   3. b   4. a   5. c   6. c   7. a
8. c   9. b   10. a

365

Chapter 37   Answer Key

A 1. contemporary   2. source   3. donate
4. lag   5. delay   6. incineration   7. preferable
8. destine   9. content   10. ferrous
11. indefinitely   12. knowledgeable   13. audit
14. standard   15. haul   16. loop   17. monitor
18. burden   19. mandate   20. hierarchy

B 1. a   2. h   3. f   4. b   5. d
6. g   7. e   8. c   9. i

C 1. monitor   2. donate   3. mandate
4. contemporary   5. haul   6. lag
7. knowledgeable   8. delay   9. preferable
10. incineration   11. hierarchy   12. indefinitely

Chapter 38   Answer Key

A 1. landscape   2. pace   3. alien
4. nonadjacent   5. vegetated   6. shortage
7. stress   8. mechanization   9. localized
10. invasive   11. output   12. assessment
13. oversight   14. distribution   15. productive
16. endanger   17. disproportionate

B 1. local/location   2. put/input
3. danger/dangerous   4. sight/insight
5. product/production
6. proportion/proportionment
7. distribute/distributing
8. inva(de)/noninvasive
9. assess/reassess   10. short/shorten

C 1. endanger   2. oversight   3. localized
4. assessment   5. vegetated   6. pace
7. distribution   8. output   9. shortage
10. landscape   11. alien   12. productive
13. invasive

D 1. overproduce   2. overgraze   3. overcrop
4. overhunt   5. overcrowding   6. overgrow
7. overuse   8. overexploit   9. overtax
10. overfertilize

Chapter 39   Answer Key

A 1. optical   2. record   3. distort
4. eyepiece   5. convex   6. refract
7. faint   8. diverging   9. magnify
10. galaxies   11. concave
12. reflect   13. orbit   14. arm

B 1. telephone   2. television   3. telegraph
4. telegram   5. telephoto
6. telethermometer
7. teleconference   8. telemetry

C 1. record; verb   2. arm; verb   3. orbit; noun
4. faint; adjective   5. reflect; verb

Chapter 40   Answer Key

A 1. g   2. b   3. j   4. e   5. a
6. i   7. c   8. f   9. d   10. h

B 1. thrust   2. stage   3. precise   4. deploy
5. penetrate   6. target   7. pilot   8. shield
9. probe

C 1. propulsion   2. atmospheric   3. orientation
4. celestial   5. attitude

Chapter 41   Answer Key

A 1. spacecraft   2. air-breathing
3. self-healing   4. payload   5. air-augmented
6. lightcraft   7. self-repairing   8. counterpart

B 1. store   2. minute   3. seal   4. sail
5. canister   6. launch   7. booster   8. dock
9. explode

C a) inflatable   b) canister   c) polymer
d) plasma   e) ribbon   f) augment
g) investment   h) returns
1. plasma   2. returns   3. polymer
4. inflatable   5. investment   6. ribbon
7. augment   8. canister

Chapter 42　Answer Key

A 1. a　2. c　3. b　4. a　5. c
　6. c　7. a　8. c　9. b　10. a
　11. c　12. b　13. a　14. b

B 1. a, noct　2. d, in　3. b, il　4. f, un/able
　5. e, com　6. c, pro

C 1. cornerstone　2. light-trespass　3. skyglow
　4. seabird　5. photopollution　6. streetlight
　7. underway

Chapter 43　Answer Key

A 1. b　2. a　3. b　4. d　5. a
　6. c　7. a　8. d　9. c　10. b　11. d

B 1. condense　2. spawn　3. fog　4. impact
　5. hue　6. uneven

C 1. flyby　2. lander　3. probe　4. orbiter

Chapter 44　Answer Key

A 1. c　2. d　3. q　4. p　5. l　6. e　7. r　8. f
　9. g　10. b　11. i　12. o　13. a　14. j　15. k
　16. m　17. h　18. n

B a) feasibility　b) penetrator　c) descent
　d) architecture　e) habitation
　f) deployment　g) simulation
　h) magnetism　i) sensor　j) sampling
　1. deployment　2. feasibility　3. sampling
　4. habitation　5. architecture　6. descent
　7. sensor　8. penetrator　9. simulation
　10. magnetism

C 1. crust　2. image　3. sampling　4. image
　5. crust　6. sampling

D 1. a　2. b　3. a　4. c　5. b　6. a　7. c　8. b
　9. c　10. a

Chapter 45　Answer Key

A 1. invention　2. useful　3. validity　4. asexual
　5. eligible　6. utility　7. ornament　8. tuber
　9. design　10. patents　11. seedlings　12. bud
　13. exclusivity　14. pollination　15. propagate
　16. article

B 1. prefix: a-; bisexual, sexually
　2. prefix: ex-; suffix: -ity; inclusivity, exclusives; exclusively
　3. suffix: -ling; seeds, seeded, seedless
　4. suffix: -ful; uses, useless, used
　5. suffix: -ion; invents, invented
　6. suffix: -ity; validly
　7. suffix: -ion; pollinates, pollinated

C a) or　b) ee　c) er　d) or　e) or　f) er
　1. d　2. b　3. c　4. a　5. e　6. f

Chapter 46　Answer Key

A 1. extent　2. burgeon　3. derive
　4. disparities　5. treaty　6. disputes
　7. paradigms　8. monopoly　9. appellation

B a) -ive: adj, exclude　b) -ion: n, protect
　c) -ion: n, promote　d) -ble: adj, access
　e) -ment: n, settle　f) en-, -ment: n, force
　g) -al: adj, transit
　1. g　2. a　3. e　4. c　5. d　6. b　7. f

C 1. c　2. b　3. a　4. b　5. b　6. b　7. a
　8. c　9. c　10. b

國家圖書館出版品預行編目資料

科技英文閱讀&練習(寂天雲隨身聽APP版)/
JoAnne Juett著；羅竹君，丁宥榆譯. -- 二版. --
[臺北市]：寂天文化事業股份有限公司, 2025.03
印刷　　面；　公分
ISBN 978-626-300-302-6 (16K平裝)

1.CST: 英語 2.CST: 科學技術 3.CST: 讀本

805.18　　　　　　　　114002356

科技英文與閱讀 二版
English for Specialized Science and Technology

JoAnne Juett Ph.D.　　著
羅竹君 & 丁宥榆　　譯

編輯	丁宥暄
封面設計	林書玉
內頁設計	洪伊珊／林書玉（中譯解答）
圖片	shutterstock
製程管理	洪巧玲
發行人	黃朝萍
出版者	寂天文化事業股份有限公司
電話	02-2365-9739
傳真	02-2365-9835
網址	www.icosmos.com.tw
讀者服務	onlineservice@icosmos.com.tw

Copyright © 2025 by Cosmos Culture Ltd.
版權所有 請勿翻印

出版日期	2025年3月 二版三刷 （寂天雲隨身聽APP版）
郵撥帳號	1998620-0 寂天文化事業股份有限公司
	訂書金額未滿1000元，請外加運費100元。

〔若有破損，請寄回更換，謝謝。〕